Resounding praise for the previous award-winning thrillers by

JAMIE FREVELETTI

"Just terrific—full of thrills and tradecraft, pace and peril. . . . Outstanding."
Lee Child, *New York Times* bestselling author of *Worth Dying For*

"While women are well-represented in crime fiction as cops, private detectives or amateurs, the female adventure story often gets short shrift. Jamie Freveletti is changing that. . . . Freveletti combines realistic scenes with believable characters in a gripping, timely plot."
Ft. Lauderdale Sun-Sentinel

"A breathless, hair-raising read, one of the most gripping thrillers I've read in a long, long time."
Tess Gerritsen, *New York Times* bestselling author of *Ice Cold*

"Harrowing. . . . Fast-paced . . . and the 'ripped from the headlines' angle adds further frisson."
Booklist

"Validates Freveletti's decision to leave [her] law career. . . . She's off to a running start."
Chicago Sun Times

By Jamie Freveletti

THE NINTH DAY
RUNNING DARK
RUNNING FROM THE DEVIL

JAMIE FREVELETTI

The Ninth Day

HARPER

An Imprint of HarperCollinsPublishers

This book is a work of fiction. The characters, incidents, and dialogue are drawn from the author's imagination and are not to be construed as real. Any resemblance to actual events or persons, living or dead, is entirely coincidental.

HARPER

An Imprint of HarperCollins*Publishers*
10 East 53rd Street
New York, New York 10022-5299

Copyright © 2011 by Jamie Freveletti LLC
ISBN 978-0-06-202531-9

First Harper premium printing: October 2011

HarperCollins® and Harper® are registered trademarks of Harper-Collins Publishers.

Printed in the United States of America

Visit Harper paperbacks on the World Wide Web
at www.harpercollins.com

10 9 8 7 6 5 4 3 2 1

For my husband, Klaus,
who taught me that life is an adventure not to be missed

ACKNOWLEDGMENTS

This book was a joy to write, and the team of people involved in bringing it to publication made the rest easy. Thanks to my agent, Barbara Poelle, for her marvelous humor and good advice. My editor, Lyssa Keusch, made my year by commenting that she was unable to put the manuscript down. Danielle Bartlett, my publicist at Harper-Collins, is more organized than I will ever be, and I'm so grateful for it! Every year I'm intrigued to see the tour and marketing ideas that she puts together. Dana Kaye at Kaye Publicity handles the rest of the myriad big and little things that go into a book launch and always manages to throw in a cutting edge concept. Thanks also to Adrienne Di Pietro for her advice on all things marketing.

This book received an outstanding cover. Thanks to Lyssa and the graphics team for creating such a standout design.

In researching for this book I roped in a long-time friend from the years at my former law firm where we handled food, drug, and medical-device matters. Thanks to Jeana Bicknell, girlfriend and FDA compliance expert, for her excellent pharmaceutical lab input and handy tip on opening a wine bottle without use of a corkscrew. You'll be seeing the second idea in book number four.

Anita Pope is a Southern girl and knew exactly who I should speak to about white lightning. No cork problems with this brew. Thank you to Michael Sims for the recipe instructions that he remembered hearing from his paternal grandfather about stills during the prohibition era.

Thanks also to my advance readers (and great writers), Darwyn Jones and Sharon Williamson, for keeping me on my toes.

I can't thank author Steve Berry enough for his wonderful blurb! When Lyssa sent me the email containing it I was ecstatic and grateful to him for taking the time to read the manuscript.

And finally, to my family, who recognized that I was caught up in writing this story and began to quietly manage the household around me until the final word was written. Thank you.

The
Ninth
Day

EMMA CALDRIDGE SAT IN THE TUNNEL AND WATCHED the rats gather around her. Their eyes glowed when they bisected the small beam of moonlight pinpointing through the jagged seam in the ceiling. Sacks of marijuana lined the walls, and metal rails ran along the floor. Emma heard the voices of her pursuers whispering to each other in Spanish outside the tunnel's entrance.

She'd been tracking their progress through the dry, dusty Arizona night. She couldn't believe her luck, coming upon an actual shipment as she did, but her good fortune changed when a straggler among them appeared at her back. She'd run through the night, chased by the coyote who was as fleet as the animal itself. The man was whipcord thin and feral and he'd stalked her with the intensity of one who knew his continued livelihood depended on catching her before she went to the police. She'd outpaced him on the flats, but he had the advantage of knowing the terrain. He'd caught up with her on the twisting path, when she found herself stumbling off it at the turns. She'd fought down the fear she felt, doing her best to focus on the trail and her pace. As an ultra marathoner she'd learned how to discipline her mind to halt any thoughts of defeat, and now she'd used that training to keep the terror at bay. She'd kept one ear tuned to the noise behind her in order to gauge his approach, and when he neared she increased her speed. She knew she could outrun him with ease as long as the trail remained visible and clear. What she didn't know was what obstacles loomed in front of her.

A second had joined him right before she fell. The tunnel's entrance was well hidden, and she'd tumbled straight down into it, legs first. She'd managed to sit up as the rats converged, but she could feel bone-deep pain in the soles of her feet where they had hammered into the packed earth floor on her descent.

She rose with a grimace, her feet throbbing at the extra weight. A whiff of air fanned her face and she dodged the dark body of a bat swooping toward her. Two more flew past and she hunched over, lowering her face to her chest. The fear fought its way upward, causing her breath to hitch. The fall into the tunnel had changed the dynamic from one where she had the whole world in which to flee to one where her flight was controlled. Now her pursuers had an edge. With one hand on the side wall and one foot along the rail, she started forward. The air smelled of dirt and grass overlaid with the distinctive odor of marijuana. At least here the shipment was inanimate. What she'd seen above was the transportation of human slaves, most of them men, being moved to locations where they would work without rest until they died.

She heard the coyote land in the passage behind her. She stepped up the pace, shuffling along, keeping her feet in contact with the rail and her hand on the wall. She'd left that evening with a camelback filled with water and a fanny pack filled with packets of running gel composed of amino acids and electrolytes to provide her with any immediate energy boost she might need. Her cell phone remained on and she'd sent a text to the main office at the first sight of the shipment. She doubted the phone would get a signal now and didn't waste any time pulling it out.

The cavern curved left, the darkness broken here and there by shafts of light from above. The men behind her had gained ground—that much was obvious by the sounds of their approach, growing louder. She stepped up to a jog, her anxiety spiking and her eyes watering with the effort of trying to pierce the gloom. Her panting echoed in the space and she sucked on the camelback spout, pulling the tepid water into her dry mouth. She came upon a handcart stacked high with sacks and for a brief moment she considered jumping on it and using the pump bar to propel the device. She discarded the idea. It would be too noisy, and she wasn't sure if the trolley required two people to move the seesaw handle.

Her hand hit some wooden supports and she felt a splinter gouge deep into her index finger at the first knuckle. She grit her teeth on the pain, doing her best not to make a sound. She kept moving, even picking up speed. The tunnel curved right and she felt the floor sloping upward. A creaking, squealing noise echoed through the enclosed space followed by the sound of the trolley wheels sliding over the rails. She ran faster, holding her right hand out in front of her and stumbling as her foot hit a small pothole in the dirt floor. She stubbed her toe on the rail when it curved once again.

Her hand knocked into a plywood wall. She ran her fingers over it, looking for a doorknob and finding none. She rubbed her palms along the walls a few feet before the door and on either side, hoping for an opening that might send her in an alternate direction, but she met with solid, packed earth. She'd reached the end.

The trolley moved toward her, the screeching metal sound filling the tunnel. Her fear choked her and all thoughts of stealth flew out of her head. She pounded on the wooden panel with both fists, no longer caring about the noise she made. The door flew open and she plummeted through the entrance, landing face-first on a linoleum floor. Bright light blinded her. She rolled over and looked up into the eyes of a man and down the barrel of a pistol.

"Welcome to Mexico, *señorita*," he said.

2

THE COYOTE STEPPED THROUGH THE DOOR AND leveled a reddened stare at Emma. He wore jeans and a black tee shirt, and his heavily tattooed arms were ropey and muscular. Behind him came the second, a stocky man with a mustache and greasy hair that hung past his ears. Both gave the man with the gun a nod and moved a bit to the side, as if they were content to let him handle her. The gunman twitched his weapon, indicating she should stand. Emma rose, dusting dirt and twigs off her legs as she did. She noted his jeans, white shirt—the sleeves rolled—expensive belt, and flat black loafers. A Rolex watch glittered on his wrist. A pistol-shaped pendant, encrusted with diamonds, hung from a thick gold chain that encircled his neck. His swarthy skin indicated that he was Hispanic, but his eyes were a bright green, like Emma's own. She stared back at him. Waiting.

"Name," he said in English.

"Emma Caldridge."

"You Border Patrol?"

Emma hesitated. She was fully prepared to lie if it meant she'd stay alive, but she wasn't sure if claiming Border Patrol status would protect her or destroy her.

"No," she said.

The man visibly relaxed. He kept the gun on her, but it was clear to Emma that he no longer saw her as a risk.

"What were you doing out there?"

"Looking for night-blooming plants. I'm a chemist for a lab that makes cosmetic products. We're always searching for plants we can use."

The gunman fired off a sentence in Spanish. The coyote answered.

"What did you see?"

"See? I don't know what you mean."

The gunman stepped closer and raised the pistol so that its muzzle was only inches from her face.

"Don't lie to me."

Emma kept her breathing shallow, but allowed the panic she was still feeling to show on her face. She knew her only hope of staying alive was to pretend ignorance of the shipment.

"I'm not lying."

"Carlos said you ran."

"He scared me and then chased me. He didn't seem friendly."

The gunman chuckled. "He's not." The gunman spoke English with only a slight Spanish accent. Not native, but not late acquired either. Emma thought he may have been educated in the States or had a business over the border where he practiced his English often.

She kept her eyes riveted on the gun, but tried to get a sense of her location. She was in a small room, maybe twelve by twelve, with gray cinderblock walls, no windows, no furniture, and one door on the opposite side. She heard the hum of fluorescent lights above her. One of the tubes buzzed as if it was close to burning out. The gunman snapped out an order in Spanish, and the coyote stepped up.

"Give him your jewelry and your packs," the gunman said. Emma handed him her watch and a chain bracelet. She left the stack of three rubber bracelets, the kind used by charitable organizations to indicate a donation, on her other wrist and the gunman didn't seem to care. She shrugged off the camelback, unclasped the fanny pack, and handed both to the coyote. He squeezed the camelback until liquid squirted out the water tube. He tossed it on the floor. He unzipped the fanny pack. Dumped her running gel, pen, pencil, handed her cell phone to the gunman, who put it in his pocket, and pulled out her GPS tracker. The coyote peered at the handset, a puzzled look on his face.

"What's that?" the gunman said.

"A GPS tracker."

The gunman snatched the device out of the coyote's hand and shoved it at her. "Turn it off. Now!"

Emma powered it down. When she looked up, the gunman knocked the tracker out of her hand

and shoved her backward, following her trajectory and pinning her against the wall with his body. She winced with the pain of the cinder blocks slamming into her spine. He dug the revolver's muzzle into her cheek. She felt his heat and barely contained anger. He smelled of weed and whiskey.

"Why do you have a GPS tracker?"

Emma swallowed once. "I'm an ultra runner. When I train I run sometimes thirty, forty miles. Not too many people can run that distance, so I'm usually alone on the trail. The tracker is in case something happens and a rescue team needs to find me." Emma held her breath. She prayed that he believed her.

"Turn around. Face the wall."

Emma's mouth went dry. Every instinct she had rebelled against the idea of turning her back on this man.

"If you're going to put a bullet in my brain do it now, while I'm watching."

The Gunman gave her a sly look. "I'm not going to shoot you."

Emma stayed still.

"Turn around!"

Reluctantly, Emma shifted. When she was face to bricks, the Gunman kicked apart her shoes. He frisked her with quick efficiency. He yanked her arms behind her and tied her hands together with plastic ties. Someone covered her face with a cotton cloth. She hissed in pain as he pulled the knot tight, because he'd caught strands of her hair. They dragged her forward. Emma moved with them, doing her best not to trip. She heard the far door squeal open and felt a rush of warm evening air flow over her. She followed along. Gravel crunched under her feet and she heard chirping crickets.

Another door creaked, and the gunman said, "You're at the back of a van. Get in and lie down." An arm steadied her as she moved ahead a step. Her thighs hit the edge of the vehicle, and she turned around to sit in the opening. She scooted backward on the metal floor and laid down, angling onto her side to relieve the pressure on her hands behind her. The doors slammed shut. Within seconds the van started moving.

Emma lay there and thought about her situation. She'd been in the area searching for night-blooming plants found in the desert regions of the western states, but she'd been asked to remain alert for any signs of drug or human smuggling, which was endemic in the areas bordering Mexico. Her plant search was funded by Pure Chemistry, the lab where she worked as a chemist, and her trafficking information was requested by Darkview, a contract security company that handled dangerous missions the world over. As she bounced along in the van, she thought that nothing either company paid her was worth the danger in which she now found herself. Still, she lay there and counted her blessings. They'd taken everything but the things she needed the most.

The thin compass in her cargo pocket and the rubber bracelets around her wrist remained.

OSWALD KROGER SAT IN A BAR IN PHOENIX, ARI-
zona, and wondered why the hell he'd taken on
this latest job. He pulled on a longneck while
contemplating the stupidity of what he was about
to do. He knew it was dumb, but years of drifting had made money scarce. Oz had only the
clothes on his back and his motorcycle. And a
near genius IQ, but that little fact was usually
only discussed by his family, who would call him
periodically to try to coax him back to MIT. He'd
left with a beautiful girl to follow a rock band
across the country. The girl had returned to college in September, but he'd stayed on with the
crew, picking up odd jobs and sleeping in parking
lots. Now he was twenty-seven years old and the
whole drifter thing was getting tired. He'd agreed
to transport some pot from Mexico to Phoenix.
Four loads, eight thousand dollars. Oz thought
the payoff abnormally high, but the guy who'd
recruited him claimed that Oz had what the
Mexican cartel didn't: a valid U.S. passport. Oz

agreed to run it. Once he had the cash, he would use it to settle somewhere and begin to put his life back on track.

What bothered Oz about the whole concept was the statistical probability of apprehension. He'd gone to the local library, logged on to the Internet, and surfed until he'd found a Department of Homeland Security report that estimated the number of arrests for the transportation of marijuana compared to the amount of marijuana believed to be imported. As far as he could tell, he had a 73 percent chance of being arrested over the course of twenty shipments. Even though he'd only agreed to four, that didn't reduce his chances of capture, because capture was random, and his chances were equal that he could be captured at the first, or the last shipment. Or he could beat the odds and never get caught. Oz was betting on the twenty-seven percent freedom quotient. Freedom with eight thousand dollars. Now that particular number he liked. Still, the whole idea was stupid and risky. If he wanted to reduce the risk, he'd have to find a smarter way to transport than the cartel did. Oz figured that a guy with his brains should be able to come up with a plan that would take the transportation to a new level. If he didn't, he'd fall prey to the seventy-third percentile.

He finished his beer, plunked it down on the bar, and headed out into the night. Oz felt the heat of the neon "Beer" sign as he passed it, shoulder height and stuck on the outside wall as it was. It glowed an amber yellow that stung his eyes and forced him to wince. His motorcycle sat at the end of a long row of cars parked in the lot of the Red Lion Tavern.

He walked up to the machine and smiled, as he always did when he saw it. He loved his bike. It was an eight-year-old Triumph Bonneville in blue with black-and-white checkerboard stripes, given to him by one of the English rockers who didn't want to take the trouble to transport it back to Britain. Oz took it in lieu of a bonus due him for crew work on the band's tour. It sported a couple of scratches from the two falls the rocker had taken while using it, but otherwise it was in excellent condition.

He lowered a full face helmet over his head and adjusted his leather jacket. His battered Wrangler jeans hung a bit on him, and he noticed a hole forming at the knee. Growing up he'd been the tall, skinny kid, unable to fit in with his peers due to his intellect. Skipping grades in school had only made it worse, because then he was the tall, skinny, little boy among the older, more sophisticated teenagers. At MIT he'd finally met people near his age who could equal, and even surpass, him in brains, but the damage was done and he'd struggled to form friendships, a skill he hadn't learned. When Karen had asked him to hit the road with her, it was the first time a girl had really paid any attention to him. She laughed with him, teased him, and showed him the way around a woman's body. He would have followed her to the ends of the earth had she allowed it. When she broke it off to return to MIT he'd been devastated.

He swung a leg over, started the engine, and rode out of the parking lot. His first stop was No-gales, Mexico, just over the border from Arizona. He'd meet his contact there, get instructions, and he'd be a quarter of the way toward freedom. He settled in for the three-hour ride, letting the wind blow over him and feeling the cycle's vibra-tion. The recruiter had wanted him to ditch the Triumph, disliking the flashy paint job, but Oz had refused. They compromised and Oz agreed to travel at night, when there were fewer people on the road to notice him. He glanced up. Stars lined the sky and a sliced moon glowed above him.

He crossed the border into Mexico at four o'clock in the morning. The patrol showed no particular interest in him or his cycle. He rode straight through the shuttered town on empty streets and kept going until he was twenty miles south. He slowed when he saw a dirt road on his left marked with a battered sign nailed to a fence post, the word "Puma" scrawled in black across it. Oz idled a moment, staring at the sign. The concept that he was at a crossroads in his life, actually and figuratively, occurred to him. He shook himself, cranked the throttle on the bike, and turned down the road.

Half a mile down the road he encountered two stone pillars spanned by an iron gate inscribed with the letter "P" in script. Floodlights and cam-eras were mounted on each. Oz stopped three feet in front and watched as the machinery piv-oted to point at him, their LED lenses glowing red in the dark. He noticed an intercom system set on a pole near the gate's hinges and inched closer and pressed the button.

"What do you want?" The voice barked at him in Spanish. Oz answered in English.

"Johnny sent me."

The speakers remained silent. Oz waited.

"Drive to the house and keep going to the out-buildings in the back." The gates emitted a buzz-ing sound as the lock disengaged. The sides swung open without a creak and Oz drove through.

He'd gone another four hundred yards when a large, two-story hacienda appeared, its white adobe walls shining in the beam thrown by the motorcycle headlight. Oz whistled at the sight of it. Terra-cotta roof tiles and elegant archways framed a massive facade. A circular driveway, lit by solar lamps, passed under an overhang that jutted out from the villa's front, framing an im-posing two panel door complete with elaborate iron handles. To the right and set back was a one-story rectangular building, with five sepa-rate doors, that appeared to be a garage. Oz skirted the house and followed the drive, heading behind and moving farther to the right. He came upon a corral with an attached stable. Next to it was a wide gravel-covered expanse that acted as a parking lot.

Oz pulled up next to a white van and killed his engine. Two men sat in the van's front seat. He heard the beep of a two-way radio and he watched as the driver spoke into a black cell phone. The guy in the passenger seat threw a glance Oz's way before climbing out of the vehicle. He moved to stand next to the van's back doors. The driver strolled around the front bumper and headed Oz's way. The sky had lightened just enough that Oz could make out the man's features, as well as a large diamond-encrusted gun pendant that he wore around his neck.

"Johnny says you're the tech guy."

Oz hesitated at that. While he could make a computer sing if he wanted to, he hadn't expected Johnny to pitch him as a tech guy to the cartel. All he wanted to do was transport the marijuana and get on with his life. He decided to downplay his knowledge.

"Low tech. Yeah."

The man snorted. "We don't need much more than that. I'm Raoul. Follow me."

Raoul headed toward the hacienda. Oz followed at a slower pace. A third man emerged from the back of the van and Oz stopped short when he saw who came out next. A woman, slender, with light brown hair and dressed in athletic clothes and running shoes stood between the van's open back doors. Plastic white strips secured her hands behind her back and a bandanna was wrapped around her head. Below the bandanna her mouth was set in a grim line. Oz felt his stomach twist.

"What are you doing with her?" he said. The two men ignored him. The skinny one pushed the woman forward, while the other man took her arm and guided her toward the stable entrance. Oz took a step in their direction.

"Hey . . ." he said. He saw the woman's head turn.

"Tech guy, come on!" Raoul yelled at Oz.

Oz stood for a moment, unsure. The two surrounding the woman kept moving her toward the stable. Oz jogged to catch up with Raoul.

"What are those guys going to do to that woman?" Oz said.

Raoul didn't bother to glance back. "That's not your concern."

"I agreed to transport some weed over the border. That's all. I don't want any part of a kidnapping."

Raoul kept marching toward the villa. "You'll transport whatever Eduardo La Valle wants you to transport. What did you think you were doing when you joined the Latin Imperials?"

Oz stopped. "I didn't join anything. I just agreed to move some weed."

Raoul stopped walking and turned to face Oz. "You joined the minute you entered that gate. La Valle won't let you go, so you'd better just follow behind me and do what he says."

Oz dug in his heels. "No! I don't want any part of that. I'm not looking to hurt anyone."

Raoul snorted. "Listen, fool, you're in Mexico now. La Valle owns this area, and the minute you stepped foot on his property, he owned you. You keep your mouth shut and do what he says, or the only thing you'll be moving is the earth that he'll make you shovel to dig your own grave."

Panic ran through Oz and his stomach clamped into a tight cramp. His first thought was to run back to his bike, throw it in gear, and drive away

THE NINTH DAY 17

as fast as he could. Raoul must have read his mind, because he shook his head.

"Don't even think of it. They'll gun you down before you hit the main road. The villa is guarded twenty-four/seven, and they shoot on sight." Raoul considered Oz for a moment. "What's your name?"

"Oswald Kroger, but everyone calls me Oz."

"Well, Oz, you're now the paid mule for one of the strongest cartels in Ciudad Juarez. If it makes you feel any better, no one's gonna touch you. They do, they die."

"What about the woman?" Oz said. "Are they going to kill her?"

Raoul shook his head. "Only if no ransom is paid."

"Will they rape her?"

Raoul shrugged. "Eventually." He gave Oz a shrewd look. "You got any money? Maybe you can ransom her."

Oz spread his arms out, palms up. "If I had any money, do you think I'd be doing something as stupid as this?"

Raoul turned, and for a moment Oz thought he saw sadness cross the man's face. "If any of us had any money, we wouldn't be doing this. Come on, La Valle is waiting. He wants to give you your first assignment. Try to act like you want to be here. He'll crush you if you show any fear, and your bones will decay in the ground with the others."

4

EMMA FELT A PUSH ON HER BACK AND SHE STUM-
bled face-first into some straw. One of her captors
clipped the wrist ties, and she sighed in relief and
brought her arms forward to rub out the creases
in the skin where the hard edged plastic had cut
into them. She heard the sound of a door slamming and the footsteps as the men walked away.
She yanked the bandanna off and looked around.

She was in a stall, ten by ten, with a half door
made of wood on the bottom and iron rails on the
top. A high square window, covered with bars,
let in a feeble ray of moonlight. The only other
source of light came from the corridor. She could
make out streaks of blood on the walls. The sight
of it made her skin crawl. She went to the door
to test it and was unable to move it. The bottom
of the door sat on heavy iron wheels set into a
track, and when she peered out of the rails, she
could see that it employed a steel bar mechanism
that shot into supports at each end, locking the
panel in place. She strained to hear the sounds

of animals, but there were none. The other stalls were empty.

Emma crouched down and pulled off the thickest rubber band around her wrist. She turned it inside out and bent the edges back. A slit ran the length of it, and when she pulled it apart she could see the red tape nestled inside. She pulled a small portion of it out and broke it off. She attached the tape to the stall door's outside corner and pulled a card out of the side pocket of her running pants. It looked like a credit card, complete with fake logo on the front and magnetic strip on the back. She swiped the strip across the wooden wall and the edge of the card lit into flame. Emma reached out to ignite the red tape.

The sound of gunshots, screams, and wailing made her freeze. She pulled her arm back in, blew out the match, put the card back in her pocket, and sat down in the stall's corner. Seconds later she heard boot heels hitting the concrete floor, coming fast. The skinny coyote peered into the stall for a moment, before unlocking the door and swinging it aside. His eyes held a frantic look and he waved her out, yelling, "Fast, fast!" in Spanish. As soon as she cleared the entrance he grabbed her by the arm and jogged her down a gravel drive.

The sun bathed the area in a soft pink glow. The coyote steered Emma toward a two-story hacienda. They passed a large swimming pool, complete with its own pool house, and an expansive terrace set up for entertaining. At thirty feet from the house, Emma heard a man's guttural

voice yelling in Spanish. She couldn't speak the
language, but the meaning was clear. The man
sounded angry, furious, but also fearful. The
coyote stepped to the French door at the back of
the house and opened it. He pushed her inside.

Emma entered a large family area, complete
with a massive big-screen television, oversized
sectional couch, and fireplace. To Emma's right,
a large wet bar, well stocked, covered half the
wall. In front of her sat three men. The man with
the gun-pendant necklace, another well-dressed
Latin man with wild eyes who was breathing
heavily—Emma guessed he was the screamer—
and a third, who looked American. The third
wore a leather motorcycle jacket, scuffed, dirty
boots, and well-worn jeans. He had long brown
hair that brushed his shoulders and a lean face
with dark eyes, angular cheekbones, and full lips.
He appeared masculine, despite the long hair.
Emma thought he was quite handsome in an as-
cetic, almost artistic way. He stared at her with
an expression of relief, as if he had been worried
but was no more. His relief was overlaid with an
edge. If she had to guess, Emma would have said
he was nervous, perhaps frightened.

The man with the gun pendant spoke first.

"I'm Raoul, and this"—he indicated the other
Latin man—"is Mr. La Valle. We need to ask you
some questions."

Emma nodded. "Okay."

"You said you were a chemist looking for plants.
Do you know anything about them?"

Emma nodded again. "I do."

"What about herbicides?"

"Yes. Why?"

La Valle turned toward Raoul and rattled off a long sentence in Spanish. He gestured with his hands, and for the first time Emma saw that he held a gun in one. He was short, with cropped hair graying at the temples and a paunch falling over his waistband. He wore a black shirt, sleeves rolled up, and dress pants with wing tip shoes. When he stopped talking he stared at Emma without emotion. It was as though he was a snake, with no thought other than his next meal. She wondered how many people this man had killed.

"The crop is dying," Raoul said. Emma raised an eyebrow. There was only one crop that Emma expected this crowd to tend.

"Marijuana?"

Raoul nodded. "I'll show you." He cast a glance at La Valle, who rose and walked up to Emma in two quick strides, and pushed the gun's muzzle against her forehead, right between the eyes. Emma steeled herself to stay still despite her jangling nerves and fear.

"You make it stop, or you die. Understand, *gringa*?" he said in English.

Emma didn't. She focused on her breathing, trying to stay still.

Raoul spoke to La Valle in a soothing tone. La Valle dug the tip of the gun farther into her skin, pushing her head back, then stepped away. She let her breath out slowly.

"Come with me," Raoul said. "Oz, you too."

The lean man stood.

Emma followed Raoul out of the house and over to the gravel parking lot. The van that she presumed had transported her sat there, as did a motorcycle and a Jeep. Raoul climbed into the driver's side of the Jeep, while Emma and the American walked around to the passenger side, meeting at the door.

"I'm Oswald Kroger. Oz for short," the American said.

Emma recognized his voice as the man who had peppered her captors with questions when she had stepped out of the van. She gave him a curt nod before sliding into the Jeep next to Raoul. Oz sat in the back. They bumped along a tree-lined dirt road for ten minutes, emerging into a meadow the size of a football field and filled with marijuana plants. Raoul cut the engine.

Emma stepped out and gasped. She had never seen a growing thing that looked as these plants did. Wart-like growths of various sizes covered the leaves and stems of the plants. Each was black or mottled red and some grew in clusters, with six or more piled on top of one another. Emma moved closer and saw that the host leaf was decomposing. It was as if the growths were chewing away at the plant's structure. The stems fared no better, with some sections chewed so deeply that the plant was leaning to one side. The entire field, which should have been green, was black and smelled of decay, the way cut flowers smell when they've been in the same water too long.

"Do you have any gloves?" Emma asked Raoul. He shook his head.

"Not here, but there are some back at the barn. I don't recommend you touch the plants."

"Has anyone touched them?"

Raoul nodded. "We have migrant workers who have."

"And? Any rashes? Problems?"

Raoul waved her back toward the Jeep. "I'll show you."

She crawled back into the car and they bounced along to a long row of cinder-block buildings surrounded by a chain-link fence topped with razor wire. A lone guard sat at the entrance in a cheap plastic chair. A rifle rested in his lap and he was reading a tabloid magazine. He got up and opened the gate for Raoul, who drove through and stopped inside.

"You want me to come?" Oz said from the back. Emma started. She'd forgotten the man was there.

"Yes. You're going to have to transport some of this, so you'd better know what you're getting into."

Emma didn't like the sound of that, and when she glanced at Oz, it was clear he didn't either. Frown lines creased his forehead. They left the Jeep and followed Raoul through one of the first doors.

They entered a small, dark room. At first Emma thought that there were no windows, but once her eyes adjusted, she could see that someone had covered them with a black cloth. The only light came from two oil lamps set in the corners. Ten men lay on grass mats on the floor in a row. Each was stripped to their underwear. A man squatted at the head of the group, rocking back and forth on his heels while making murmuring noises. In the corner sat a terra-cotta pot filled with leaves. The smoke in the room was suffocating, thick, and filled the area with a sickly sweet smell.

Two of the men on the mats were breathing in short gasps and their eyes were open, but they stared at nothing. A man on the end giggled uncontrollably. Emma watched his emaciated shoulders shake with mirth. His eyes, though, remained lifeless. The men's skin was covered with the same growths that had been on the plants. One man's calf had a curved section eaten out of it. Their hands were the worst, though, and in some cases the fingers could no longer be seen; just a mass of wart growths covering their skin.

"Jesus," Oz said.

Raoul pointed to the squatting man. "He's a medicine man. From Mazatec. He's given them a potion to incite hallucinations in order to gain an insight into what is eating them alive."

Emma noted that Raoul sounded scared. She thought he had every right to be. What was happening to these men was hideous.

"Have they been seen by a doctor?" Emma crouched down to take a closer look at the growths covering the nearest man's skin.

"A dermatologist and an internist. They had no explanation. At first they thought it was a type of fungus, but their tests came back negative."

"Did they attempt any treatment? If they thought it was a fungal growth, there are several antifungal drugs out there."

Raoul sighed. "They gave those to the first batch."

Emma straightened. "First batch?"

Raoul nodded. "Of migrant workers."

"And?"

"They died."

"How long did it take these growths to appear?"

Raoul fired off a question in Spanish to the medicine man. He answered in a low voice with a slow cadence.

"He says the growths appeared in forty-eight hours. The first batch died seven days after that."

"Any other diagnoses? Treatment attempts?"

"The internist thought it was the same disease described by that man they call the tree man in Thailand. He sent a sample to the Thai's treating physician, but that, too, didn't pan out. The internist administered antibiotics to try to slow their growth, and then chemotherapy drugs to kill any unusual cells. It didn't work. The second batch died as well."

"What batch is this?"

"The sixth."

Emma swung around to face Raoul. "You continued to send men out there? Why?"

Raoul looked angry. "The crop is worth millions! We need to save it. The men are expendable."

Emma heard Oz's sudden intake of breath. Clearly he wasn't used to the idea of human beings as expendable. She wasn't sure how this Oz character got caught up with this bunch, but she could tell that he was out of his element. Far out.

"But now you must stop this, because something terrible has happened," Raoul said.

Emma waved at the men on the mats. "Worse than this?"

Raoul nodded. "La Valle's mistress just discovered a spot on the tip of her finger. She's never gone near the plants." The medicine man stopped murmuring. Emma walked to him and squatted down to his level. He looked to be in his forties, with hair just starting to gray at the temples, broad, flat features, and a compact, wiry body.

"Please ask him what he thinks is happening here," she said to Raoul.

Raoul started to speak, but the medicine man waved him off. "You are American." He spoke to Emma in English. Emma was relieved to be able to communicate directly with him.

"I'm a chemist. From America. I know something about plants as well."

"Do you know anything about curses?" the medicine man said. "Because La Valle is cursed, as is everyone who has contact with him. This sickness will spread throughout. All will die."

Raoul stalked to the medicine man and hovered over him. "Either you fix this problem or you won't just be cursed, you'll be dead! Did you hear those shots? That was the medicine man from Chiapas. He, too, talked of a curse and La Valle put a bullet in his brain. Perhaps you want to end up like him?"

The man stared back at Raoul without fear.

"Your threats and bullets will not stop this, so why do you persist?"

Raoul jerked his head in the direction of the door and Emma and Oz filed out. The sun hit her face along with fresh air, and she was grateful to breathe it in.

"Have you seen this before?" Raoul's voice was harsh.

"No," Emma said. "Never."

"Can any chemicals create this?"

It was an interesting question. Emma thought a moment.

"You asked me about herbicides. Why?"

Raoul turned and continued toward the Jeep. "The American government does random flyovers and dumps herbicides in an attempt to eradicate the crop. It's never worked before, but perhaps now they have something different."

Emma saw his point, but she doubted the damage she was seeing was from an herbicide. She filled him in.

"Drug-dusting herbicides are the same as those you can buy in any agricultural store, with the exception that their ingredients are augmented with surfactants or some other toxic chemical to heighten their effect. But none of the additives that I am aware of could create these growths."

"Then perhaps the negative report the internist received about the fungus was wrong. I saw a picture of that Thai man with tree-like warts on his hands. They looked a little like this."

Emma shook her head. "I know the case you're describing. That *was* a fungus. The difference here is that the growths aren't growing *on* the skin, they're eating *at* it. Devouring it and the tissue beneath it at an incredibly fast pace. Let me speak to the dermatologist and internist. I'd like to know what drugs they've used so far."

"You can't. La Valle had them killed when they said they didn't have the answer."

Oz groaned and rubbed his face with his hand.

Raoul stepped closer to her. "You need to discover what's going on here, and fast. La Valle is panicked now that his woman has it. He's convinced it's the herbicide. He's launching an offensive at the American government's Department of Defense. They ordered the dusting."

"Offensive, in what way? Any offensive against the DOD will fail, and once they get wind of it, they'll come after him."

Raoul spit on the ground. "They'll never make it to Ciudad Juarez. La Valle owns the police, the judges, the lawyers, everyone. No one will reach him here. Get back in the Jeep."

Raoul drove along the edge of the ruined field until they came to an intersection, where another dirt road bisected theirs. On the opposite side was a second field. These plants were tall, green and healthy-looking. Workers moved among them, cutting the stems and stacking the plants onto flat trailers. Guards holding rifles stood at various locations along the field's perimeter. Raoul stopped and they watched as a black Mercedes with tinted windows pulled up. La Valle emerged from the car, along with two armed men. La Valle pointed to the ruined field. The workers froze in their tracks. La Valle screamed at them in Spanish and they started to move, heading toward the decaying plants.

Emma grabbed Raoul's arm. "Stop them!"

Raoul shook her off and climbed out of the Jeep. Emma swung out from her side, as did Oz. The three of them stood there and watched the proceedings. Oz's entire body vibrated with tension. The first migrant worker to reach the ruined field chopped several of the blackened plants down with a machete. He dragged them to the trailer and threw them on top of the healthy foliage.

"Why are they doing that? They're contaminating the shipment," Oz said.

Raoul nodded. "Exactly. And that's the shipment you're taking to the United States. Your country will reap what it sowed." He looked at Emma. "You have nine days to figure out what's killing the men. You fail, you die."

5

EMMA STARED AT RAOUL AND DIDN'T BOTHER TO hide her astonishment.

"I'm a *chemist*. I know about plants in cosmetic applications, herbicides, chemical reactions and lab techniques, but I'm *not* a medical doctor. Nine days to diagnose, treat, and cure a progressive disease that two doctors and two medicine men have never seen before? Are you serious?" Raoul stormed up to her, only stopping when they were toe to toe. He pulled his ever-present revolver out of the waistband of his pants and shoved it against her jaw.

"You want to die now? Just say that you can't do it, and I'll be happy to shoot you."

Emma was done with the threats and something told her that showing fear before Raoul would only escalate his behavior. She steeled herself and stared him in the eyes. "One more person shoves a gun in my face and you might as well shoot me, because I'll refuse to help you and La Valle's mistress will surely die in the next nine days. I'll let you explain why you thought it best to shoot me before I even started." Raoul opened his mouth to speak, then stopped. Emma gave a pointed look at the gun. "Lower it. I mean it."

Raoul lowered the gun.

Emma took a deep breath. "Take me to the mistress. I need to speak to her."

They climbed once again into the Jeep and Raoul drove to the hacienda. They stepped back into the family room, empty this time, and Raoul disappeared into a hall that branched off from the opposite end of the room.

"Wait there," he called back behind him. Emma heard his footsteps fade as he walked away. She looked at Oz.

"How the hell did you get caught up in this mess?"

Oz sighed. "Money. I've been drifting, working as a roadie, for years. I'm broke. A guy that hung around the last band I worked for claimed that I could make eight thousand, easy, by running drugs from Mexico to the States. I bit at the chance."

"How many shipments have you transported?"

"None. This is my first," Oz said.

Now *that* was some unfortunate timing. For a brief moment Emma hoped that his bad luck hadn't become hers. There came the sound of footsteps, two sets this time, coming toward them.

Raoul entered the room followed by a tall, thin Latino woman. Her hair looked chemically lightened to an even honey color that was a beautiful contrast to her brown eyes. She wore a too-tight corset top that emphasized a chest swollen completely out of proportion to her figure. Emma assumed she'd had implants. Large hoop earrings swayed in her ears, and several bangles, all gold and some encrusted with diamonds, encircled her wrists. She wore tight jeans and stiletto heels. Emma noted that Oz perked up, and looked at her with interest. The mistress, though, looked frightened. Her eyes locked on Emma's.

"Are you the chemist?" she said in English.

"I am. Can you show me the spot?"

She walked toward Emma with a swaying motion and thrust her hand out. "Here."

Emma moved in closer. A small red wart-like growth covered the tip of the woman's little finger. It matched the growths on the men and the plants exactly.

"You haven't touched the plants?" Emma said.

The woman shook her head. "No, never."

"Do you smoke them?"

The woman nodded. "Yes. Eduardo and I do. We all do." She waved a hand in Raoul's direction. "But only leaves taken from the healthy field. Not the sick ones."

Emma doubted that the healthy field was as healthy as it appeared. Presumably the herbicide dusting planes managed to cover both fields, not just one, and even if it missed one area with a direct hit, some part of the herbicide would float or be blown onto the nearby plants. It was likely both fields were contaminated, but one more heavily than the other, and the healthy one just wasn't showing the decay yet. She kept this thought to herself, though, as she didn't want to frighten the woman further. Emma noted that the woman's hand shook as she held it out to Emma to analyze.

Emma stepped back. "When did this appear?"

"This morning. I told Eduardo first thing."

Raoul watched Emma with an unfaltering stare. Emma made a mental note to control her emotions in front of him. His eyes were far too sharp, and she sensed that he would use the slightest hesitation on her part as an excuse to undermine her. There seemed a tension between him and the mistress, but Emma couldn't get a grip on what the tension meant. Whatever was going on here, Emma needed to keep him cooperating with her and giving her the information she needed. As she stood there, Emma caught the smoky, tangy smell of cooking bacon. Her stomach growled, audibly.

The woman said, "You are hungry? Let's have breakfast. You can ask me more questions there, though I doubt I'll be able to eat a bite." She spun and marched to a second door on the right side of the room and pushed through it. It swung in and then returned. Oz caught it on the backswing and held it for Emma and Raoul.

The hacienda sported a spacious kitchen with top-of-the-line stainless-steel appliances and cherrywood cabinets. A cook moved bacon from a fry pan onto a plate lined with a paper towel. She glanced up and gave a slight nod at the mistress, but no smile crossed her lips. Emma wondered if she was another unwilling recruit like Oz.

Emma's mouth watered at the smell. A large wooden kitchen table with matching wood chairs nestled in a bay window area to Emma's right. The table was set for three, with bowls of fruit, biscuits, and a platter of sausages arranged in the center. A coffee carafe dominated one corner. The cook opened a nearby drawer and pulled out an additional place mat. She moved with a practiced efficiency and in utter silence. When they had all taken their seats, she handed Emma the coffee carafe before returning to the stove.

"I am Serena," the mistress said. Emma warmed to the woman despite her association with La Valle. The offer of food was gracious. She could have simply gone herself to the kitchen and left Emma and her empty stomach for someone else to address. They filled their plates and ate in silence. The scraping sound of utensils on ceramic was the only noise in the room.

Emma broached the subject that hung heavy in the air.

"You need to go to Mexico City. To the finest hospital you can find," she said.

Serena shook her head sadly. "I can't."

"Why? Your life may depend on it."

"I'm wanted in Mexico. The army knows that I'm La Valle's girlfriend. They'll lock me up for the rest of my days. I'd rather die quick here, than slowly there, year after year." She shook her head again. "I'm wanted."

"Wanted for what? Being his girlfriend?" Emma said.

Serena snorted. "And for murder."

Oz stopped chewing and looked up from his plate. He slid his eyes sideways at Emma. Raoul returned to staring at her, a hint of a smirk in his eyes.

Nest of vipers, Emma thought. She felt a stab of fear and panic, but tamped it down. She would do what it took to stay alive, and if that meant trying to unlock the secret of the disease infecting the men and Serena, then she'd apply herself to solving it.

"I'll need to talk to the medicine man again." She slid her chair back and stood up. Raoul shook his head.

"Sit down. I'm not done," he said. He continued to shovel his second helping of eggs into his mouth.

Serena hit him on the arm. "Shut up, Raoul. She needs to go now. I'm sick and you're worried about eating?" Serena turned to Emma. "Go. Do what you must. But whatever you do, do it fast." Raoul shot Serena a look filled with loathing, but when he spoke, he spoke to Emma.

"Don't think you can get away. The entire compound is under surveillance. You try to run and we'll get you. You won't like what we do to those who run." A look of dismay ran across Oz's face. Emma didn't reply. She gave Oz and Serena a curt nod and headed back to the swinging door.

The temperature had risen and the heat would soon be upon them. Emma walked down the path toward the migrant workers' huts. All the while she did her best to act nonchalant, like she belonged there. She used her peripheral vision to search for the video surveillance that Raoul claimed existed. She spotted a camera high up on the hacienda's roofline, under the eaves at the corner. She turned a bit and checked another corner. Another nestled there. They both pointed to the backyard, triangulating it.

Emma kept strolling, using the slow pace to scan the area. She saw a third camera attached high on a tree. That one pointed further out, toward the migrant huts. The path turned into the wooded area, and she welcomed the cool darkness. After fifteen minutes she emerged at the place where the sentry sat on the chair. This time he held a *Maxim* magazine. He nodded and opened the gate for her.

She glanced up. Two more cameras were mounted on high poles located at the chain-link fence corners. These turned inward, toward the row of migrant housing. Emma took a deep breath and steeled herself to enter the sickroom.

The medicine man leaned over the last man in the row and didn't look up when she entered. Emma watched him reach out and close the man's lids over his eyes. He made the sign of the cross over the body and murmured a prayer in Spanish. Despite the language, Emma knew what he said: the Lord's Prayer. She mentally recited the words as well. The medicine man leaned back and peered at her through the gloom.

"I'm sorry," Emma said. The man didn't reply.

The other patients were in the same position that they'd been in when she'd first seen them. They lay on the mats, still, appearing to be sleeping.

The man rose in one graceful motion and moved toward her. He wore faded jeans, a short-sleeved western shirt with piping on each shoulder in a scroll pattern, and dusty cowboy boots.

"Let's go outside."

He turned right outside the door and walked away from the migrant huts. They once again entered the trees and walked along a path. Emma spotted three more cameras, placed high among the branches. She heard a mechanical whirring sound as the equipment swivelled to follow them.

"Do they have audio?" Emma asked the medicine man.

"No. You can speak. They won't hear." The path curved left. Through the branches Emma spotted the glint of sun on steel. They were still within the boundaries of the chain-link fence and its razor-wire deterrent.

"I'm Emma Caldridge."

"Octavio Guzman." Octavio looked at her with a hint of amusement in his eyes. Emma couldn't tell if the name was real.

"What do you think is killing these men?"

All amusement fled from his eyes. "I told you, La Valle is cursed. As are all in his radius."

Emma felt her irritation rise. "I don't mean to belittle curses, but—"

"But you are a scientist and don't believe in them," Octavio shot back.

"*But* I don't believe that innocent men can be cursed. La Valle, yes. The men and women held on this compound against their will? No." Octavio stopped walking and turned to her. Emma felt a grim satisfaction to see the surprise in his eyes. "What?" she said. "You expected me to scoff?"

Octavio nodded. "Yes. Scientists, especially Western scientists, have long ago dismissed nature's ways from their scrutiny."

"I spend a lot of time in nature. La Valle's men chased me down while I was scouring the desert for night-blooming plants that might have a medicinal effect. Please tell me what you suspect is happening."

"You know La Valle doesn't just deal in drugs?"

The question sounded rhetorical, but Emma answered it anyway. "I presume he traffics humans as well."

Octavio nodded. "But he also sells human organs."

Emma stopped walking. "Does he sell them on the black market?"

"There are hundreds of murdered women from Ciudad Juarez, and many are La Valle's work. He kills men, too, but not for the same reasons." Octavio blew out a long, slow breath. "In truth, he doesn't discriminate. He prays to Satan and those prayers have brought this curse upon himself."

Emma returned to Octavio's side. The trail widened so that she could stay shoulder to shoulder with him. She clenched her teeth to stop them from chattering in fear: not at Octavio's claims of a curse, but at his revelation that La Valle was a killer on such a level. If Octavio was correct, Emma's own chances of survival just went even lower.

"How does one reverse the curse?" Emma said. Octavio halted and faced her.

"You wish to keep Satan's messenger on Earth alive?" His voice held a harsh note and his eyes sparked with anger.

Emma frowned. "Of course not, but I don't see any sores forming on the messenger, do you? They're all forming on his victims. I will stop *that* destruction if I can."

Octavio's belligerent stance subsided a bit. "I understand your dismay at the unfairness, but they will all die. None will escape."

"And you?"

Octavio gave a small nod. "All of us. Even me. It's fate."

Emma's own barely contained anger roared upward. She struggled to regain her composure before she spoke. Anger was a wasted emotion that would cloud her judgment. She needed to remain calm.

"It's not *my* fate. *Nothing* is fated," she said, still a little too forcefully. Octavio's face held a resigned look. It seemed clear that he didn't believe her, but he wasn't planning on arguing with her either.

They'd reached a clearing. In the center sat a canvas tepee. Its sides were bleached white in some places, baked yellow in others. The color reminded Emma of the dirty maize of a pair of canvas gym shoes left in the sun to dry.

"A tepee?" Emma said. "Is this yours?"

"It's La Valle's. He loves American-Indian folklore. He's fascinated with it. The tepee is just one of his affectations. The other is the wearing of totems. He believes in their power. Of course, while the real Indian tribes created totems out of rawhide and carved wood, La Valle's are made out of platinum and encrusted with diamonds. I use the tepee because I don't want to go near the hacienda."

"Tell me what you've attempted to treat these men with and I'll begin my own testing."

"I wash their wounds with a tincture of chamomile, thyme, rosemary, and oregano. They're sleeping in response to a concoction that I create from valerian and other herbs, and this afternoon I'll use salvia."

Emma raised her eyebrows. "The hallucinogen? Well that should be interesting."

Octavio frowned. "We don't use it the way those in the North do—just to obtain a temporary high. We use it to illuminate a man's psyche. Delve into his thoughts."

"What time?" Emma said. She wanted to be present to watch Octavio probe into the migrant workers' subconscious. The only time she'd seen salvia utilized, it was at a base camp in a small town in Panama, where the smokers fell into a trance and then to sleep.

"Two o'clock," Octavio said.

"I'll be there."

Octavio gave her a thoughtful look. "What do you think it is? The herbicide?"

Emma considered the question. "The herbicide is getting its share of detractors. Especially in Colombia, where they've been using it for years. Neighboring villages are claiming that it causes cancer clusters, skin diseases, and strange maladies, but I haven't heard of anything on the magnitude of what you're seeing here."

"They're harming nature. Upsetting the balance."

"La Valle is harming a lot more than nature and he doesn't really give a damn about human life. Even Serena's. If he did, he would have taken her to a hospital already. Demanding that I do something is just show. A smokescreen to keep her thinking she has a chance."

"But you do know a lot about the herbicide."

"But very, very little about medicine."

"There's a field over there." Octavio pointed to the west. "With a bulldozer. Seventy-two people are buried in that place. La Valle killed them."

Emma swallowed. She couldn't imagine seventy-two dead people. Didn't want to imagine it.

Octavio gave her a sympathetic look and disappeared inside the tepee. Emma glanced up. A camera lens pointed at her from a tree opposite the tepee's flap opening. Its red eye glowed in a steady stare.

6

EMMA FOUND OZ SITTING ON THE PATH, HALFWAY
between the migrant huts and the hacienda,
smoking a joint. She yanked four leaves off a
nearby tree, stacked one on the other, and placed
them on the dirt in front of him.

"Put it out on the ground and wrap it in these,"
she said. "Fast."

Oz gave her a dreamy look. "What? I'm not
done."

"Oh yes you are. Are you crazy? What in the
world possessed you to smoke that thing?"

Oz inhaled and blew out a stream of smoke. He
gave Emma a goofy smile. "I smoke every day.
Have for the last eight years. Since I left MIT."

Emma let her surprise show on her face. "MIT?
What's your degree?"

"No degree. I quit after the second year. I took
physics and computer science," Oz said.

Now Emma was confused. "Why did you leave?
Half the world would kill for a chance to go to
MIT."

Oz nodded. "I know. Well, I know that *now*. It was supposed to be just for a summer, but it was so much easier following the band that I decided to extend my leave for a year." He inhaled again. "That was seven years ago. I never went back. Just worked the concerts at night and got high all day."

"So that explains the complete lack of motivation," Emma said.

Oz rolled his eyes. "You're one of those."

"What do you mean by that?"

Oz shrugged. "One of those driven kind of people. I met all kinds of them at MIT. Each one smarter than the last and each one gunning for the other's back. Racking up degrees and awards just so you'll feel good about yourself."

Emma pointed at the leaf bed. "Drop it, Oz. I mean it. You have no idea whether it's contaminated."

Oz shook his head. "Nope. This is from La Valle's personal stash. Serena gave it to me." He leaned forward. "And it's excellent, let me tell you. The guy's an asshole, but he sure knows his drugs."

Emma crouched down to Oz's level. "Serena's got a sore on her finger. Or did you forget?"

Oz froze. He seemed to struggle to concentrate. Emma grit her teeth to avoid snapping at him. She couldn't imagine how a man so obviously smart could act so patently stupid. Oz tilted his head to one side as he looked at her. Emma noted that his pupils were huge.

"But La Valle doesn't, and Serena says he smokes every day. It couldn't be his stash that's causing the disease in Serena."

"But it could be. Put it out. And don't touch any more until I figure this thing out," Emma said. Oz made an irritated sound and rubbed the joint's lit end in the dirt next to his leg. He tossed the butt onto the bed of leaves. Emma reached out and started to roll them toward the joint. When she was finished, she had a tightly curled tube with the joint wrapped in the center.

"This situation is so damn frightening, that's the only way I'm going to get through it." Oz indicated the leaves.

Emma could sympathize, but not to the extent that she would allow him to infect himself, however unknowingly. She looked up, into the trees. Oz followed her gaze.

"Looking for cameras?" he said.

Emma nodded.

"I took a walk around and counted them."

Emma settled onto the trail next to him. "So tell me what you learned."

Oz heaved a sigh. "The entire compound is a thousand acres. It's enclosed at the farthest edges by a regular wooden-rail fence. No barbed wire, nothing. Fence is only four feet high."

"The migrant huts are surrounded by chain-link and razor wire," Emma said.

Oz nodded. "Yeah, but that's the only place that is. Turns out that the surrounding landscape is impossible to cover by car. There's only one road in, and one out. You get off that road and even the toughest four-wheel drive can't manage the terrain. It creates a natural barrier. You'd go miles in any direction before you'd hit a town. The rest of the acreage looks to be like a former working ranch that La Valle bought for himself. He's even got a farm on the far end, where he has some cattle, horses, and armadillos."

"Armadillos?" Emma said. "What's he doing with armadillos?"

"Who the hell knows? Guy's not all there." Oz tapped his temple with a finger.

"So what's keeping the migrant workers here? If they plan it right, once they're outside of the fortified area, they can just sneak off the ranch over the wooden fences."

Oz shook his head. "Nope. That's where the cameras come in. They're everywhere. Every one hundred feet at the perimeter, four on the outside of the hacienda and God knows how many more inside. Three on the stable's exterior wall, two interior with a view of the breezeway down the center. One camera sits on top of what looks like a cell-phone tower outside the compound that captures a view of the road leading to the house. Even if these guys managed to get over the fence, they'd have to run a long time to the nearest village, and then they'd probably get turned in by La Valle's flunkies. He pays everyone in town for their silence." Oz batted at a fly that landed on his sleeve. "I'm stuck. I'm going to have to deliver that shipment." His voice held a desolate note.

Emma stood. "You're not stuck. Something will break." Oz gazed upward at her. He rose, smacking dead leaves and twigs off his jeans as he did.

"I wish I shared your conviction. What did the medicine man tell you?"

Emma started back toward the hacienda. Oz fell in step next to her. "Not much. He repeated the claims of a curse. He says La Valle dabbles in black magic."

Oz groaned. "The guy is looney tunes."

Emma nodded. "The medicine man called him Satan's messenger."

"Lovely," Oz's voice was dry. "Raoul told me they caught you running in the desert. Just what the hell possessed you to run through the desert at night that close to the border? You had to know that the coyotes were out there, shuttling their humans around."

"It's my job," Emma said.

Oz snorted. "And to think just two days ago I would have killed for a job." They walked some more. "Raoul also said that you know about herbicides. Do you think the herbicide is creating the disease?"

"I doubt it, but at the same time wouldn't rule it out. It's possible the DOD is using a new concoction that I'm unaware of. As it is, the usual herbicide is boosted with so much deadly stuff that some countries are claiming that the residue creates rapid birth defects and cancer cases. But I've never heard of a massive, systemic disease on the level of what these men are experiencing."

As they moved Emma watched the tops of trees for video cameras. They reached the hacienda and reentered the family room. La Valle was there, talking on a small cell phone. Raoul sat next to him, listening to La Valle's end of the conversation. Emma stayed by the door and waited. She was loath to get any closer to La Valle. When he was finished, he turned his eyes on her.

"I need some equipment," Emma said.

"What type of equipment?" Raoul said.

"A microscope, petri dishes, slides. In short, I need a laboratory." Emma felt some satisfaction when she saw La Valle frown. That's right, jerk, I need more than you can provide, she thought.

"Isn't there a microscope over at the farm?" Raoul addressed his question to La Valle, who nodded. Raoul waved a hand in the general direction of the backyard. "There's a farm at the far end of the property. Ask Miguel to show you where the medical supplies are kept. I think they have a microscope there for the veterinarian's use when she comes. Oz, you've seen it. Take her there."

Oz gave a curt nod.

"What did Octavio tell you?" La Valle asked. His eyes bored into Emma's.

"That he's used a tincture with herbs on the sores and this afternoon he'll administer salvia."

La Valle grunted. "The magic mint. That's good. I expected him to do that first thing. Don't know why he waited."

"Magic mint? What's it do?" Oz asked.

Emma tipped her hand from side to side. "Salvia is a hallucinogen. Makes people laugh, cry, but mostly just stay stock-still while a movie plays in their brain. Once the hallucinations start, the medicine men believe that the patient will speak the truth of what's actually attacking his system."

"It's a magical leaf," La Valle said. Emma didn't

respond. La Valle's belief in magic would be his downfall, one way or another. The only question was whether he would bring her down with him. She turned and walked out into the sunshine. Once there she took a deep breath, happy to be out of La Valle's orbit. She heard the door behind her open and close.

"So what's your next step?" Oz said.

Break out of here, Emma thought.

7

"TAKE ME TO THE FARM," EMMA SAID. OZ STRUCK
out to the right, headed toward the stable. When
they reached the graveled area that acted as a
parking lot, he swung a leg over a flashy motorcycle parked next to the Jeep Raoul had used to
drive them to the fields.

"Hop on," he said.

Emma joined him on the back and wrapped
her arms around his waist. His body felt warm
through his tee shirt. He kicked the cycle alive,
and the engine's noise sent a group of blackbirds
flapping out of the trees. They cruised on a dirt
road that ran along the inside of the wooden rail
fence. Emma scanned the trees. No video cameras that she could see. Then a wooden pole,
much like an electrical pole, came into view. At
the top Emma spied a small wireless camera.

Oz turned his head toward her. "See it?" he
yelled over the roar of the engine.

She nodded against his back.

During the trip she determined that Oz was

right. The poles appeared in formation, and each one sported a camera. Video surveillance monitored the entire compound. Oz drove up to a gate and killed the engine. A pole sat twelve feet from them. The gate bisected the fields, creating a separate area. Emma counted ten horses grazing in the distance.

Oz waved at the meadow. "This is where the farm starts. The outbuildings, stables and a ranch house are up ahead." He started the motorcycle up again. After a minute or two more, the outbuildings came into view. In front of them was a one-level house painted white, with a large carport attached to one side that was wide enough for two cars. A black SUV was parked in the spot nearest the side door.

Behind the ranch house Emma saw a round paddock and two more stables, these more modern-looking than the one back at the hacienda. Several smaller corrals held pigs, and cows grazed in an adjacent field. Oz parked the cycle next to the SUV. Emma swung a leg off and stood up while he killed the engine. She walked to the vehicle and peered inside. On the passenger seat was a stack of invoices, with the name "Luisa Perez" at the top and the acronym "M.V.Z."

"The veterinarian is here," Emma said. "Let's go inside."

The first room consisted of a combination dining and kitchen area. A round wooden table with chairs painted white sat in the center of the dining area, which opened into a square space with a kitchen. Emma pushed through another door on the far side of the room and stepped into the laboratory.

A young Mexican woman, her hair pulled into a ponytail and wearing jeans and a blue chambray shirt, worked at a counter lined with a microscope and several round glass containers, each with their own aluminum top. She looked up when Emma entered. She had a lovely face, devoid of makeup, and skin that glowed with good health.

"May I help you?" she said in English. Emma introduced herself and Oz, who had stepped up behind her. "I'm a chemist. Are you the vet?"

The woman nodded. "Luisa Perez." Emma reached out her hand. Dr. Perez hesitated. When it became obvious that the woman wouldn't shake her hand, Emma slowly withdrew it. Dr. Perez's face flushed, and she looked down in embarrassment.

"Are you afraid that I have the migrant workers' sickness?" Emma said.

Perez grimaced. "I'm sorry. I just can't take the risk. I'm here for only a moment. One of the mares is due to give birth, and I wanted to check on her."

"Have you told the authorities about what's going on here?" Emma said.

Perez got a panicked look on her face. "Absolutely not! La Valle would have me killed if I spoke out of turn. I care for his animals, and in return he pays me and leaves me alone."

Oz turned abruptly and stalked out of the room. The walls shook when he slammed out the door one room away.

Perez sighed. "I apologize, but La Valle is not a man to take lightly. He is quite powerful, and I don't wish to have any trouble. I do my job and don't ask any questions."

Emma felt her anger rising again. She had hoped for more from this woman despite the fact that she knew La Valle was a force in the area. How could Perez help the animals he housed but not the humans he abused? Emma took a step closer. Perez took a step back.

"I'm here against my will. I didn't ask to be involved in this mess, but now that I'm here I can't just turn my back. The men are dying. They need to get to a hospital. Preferably a large teaching hospital, where their condition can be diagnosed and treated."

Perez shook her head. "I can't help you. Or them. Octavio told me that he believes they will die whether they go to a hospital or not."

"They deserve a chance. Octavio could be wrong."

Perez pushed past Emma, headed toward the door.

"Wait!" Emma said. Perez turned and gave her a wary look. Emma sought to placate her. "Can you tell me what medications you have here? Maybe show me the farm?"

Perez took a deep breath. She jerked her chin at the cabinets that lined the walls above the countertops. "I have liniments for the animals, tranquilizers, syringes, and some very general medications for various routine ailments. Heartworm, rabies vaccinations, things like that."

"I want to take scrapings from the men's sores and look at them under the microscope. I'd also like to draw some blood and have it analyzed. Do you have fresh slides, a scalpel, and some gloves? A petri dish would be great as well."

Perez reached into the cabinet and began removing supplies. She assembled them on the counter before reaching below and opening a brown paper bag. She loaded the tools in, added gloves and packets containing alcohol swabs, curled the top and handed it to Emma.

"Thanks. Once I draw the blood, could you take it to a lab in town?"

Perez shook her head. "Not unless La Valle orders it."

Emma gritted her teeth at the woman's complete lack of a spine. "La Valle ordered me to investigate the disease and treat it. To do that I'll need the use of a lab. I think he'll understand."

Perez got a dubious look on her face. "If it's all right with him, then I'll do it."

Emma tried a different tack. Maybe the woman would open up more if she felt Emma was on her side. "What animals do you treat here?"

"All of them. Even the armadillos."

"Ahh, yes. I'd heard that La Valle keeps armadillos. Do you know why?"

Perez grimaced. "La Valle believes in the folklore surrounding them that says an armadillo's hard carapace covering makes it impervious to injury."

"Impervious to injury? Seems like most of the roadkill in the west consists of armadillos."

Perez nodded. "I know, but that doesn't sway La Valle. He kills them and grinds their plated back armor into a fine powder."

Emma was intrigued. "What does he do with it?"

He sprinkles it around the hacienda in a border. He believes it protects the home from evil spirits. The theory is that evil won't cross an armored line. He's surrounded this barn with it as well."

"That's nuts. Besides, if evil can't cross the line, then La Valle himself would be stuck inside his hacienda." The words were out before Emma could censor herself.

Perez gave a grim laugh. "You and I don't believe these stories, but we're scientists. He also feeds their meat to the migrant workers to make them strong."

"I've never heard of eating armadillos. That's disgusting."

Perez nodded. "Lots of people eat them. La Valle doesn't, though. She waved Emma toward her. "Come, I'll show you the armadillo pens."

The ranch house's backyard held only a few scrub plants. The sun hit Emma full bore when she stepped outside. Perez angled right to one of the smaller pens at the end of one of the stables. A five-by-five fenced area, walled on one of the sides by the stable, held a small low-lying wooden platform, about ten inches off the ground. Underneath it, Emma saw an armadillo curled into a ball, sleeping. A dog door set into the stable wall gave the animals access to the inside.

"They're sleeping. Let's check the interior. They like it when it's cool and dark." Perez walked around to the end of the building and stepped inside. Emma followed, and was relieved to be out of the sun's glare and in the stable's gloom. The area smelled of animal hair and straw. Emma glanced at the ceiling, and in all four corners. No cameras anywhere. It appeared as though La Valle's security team had overlooked the barn.

Perez waved at another penned area. In this one, several armadillos lounged under wooden slats set up as houses, or were curled up in deep pits that they had dug for themselves. Most of the animals were gray, but in one corner, separated from the rest by a low barrier, was a bundle of pink fur and claws.

"That one's beautiful," Emma pointed at the pink creature.

Perez nodded. "It's called a pink fairy. Very rare. La Valle has four of them. The rest are your average nine-banded armadillos. Nothing to write home about."

"Still, it's a strange obsession, but La Valle seems to have a few. The medicine man showed me the tepee and told me about La Valle's fascination with American-Indian folklore."

Perez turned somber. She seemed to be struggling with herself. Deciding whether she should say something. Emma prodded her.

"Tell me."

"La Valle's interest in armadillos grew out of some other folklore that I haven't told you about. Armadillos are called gravediggers."

Emma didn't like the sound of that. "Why?"

"They use their claws for burrowing. They're quite good at it. The folktales say that the armadillo digs into the graves of humans and dines on the bodies it finds. La Valle tells his enemies that he will exact vengeance even after they're dead. He'll bury them and send his armadillos to eat their flesh."

Obsession indeed, Emma thought.

8

EMMA FOUND OZ LEANING AGAINST A RAILING about thirty feet from the ranch house, watching the horses graze. She leaned on the fence next to him. He glanced at her once before returning to watch the field.

"I saw the armadillos. Kind of interesting," Emma said.

Oz said nothing.

"I need to get back to the men. I want to sample the sores. Will you drive me? It'll save time."

"Can you cure them?" Oz said.

"Given access to a lab and unlimited time, maybe. In nine days without benefit of testing equipment? Not likely."

Now Oz bent his head to look at her fully. His eyes were gray with flecks of blue. They held a somber, intelligent look. Emma thought the planes of his face were elegant. He was handsome in a startling, classic manner, and this close up she could see the beginnings of a five o'clock shadow.

"So what are you going to do?"

Emma took a deep breath. "Escape. Once I'm out I'll notify the authorities. It's the best chance they, and Serena, have."

Oz lifted an eyebrow. "And me."

Emma swallowed. She knew that a man with his intelligence would have figured out the end game. She was impressed with his calm.

"If you're forced to transport the shipment, wear gloves and try to avoid touching the leaves. You shouldn't get close."

Oz held her gaze a moment. "Even if I manage to avoid infection, they'll kill me at the last stop."

Emma looked away. He was right, but she didn't know what to say.

He sighed. "You won't be able to escape. Not with those cameras."

"I'll think of something," she said.

"You'll need help."

Emma turned to face him. Only inches separated them. He was still looking at her, but this time there was determination in his eyes.

"It's very, very risky. The odds . . ."

Oz gave a mirthless laugh. "Eighty-five to one." He must have caught her surprise, because he offered a further explanation. "That's what I estimate to be the odds based upon the number of cameras stationed around the area. You'll need to cross the yard, hit the road, and from there make it to a nearby town, all without being seen by one of them. If by some miracle you get past the security, how will you get to town? Steal Raoul's Jeep?"

"You're assuming I'll take the road, but that's the first place they'll look. I'll head out across the fields."

Oz shook his head. "Won't work. I drove in here and we're at least ten miles from any real town."

She refrained from telling him that ten miles was a stroll in the park for her. At a conservative seven-and-a-quarter-minute miles, she could reach safety in a little over one hour.

"We'll take the motorcycle," Oz said.

"*We* won't take anything. *I'm* leaving. You stay here and wait for the troops to arrive," Emma said.

Oz gave her an incredulous look. "Are you serious? You mean to do this alone?" Emma pushed away from the fence.

"I do." She spun around to walk toward the cycle. Oz grabbed her arm, stopping her mid-stride.

"I'm going with you," he said.

It wasn't an option. He'd only slow her down, something she couldn't afford.

"You're not. The safest thing for you to do is to wait here until I send the authorities. They need you to deliver the shipment. They won't hurt you until that's completed." She tried to continue toward the motorcycle, but Oz wouldn't let go of her arm. She watched as the surprise on his face turned to anger.

"You are *not* leaving me here. You break out, I do too."

Emma was acutely aware of the camera on the pole not twenty feet away. If anyone was watching, they'd see that she and Oz were arguing. That was good. She needed them to view Oz as her adversary, not as part of a team. He'd be safer once she left. She jerked her arm out of his grip in an exaggerated motion and pointed a finger at him.

"Listen to me. What I'm going to do will probably kill me. If I manage to elude the cameras, they could catch me in the field. They caught me last time when I landed in one of their hidden tunnels. That could happen again. My only edge is that they'll have to navigate the terrain in their Jeeps, and that's going to slow them down, but if they take one of those," she pointed at the horses grazing in the field, "then it's going to be an interesting proposition. Who's faster? Runner or rider?"

Oz looked over at the horses. "Rider," he said.

Emma shook her head. "Not necessarily. There are ultra runs that match horses against runners. Some are called ride and tie, because two runners on a team take one horse. The first teammate rides the horse, ties it up, and continues on foot. The second runner runs to the tied horse, hops on, and rides past the first. In this case the horse usually moves ahead because it gets a rest in between. But in a straight race on an uneven trail, runner against horse, the best horses will beat the best runners, but not *all* the horses will." Emma looked at the animals grazing. "I'm one hell of a fast runner. Close to the best. We'll just have to see what kind of horseflesh La Valle has invested in. No matter what, though, I'll need to be fast and nimble to stay ahead, but I can't do that if you're with me. You'll fall behind, they'll find you and kill you."

"I can run too. Especially if I know it's going to get me out of here."

"How fast? Six minute miles? Seven? For how long and how far? You said town is ten miles away. Can you maintain that pace over difficult terrain for sixty minutes?"

Oz paused. "I have no idea how six- or seven-minute miles would feel." At least he was honest. Emma had to give him that.

"Let me tell you; an untrained runner couldn't do it. Even for a trained runner, ten miles at six minutes per mile would feel like agony. Your heart starts pounding in your chest and you can't catch enough breath. Dragging your legs forward time after time begins to feel like an impossible task, you trip when your legs don't cooperate, and each step feels like you're running through water. If you've eaten it's likely the food comes up and you'll have to stop to throw up. It's a rare person who could run that fast without extensive training. Most amateur runners that *are* trained can't sustain such a pace. It's that hard to do."

She stalked to the motorcycle and waited for him to join her. When she looked back, she saw that he was still standing near the fence. After a moment he started toward her. When he stepped from the bright sunlight into the carport's shade, she saw that he was furious. His brows pulled together in a frown and his mouth was set in a straight line. He climbed onto the cycle and waited. She slid onto the back and once again put her arms around his waist. His entire body felt rigid with anger.

He swung the bike around and gunned it back the way they came, curving toward the migrant huts. This time the sentry didn't rise from his resin chair. He simply nodded and went back to talking on a cell phone that was pressed to his ear.

Emma took her kit and marched straight to the hut containing the patients. She stopped right before the entrance to slip on the surgical gloves Perez had given her. As she opened the door she heard the cycle's engine roar as Oz revved it. She didn't glance back. She listened to it fade in the distance as he drove away.

The hut's interior baked with the escalating heat of the day matched by the warmth of the men's bodies. Some were shifting, moving on their mats, but none looked alert enough to be conscious. Whatever sleeping potion Octavio had given them, it was powerful. She crouched down next to the closest man and analyzed his sores. Raw and inflamed, with black around the edges, they appeared almost gangrenous. Emma assumed the internist had considered gangrene brought on by some sort of infection first, but she would check for it as well. She thought about herpes, shingles, a virulent form of measles, chickenpox: the list was endless. She picked up a scalpel and used the blunt side of the blade to begin scraping cells onto the small glass slides. The skin peeled easily, and when it did, it gave off a sickly sweet smell. Emma would not be surprised if gangrene was the answer.

She collected specimens from each man, working her way down the mats. So intent was she

on the process that she failed to notice that the
oil lamps had burned low. One guttered and the
room went blacker. She sat back on her heels,
waiting to acclimate to the new darkness.

A hand grabbed her by the forearm. The sores
on the man's palm scraped against the top of her
arm, and Emma felt herself begin to panic when
she realized that the man's infected skin was in
direct contact with hers. She would have jerked
her arm out of his grasp, but she was afraid that
such a violent movement would only rip the sores
open, with the end result that she'd be further at
risk. She froze.

"Let go of me. Quickly," she said.

"It's the revenge. He was right," the man hissed
in a sibilant whisper. His English was heavily
accented, but Emma understood him. That he
shook in fear needed no explanation.

"Let go of my arm. You'll spread the infection."

"He sent them to eat us."

Emma did her best to breathe normally. The
man still had her by the arm. "Eat you? Do you
mean the armadillos?"

She felt the man's movement as he nodded.
"Yes. He sent them to eat us. And now, we die."

"I'm here to help you. Let go of me."

He let go. Emma ripped open an alcohol swab
and rubbed it across her arm, covering every inch
of it. When she was done, she took out a second
and repeated the action. The tangy smell of iso-
propyl alcohol stung her nose and she felt her
eyes watering with the combination of antiseptic
and smoke that hung in the air.

"Please save us. Save me," the man said.

The desperate plea made Emma's throat swell with unshed tears. She would not cry in front of this man. She swallowed once, and, when she regained control, she nodded.

"I'm going to solve this. I won't rest until I do," she said. She imbued her words with as much certainty as she could. It was easy to do so, because she spoke the truth. She would not leave these men to die. The patient fell back on the mat. His eyes closed.

The door swung open, bringing with it a triangle of sunlight that pointed into the room. Octavio stepped into the hut. He held a small burlap sack gathered together and tied at the neck with twine. He held it up to her.

"I bring the salvia," he said. "Do you wish to stay?" Emma collected her slides, placing them carefully in the brown paper bag.

"I can't. I need to look at these under a microscope, but I'll return as soon as I finish."

"It will take a while to start. Perhaps an hour."

Emma nodded and walked past him through the still open door into the fresh air and sun. She tilted her face upward, basking in it. On an impulse, she turned her arm, the one the man had grasped, and angled it into the sunlight. She held it there, feeling the heat warm her skin. After a moment she jogged out of the enclosure and headed into the trees. Once in the shade she picked up her pace. Running always had the effect of soothing her, no matter what the circumstances. She kept moving past the hacienda, stable, and

onto the dirt road headed to the ranch. She held
the bag as steady as she could, keeping the arm
that clutched it still and swinging the other in
rhythm. After a moment, the ranch house came
into view. Perez's SUV was gone, but in its place
was Oz's motorcycle.

Emma stepped into the kitchen and found Oz
sitting at the table, eating a sandwich. A brown
paper bag sat in front of a nearby chair. He glanced
up at her, then jerked his chin at the bag.

"That's a sandwich for you. Raoul said to bring
it. He wants you to keep working." Oz spoke in
a formal tone and returned to eating, making it
clear he was still angry with her. Emma set the
slides down next to the sink and washed her
hands. She slid into the chair next to Oz's and
pulled a sandwich out of the bag. "I have some
bad news," Oz said. Emma bit into the sandwich,
a turkey club with fresh tomatoes. It wasn't until
that moment that she realized how hungry she
was. She nodded at Oz to continue. "Perez went to
the hacienda and asked La Valle if she could take
your samples to a lab for analysis. He said no."

Emma stopped eating. "Why not?"

Oz shook his head in disgust. "Seems La Valle
doesn't want anyone on the outside to get wind
of what's happening here. Raoul said he's afraid
the other cartels will learn of it and see it as a
sign of weakness, and if the government hears
that a strange disease is sweeping through the
area they'll feel compelled to send their own scientists."

Emma wasn't surprised at La Valle's decision.

A man like him never worked within the system, and his fears of government scientists descending on the ranch were probably right on target. He was maneuvering himself into a corner, letting his fear of arrest cloud his judgment. Emma was pleased that Perez had asked, though. Perhaps the woman had a conscience after all.

"When do you make your move?" Oz said.

"Tonight."

EMMA JOGGED BACK TOWARD THE MIGRANT HUTS, having declined Oz's offer of a ride. She wanted to count cameras and get the lay of the land. Outside the fence lay expansive fields dotted with scrub, trees, and low-lying brush. Oz had told her that the town lay due south. Halfway down toward the hacienda she saw a guardhouse next to an electrical pole. She knew there were four others: one located close to the main entrance, and the other three positioned along the perimeter. Each held two guards, and the far ones also included dogs. She wondered how many screens each position maintained. It made sense that the house at the main entrance held the most equipment. Oz had told her that it was by far the biggest of the five. He opined that the "satellite" stations monitored only the perimeter areas closest to them. Emma certainly hoped he was correct, because it would simplify her mission immensely. If he was, then she could disable the guardhouse at the main entrance and run from there, but the others would not see her leave.

She hugged the fence line and worked her way around the hacienda, neither speeding up nor slowing down. When she reached the driveway leading down to the gated entrance, she turned to run that way, keeping her pace, hoping she looked to all as though she was simply out for a run. After a couple of minutes, both the primary guardhouse and the entrance gates appeared. She ran toward them both, but slowed.

The guardhouse lay fifty meters back from the gate and to her left. It was a two-story building made of the same materials as the hacienda, and bearing the same terra-cotta tile roof. Tinted windows lined all four sides of the second level, and the roof bristled with antennas and a cluster of satellite dishes. Each corner boasted a camera along with a spotlight and megaphones, and at the very top, in a sort of cupola, was a revolving spotlight, like a lighthouse. Presumably the guards left it off until it was needed.

Emma slowed to a walk, her hands on her hips, and did her best to appear as though she was tired. She drew even with the guardhouse and heard a whirring sound. The closest camera moved slightly, tracking her. She walked in a circle and continued back toward the hacienda along the driveway. She heard the whirring sound again as the camera followed her progress.

During the entire time she was acutely aware of the camera, pointed at her back. She wondered if a gun was pointed there as well. She breathed a sigh of relief when she disappeared from view around the corner. The sentry at the migrant area didn't bother to look up when she walked past him toward the migrants' building. His indifference was heartening. She only hoped the entrance guards were as lax, but somehow she didn't think so. She pushed open the door to the patient hut.

A blast of fragrant smoke hit her full in the face. She stepped out, took a deep breath of fresh air and stepped back inside.

The patients were in varying degrees of intoxication. Some giggled uncontrollably, while others batted at the air around them. The majority lay perfectly still, their eyes watching something that only they could see. Octavio squatted near the head of one while he conducted an intense conversation. The man babbled in Spanish, stopping only to take a breath. Octavio appeared to be prodding him along, asking questions in a low voice.

Emma felt her own senses release, and her body started vibrating in slow motion. A languid feeling crept over her. Her thoughts became disjointed, and it was all she could do to remain focused. A low humming noise began in her inner ear. All her resolve and ambition to move disintegrated, and she wanted only to remain still. A series of thoughts and images ran before her eyes.

She was back in the jungle, running. Large palm leaves slapped her face and she could feel the soft earth below her feet. The image morphed into one where she stared through a small porthole as a pointed rocket head raced toward her. Oz's face appeared, followed by that of Cameron Sumner, a man she knew. He smiled at her and held his hand out as if to pull her toward him. His image exploded and blood splattered over her.

She shook her head and was surprised to note that she'd managed to move in real time, not in a dream. Her eyes refocused, and she was back in the hut, with the dying men all around her. Octavio had moved to yet another patient, and appeared to be interviewing him in the same manner as the first. Emma needed to get to him, but she didn't trust her balance if she stood. Instead she crab walked around the mats to reach his side. Octavio glanced at her out of the corner of his eye.

"Ask him if the armadillos come at night," Emma said.

Octavio raised an eyebrow at her. "The armadillos?"

Emma nodded. Octavio fired off a question in Spanish to the man. The patient became agitated. He tried to sit up, and when Octavio held him down, the patient batted at his hands. All the while he babbled in Spanish.

"What's he saying?" Emma said.

Octavio frowned. "He said that the beasts come at night, digging with their claws. The animals chew on them, then leave."

Emma felt herself come to full awareness. There was something here, a clue, she could sense it. She only wished she could discern how much of what the man said was real, and how much was salvia-induced fantasy.

"Ask him if he thinks it's a dream, or real."

Octavio looked at her. "I don't have to ask. I'm here every night, watching over them. When I sleep, another man guards them in my stead. There are no armadillos. The only thing that comes at night is darkness, and their own fears."

"Still, ask him. Please."

Octavio got an annoyed look on his face, but he rattled off a question in Spanish. The nearest patient answered. When he was finished, Octavio looked wary, and a bit baffled.

"He says that he has seen the armadillos, and it could be a dream, or it could be real, but no matter whether fantasy or reality, the beasts are symbolic of La Valle, and they do his bidding." Emma tried to imagine what the man had actually seen that he mistook for an armadillo.

"What do you think about this?" she asked Octavio. He pursed his lips as he pondered the question.

"I think he saw something. I never saw an animal enter this cabin, but perhaps I nodded off to sleep and it occurred then." Emma stared at the assembled men, all of whom were muttering and tossing.

"They have a lot of chemicals running through their systems. The sleeping potion that you gave them, the salvia now, it's entirely possible that what they are seeing is a hallucination, nothing more."

Octavio looked dubious. "That doesn't account for the salvia. When a man speaks through the salvia, he speaks the truth." Another patient began talking, holding an entire conversation with himself. He nodded and then laughed, as if there was a person in front of him, not blank air. He stopped laughing and crossed himself while intoning words in a prayerful cadence, and he reached out to Octavio and fired off some more sentences. The man's eyes held a pleading note. Octavio listened, and then sucked in his breath. The man subsided back onto the mat, mumbling.

"What did he say?" Emma asked.

Octavio stood and began gathering up his things. He retied the twine around the bag containing the remaining salvia and blew on the leaves burning in the shallow terra-cotta pots he'd placed around the men. When he was done, he looked at her with a sad expression in his eyes.

"He asked for a priest to say his last rites, and suggested that we do so as well. He said death visits us all after the clock strikes three."

10

EMMA BURST OUT OF THE HUT, WITH OCTAVIO right behind her. He reached out to grasp her elbow and held her in place.

"I'm sorry, but I believe the man speaks the truth."

Emma shook her head. "His truth, not mine. Tomorrow is *not* my day to die."

Octavio contemplated her with a serious look on his face. "Why do you insist that death is not coming? It comes for all of us."

"Not now. Not for me," Emma said. She indicated the salvia bag. "May I have the rest?"

Octavio handed it to her. "Please, take it. I have more." He gripped her elbow tighter. "What did you see when you inhaled the salvia?"

"Not much. I didn't really smoke it, I just breathed in the fumes."

"Yes, but inhaling the smoke should have induced a mild hallucination. What did you see?"

"I didn't see my death, if that's what you're asking." Her answer didn't seem to satisfy him, because he waited with an expectant look in his eyes. Emma sighed. "I saw the past and two men that I know. I didn't see the future."

"Are the men living?"

"Very much so."

Octavio let go of her arm. "Watch behind you every waking moment. Especially tomorrow. Don't be afraid to retrace your steps to find the answer."

Whatever that means, Emma thought, but the request seemed easy enough. "I will."

This time her answer seemed to satisfy him. He gave her a curt nod and began walking toward the clearing where his tepee was set up.

"Octavio!" Emma called out. He turned to face her.

"Is tomorrow your day to die?"

Octavio nodded. "I believe the man."

Emma watched him disappear into the trees. She struck out toward the fields. Oz had told her he'd be there, watching them as they prepared the shipment for travel. "If I'm going to transport the thing, I at least want to have some say in the method," he'd told her. At that moment she needed to talk to the one sane person in the entire compound, and that was Oz.

She found him, Raoul, La Valle, and three other men standing in the road between the two fields. If anything, the ruined field appeared even worse than it had just a few hours earlier. The smell of decay had increased, and the black color of the infected leaves seemed more pronounced. Very little green color remained.

All of the men stood in front of an ambulance. When Emma stepped closer, she saw that the sides and floor of the vehicle had been removed. The migrant workers were busy packing burlap bags of leaves into the space. They finished lining the bed, and then replaced the steel bottom over the sacks. It snapped into place. They then turned their attention to the walls. Thick elastic cords ran vertically from top to bottom, spaced about three inches apart. The men stacked bricks of marijuana one on top of another behind the cords. The columns increased. When they were done with one side, they replaced the steel wall. They turned to the next side, and began stacking again. Once the walls were in place, the men began to reassemble the interior, adding a collapsible gurney, packets of gauze, breathing apparatus, syringes, and bottles of anesthetic. The ambulance resumed its usual appearance.

La Valle turned his beady eyes on her. "The vet spoke to me. You tell anyone else about the disease here and I'll slit your throat."

"I need access to a lab. I told you that," Emma said. She leveled a stare at La Valle. "Serena will die unless I can narrow down her symptoms. She may even die with it."

La Valle pointed a finger at her. "She dies, and you do, too."

Emma didn't bother to respond. She wouldn't be there long enough for any of it to matter. She was leaving that night. Once she notified the authorities, she would see that Serena and the men were taken to a real hospital for treatment. La Valle could burn in hell for all she cared.

La Valle spit on the ground. "No lab. And forget about trying to get anyone here or in Ciudad Juarez to help you. They know that I am the real government." He moved to his Mercedes and crawled inside. Raoul smirked at her and followed La Valle into the vehicle. The motor roared to life, and the car shot off, its back wheels churning up dirt and gravel from the crude road.

She walked to stand next to Oz. From that angle she saw a black Cadillac Escalade parked behind the ambulance. The back doors were thrown wide and the workers were busy lining the interior of that vehicle as well. Behind the SUV was a black BMW 850 with its wheel wells exposed. The migrants packed the opened space with more bricks. Emma moved to the side to peer into the interior. The cavity that usually contained the glove compartment was exposed and it, too, was being filled. The trunk lid was up and the migrants worked their way back and forth.

Oz took a swig from a plastic water bottle. "What happened at the hut? Did they smoke the salvia?"

"It didn't go well."

He raised an eyebrow. "What happened?"

"One of the men claimed that we were all going to die tonight when the clock strikes three."

Oz groaned. "More hocus-pocus. These guys believe in more shit than the rock groups I've dealt with for the past eight years, and I thought the rockers were nuts. They were on as many drugs, that's for sure. What did Octavio say?"

"He agrees with the men. He thinks he'll die then."

"And you?"

Emma shook her head. "No. Not me."

Oz gazed at her. "You still going to try to escape tonight?"

Emma nodded.

Oz looked down at the ground. "I'll help you." She opened her mouth to protest, and he held up a hand. "I don't expect to come with you. But you'll need my help with the cameras."

Before Emma could ask him what he meant, a worker waved Oz over to the BMW. Oz joined him to stare into the trunk. After a moment, he returned to her side.

"I assume the trunk has a false bottom?" Emma indicated the BMW.

Oz nodded. "We'll try to cross the border with all three, spaced at close intervals. If one gets stopped, the other two will try to slip by. My theory is that there are only so many guards at each gate, and if we occupy them with one, the second will be ignored."

"We?" Emma said.

Oz grimaced. "It seems as though I'm not to be trusted. Raoul informed me that four guards will escort me the entire time."

"Why do they need you at all? Why not have the guards handle it?"

"Presumably for my U.S. passport. Raoul claims that the fakes they've been using are being detected more often than not. At least that was what I was told when they recruited me. But now I know that's not exactly true." Oz hesitated. "They actually need my expertise."

Emma glanced at him. Now it comes, she thought. "What expertise?" She sounded sharper than she intended, and the way that Oz looked at her made it clear that he'd caught the tone in her voice.

"I'm good at computers. All things electronic, actually. I have a knack for it. Always did."

He didn't seem willing to continue. Emma pushed him. "And?"

"And they need me to disable the security devices used at the Department of Defense."

EMMA SNORTED IN DISBELIEF. "IS LA VALLE CRAZY?
He can't disable the devices at the Department of Defense. For one thing, the security isn't only technological, it's human. They have guards there. Well-trained ones."

Oz nodded. "I know. I explained to Raoul that even if he could block the cameras, he'd still have the human security to contend with. He said that was no problem. His guns are bigger. But it's all cartel bravado. These guys are so used to getting their own way here, they can't envision a scenario where there is actual resistance."

"And that resistance would continue every step of the way into the building. The offices are loaded with current and past military personnel. Male and female. This isn't your usual corporate crowd. These people know how to defend themselves." Emma felt panicked at the very idea of Oz trying to blast his way into the DOD. He would die in a hail of bullets. On the heels of the thought came the realization that Raoul and La

Valle had to know this. All they wanted was to get the shipment into the building. Once inside and Oz was dead, investigative personnel would descend on the shipment, touching it, inhaling it, and possibly spreading the disease. Oz was expendable. It was a suicide mission.

"You can't deliver that shipment. You know that, don't you?"

Oz gave her a grim look. "I'm going to do what it takes to stay alive. If that means I take out the DOD security, then I will."

Emma could see he was serious. "I won't let it come to that. I have friends who work there. I won't let La Valle hurt them, or you."

Oz stared at her a moment, then sighed. "I'll help you escape." She wanted to tell him to join her, and almost did, but clamped her jaw shut. He wouldn't make it.

"I'm headed back to the far end to look at some slides. Let's talk about this after dinner. I can't make a move until it's dark in any event."

Emma returned to the ranch house by the stables and began preparing the slides for review. She used some of the scrapings from the sores to innoculate petri dishes containing various mediums. She wanted to see if the disease grew under various circumstances, not just when offered a plant or human host upon which to feed.

The camera attached at the center of the ceiling contained one glowing LED pin light underneath a dark glass globe. While Emma worked on the slides, her mind was elsewhere, creating and discarding escape ideas. She wanted to attempt it without including Oz if she could. She didn't know him well enough to be sure that he wasn't acting as the "good cop" in a "good cop, bad cop" scenario, but her gut told her he was just as desperate to leave as she was. Even so, she would rather not involve him.

Her mind wandered to the world outside the compound. By now her absence from her office would be noted, but she doubted that anyone would have begun worrying about it. The plants that she scoured the earth for were often in remote areas accessible only on foot and after hours or days of hiking. As a result, she routinely slept in the field, and had become adept at carrying her own tent, water, and all the supplies she would need for an overnight. Her colleagues knew this. Banner, the CEO of Darkview, might grow suspicious, but if he was in the field as well, there was no telling how long she'd be gone before someone worried about her.

She completed her work and put the petri dishes aside. She placed a slide under the microscope and peered through it at the tissue. The image sprang into focus, a large red scale with irregular edges. Emma recognized nothing unusual.

She blew out her breath in irritation. Solving this problem with such inadequate tools was impossible. Emma removed the slide and added another. Same picture, same problem. Ten minutes later she'd viewed them all and was no further enlightened. She pushed away from the counter and headed to the armadillo barn.

The sun had long since peaked and was head-

ing downward. The air remained heated, but
large clouds of gnats flew low, keeping below the
tree line. Emma glanced at the sky. Heat lightning flashed in the distance. Cameras placed at
the corners of the armadillo barn remained stationary despite her movement. A glance at them
revealed that they were mounted on rigid arms.
These eyes, then, were fixed. Staring. Their LED
lights didn't glow. They were the only ones she'd
seen on the compound that remained dark.

"Dummy cameras," she thought with satisfaction. La Valle must have thought the ground-
armadillo-plate border would protect anyone
from taking his pets, though Emma thought it
more likely that no one wanted the damn things
anyway.

She passed into the barn and was once again
struck by the smell of animal dander, straw, and
the funk of old water and dried dung. Emma
loved the smell of horses and liked the smell of
dogs. She was less than thrilled at the smell of
armadillos. Not overwhelming, but not familiar either. She walked up and down the center
aisle, peering into each enclosure, and glancing
upward whenever she could to peer at the ceiling. The dark rafters were bare of any surveillance technology.

The best place for her escape was right there.
While there were cameras inside the house, they
did not extend to the barn, and the nearest exterior camera focused on the perimeter. By Emma's
estimation, she could take out the one functioning
camera, and the others on the barn were fakes.

She removed her rubber bracelets and peeled apart one. It ripped in half easily, and had striations running the length of it. She pulled on the striated section and was left with a long piece of rubber the thickness of an ordinary rubber band. She strolled out of the barn and over to the pole that held the one camera that she thought was functioning. Its red eye glowed at her.

Pretending nonchalance, she leaned against the pole with her hands behind her. As she did, she took the thick part of the rubber bracelet and pressed it onto the wood, flattening it like clay. The remaining thin band she slid into her pocket. She removed her compass from the other pocket and spotted due west.

With her weapon in place, she was free to stroll back to the main house. She'd eat and rest. When the darkness came, she'd make her move.

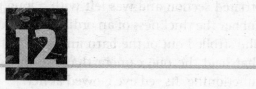

12

HALFWAY TO THE HACIENDA, EMMA HEARD THE sound of pulsing dance music and murmuring voices punctuated with the occasional high-pitched laughter of a woman who sounded well on her way to being smashed. As she neared the pool, Emma spotted the source of all the merriment. At least fifty people were scattered across the yard and Emma could see more inside the hacienda's family room. The french doors were thrown wide to allow the guests to move freely between the house and the pool.

Flaming torches placed in the ground about ten feet apart smelled of citronella oil and smoke, the tangy scent floating on the air. Several people sat on the chaise longues arranged poolside. Two thickset men smoked cigars and conversed, while others smoked rolled joints. The pot smokers handed theirs off to a group of nearby women. A rolling cart loaded with liquor bottles sat at the pool's edge. The containers glowed amber in the yellow light thrown by the torches.

Someone cranked up the music and the milling crowd started dancing, moving in the evening air. Emma changed direction to walk in a large semicircle, skirting the pool area. She was half-way past the hacienda when Raoul rounded the corner. The skinny coyote walked next to him.

"You go back to the stable. Carlos will take you there."

Emma hadn't planned on spending any more time locked in the stall. "I need to eat and get back to the farm. I should keep working." She improvised her answer.

Raoul fixed her with a frown. "No more working tonight. The others are here. I don't want you to be seen. Carlos will bring you dinner. Get moving." He waved a hand at Carlos as he said this.

"I can go the long way around the house to the stables. No one will see me. I need every available minute to try and solve this problem." Emma put some steel into her voice.

"Enough!" Raoul said. He gave Carlos a curt nod and cut away, heading toward the pool and the lights.

"La Valle won't like this!" Emma called to Raoul. He turned and smirked at her.

"La Valle is having a party. While he does, he won't give a damn about anything."

Carlos grabbed her arm and started dragging her away from the hacienda, back to the stall. He pulled a pistol out of his waistband and held it in his free hand, making sure she saw it. They reached the stable where she'd been that morning. A quick glance at the cameras placed on the outside confirmed that they were live. Red lights glowed. Carlos dragged her into the stable's breezeway. She spotted two more cameras at either end, but neither had a red light. More dummies, she thought.

Carlos got to the stall where she'd started her day and shoved her in, sliding the door after her. She heard him snap the locks closed and walk away.

Emma checked the rubber band she'd placed that morning. It was still there, stuck on the side of the door. Satisfied, she settled onto the straw. Her stomach growled, and she did her best to ignore it. She hoped that Carlos would remember to bring her food.

The moon shone through the bars on the high rectangular window, lighting the area enough so that Emma could once again see the streaks of blood on the interior walls. She moved as far into the center of the small space as she could and settled into the hay, bunching parts of it into a pile to form a makeshift bed, and waited.

Twenty minutes later Carlos reappeared with a plate in his hand. He opened the stall door and handed it to her, along with a bottle of water. He closed the panel with a thud, and snapped the locks closed once again.

Emma tore at the shredded pork and munched on the corn bread that accompanied it. She washed the entire meal down with the water. When she was finished, she subsided again onto the straw. The party noises increased, with the shrieking of high-pitched voices growing more shrill and coming more often. Every few minutes she heard a splash as a guest jumped into the pool. The water landings were each time followed by laughter and a smattering of applause. Electronic dance music punctuated the splashes. The party sounded like it was getting louder, the attendees wilder. Emma would wait a little longer before making her move. She settled into the straw for a short nap.

She woke with a start, disoriented. The music cranked higher, blaring across the empty area. The splashes were constant. It seemed as though the entire party had migrated to the pool. Somewhere a dog barked incessantly, its flat tone cutting through the synthesized music. Now the smell of marijuana reached her, carried on the soft breeze. The moon had moved only a little. Emma estimated she had slept for half an hour, no more. She heard the faint buzzing of a mosquito in her ear. She batted at it with the back of her hand.

It was time to leave. She rose in one movement and walked to the rubber band. She removed the pack of matches she'd stolen from the stable, twisted off a single one, and scratched it across the pack. It lit with a fizzing noise, accompanied by the smell of sulphur. She reached through the bars to get the flame as close to the band as she could.

She froze when she heard the sound of boot heels hitting stone. She yanked her hand back inside and blew out the match.

Oz appeared in front of the stall door. He gazed at her. Gray shadows and milky white light covered his face. He looked drawn, tired, and grim, yet he was the only friendly face she'd seen in a while, and she smiled a tentative smile. His responding smile was sad. Poignant, almost. It seemed as though he had accepted his fate.

"I came to get you out of here," he said. She released a breath that she didn't realize she was holding. He walked to the end of the corridor and stared in the direction of the pool. While he did she gently removed the band from the door. She shoved it in her pocket for use at a later time.

"Aren't you worried about the cameras?" she said.

"The ones in here are fakes. As for when the others catch sight of us, I'll make up some sort of story." His right hand was wrapped around a longneck beer, the other holding something that Emma couldn't see. He lifted it up, and she saw that he held a large ring with a mass of keys attached.

"I bring you the key to heaven. Or at least to freedom from that tiny box they've put you in." Oz took a swig of the longneck and placed it on the ground at his feet. A messenger bag, its strap slung over his shoulder diagonally, swung against his hip. "Now it's just a matter of finding the right one." He inserted a brass key into the lock. Emma watched him try to turn it. It didn't move. He glanced up at her. "Clearly not the right one." He inserted another. No go. He moved the next into position. Shoved it in the lock and tried to turn it. From the hacienda came the sound of a huge splash and the yells of the partygoers.

"Are they all in the pool?" Emma asked.

Oz kept his eyes on the lock in front of him. "The men are cannonballing into the deep end and the women are congregating at the shallow end. The wet bar area is covered with little piles of every type of drug imaginable. Cocaine, meth, marijuana, 'shrooms, little pill piles of oxycontin, you name it. It's like a drug buffet. Every one of them is blasted and washing their powders down with alcohol. At some point they're either going to fall unconscious or fight."

He shoved yet another key into the lock and Emma wanted to shout with joy when she saw it turn. "Got it." He pulled the door aside.

Emma stepped into the center corridor. "Thank you," she said.

Oz retrieved his beer and took a full gulp. He handed it to her. She took it and swallowed a mouthful. It was smooth and still decently cold. It tasted like heaven.

"Let's get out of here." Oz replaced the panel and locked the stall. "Stay close to the stable walls. They're so hammered at the pool that I doubt anyone will spare a glance this way, but you never know."

"I want to head to the farm," Emma said.

Oz raised an eyebrow at her. "Any particular reason you chose that area?"

Emma moved to the edge of the stable wall and peered around it, doing her best to keep herself out of sight, both from the revelers and the cameras on the corners. Through the trees she could catch glimpses of the men as they moved back from the pool in order to get a running start for their cannonballs.

"The cameras on the barn are dummies. I'm almost sure of it. The only one that needs to be disabled is on the high pole next to the ranch house."

"How do you intend to do it?" Oz asked. Emma turned to face him.

"Blow it up."

Oz's mouth dropped open. "You mean, like a bomb?"

Emma nodded. "Just like that. Let's go."

"Wait a minute. You can't blow up that camera. The guards at the front are hardly going to miss an exploding camera. They'll be all over you in a minute."

Emma shrugged. "There are too many cameras to allow me to slink away unnoticed. Even if I could quietly disable one, they would be alerted once it went off line. Blowing it up has the same effect. The key point is that they won't see the crucial information, which is the direction I take over the fence."

"That will never work," Oz said.

Emma put her hands out. "It's all I've got."

"I have a better idea."

Emma paused. "And that would be?"

"I'll block the camera. Hijack its frequency and play them a fake tape. You can leave from the ranch, and they'll never see you go, because they'll be otherwise occupied." He hoisted the bag off his hip to show her. "I've been thinking about this all day, and I'm pretty sure it will work. I have everything I need to do it right here." Emma walked over and flipped the top off the bag to peer inside. What looked like a metal laptop was all she saw.

"That's all it takes to block the cameras?"

Oz shook his head. "Not *all* of the cameras, just those that sit within twenty or thirty feet of where I place this, so you'll have to pick your location wisely."

"Let's get to the ranch. We can try it there."

"After you," he said. They walked toward the parking lot where the ever-present white van sat, as well as Oz's motorcycle. He climbed on and she moved behind him. More shrieks came from the pool.

"Think they'll notice the sound of the engine?" Emma asked.

"Doubtful. They're pretty far into party mode now."

They headed to the ranch, the darkness broken only by the flickering headlight. They made it to the carport and killed the engine. A camera placed high at the ranch house's corner glowed red, but it was pointed away from them.

"Ready?" Oz said.

Emma nodded. "You have no idea how ready."

"Then let's go." Oz reached into the messenger bag and pulled out a small, portable DVD player and his laptop computer. He connected the two, turned on the DVD and waited. The screen sprang to life, and showed an image of the ranch house's yard. The only movement was the flitting of insects as they shot through the glow thrown by a lit porch light. Oz pointed at the screen.

"That's what the guards are seeing right now. I've rigged the player to send a wireless signal, and I've set it to use the same frequency as the security cameras."

"Where did you get this?" Emma said.

Oz smiled. "I asked Serena if she had any portable DVD players. Told her I wanted one for my room to watch a movie. She gave this to me, and offered some discs from La Valle's personal collection."

"Does this mean that if I walk across the lawn, they won't see my image, but just this?"

Emma pointed at the screen.

"No. That's live. If you walk into the frame, they'll see you do it. Once I start the player, the movie will play and the security cameras will pick up that image instead of the yard."

"Are you sure?"

Oz nodded. "You've heard of people in a neighborhood who have their baby monitors set to the same frequency? One picks up the signal from the other's house and, bingo, you get an image of whatever the other monitor is viewing. This," he indicated the player, "is going to do the same thing. Except they won't see the interior of a room, they'll be seeing the movie."

"What did you pick?"

Oz gave her a sly grin. "La Valle had an extensive porn collection. I figured once they saw it, they wouldn't be in any great hurry to run out and stop it."

Emma laughed. "That's brilliant."

Oz nodded. "I hope so." He sobered. "When do you want to leave?"

Emma took a deep breath. She put a hand on his arm. "If I make it to the village, I'll call for backup. Just stay out of sight as much as you can until they arrive."

Oz nodded. "I can't wait."

She jerked her chin at the player. "Hit it."

Oz pushed "play."

The image of a writhing couple came into view on the screen. Emma didn't stay to watch, she inhaled and took off running.

13

EMMA SPRINTED INTO THE YARD AND RAN ACROSS the lawn, heading to the fence. A quick glance at the camera on the pole showed that the red light still glowed. She felt her heart skip a beat, but she ignored the fear that wanted to grab at her. She could only trust that Oz's plan was working and the guards were seeing the couple, not her.

She leaped onto the lowest rail, threw her leg over, landed on the other side, and dug her heels into the ground to catapult herself forward. She stumbled once when her foot dropped into a small depression in the ground, but recovered her balance and kept going, dodging brush and cactus on one side, and darting through a small stand of trees. The moon glow was weak and nowhere near enough to reveal every little divot or hole, but enough to allow her to dodge larger obstacles. Once she cleared the trees she picked up the pace to a speed that felt faster than her familiar training pace. A large beetle of some sort, like a June bug, smacked into her cheek. She did her best to ignore it.

The first hill loomed ahead. Emma glanced right and left, looking for a cut through, but the hill face extended on both sides as far as she could see. The ground rose straight up, starting at a forty-five-degree angle, but rising to a nearly sixty-degree angle at the top, with no visible trail. Shrubs, a few cactus, and a couple of meager trees dotted the hillside, but she would be exposed for the duration of the climb. Loose gravel, larger rocks, and deep, soft dirt covered the ground, providing no real footing. Her feet sank into the loose topsoil and skittered downward before she was able to dig the tips of her shoes into a small depression. She continued upward, and began to feel the burn in her calves as they took the brunt of her weight at the canted angle. On the next step her treads failed to grab and she slid downward three feet. She leaned forward and kept going. The climb grew steeper, but she kept the pace, hustling up the hill.

An alarm rose through the night. Emma looked back, dismayed to see the large, circling spotlight flash in the distance. La Valle's men were well trained. She'd only gained fifteen minutes at the most. She started calculating the time it would take for them to reach the foothill. In a Jeep, five minutes, maybe ten, maximum. While they'd have to stop at the base, they could simply look up and see her making the climb. With a decent rifle they'd pick her off. She needed to get to the top and over before they made it there.

On a horse it would be a bit longer, because they'd need to saddle up before riding out. That would chew up at least twenty minutes, and then it would take ten more to make it to the base of the hill. Better for her initially, because she would be over the top before they got there and out of rifle range, but worse in the long run, because they would continue their pursuit. Her heart pounded in a fast rhythm—equal parts exertion and fear. She was closing in on the summit, and slowed to a climbing pace as the angle steepened. She pushed with her feet and clawed with her hands, inching her way higher. She heard the sound of an engine rising and then cutting out when it bounced into the air and presumed it was a Jeep or all-terrain vehicle lurching over the small hills that dotted the area before the massive rise.

She didn't look back, didn't waste the time. She propelled herself upward even faster, her legs burning with the exertion. Now the angle was such that she could grab at the brush with her hands while staying relatively upright. Her left shoe lost traction and she went down on one knee, banging her kneecap onto a small stone. She winced at the sharp pain, but straightened out and kept moving.

She was ten feet from the peak. The engine noise filled the air. She glanced back to see the headlights bouncing, thirty feet from the hill's base. It was an ATV, with an open carriage, a roll bar and two passengers. One held a gun with its butt on his thigh and the long muzzle pointed to the sky. The noise stopped. Now it comes, Emma thought. She strained up, only three feet from the summit. She flung herself to the side, straight left. A rifle shot cracked through the air and bits of dust from a hit only two feet away flew into her face. She propelled herself upward, uncoiling in an explosive push the final two feet, and crawled over the ridge.

She was back on her feet and racing down, now reversing her weight distribution so that she leaned back into, rather than away from, the hill. The pounding on her shins increased three-fold, as she slammed downward with both her weight and the force of gravity, but she'd trained enough to know that her legs would survive it. She reached the bottom in half the time it took for her to climb to the top. At the base the ground leveled out. The next hill sat over three hundred yards ahead, and she began to sprint toward it. No sound came from behind her.

She pushed her speed up a notch, racing over the uneven ground and up and down two small rises before she pulled her compass out of her pocket and pressed on the glow button to check her direction. She was running dead south. Right where she wanted to be.

She heard nothing behind her. Not the sound of alarms, motor engines, yells, or even other animal calls—only the crunching noise made by her shoes as they hit the dirt and stones in a rhythmic cadence. Her breathing evened and she felt her body settle in. This was the best part of a run, when everything functioned as a unit. She knew that any minute a feeling of well-being would wash over her, and her mind would detach and grow peaceful as though she was meditating. In her current state of conditioning, she could maintain this pace and feeling of ease for the next two hours.

The clouds scudded across the sky, and the moonlight bathed the area. Emma dodged a small cactus with only inches to spare. The light stayed constant. Another bug hit her face, and the crunching noise of her footfalls continued. Small potholes and divots covered the ground. If the guards reverted to horseback they would be required to go slowly on the flats in order to avoid having the animal step directly into a hole. Emma doubted any rider would simply race an animal over the terrain. The odds of the horse landing in a depression and snapping a leg were too high. Emma stumbled, regained her footing, and barreled to the next hill, powering into the rise. This one remained at a steady climb the entire way up, and she was at the peak and over with much less exertion. Still, she heard nothing more behind her. My God, could it be this easy? she thought.

She ran for forty-five minutes, scrambling over each hill and running flat out over the fields. After another twenty minutes she saw the occasional light from a farmhouse. In the distance in front of her the village's clustered buildings were pinpoints, growing larger. It was nestled in a slight valley, and Emma was on the rise above it, and able to see the boundary lines where the houses began in earnest. Now other noises mingled with the sounds she was making. Out of the darkness came the sharp report of a gunshot.

Emma's heart skipped and she felt her nerves jangle to the fore. She snapped to attention and raised her speed a notch. Her arms pumped faster and her breathing labored for a minute. Once again it evened out as her body settled into this new, faster pace. She strained to hear above the noise she made as she ran, doing her best to pick up all ambient sound that might indicate pursuit. There came another shot. This time it was clear. It came not from behind her, Emma was sure, but from the direction of the town in front of her. She slowed for the first time in an hour. Several more shots rang out, followed by the boom of an explosion. Emma saw a flash of fire. The village was under attack.

She heard a mixture of voices and screaming from the area in front of her, the sound carrying on the wind, but still faint in the distance. She kept running forward, but now she wasn't sure what to do. Her original plan had been to find the nearest bar, ask to use the phone, and call Banner, the one man she knew could mobilize a crew to assist her. She hadn't counted on running into hell.

Another explosion ripped through the night, and to Emma it felt as though the earth shivered with the impact. This time she saw the fire leap up into the air along with flying clods of dirt and what looked like cement from a building. She could see forms fleeing, their shadows lit by the flames. The rattling report of a semiautomatic gun firing round after round cracked through the air. Sweat from her armpits ran in rivulets down her arms, not so much from the exertion, but from the fear.

She hit an asphalt road and turned onto it, notching her stride up a bit now that she knew she was unlikely to trip on a small hole. The gunshots continued, both in front of her and to her right. She veered left, and back off the asphalt, hoping that direction held more security for her.

Another road appeared, this one running perpendicular to the first, and she stepped onto it. More gunshots, but this time it sounded like the shooter was to her right. She kept on the road, and again picked up her pace, taking advantage of the even terrain. She hoped to be on the other side of town before whoever was shooting decided to expand their horizons and turn her way.

What worried her the most was the complete lack of vehicles on the streets. It was as if the townspeople were already dead. The gunshots continued in earnest, with so many reports that it was clear there were several shooters. The screams were increasing as well. Emma could hear the guttural voices of men, whether the shooters or some other people, she couldn't tell. Two more explosions rocked the town, the second spewing bits of boards into the air. Now Emma could see a few people running, darting out from between the houses and racing down the road.

An armored vehicle turned a corner and entered the main street. Its hood was a wedge shape that enabled it to push objects in front of it, and in the back an open bed contained several men dressed in military fatigues and holding weapons. One man bit off and tossed something small in the direction of a nearby house. It landed on the front lawn and rolled toward the stoop.

The men yelled a warning, and the armored car accelerated away.

Seconds later, the grenade exploded, splintering the porch and shattering the house's front window. More screams filled the air. Emma cut further left, but now the explosions and gunshots were coming from all sides. She cut behind a tree and leaned against it, her breath heaving. She tamped down the panic she felt at the chaos all around her. She couldn't go forward into the town, or sideways around it without risking getting hit by a stray bullet. Backtracking was even less of an option. If La Valle caught her again, she had no doubt he'd torture her, kill her, and give her body to the armadillos to be eaten. She leaned against the trunk and shivered.

The sound of a car, coming fast, made her look around the tree. A black Range Rover barreled toward her, driving across the dirt. The body of the car bumped along in a crazy, jerky pattern. Emma looked down and saw that the front right tire was dangerously low. The car made a slight turn and she saw that the rear tire was low as well. The Rover hit a pothole, and a silver hubcap detached from the side and careened away, rolling on its edge. The car kept coming. Emma ducked back behind the tree and pressed herself tightly against it, trying to make herself as small as possible. The Rover drew even with the tree, and came to a stop. It idled there a moment. Emma watched the passenger window roll downward. Luisa Perez's frightened face came into view.

"Get in the car, now! They're coming!" she said.

Emma sprinted to the Rover and yanked the door open. As she clambered inside, Perez hit the gas and they moved out. Emma grabbed at the door to swing it closed while the car once again began its crazy, jouncing pattern. "La Valle's men alerted the town that you'd escaped. They want you recaptured when you arrive. Of course that was before the trouble started," Perez said.

"What's going on down there?" Emma said. Perez yanked the wheel to the right and Emma bumped against her door. She reached up and pulled her seat belt down, snapping it into place.

"That's the Mexican army. They're wiping out the town."

Emma did her best to contain her shock. "The army? Aren't they the good guys?"

Perez shook her head. "Not necessarily. They think the town is controlled by La Valle. They intend to kill everyone in it to prove that the army is bigger than the cartel."

"Does La Valle control the town? Is everyone under his thumb?"

"Yes, of course, but that doesn't give the army the right to kill them all. There are blameless women and children living there." Perez spoke without removing her eyes from the area in front of the car. Emma heard the scrape of a cactus's needles as they raked the Rover's side.

"I need your cell phone. I have to make a call. Right now. I know the people in charge of a security company in the States. If I call them, they'll come to my aid, no questions asked." Emma held her hand out to Perez.

Perez shook her head. "I don't have a cell phone. I escaped out of the back of my house into the garage. I keep the car keys in a box in the garage, but my cell phone I keep in my purse, which was in the front of the house. The army was busy breaking down the front door, so there was no time to get the phone." Emma leaned back against the seat, and for a short moment she thought she wouldn't be able to control her despair at the knowledge that Perez had no phone.

"Then stop and let me out. I'll take my chances with the army."

Perez snorted. "Are you loco? They'll shoot you first and not even bother to stop and ask your name."

"Where are you going?"

Perez shot her a glance. "To La Valle's, of course."

Emma groaned. She'd run over an hour through the desert night, only to hitch a ride back to where she began.

"Why La Valle's?" she asked.

"If we can make it to the compound, his people might be able to hold them off," Perez said. Emma gaped at her. The idea of holding out at the compound while the Mexican army surrounded it was too ludicrous for words.

"How many soldiers are sacking that town?" Emma said.

Perez yanked the car to the right so violently that Emma smacked the side of her head against the passenger-side window. Perez straightened the wheel once again.

"I don't know. I saw at least forty."

"What makes you think that La Valle can hold them off?"

"He has over thirty security personnel, an entire arsenal of weapons stored in a shed near the ranch stables, and the guts to face down anyone who steps in his path. *That's* what makes me think this way."

"Let me out. I mean it. I'm not going back to La Valle's," Emma said.

"Fine. Go."

Perez slammed on the brakes. Emma jerked forward, then slid back. She threw open the door and jumped onto the grass, slamming the panel behind her. Perez gunned the vehicle, forcing Emma to leap out of the way as it went forward. She turned to see the armored truck with the battering-ram hood heading straight for her but still a fair distance away. The headlights bounced up and down as the vehicle navigated the terrain. Emma raised her hands in surrender.

Bullets struck the dirt all around her. She dove onto the ground. When the noise stopped, she lurched upward and raised her arms again. The truck curved to a stop. More bullets hit the dirt.

She spun and ran on the diagonal. The thunking sounds of ordnance hitting all around her lent wings to her feet, as did the roar of the truck's engine as it started again. She sprinted one hundred meters, then switched left. Perez's Rover was to her right, and Emma watched it circle back toward her. It stopped fifty feet away, kicking up dirt all around. Emma skirted behind it and grabbed at the passenger door. She yanked it open and dove back in. Perez hit the gas.

"Next time you listen to me!" Perez yelled at her. Emma didn't bother to answer, but checked the side-view mirror. The armored vehicle kept coming at them. While it was clear that it was going half the speed of Perez's Rover, it was also clear that once it caught up, the game was over. Five soldiers stood in the truck's bed, grasping the vehicle's sides as it came toward them. Emma cut a glance at the fuel gauge on the Rover. Perez had a fourth of a tank left.

"Can we outrun them?" Emma asked.

Perez, too, glanced at the gauge. "If my gas holds up and theirs fails."

A shot echoed in the night. Emma flinched, but nothing hit the car. Another quick glance in the side-view mirror revealed that the soldier on the left had fired. He took aim once again.

"They're targeting us. Do you have a gun?"

Perez nodded. "There's one in the glove compartment." Emma snapped open the compartment to find a weapon nestled on top of a stack of warranty books. "There should be a fresh magazine. Under the manuals. And a box of bullets." Emma found both, but the magazine had only two bullets in it. She put the box of ammunition on her lap, picked up a bullet, and started to fill the rest of the magazine. It held seventeen rounds. She snapped the magazine into the gun and lowered her window. Perez swerved toward the asphalt street.

"I've had enough of this terrain. I thought it would slow them down, but now I think I should get on the road and outrun them," she said.

Emma turned back and braced herself against the side door, with her left shoulder pressed back against the window frame. When she stuck her head out she got her first clear view of their attackers.

The truck looked like a converted Hummer, with a heavy steel grill guard on the front and an open bed in back. The men riding along were dressed in fatigues. They were running on adrenaline, making whooping noises each time the car slammed into a hole and bounced back up.

Emma raised the gun, holding it with two hands and doing her best to keep it steady despite the rocking car. She heard one of the men yell. A man on the side raised his rifle. She squeezed off three shots. The gun recoiled with each one, but she could have sworn she hit the truck. The men inside dropped below the side walls, and the one with the rifle positioned himself in a corner next to the cab. He put the barrel of his gun on the rail, pointing in their direction.

"Perez, swerve left, now!" Emma said. Perez responded with a vicious yank on the steering wheel. At the same moment, the Rover hit a large boulder. The car's entire right side rose into the air, riding on two wheels. They stayed that way, perched on the left tires, for a few seconds, before the car slammed back down. Perez drove it straight onto the asphalt road and gunned it.

The Rover engine gave a louder roar as it accelerated. Emma watched as they pulled away from the Hummer. It responded with more speed, closing the gap they had just made.

"Faster. They're gaining," Emma said. She felt the car surge forward again.

"My foot's to the floor," Perez said.

A huge explosion rocked the air, followed by a large fireball that was released over the edge of town. The Hummer visibly slowed. A second explosion ripped through the night, even louder than the last. Black smoke cut with red fire belched into the sky. The Hummer curved to a halt, with its side facing Emma. The last thing she saw before it faded from view was the taillights as it turned and raced back toward the town.

PEREZ LAID OFF THE GAS PEDAL, BUT KEPT THE speedometer at eighty. Emma returned to sit in the seat, and pulled the seat belt back into place. She closed the window. Neither of them spoke. Perez leaned into the windshield, and from the strained look on her face, Emma guessed that she was having a hard time seeing the road.

The darkness *was* complete. Emma was struck by how dark it actually was, and for a moment she wondered just how she had managed to run all that way without breaking an ankle. She tamped down the anxiety she felt rising at the thought of returning to La Valle's. It was clear she couldn't go back.

"If I head east or west from here, how long before I hit a town?" Emma said.

Perez seemed to contemplate the question. "Close to twenty-five miles east, and farther to the west." Not great distances, but still another four hours of running through the night. Emma didn't relish the idea, yet she'd do it if it was her only shot.

"And if I skirt around La Valle's and keep going straight on the other side?"

"Ten miles, no more," Perez said.

So that was the best option. "Let me out two miles before the ranch. I'm not going back there," Emma said.

Perez nodded. "I know. I figured as much."

"Come with me," Emma said on an impulse. "I'll call my friends and you'll be safe."

Perez kept her eyes on the road. The silence stretched out. "I can't take the risk. La Valle learns that I helped you, I die."

"How cowed are you by this man? I'll do my best to get you out of here. You can go to Mexico City, anywhere. Going back to your house is not really an option, anyway. Perhaps you can enter the States as a refugee."

Perez snorted. "Not likely. I'll be sent back here immediately. Once I am, La Valle kills me. Slowly."

Something flashed in the headlights' beam.

"Did you see that?" Perez said.

"I did. Are your high beams on?"

Perez flicked a switch and the resulting light pierced farther ahead. There came another flicker, then nothing. Emma felt her scalp prickle, as if someone or something was watching her.

"Slow it down. I have a bad feeling."

Perez took the car down to forty, then twenty, miles per hour. Emma kept her eyes focused in front of the car. The feeling of being watched increased. A terrible thought came to mind.

"Perez, do you think the army has surrounded

the compound already? Maybe they're waiting for a signal to attack?" Perez brought the car to a complete stop, turned off the headlights, and cut the engine. She lowered her window, and Emma did the same on her side. They sat there, listening.

The only sounds were the scratching of insects and the occasional whistle of the breeze as it swooped past the car. From somewhere in front of them, still a distance away, Emma heard the scraping of metal on metal, and the beep of a walkie-talkie, quickly silenced.

"They're out there, waiting," Perez whispered.

"Is there another road parallel to this one? Can we skirt around them in much the same way as I wanted to run around?"

Perez nodded. "The main road to the compound is monitored by cameras starting at about two miles out. If we can circle around them here, maybe we can find a gap. That ranch is so large, they can't possibly ring it completely. There have to be some unguarded sections."

"The most likely spot for a gap is from the front. Especially if they know about the cameras. I would think they'll stay to the sides and back."

"I hate to turn this engine back on. They must have heard us coming."

"I doubt they'll leave their position to come for us, though. They'll stay in place and wait for us to drive right up to them." Emma checked the gun again. "Let's go around to the main road. We'll head for the front entrance."

Perez shot her a look. "We? I thought you were leaving."

Emma shook her head. "Not anymore. Oz is in there. If I can, I'll try to warn him. If not, I'll do my best to help him escape. From all of them."

Perez got a sad look on her face. "There is no escape. We'll be lucky to get out of this alive."

"Today is not my day to die," Emma said. She jerked her chin at the ignition. "Let's go. There's no gain in waiting."

Perez inhaled, turned the key in the ignition, flipped the lights back on, and moved out, dropping off the road and driving parallel to the direction of where they thought the compound's fence lay. Emma kept a watch on the surrounding countryside, but the night was so dark that she doubted she'd see anything until it was upon them. She leaned a little out the window, peering around the side of the car and casting regular glances at the side view mirror to see if anyone was following them. The darkness was unbroken behind them as well. Her eyes watered with the intensity of her stare, and she blinked to keep them moist. Two bugs went splat against the windshield, leaving behind a yellow, pus-like smear. They kept moving. After fifteen minutes, Perez began to angle right, cutting back toward the compound.

"You see anything?" Perez said.

"No. You?"

Perez jerked her head "no." "I think we must be just a couple of miles away from the main road by now."

"Be prepared to turn that wheel and run again if you see anyone." Emma was glad for the relative lack of trees or other tall plants. Scrub bushes, "teddy bear" cactus, and low-lying dry-weather flowers were all that populated the area. There was nowhere to hide, both for the army and for them. She opened the glove compartment and fished around.

"Do you have a piece of paper in here? A pen?"

Perez nodded. "There should be." Emma found both, and wrote the words "Edward Banner" and "Carol Stromeyer" on it, followed by cell phone numbers for both. She held it up for Perez to see.

"Here are the numbers for my friends. You get into trouble, call them." Emma put the paper in the glove compartment and closed it.

"I'm not going to call anyone in the States," Perez said. "Those men may help you because they know you, but they're not going to help me."

"One's a woman, and they *will* help you. They specialize in contract security forces for the Department of Defense. If anyone can stand up to La Valle, it's them." Perez didn't reply. She kept her eyes on the road. "See anything else?"

Perez shook her head. "Nothing."

Emma's feeling of dread remained, but as Perez headed in what she thought was a path that would intersect with the main road, the feeling didn't increase. She didn't see any metallic flashes or any other indication that someone was out there. After ten more minutes, a road appeared in the Rover's beam.

"That's it!" Perez's voice held a note of excitement. Clearly she thought they were close to safety.

Emma wished she shared Perez's faith in La

Valle and his henchmen. She thought it unlikely that La Valle would come out on the right side of a firefight against the Mexican army, no matter how many guns he had and guards he employed. The army had the advantage that it could move freely around the compound in any direction, and if the siege lasted for a while, could replace men by driving them in from the surrounding countryside. La Valle, on the other hand, would be trapped in his ranch, forced to fight wave after wave of the army.

Emma shook off the thought. If there was one thing she'd learned in the last few years of working with and around the Darkview security personnel, it was that not everything went as planned. Not at all. When that thing went awry for the Mexican army in their attack, Emma would seize on it and use it against them.

"Get ready," Perez said. "I'm going to drive as fast as I can to the front entrance."

"Wait! What if they think we're an intruder and fire on us?"

"They know my car. They won't fire."

Perez hammered the pedal down, and the Rover hesitated a moment, as if it hadn't quite decided that she was serious. Then the car surged forward in a squeal of wheels and shooting bits of gravel. Emma watched the speedometer needle move upward in a smooth motion. It passed fifty, sixty, seventy, and soon was inching ahead of ninety-five.

The car shot down the asphalt road. Emma watched the foliage whip by, but nothing else seemed to impede their progress. The entrance gates came into view, with their scrolled "P." Emma watched as they slowly opened. Perez dialed down the speed and she shot through the gates and hammered on the brakes. The car skidded to a stop.

Perez was out of the Rover in a flash. She left the car lights on, the key in the ignition, and the door hanging open. The repetitive dinging of the warning bell set Emma's teeth on edge. She reached over, yanked the key fob out and tossed it on the front seat. She slid the revolver into her waistband at the small of her back and covered it with her shirt. Raoul jogged toward the car, with Carlos hot on his heels, his ever-present gun in his hand and his usual angry expression. Three other men that Emma didn't recognize appeared from the guard station. They all looked worried. Emma climbed out of the car. Raoul stopped, took one look at her, and pointed his gun.

"Where the hell did you go?" he said.

Perez stepped between them. "There's no time for that. The army surrounds us. They attacked the town, shooting at anything that moved. I think they're coming here next. We saw some lying in wait on the west end."

From somewhere in the distance came the shrill sound of a woman laughing and the bass beat of electronic dance music.

"Is the party still going?" Emma said. It seemed like a lifetime ago that she'd leapt the fence.

Perez gave Raoul a sharp look. "Party? Who's here?"

Raoul grimaced. "The Ginoas and Chandos."

"*All* of them?" Perez sounded shocked.

Raoul nodded. "At least the main guys. Felipe, Juan, and the ladies. The lieutenants, too. Jorge and that skinny one with one eye."

"They call him 'Churro.' I've never learned his name," Perez said.

"What condition are they in?" Emma said.

Raoul pointed the gun at her. "Shut up. You have nothing to say here."

Perez once again waved him off. "It's an important question. If they're staggering drunk they're going to be no use. Do we tell them?"

Raoul shot off a rapid sentence to one of the nearby guards and jerked the tip of his gun in the direction of the hacienda.

"Come on. You two are going to tell La Valle what you know."

Perez jogged up to Raoul and fell in step beside him. Emma followed at a considerably slower pace. She thought of and discarded several plans in the space of a minute.

The worse fact was that now she was not only back on the compound, but she was in an even more precarious position than before, if such a thing was possible. La Valle could choose to kill her after she finished telling her tale, and if he didn't kill her, she'd have to stand and fight should the army attack.

ONCE THEY TURNED THE CORNER TO THE BACK OF the hacienda, the full extent of the party was revealed. The shrieking women were dancing by the pool, wearing only their diamond necklaces and bikini bottoms and stiletto heels. All looked smashed. None appeared capable of staying upright much longer, much less holding a gun and shooting it to defend themselves.

Emma noted that the men were in even worse shape. Two lay passed out on the chaise longues lining the deck area, and another was busy throwing up in the nearby bushes. One man staggered past the women without a glance, a bottle of Patron tequila in his hand. He raised it to his lips and took a huge gulp before continuing to sway in the hacienda's direction. Neither La Valle nor Serena were in sight.

Raoul must have seen this as well, because he veered off toward the house and the family room. He, Carlos, Perez, and Emma stepped through the french doors.

Loud music assailed them. The stereo on the built-in cabinets on the wall blared a screaming rap song. La Valle sat on the couch, smoking a cigar with Serena in his lap. On the cocktail table before them was an elaborate hookah, with its water-filled lower bowl and three tubes.

Next to La Valle sat another man Emma didn't recognize. Serena took a drag off the hookah. Jasmine-and-rose-scented smoke filled the air. Oz sat in a leather chair on the right of the room. He held his own hookah tip to his lips. His bloodshot eyes looked glassy and his face was lined with exhaustion. He glanced over at Emma, and his eyes widened. He sat up straighter.

La Valle fixed Emma with a stare and nudged Serena off his lap. She landed on the couch next to him. Her heavy-lidded eyes telegraphed her drunken state. Emma took a quick glance at her finger. The spot now covered half her hand and the fingers from the first knuckle to the tip. Emma felt some sympathy for the woman. She, of all people, had a reason to be smashed this evening.

Raoul walked over to the stereo and swung the volume control down. He turned back to La Valle. "Something's happened," he said.

"Why isn't she locked up?" La Valle responded.

Perez stepped forward. "The army attacked the town. I barely got out of there alive. We came here on Quinona Road and saw some more soldiers camped out." Perez waved in the direction of the stables. "Near the farm. I think they're planning to attack here next."

"How do you know they were army?" La Valle said. He stood up.

"They wore the uniforms. They came in army-issue trucks," Perez said.

La Valle remained still, thinking. The only sound in the room was the bubbling of the hookah as Serena continued to inhale. Her head rested against the back of the couch, and her eyes were closed. She didn't seem to be listening to the conversation. Emma flicked a glance over to Oz. He had put aside the tube on his own hookah, and rose off the couch, slowly. He pinned Emma with a look that seemed to say, What the hell is next? The party continued outside and the cacophony of voices mingled with the music that poured from the exterior speakers. Emma estimated there were fifty people in the pool area alone.

A man stepped into the room. About forty-two years old, he was of medium height and weight, with hair that was cut close to his head. He wore expensive jeans, a polo shirt, and had a revolver clipped to his belt. Three heavy gold chains looped around his neck, and the letter C in script and studded with diamonds sparkled on one. He directed a string of Spanish at La Valle, who answered. The man's eyes flickered, but Emma thought he did an excellent job hiding his astonishment. He turned to Emma and spoke to her in Spanish.

"He wants to know who you are," Perez translated.

"Emma Caldridge. An American chemist."

The man's eyes narrowed at her. "What were you doing out there?"

Emma went for the truth. "I was running away, what do you think I was doing?"

"Why did you come back here?" He'd switched to English. "Why didn't you stay with the army?"

"She tried to go to them," Perez explained. "They shot at her. You know how they are, they shoot first and ask questions later."

"They don't act like any army men I've ever encountered," Emma said.

La Valle snorted. "That's because they're not. What do you think, Chando? Are they the ones controlled by Duarte?"

Chando nodded. "Probably. They think to ambush us all while we party."

"How did they find out about it?" Raoul said.

Chando inhaled. "Someone betrayed us, La Valle."

La Valle nodded. "I've got thirty guards. They should be sober. And Ginoa and his lieutenants? What condition are they in?"

Chando grimaced. "Juan is passed out in the bushes. Churro is so drunk on Patron that he's ready to piss himself, and the others aren't far behind. They left with some party girls for the stables, to look at the armadillos."

"And Ginoa?"

Chando shrugged. "Ginoa is always good for a fight, no matter how drunk he is. He brought ten of his own guards, so they should be okay, and I have a dozen with me. With your thirty, it makes enough to show the bastards that they made a mistake coming here."

La Valle waved at Raoul. "Tell the guards to go to the shed and get their body armor on. I'll meet them there in ten minutes. Raoul, you, Carlos, and the gringo"—he indicated Oz—"get to the trucks containing the shipment. Drive it to the fields by the access road. When you hear us start firing, move out."

"And her?" Raoul said.

La Valle turned his attention to Emma. "Have you gotten any answers?"

Emma shook her head. "I need access to a lab. I told you that." La Valle crossed the room in two strides. He cocked his arm to hit her, with his hand balled into a fist. Emma stepped back, bumping into Raoul behind her. He pinned her arms close to her torso and held her in place.

"Eduardo, no!" Serena's voice came from behind La Valle, and Emma saw Serena's hand wrap around his bicep, keeping him from punching Emma. "I need her. Look at my hand." Serena shoved her hand in La Valle's face. He flinched away from the open sore. "You can't keep killing the doctors. I'll die. Let her go to a lab."

La Valle said something in Spanish to Serena. Whatever it was, it calmed her. She sat down on the couch, grabbed the hookah's tip, and once again leaned her head back with eyes closed as she inhaled. La Valle looked back at Raoul.

"Take her with you and the shipment. If you

cross the border successfully, she can use Tico's lab in the mountains."

Emma felt her stomach plummet in fear. It appeared as though she was going to get up close and personal with the shipment. She only hoped that packing it in plastic and behind the false vehicle walls would be enough to keep it from contaminating all of them.

Raoul was already barking into a walkie-talkie. He herded her toward the exit. As Emma turned to go, Perez grabbed her arm.

"You may be in the States again, soon."

"If we make it out of here, and if we get to Tico's lab, and if we don't get infected on the way," Emma said.

"The odds are slim, aren't they?" Perez said. She walked with Emma, out toward the pool area. Once they cleared the trees a breeze played around them. Emma shivered. Her clothes were wet with sweat from the run, and the night air had cooled.

"Tell me about the lab, is it what I need?"

Perez shook her head. "It's a meth lab in the Arizona mountains. Tico likes to experiment with mixing chemicals, so he keeps a minimal amount of equipment there. It's rustic and simple. Nothing sophisticated, and I doubt he'll have the tools you'll need."

A crack pierced the air. Perez's body dropped into a heap. The back of her head was blown away. Emma stared at the mess in horror and dropped to her knees next to Perez.

"Go now! To the huts. The cars are there," Raoul screamed. He held his gun out in the direction of where the shot originated, but all Emma could see was darkness. She pushed off the ground and started running in the direction of the huts. Oz pulled up on her right, running alongside her. Carlos ran on the other side of Oz. Raoul followed them all.

An exploding noise came from behind them. Emma looked back, and saw that the hacienda's roof had a large, gaping hole in it. The screams that followed were evidence that the partygoers were now fully aware of the danger. Three more blasts rang in Emma's ears. She kept running, praying that a bullet wouldn't hit her in the back. She heard the reports of rapid shots and return fire. As they neared the migrant huts, they saw the workers running in all directions. Most disappeared into the trees. Octavio appeared on Emma's left. He turned toward the migrant huts as well. They reached the gate where the guard usually sat, and found it open. The guard was gone. The converted ambulance, SUV, and BMW sat parked in a row, along with two other Mercedes and a long black limousine.

Emma was running toward the BMW when she heard the hissing of a rocket, a sound she had heard before, and hearing it again sent chills through her. It was a rocket-propelled grenade, heading toward them.

"Down!" Emma yelled. She hit the dirt just as the grenade struck the first hut. It burst into flames.

Emma scrambled upward, with Octavio next to her. Another shot pierced the air, and Octavio flew forward. Emma turned to catch him in her arms. She staggered with the added weight, but managed to lower herself to her knees while still holding him. His chest was against her arm and his back faced up. Blood hemorrhaged from a hole there. Emma watched it surge out, the flow increasing and decreasing with each pump of his heart. She put her hands over the wound and pressed.

"Octavio, can you hear me?" she said.

He coughed once. "Turn me over."

"I can't." Emma's voice cracked on a welling sob. She swallowed and tried to pull herself together. "You're injured and I'm pressing on the wound. We need to get you to a hospital."

"Turn me over. I want to see the sky when I die." He started to struggle and Emma released him, helping him to roll onto his back. She laid him down. Her vision became blurry as the tears welled in her eyes. She blinked them away. Oz knelt next to her, and she heard him say, "Oh no."

Octavio looked pale, but he stared up at the night sky. He turned his head to look at her. Emma heard the fizzing of another rocket, heading their way. She gritted her teeth and focused only on the man lying in her arms. She couldn't outrun it anyway. Octavio frowned at her.

"Run. Go."

Emma shook her head. "Let's go to the ambulance. I can bandage the wound and slow the bleeding. Then we'll get you to a hospital. Come on. It's only a few feet away, you can make it."

Oz lowered himself on the other side of Octavio and slid his hands under the man's shoulders in preparation to lift him. Octavio shook his head. He groaned, closed his eyes, and opened them again.

"It's better. I can see heaven." He smiled, exhaled with a rattling sound, and then was still.

Emma stared at him, not quite believing that he was gone. She felt Oz wrap a hand around her arm.

"Let's go. We've got to get out of here."

Emma said a short prayer and left Octavio lying on the ground, his face to the stars.

16

EMMA RAN NEXT TO OZ, HEADED FOR THE LINE OF
vehicles. Gunfire rang all around them, peppered
with loud explosions. The migrant huts burned,
the flames meeting each other in a conflagration.
Emma thought about the patients. She doubted
any of them managed to get out alive. She could
only hope that they still were sedated when the
grenades hit. Raoul waved Oz and her into the
Escalade. Two more grenades hit the surrounding trees. The healthy field burned with billowing
black smoke. Ash floated in the air. Emma inhaled, and the pungent smoke hit her lungs with
a searing feeling. She started to cough. Oz joined
her, coughing and holding his hand to his face.

"I'll take the BMW. Follow me," Raoul said. He
yanked the driver's-side door open.

"Do you have a gun?" Emma yelled to Raoul
over the noise of gunfire and crackling flames.

"You don't get a gun," Raoul said. "Headlights
off. Drive slow." He paused for a moment and

stared in the direction of the hacienda, watching the compound burn. Emma looked, too.

The night sky glowed orange, and the rapid, staccato sound of assault weapons filled the air. From out of the bushes came La Valle, Chando, Serena, and another man. The last was ringed by several guards, who swung their heads from side to side, scanning for danger.

Ginoa, Emma thought. The man carried himself with an air of power. This last group piled into the limousine, with the two guards jumping in the front. The rest of the guards climbed into the ambulance, and two hopped into the Mercedes.

Emma crawled into the driver's seat of the Escalade, and Oz climbed into the passenger side. "They made us drive the biggest damn target there is," she said to Oz. "With the possible exception of the ambulance." She turned the car on and it responded immediately. "At least it runs. Remind me where the leaves are."

"In the glove compartment, behind the fake radio, in a dummy panel between the sides of the car and the footwell . . ." Emma pulled her leg away from the side panel. ". . . and under the bench cushions in the backseat." Oz ended his speech in a coughing fit.

The BMW moved out, and Emma followed. They wound their way down the frontage road. The darkness made it difficult to stay on the path, but Emma breathed a sigh of relief when they entered a short stand of trees. It lent a feeling of security. A false one, Emma knew, but it still felt better than being out in the open. After a couple of minutes of driving, during which Oz said nothing and the reports of gunfire faded, they reached the beginning of the fields.

Raoul slowed, and then stopped. Emma braked as well. Behind her the limousine idled, with the ambulance next and the Mercedes last. The lights on the BMW switched on without warning, and Emma heard the wheels squeal as Raoul must have pushed the gas pedal all the way down. The BMW shot off in a fog of smoke and flying dirt.

Emma flicked her own lights on and the Escalade responded, albeit somewhat slower than the BMW, but it still managed to reach a decent speed quickly. Emma glanced in the rearview mirror and she watched the sky glow red with fire and flashes. She turned her eyes away and drove into the night.

17

"EMMA CALDRIDGE IS MISSING." EDWARD BANNER held the phone to his ear and tried to process what Carol Stromeyer, the vice president of his company, Darkview, was saying. "I'm sorry to bother you on vacation, but I thought you'd want to know," she said.

Banner sat up on the edge of the bed, doing his best not to disturb the sleeping woman beside him. Her long brown hair flowed over the pillow. A quick glance at the bedside clock told him it was four in the morning. He got up and left the room, closing the door behind him and stepping into the living area of the suite. He flicked on the light by a desk and settled into the chair.

"No, you're right to call. What can you tell me?"

"Not much, unfortunately. She failed to appear for work in the morning. The lab didn't think much of it. She was on an excursion to find some plants in the desert, and they assumed that she had camped out overnight."

Banner yawned. "Sounds reasonable. So why the worry now?"

"They're not worried, I am. She sent a text that she'd seen a group of people being smuggled over the border and gave the coordinates. But the coordinates were located in Arizona." I just got back in town and checked the status on that GPS locator watch you gave her. Its last transmission came from Ciudad Juarez."

Now she had Banner's full attention.

"Kidnapped?"

"I think we have to assume so, yes.

"Who would she tell them to call for ransom?"

"My bet is on you. Or Cameron Sumner."

Banner ran a hand through his hair. He was due to fly home later that day, connecting through Miami.

"Is Sumner back in Key West?"

"Yes. He's conducting a training session there. I thought I'd arrange a quick charter to the Keys for you instead of to Miami. This way, whichever one of you they call, you'll be together and can coordinate something." She rattled off the flight information. "How's the vacation? Did you get some rest?"

"I did. I want to thank you for insisting on it. I'm going to insist on the same for you when I get back."

Banner and Stromeyer had been working eighteen-hour days repairing the damage done to Darkview by a congressional probe into an earlier matter undertaken in conjunction with the Department of Defense. While Darkview's actions were ultimately determined to be appropriate, it had taken months to acquire additional DOD assignments. They'd been unable to pin down the source of the lies that started the probe, but put that goal aside while they rebuilt the company's balance sheet. As a result, Banner was exhausted, and once the company regained its footing, Stromeyer had insisted that he take a break. For a brief moment he'd almost forgotten himself and asked her to join him, but pulled back in time. She was his colleague, the request would have been inappropriate, and he didn't know if she had any thoughts about him that went beyond friendship. Not to mention that he needed her at the helm in his absence.

Now Banner hung up and pondered the situation for a moment. He sighed, switched off the light, and walked back into the bedroom, navigating his way to the bed. He carefully lowered himself down onto it again.

"Let me guess, that was the wife calling." Her voice came out of the gloom. Banner smiled in the dark at the idea of Stromeyer being his wife. Once again, he pushed the thoughts aside.

"I'm not married," he said. "And you should have asked me that long before this."

He heard her give a small laugh. "I was busy."

"The whole week?"

"You were there," she said. "Besides, you never asked me, either."

Now it was his turn to laugh. She was famous the world over. With paparazzi following her slightest move. He knew everything about her, not because he read the tabloids, but because information about her was so ubiquitous that even he couldn't escape it. He knew she wasn't married. Had never been.

He'd met her the first day of the vacation, when he'd gone to the resort bar to relax after the long flight. She'd been surrounded by people; the curious stared at her, the bodyguards kept close. Through it all she'd sat, gazing into her drink, looking pensive. He knew from the tabloids that she'd just ended a relationship, so he wasn't surprised that she was alone, but what did surprise him was that she'd managed to use a trip to the ladies' room to slip away from the bodyguards. He'd thrown his money down on the bar and followed her into the dark, keeping his distance as she walked the exclusive and empty beach alone. His position as CEO of Darkview made security second nature to him, and he didn't like to see her taking such a risk. He assumed she'd hired the guards for a reason, and shaking them to be alone wasn't a wise move.

He'd tailed her easily, enjoying the soft night breeze and listening to the waves lap against the shore; giving her plenty of space, but watching for any signs of threat. At the turnaround they'd met, and he'd simply nodded and turned with her, saying nothing and strolling along. She'd spoken first, commenting on the beach's beauty, and they'd walked and talked the length of the return and then two more laps. By the end of the evening he'd asked her to have lunch with him the next day.

"That was work calling. Something's happened that requires me to divert from Miami. We won't be able to fly back together. I'm sorry." He heard her sigh.

"Actually, that's better. Your face would be plastered all over the tabloids if you did, and I know enough about you already to know that you'd hate that."

Banner thought her turning the situation to one that benefitted him was a bit of deft handling on her part. He knew that she had no intention of making their liaison public. She guarded her privacy even more than he did, and, as the president of a contract security company that routinely dealt with classified missions the world over, he kept his private life buried very deep. That she was as fanatical about hers said something.

She was right, of course. He would hate to have the press focus on him. He had dealt with the media often enough to realize that there was no way to appease their insatiable appetite for news. While he found her funny, charming, beautiful, and endowed with a personality that filled a room and a movie screen, he didn't wish to be sucked into the vortex surrounding her, even had she allowed it. At least not on this short of an acquaintance. If he saw her again, he wanted it to be in private. He knew that she would, as well. He reached for her in the dark.

"Let's make these last hours count."

Banner stepped onto the tarmac in Key West and squinted in the bright sunlight and the heat. He spotted Cameron Sumner leaning against a

Jeep, with his sunglasses on and his arms folded
across his chest. Sumner stood a little over six feet
and was lean, with brown hair and a face that
was handsome in a masculine, slightly rugged
manner. He dressed conservatively in khaki pants
that looked well worn and a polo shirt that may
once have been navy in color, but was now faded
to a softer blue. He looked cool, collected, and
calm. In all the time Banner had known Sumner,
he had never seen the man react with fear, nervousness, or even extreme anger. Sumner never
lost his temper. As Banner walked toward the
Jeep, he did notice that Sumner's mouth was set,
and his jaw seemed clenched. Banner had an idea
what Emma Caldridge meant to this man, and he
admired his composure in the face of this latest
bad news. He reached the Jeep and held out his
hand.

"Any news?" he said.

Sumner shook his hand. "Nothing. No call, no
text, e-mail, nothing."

Banner thought about that a moment. "Isn't
that a bit unusual?"

"Highly. On average they make contact within
twenty-four hours of the event. Assuming the
victim is alive, of course."

Banner frowned. "Any Jane Does been found
in the Ciudad Juarez area?"

"You mean other than the four hundred already murdered women?"

Banner grimaced. Sumner was right, of course.
Over the last twenty years, hundreds of women
had disappeared from Ciudad Juarez. Some be-

lieved a serial killer worked the town with impunity. Others thought human trafficking was the cause, but all believed that the perpetrators were known to the police, who turned a blind eye. Sumner pushed off the Jeep.

"No recent bodies. Of course, if she fell afoul of whoever is killing the women of Ciudad, then there is a good chance we'll never hear from her." Sumner's voice sounded harsh as he made this last observation. He waved Banner into the Jeep. "Come on. I'll take you to the radar center and we can talk there." Banner threw his bag into the back of the car and slid into the passenger seat. Sumner circled the tarmac and left off a frontage road.

"How's the drug busting going?"

Sumner worked for a branch of the Southern Hemisphere Defense organization responsible for detecting cartel drug planes that attempted to enter U.S. airspace from the south. His main responsibilities involved the "Air Tunnel Denial" program, a group charged with identifying these low-flying aircraft and intercepting them. Once they pinpointed a target, Sumner's group had the authority to demand that the intruder identify themselves, scramble their own planes to intercept the suspicious flight in cases where the response is inadequate, and, if required, shoot the foreign aircraft down.

"We've intercepted two hundred flights in the last three months. Now the cartels are moving underwater. The Coast Guard is reporting a rash of homemade submarines."

Banner snorted. "Homemade submarines?" He shook his head. "Never ceases to amaze me how ingenious the cartels can get. Do the subs work?"

Sumner cleared the airport runway and shifted into third. "Pretty well, considering how crude they are. They have fiberglass bodies and use PVC plumbing tubes that they jam into the top. The pipes pierce the surface, providing air. Of course, we have no idea how many sink en route."

"And the poor mules driving them sink right along with them," Banner said.

Sumner nodded. "The cartel doesn't worry too much about losing them. As long as there are broke people desperate to make some cash, the cartel is insured a steady supply."

Sumner drove along the frontage road to the far tip of the tarmac and slowed in front of a heavy metal gate bearing a sign with PRIVATE PROPERTY, KEEP OUT and the usual picture of a stick figure getting caught in the gate as it closed. Sumner reached up and pressed a door opener, and the gates swung wide.

The Air Tunnel Denial offices were located in a second control tower at the end of the existing airport. The hexagonal building held six employees on an eight-hour shift. Enough people to monitor suspicious flights around the clock. Sumner parked the Jeep in a reserved spot at the base of the tower and waved Banner into it.

"I'll show you the control center first. That building"—he indicated a low, ranch style structure thirty feet from the tower—"is the main office."

They took a flight of stairs and entered the control tower, and Banner was struck by the quiet in the room. Three men sat in front of radar screens populated with various dots moving across in formation. None spoke, though all cast a quick glance at Sumner and nodded a greeting before returning their attention to the screens. The third man indicated to Sumner that he should come closer.

"Got something?" Sumner said.

The man pointed at a dot on his screen. "Been watching this one since Colombia. Guys at Apiay told us that it's likely hauling coke. It's been flying so low that it drops off the track, but it keeps reappearing, and when it does, it's clear that it's on a path here. Maybe not the Keys, but definitely somewhere in Florida."

Sumner leaned into the screen and watched the dot track along the path. "Did the Colombians hail it?"

The man nodded. "They did, and the guy responded with a dare. Told them they'd never catch him, he was too good. They said he spoke in English with a strange accent. They couldn't place it. When they addressed him in Spanish, he told them he spoke English only, and they should, too."

"That a problem for the Colombians?" Banner asked.

The man chuckled. "Not at all. We're all bilingual in the Air Tunnel Denial program. But an exclusively English-speaking cartel pilot is rare. I've never heard of it in the five years I've been

dealing with these cartel flunkies. Have you?"
The man directed his question at Sumner, who
shook his head.

"Never. Always Spanish-speaking pilots."
Sumner pointed at the dot. "That him?"

The employee took a sip of coffee from a mug.
"Yep. And he *is* good. They scrambled Jorge to intercept and he said that they played tag in the air
for over fifty minutes before Jorge hit maximum
range and had to turn back. He said that the guy
flew like a stunt pilot. Jorge was impressed, and
you know how hard it is to impress Jorge."

Sumner straightened. "Keep me posted on this
guy. He enters our airspace, I want to hear about it."

"Will do," the man said.

Sumner waved Banner back out the door. "Let's
go to my office. We can talk there."

Sumner's office was stark white with a black
wooden desk in a modern style, a chrome archi-
tect's desk lamp with a bright halogen light and
a laptop in a docking station. On the wall behind
his desk was a black-and-white photograph of a
figure, its body a black smudge surrounded by
a dense fog. The tips of trees appeared at various places where the fog thinned, and in one
corner Banner could see a lake or pond behind
the figure. The scene appeared quiet, eerie, and
the image was arresting with its stark beauty.
Sumner saw him staring at it.

"That's a picture I took of my grandfather two
months ago as he walked along a lake in Minne-
sota. We would go there every year, along with
my father and uncles to hunt and fish. One morn-

ing the fog was so dense that we couldn't see far enough in front of us to even take out the boats. He went to check on some lines we'd strung by a dock, and I snapped the shot as he walked back toward our cottage."

"It's an arresting photo," Banner said. Sumner appeared pleased. He gazed at the picture a moment before looking back at Banner.

"I checked out the odds of Caldridge being killed prior to being ransomed. It's an uncommon occurrence. Apparently hostages are rarely killed, though they are tortured. Dead hostages aren't worth much."

Banner grimaced. His mind refused to even consider that Caldridge was dead, but he hated the idea of her being tortured.

"I have to think she's alive, and I also think that she can hold her own in most scenarios. I don't think she'd lose her cool."

Sumner sighed. "I agree. Her ultra training is going to come in handy in this instance. You need a strong mind to endure running more than one hundred miles without stopping, but you need an even stronger mind to overcome the despair that comes from torture." He shook his head. "I just wish they'd contact us, already. Get the ransom ball rolling."

Banner couldn't agree more. "I have six operatives in Mexico currently, but they're in deep cover and hundreds of miles south of Ciudad. I'm considering moving them into position to attempt a rescue."

"Where are they now?"

"Sinaloa."

Sumner whistled. "That's home to the worst of the worst. Weren't they responsible for the beheadings?"

Banner nodded. "They took the heads to Mexico City and tossed them on a dance floor."

Sumner tapped on his computer screen. He turned the laptop so that Banner could see the monitor. On it was a picture of a swarthy man with small eyes and thick lips. Sumner pointed to him.

"That's a guy named Eduardo La Valle. He operates out of Ciudad Juarez. Ever hear of him?"

Banner had. "They call him 'the Tailor,' because he is believed to mutilate his victims in strange ways and then stitch up the bodies. There are rumors that he's behind the hundreds of killings in Ciudad, but it's never been proven."

Sumner gazed at the photo. "I intercepted ten of his planes last month alone. Only one landed when we converged on it. The rest flew their equipment right into the water."

Banner raised an eyebrow. He hadn't heard a thing about the downed planes. "They commit suicide rather than be arrested? Strange."

"I thought so, too. The transporters for the other cartels will surrender quickly once they're on U.S. soil. They know the prisons here are far better than the ones in Mexico. When I interrogated the one that didn't kill himself, he told me that most of La Valle's mules would rather die quickly than have to go back and endure torture at La Valle's hands. He said no one who fails lives longer than twenty-four hours, and those last hours are horrific."

Banner stood. "I'll ask Stromeyer to start moving some operatives toward Ciudad. If this La Valle has Caldridge, we'd better be prepared to move quickly."

"He owns the towns in a one-hundred-mile radius. It's not going to be easy to infiltrate his organization in the small amount of time we have. And if he doesn't have her?"

"Then we start searching every house until we find her." *Or her body*, Banner thought.

18

EMMA DROVE THROUGH THE DARKNESS, KEEPING the taillights of Raoul's BMW in view. Oz sat in the passenger seat next to her, with Carlos and another guard, named Mono, in the back. Mono looked like a small, mean frog, with protruding eyes and ears that bent outward. He had a large, raised slash scar on his neck. Both men smelled of alcohol, sweat, and weed. Emma opened the window to let in some air. She hoped that these two had been enjoying the party along with the other cartel players, and with any luck they'd fall asleep as time wore on. Once they did, she intended to watch for an opportunity to ditch them both.

Oz stared glumly ahead. He, too, looked exhausted, but Emma doubted he would sleep anytime soon. The worry on his face was clear, and his edgy nervousness was palpable. Emma kept her eyes on the road and her attention focused on driving. She was forced to drive at speeds upwards of ninety miles an hour just to keep the BMW in her sights. The ambulance rode behind them, at times tailgating, forcing Emma to increase her speed. The two vehicles effectively sandwiched her, an occurrence that was not a coincidence. It appeared that they had no intention of letting her escape again.

Emma's mind raced with ideas. One seemed to provide the likeliest chance of both she and Oz escaping from this nightmare, but none would solve the mystery of the decaying shipment.

The sky to the east began to lighten, and Emma checked in the rearview mirror yet again to see if the men were sleeping. Both were.

"Are you okay?" She spoke to Oz in a low voice.

"Yes. Depressed as hell, but okay. I'm sorry you didn't make it out."

Emma sighed. "It was a bit of extreme irony. I ran out of there and into hell."

Oz put his head against the headrest and turned to look at her. "You look beat. Want me to drive?"

"I don't think we can stop unless Raoul allows us to. But at least he's slowed down." Emma slowed to a reasonable seventy-five miles per hour, and easily kept up with the forward car.

"Are they asleep back there?" Emma asked.

Oz turned to check out their jailors. "Yep."

Oz once again faced forward. "Do you speak any foreign languages?"

Emma smiled. "You mean other than Spanish?"

Oz nodded. "That's exactly what I mean."

"German and Latin. And you?"

"French and Italian."

"Hmmm, guess we're stuck with English. You think those two in the back know it?"

Oz seemed to consider the question a moment. "Carlos, not likely. I have no idea about the other guy."

"So we can't speak freely."

The car in front of them slowed. "Raoul's dialing it way down." Emma watched as the Mercedes pulled to the side of the road and prepared to stop, the BMW right behind. "Looks like we're going to take a break."

Emma pulled to the side as well and shifted into park. Moths and flying gnats danced in the glow thrown by her headlights. The sky to the east continued to lighten. Soon it would be dawn. She watched as Raoul emerged from the back of the BMW. He walked toward the car, a gun in his hand. He shook it to indicate that she should lower her window. When she did, he shoved the gun against her cheek.

"Don't think I will forget that you tried to escape."

Emma moved her head away from the cold metal tip. Her anger rose. She swallowed to settle back down and thought of what Sumner had once told her. Never let your emotions rule your intellect in a fight. The one who maintains her focus and calm will win. Raoul smirked at her. It was clear to her that he misunderstood her swallowing to be fear. Out of the corner of her eye she saw that Oz was sweating. He clenched his hands in his lap, as if it was all he could do not to attack Raoul. She tried to will him her calm. Oz needed to be allowed to roam freely, and he wouldn't be if Raoul thought they were conspiring against him and La Valle.

"How far to Tico's lab?" Emma said, mostly to change the subject. She had no intention of staying with the caravan long enough to reach the Arizona mountains.

"Five hours. We have to cross the border first." Raoul leaned farther into the car to look at Oz. "You got your passport?"

Oz nodded. "It's in the ambulance along with my spare set of clothes and the Triumph. We put it there this afternoon. Good thing, too, because I would have forgotten it otherwise."

"You brought the motorcycle?" Raoul said.

"Damn right I did." Oz gave Raoul a defiant look.

Raoul shrugged. "Whatever. We'll wait until seven thirty. That's when the morning commuters are the heaviest, and the customs agents work to get everyone across in time to make it to their jobs."

"How will I get across?" Emma said. "I don't have a passport."

Raoul tossed her wallet in her lap. She hadn't seen it since he confiscated it over eighteen hours earlier. Raoul followed up the wallet with a blue passport embossed with the gold seal of the United States of America. Emma opened it, and found her name next to a picture of Serena. Emma peered more closely at the document. It looked close to authentic, right down to the stamps on the pages from locations where she'd supposedly vacationed, but it felt thinner than she recalled her actual passport to be. As if it was made with cheaper paper, and cardboard.

"When we get to the border, I want you to enter the fourth lane from the left. There should be a bald man there. His name is Kurt. You hand him the passport, and tell him you work for Wallenda's Textiles."

Emma held the passport up. "This is Serena's picture. Won't he notice that I don't look anything like her?"

Raoul shook his head. "The picture doesn't matter. He's being paid, he'll let you through. Don't think you can tip him off that you're a hostage though, he doesn't know about that and if you try, Carlos there will have a gun pointed at your back. Anything goes wrong, and he'll kill you first." He leaned farther into the truck and directed his attention at Oz. "You're going to drive the ambulance. You pick lane six. You tell them you're headed to get a medical transfer. Your patient is waiting at the hospital."

"Is my guy on the take too?"

Raoul shook his head. "We've only got three, and they don't all work at the same time. We figure since your passport is real, you have a shot at getting through."

"And if they bring out the sniffing dogs?"

"Then you're done. That ambulance is gonna make them howl at the moon."

Raoul sauntered back to the BMW.

Emma settled down into the seat and leaned her head against the glass. "Wonder if we'll make it," she said.

Oz sighed. "We've got a twenty-seven percent chance."

Emma looked at him. "That sounds pretty precise. How'd you come up with that figure?"

"I did some research before I took the job. Seventy-three percent get caught within four shipments."

Emma thought about that for a moment. "I wouldn't take those odds. What in the world possessed you to?"

Oz shrugged. "I was broke. I was tired of being broke." He gave a grim laugh. "But now I'm just tired of everything." Emma thought about the ambulance going through aisle six. The "clean" aisle. She leaned closer to Oz.

"You need to try to tip off your agent. You've got the 'clean' guy."

Oz nodded. "I know. I'm already thinking of what to say."

The sun rose higher, bathing the dust-brown road with a pink tinge. Emma watched it ascend and thought, I'm alive to see another sunrise. A picture of Octavio rose in her mind, as he looked up at the sky. A lump formed in her throat.

She heard Raoul's engine roar to life. His brake lights flashed once, and he squealed away from the shoulder. Emma turned the key and hastened to catch up with him. The ambulance took its usual spot behind her. The sound of the car revving woke Carlos. Emma looked in the rearview mirror and watched him take in his surroundings. He yawned.

They wound down the road, but now at a more sedate pace. It seemed as though Raoul became more cautious with each mile closer to the border.

Emma kept her eyes on the road, but her mind worked up a plan to escape. She'd make her move close to the border patrol. Carlos and Mono were awake, and Carlos sat in the center of the seat in an attitude of watchfulness.

The sun rose higher, and soon it was full day. Raoul, Emma, and the ambulance were the only cars on the road. They shot down, doing seventy and remaining in formation. Soon Emma saw the border crossing loom in the distance. It rose out of the shimmering effect thrown by the sun's rays on the asphalt. They slowed when it became clear that the line was snaking over a mile long. Emma envied the cars in a nearby lane that seemed to fly compared to hers. A quick glance ahead told her why. The lane was marked STUDENTS ONLY. Seemed the kids getting to school were given their own lane.

Raoul pulled to the shoulder and put on his hazards. Emma did the same, and a quick glance in the rearview mirror displayed the ambulance right behind them. Emma watched Raoul exit the car. He stormed toward Emma and it was clear that he was angry. He ignored her and pulled open the passenger door. He rattled off a sentence in Spanish to Carlos, who sidled sideways out of the car. Raoul leaned into the doorway and placed the muzzle of his revolver on the seat next to Emma's headrest.

"Get out of the car," he said.

"What's happened?"

Raoul gave the side of her head a shove with the tip of the gun. "Our guy says your face is plastered all over the border patrol's offices. They're saying you work for the DOD. They know that you've been taken to Ciudad. You lied. You made a call from the village. Tipped them off."

Oz shot her a frantic look. Stay cool, she thought, but she couldn't help feel a thrill of hope at the news that the authorities were looking for her. She figured either Banner or Stromeyer was behind the alert. She scrambled to back off Raoul.

"I did not tip off anyone. I never had the time, you know that, and Perez confirmed it. I never made it to the village."

"Get out."

Emma reached to turn off the car and saw that her hand was shaking. Oz sat rigid next to her. She saw him put his hand in his pocket and slide out a knife. She doubted that Raoul could see the movement or the knife from his angle. She placed her hand over Oz's wrist, stilling his movement. He gave her a hard look, but she shook her head. He subsided, keeping the knife out, but nodded back at her, as if he understood that he wasn't to attack just then.

Emma swung the door open and stepped into the sunlight.

The sun hit her face, along with a dry breeze. Seven fifteen and already it was stifling hot, with a dry heat that baked the skin. Raoul stepped next to her, the gun held low and pointed at her side. Any car driving past wouldn't see the weapon. Emma felt her stomach muscles contract, waiting for the moment he'd pull the trigger. Out of the corner of her eye she saw Oz's door fly open and he stood up.

The Mercedes's rear door opened as well. Serena filled the opening, with one hand on the edge of the door, and the other pushing against the car.

"Raoul, stop!" she shrieked.

Raoul held his stance, his eyes never leaving Emma's. She stared back, doing her best not to move an inch. She was breathing in shallow breaths, and her head buzzed from the combination of adrenaline and fear.

"She works for the DOD, Serena. It's about time you stop protecting her," Raoul said.

Serena marched over to Raoul. "You don't want them to see her, you put her in the back of the ambulance, but you don't kill her, you understand? We go to Tico's lab."

Carlos stepped next to Emma and grabbed her arm. He spoke to Raoul, and shoved her toward the ambulance. Raoul kept the gun pointed at her the entire time. The ambulance drivers climbed out and opened the back for Carlos. He gave her a final push and she fell face forward, between Oz's small duffel bag and the Triumph, which was held upright against the wall with bungee cords. Carlos produced a set of plastic ties and tied her hands behind her back. He did the same for her ankles. He grabbed a roll of gauze and wrapped it around her mouth as a gag. The last thing Emma saw was the ambulance door close and darkness descend.

EMMA LAY SWEATING IN THE AMBULANCE AND thought about how Serena saved her life a third time. It was clear that neither La Valle nor Raoul had any use for her as a hostage, and the moment she solved the mystery of the infection, they would eliminate her. The heat in the ambulance was stifling, but that discomfort was nothing next to the aches in her shoulders and legs. The hours without sleep, the long run, and the stress were all working on her. She hit her back on the ambulance's steel floor with each bump in the road.

After twenty minutes she felt the car slow. It began to move, then pause, then move again. They were nearing the border crossing. Emma waited, hoping she could hear something that would indicate how close they were to the border guards. She waited ten more minutes, during which time the ambulance moved and paused a few more times. When she thought they were close, she started pounding her heels on the floor.

Alternating fast and slow, attempting an SOS signal. The ambulance continued to start and stop. Emma continued to pound out the rhythm. This seemed to go on forever. Emma's stomach ached with the strain of holding her legs up in the air while she made the noise. The ambulance continued its sporadic movement.

Twenty minutes later she felt the vehicle accelerate up to speed and remain there, humming along. Emma stopped the SOS signal. They must have gone through the crossing and on the interstate on the Arizona side. She fought down the depression that threatened to engulf her at this latest setback. She needed to keep thinking, keep planning.

The air in the ambulance grew stale and the heat rose. Emma smelled the musty odor of the leaves. She took shallow breaths, hoping that it would save her from inhaling the spores from the diseased leaves deep into her lungs. Every minute it seemed as though the smell grew stronger. It was as if the heat on the outside of the ambulance walls created an oven that was baking the leaves and releasing their deadly sickness into the air.

After what seemed like hours, the ambulance slowed and stopped. Emma heard the doors at the front slam and the crunching sounds of a man's shoes as they walked over gravel. The back panels swung open.

Carlos stood there. He waved her forward, and she scooted toward him. He took out a pair of short pruning shears and cut the ties on her wrists and ankles before cutting away her gag. He stepped aside so that she could exit.

Emma scrambled out of the ambulance as fast as she could. The air, while still unbearably hot, felt fresh compared to that in the ambulance and she happily inhaled her first full breaths in hours. She glanced around.

They were high up on the side of a mountain, parked in a stand of trees. In front of her and off to the left was a beat-up trailer home. It sat three feet off the ground on cinder blocks. Broken beer bottles littered the ground, and the hulk of a rusted car body rested five feet from the back. A couple of discarded tires were stacked next to the car's shell. The trailer's screen door hung off the frame in a lopsided manner. Aluminum foil lined the windows. Three more trailers, spaced twenty feet apart, ringed the area, with a row of motor-cycles parked in front of the third. In between the trailers sat picnic tables loaded with used liter bottles filled with liquid. The entire area reeked of a chemical smell so horrible that Emma's gorge rose as she inhaled. Oz walked to her side and began to cough.

"Jesus, what is that smell?" he said.

Emma knew what it was without question. "That's the smell of crystal meth being cooked. We're at Tico's lab."

Oz took in the trailer and trashed car. "You've got to be kidding me. *This* is the lab? Are they out of their minds? I thought we were going to a real facility."

"Where's the BMW? And Raoul and Serena?"

"Don't know. They broke off about four miles earlier. It's just you, me, Carlos and Mono." The last two hung back by the ambulance. They lit up cigarettes and were smoking them while leaning against its side. Both had rifles slung over their backs. Oz held up a car key. "They're going to drive the ambulance next, and I have the keys to the Escalade."

The door to the trailer creaked open and a man dressed in battered jeans and a white wife beater stepped out. He had long salt-and-pepper hair that flowed down his back, a full beard, tattoos on both arms, and a leather bracelet with studs around his wrist. A woman hovered in the doorway behind him. She was thin, with dirty-blonde hair that hung in clumps and sunken, black-rimmed eyes. She wore a blue tank top over jean shorts and pulled on a lock of hair in a nervous, childlike gesture, though Emma estimated her to be in her mid-twenties.

"You must be Tico," Emma said.

Tico looked around at the assembled group of them. He spit on the ground and jerked his chin at Carlos. "I know those guys, but who the hell are you two?"

"That's Oswald Kroger." Emma pointed at Oz. "And I'm Emma Caldridge. I'm a chemist. I need to use your lab."

Tico raised an eyebrow. He turned his head to acknowledge Carlos. "*Cerveza*?" he said.

Carlos smiled a broad, tobacco-stained smile. "*Si*." Tico snapped his fingers, and the woman behind him trotted up. Like a dog to its master.

"Get them a couple of beers." The woman scuttled off back into the trailer, slamming the crooked screen door behind her. She reemerged with two Coronas in hand. She kept her eyes down as she delivered the beers. Bleeding sores covered her arms. Oz gazed at them as she walked by.

"You see those sores? They look just like Serena's." Oz spoke to Emma in a voice low enough for only her to hear.

"They're not, though," Emma said, keeping her voice just as low. "Those are called 'crank bugs.' They're from her body trying to release the meth toxins from her system through her skin."

Oz grimaced. "That's awful."

Emma nodded. Oz had it right. Meth was awful.

Tico took a drink of the beer that the blonde handed him. "You need one?" Tico said to Oz.

"I need two." Oz pointed at Emma. "One is for her."

Tico spit again. "I don't waste my beers on women." Oz's eyes narrowed, and she saw him reach into his pocket where he kept his knife, his angular face even more arresting in his anger. It was like watching Beauty and the Beast face off, except Emma had no time for it. She held up her hand to stop him. Oz subsided a bit, but still looked ready to kill. Emma ignored Tico and headed to the end of the first trailer. The smell grew stronger as she approached it.

"Hey!" Tico said. "Where the hell are you going?"

Emma kept walking away.

"I *said* where the hell are you going?" Emma was pleased to hear that Tico was pissed off. She kept moving.

"I don't waste my breath on assholes," she called behind her.

"You stay away from my goddamned lab," Tico was bellowing now.

Emma stopped at the corner of the trailer. From that angle she could see more rows of plastic liter soda bottles filled with cooking meth. Coolers lined the ground, containing more. Behind them was another, smaller trailer. A sign featuring a skull and crossbones in red and black was tacked on the door, and under it the words, "Keep Out." Next to the trailer sat a gleaming, tricked-out Harley Davidson motorcycle. Black saddlebags hung from behind the seat. The symbol *1%* was embroidered in gold on the side of one. She glanced at Tico.

"I told you, I'm a chemist. I need your lab. La-Valle's men brought me here to use it. And it's a good thing, too, because you can't make meth for shit. You used too much ammonia. Damn bottles are going to blow."

"How the hell do you know?" Tico said.

"I can smell it. Too much of it. And let me guess, instead of red phosphorus you used hypophos-phorous acid."

She heard Tico inhale, confirming her suspicion. Hypophosphorous acid was an extremely dangerous acid that worked as a substitute for red phosphorus, but was so volatile that the slightest mistake in temperature, or capping the cooking bottle too tightly, would cause it to blow. Emma figured Tico got the substitute cheaper than the regular ingredients, and took the risk to save cash.

"I ain't worried. Lots of guys use hypophosphorous acid. This is my second batch with it and so far it's been fine. Should've switched sooner."

She resumed walking toward the second trailer. The smell grew even more noxious as she approached. She veered away from the picnic table set up and went straight for the lab. God, this is depressing, she thought. That Serena's life hung on the fortunes of a two-bit meth lab that wasn't a lab at all, but just a broken-down trailer in the middle of the mountains was unconscionable. Whether Serena deserved her fate or not, no one should die by being eaten alive.

She opened the lab's door and gazed inside. The interior smelled like cleaning fluid, alcohol, and rotten eggs. Tico must have been cooking inside as well. Emma moved in farther. The trailer was a long rectangle, with a galley kitchen to her left and a small eating area to the right of that. A pile of decongestants of every brand and description were stacked in one corner of the counter next to a blender. Empty mason jars filled the opposite counter, along with a pile of lithium batteries. A pair of pliers lay next to the batteries. Oz stepped in behind her. He gazed around, and his eyes fell on the various ingredients piled on the counters.

"I know they use decongestants. But batteries?"

Emma nodded. "They take them apart and

pull the silver lithium strip out of the middle. The pseudoephedrine in the decongestant tablets"—Emma pointed to the pile—"is ground into a powder, added to an accelerant, or precursor, such as drain cleaner, and the lithium strips punch up the chemical reaction."

"Batteries, pliers, and a blender. This is a joke," Oz said.

Emma sighed. The trailer contained everything needed to cook meth, but nothing that even resembled equipment that stocked an actual lab.

She moved closer to the sink. Portions of the Formica showed rings of dust and dirt, as if something had been there but was removed. She walked to the refrigerator and opened it. Two small propane tanks sat on the refrigerator's main shelf. More meth ingredients. She stepped out of the trailer and into the clearing, with Oz behind her. Tico stood next to the cycle.

"That's not a lab at all," Emma said.

Tico bristled. "I had to pawn most of the equipment to pay some debts. La Valle wants it, he can still get it back. My month isn't up at the pawn shop. They haven't sold it yet."

Oz gave a low whistle and walked toward the motorcycle.

"What the hell you whistling at, pretty boy?" Tico said, a sneer in his voice. Oz didn't seem to hear him. He just stared at the cycle.

"I didn't see this before. Damn, that's a great bike," Oz said.

Tico stopped cold. After a moment of confusion,

where he didn't seem to know how to feel about Oz's change of subject, a look of pride entered his eyes. He puffed up his chest. Emma noted that even then, his belly loomed huge over his pants.

"That bike's been all over the country and back. Not a scratch on her."

Oz stopped a few feet away from the bike, off to the right. "How old?"

"Ten years."

The skinny blonde appeared with two beers in her hand. She handed one to Oz, before passing behind Tico and offering the second to Emma.

Tico frowned. "I didn't say she could have one."

The girl froze in her tracks, with the beer extended to Emma.

Oz frowned at Tico. "But I did."

The girl gave Oz a sidelong look. Emma took the bottle from her.

"Uncap those liter bottles very carefully," Emma said to Tico. "If you're going to use the 'shake and bake' method, then you have to keep them cold. The sun's going to warm them enough to cause the chemicals inside to detonate." She took a gulp of the beer. It tasted crisp, but did little to quench Emma's thirst or quell her growing hunger. Emma watched the skinny blonde step back, her eyes wide. She resumed playing with her hair, staring at Emma.

Tico leaned toward her. "I don't waste beer on women, and I don't take orders from them either. If you wasn't sent by La Valle, I'd have killed you when you first opened your mouth."

Emma took another drink from the bottle. "Then I guess Oz and I will be moving on. I don't want to be around when your yard explodes."

Tico snorted. "It ain't gonna explode. I been making meth for five years, and never once lost a batch."

"Every one of those is going to combust." She took another large gulp and started back to the front yard. Out of the corner of her eye she saw Oz take one last look at the cycle before he, too, began to make his way back to the Escalade.

"Hey, pretty boy," Tico said.

Oz stopped walking. He spun on his heel and leveled a stare at the man.

"You call me 'pretty boy' one more time and you're not going to like what happens."

Tico put his arms out in a placating gesture. "All right, relax. I didn't mean nothin' by it. Carlos told me that *she*"—Tico pointed at Emma—"is a hostage. If that's so, why don't you leave her here? I'll handle the ransom, everything. We'll cut out La Valle. I'll give you, Carlos, and Mono forty percent of what I collect." Emma was truly surprised that Tico had such duplicity in him.

"You really want to take on the biggest cartel leader in Ciudad Juarez?" she said to Tico. "Do you think that's wise?"

Tico pointed a finger at her. "You keep out of this."

Oz shook his head. "Forget it."

Tico took a step closer. "Why not?"

"Why not? I'll tell you why not. La Valle will

come and kill us all, that's why not. You think you can beat him at his own game, good luck."

Tico pointed at the *1%* symbol on his saddlebags. "You know what that means?" Oz put his hands on his hips, but said nothing. "It means that I'm a lieutenant in the Black Eagles. The Hell's Angels and Outlaws can't lick our boots." Oz just kept moving around the trailer. Both he and Emma stepped onto the front lawn. Tico followed them. "You see those bikes?" He pointed to the four tricked-out motorcycles parked in front of the other trailers, all Harleys, and all gleaming. Saddlebags on the back of each bore the crest of an eagle crisscrossed with two pistols. "La Valle comes at us, my crew will protect me. Come on. We all stand to make some money. I'll give you her," he pointed at the blonde.

Oz snorted in disbelief. "You've got to be kidding me."

Tico shook his head. "I'll even throw in a case of beer."

Emma laughed. Her response caused Tico to frown. She supposed she shouldn't goad the moron, but the ridiculousness of the conversation invited derision.

"I guess women are worth some beer after all," she said to Oz, who didn't smile. He continued to look at Tico with an incredulous expression on his face.

"Are you brain-dead? You act like you can just offer someone up like that," Oz said.

Tico shrugged and pointed at the blonde. "She'll do what I say. She'll go with you." The blonde got a hopeful look on her face, which cut Emma to the core. The girl viewed herself as chattel.

Oz pointed at Emma. "*She'll* kill you in your sleep. And that would be after she killed me for even thinking about it." He stalked past Emma. "Let's get out of here. This guy's crazy."

Two men stepped out of the front door of the second trailer. One bald, wearing black combat boots, jeans, a gray tee shirt, tattoos running up his neck to his chin, and a studded wristband as a bracelet, smoked a cigarette. The second man was small and wiry, with ropey arms and a bandanna wrapped around his head. He held a beer in his hand. The two men's eyes locked on Emma, and the one with the bandanna raised an eyebrow. He spotted Mono leaning by the ambulance.

"Looks like you've traded up, Mono," he said.

Mono shook his head. "She's cargo." He jerked a thumb at the Escalade. "We've got twenty in the back for you. You want 'em?"

The wiry man nodded. "If it's good."

Mono snorted. "The best Mexico has to offer." He pronounced "Mexico" like "Mehico." The wiry man shrugged.

"We'll test it, like we always do." He jerked his chin at Emma. "Come on inside."

"You carry the shipment in?" Mono said.

The second man, who up until this point hadn't said a word, started toward the Escalade. Emma felt her nerves stretch as he approached the car.

"You got any gardening gloves? Maybe you get them before you start unloading," she said.

The man stopped and looked at her in surprise. "Why? To protect my soft hands?"

Mono chuckled in an unconvincing manner and waved the gun at her. "You stay quiet."

The man kept going. He swung open the back door and reached inside. Emma couldn't watch anymore. She started to the trailer, moving past the tattooed man, who still stood in the doorway.

The house was dark and oppressively hot, even though the windows were open. A fitful breeze blew the curtains around, but did little to lower the temperature. A tattered couch shoved against a far wall dominated the living room, and a ring-stained coffee table held two bongs, one filled with sludge water. Emma could see a portion of the kitchen. Stacks of pizza boxes were on the floor, along with several beer carriers, each holding empty bottles. The entire house smelled like stale beer and old cigarette smoke.

The two men entered, each holding a brick of the shipment. Mono walked in behind them. He held his gun, but no bricks.

The wiry man settled onto the couch and prepared a bong using the brick. The second man tossed his onto the cocktail table before joining his buddy on the couch. The wiry man packed the bong in no time and held it to his lips as he lit it. Emma heard him inhale.

"I need some fresh air," she said. She spun around and moved past Mono, who watched the two men smoke with a knowing look on his face. She hit the screen door and pushed it open. It slammed shut behind her with a sound like a gunshot. She

looked around at the dilapidated trailers and littered lawn and hoped that not all of rural America
had become so worn down, so sad.

The screen door gave a second report and she
looked over to see Oz coming toward her, with
Mono at his heels.

"Let's go," Mono said. "Fast." He jogged toward
the Escalade, and some of his urgency transmitted to Emma.

"What's going on?"

"They're smoking the sick leaves," Mono said.
"We got to get out of here now." When he saw
Emma and Oz staring at him, he became impatient.
"Come on! We don't have much time. Get the hell
out of here. Fast. Before they realize they're dying."

"They have nine days," Oz said.

Mono shook his head. "Not these guys. When
they smoke the bad leaves it goes fast. We've got
to get out of here."

The screen door slammed. One of the men staggered out onto the lawn. Blood poured from his
eyes, nose, and mouth. He took an unsteady step
toward them. He fell to his knees and landed
on his face in the grass. He twitched once, and
stilled. Emma saw the second man stumble out of
the house. He, too, was covered in blood.

"Jesus," Oz said.

"Go! Now," Mono yelled.

Before Emma could respond, the first bottles on
the picnic tables between the trailers exploded.

Emma felt the heat and force of the blast, which
knocked her backward onto the ground. She hit
the dirt, and lost her breath. Oz fell next to her.

More bottles exploded, followed in rapid succession by the others. One by one Emma heard the stash in the backyard begin to combust. Tico gave a guttural scream, which was followed by a high-pitched one from the blonde. Emma scrambled into a crouch and grabbed Oz's arm. She hauled him upward as the next group of bottles exploded, creating a large fireball that belched into the air. She started running toward the cars and nearly ran into Carlos, who appeared from around the corner. Flying bits of metal, rocks, and dirt hit the back of Emma's head.

Carlos yelled at her in Spanish. She didn't know the words, but she understood his intent. She ran right behind him as they sprinted to the vehicles. Carlos veered off toward the ambulance. More explosions rocked the area. Flames spewed up from the lab. Oz threw open the door to the Escalade's driver side. Emma ran to the passenger door. Mono crawled into the back.

Oz started the car and hit the gas. He pointed down the dirt road away from the trailers. Explosions triggered behind them, filling the air with sound. Emma craned her neck to see. Flames engulfed the lab, creating black smoke that billowed into the sky.

Oz gunned the Escalade, keeping it close to the ambulance, which filled the road in front of them. No one spoke for several minutes.

"There goes Serena's chance," Oz said.

Emma gazed out the window, watching scrub brush and twisted cactus flash by. Mono remained silent in the back, his ever-present rifle by his side and a gun on his belt. Emma was still trying to wrap her head around what she had seen. Oz was quiet, brooding.

"Guess they'll never steal from La Valle again," Mono said. After a moment, Emma heard him chuckle.

20

BANNER LURCHED TOWARD THE RINGING CELL phone, reaching it before Sumner could. The display showed that Stromeyer was calling.

"Tell me some good news," Banner said.

"Good? No. Weird? Yes. I just received a call from some investigator with the Mexican army. Seems that they found a Range Rover that contained a piece of paper in the glove compartment with both our cell-phone numbers written on it." Banner switched the phone to speaker and placed it on the desk so that Sumner could hear.

"Whose car was it?"

"It was registered to a woman named Luisa Perez. She was a veterinarian."

"Did she say who gave her the numbers?"

"Unfortunately, no. She's dead. They found her body inside a compound owned by one Eduardo La Valle." Sumner groaned. "I know, I didn't like that either."

Sumner leaned toward the cell phone to speak

to Stromeyer. "But I thought the GPS transmission was coming from Ciudad. La Valle's compound is one hundred and fifty miles south of there."

"Perhaps Caldridge made it out of Ciudad."

"You said they found this woman's body. What happened at the compound?"

"The army raided it early this morning. La Valle's men put up a fight, and a whole group of cartel dealers died. Apparently the Mexican army had a tip about a cartel gathering there, and they planned the raid to coincide with it. Half the partygoers died before they knew what hit them. Sumner, would you recognize Caldridge's handwriting?"

"Yes."

"Then let me fax you this note. I received it by fax as well, so it's going to be a bit blurry, but perhaps you can rule out her writing."

Sumner's office phone rang. He punched on the speaker and answered. A voice that Banner recognized as the man in the control tower poured out of the speaker.

"You wanted to know about this air jockey, right?"

Sumner nodded, then seemed to catch himself. "Yes I did."

"Well he disappeared for a while, then reappeared, but he's changed his course."

"Okay," Sumner drew out the word. "Where's he going now?"

"The Midwest. Not Miami."

Sumner frowned. He thought a minute. "Then he's not hauling cocaine. Miami would be his first stop if he was. Midwest route through Chicago?"

"Most likely."

"So he's hauling either meth or marijuana," Sumner said.

"Yep. You want to fly intercept?"

"You bet I do."

"Think you can beat this guy? I mean, Jorge couldn't."

"No disrespect to Jorge, but I think I can beat this guy," Sumner said.

Banner heard the man laugh over the line. "Okay. I'll keep you posted." Sumner got up and walked over to the fax machine to remove a piece of paper. He gazed at it a moment.

"Well?" Banner said.

Sumner nodded. "It's Caldridge's handwriting."

Banner heard Stromeyer blow out a breath. He felt the same way, as if he'd been punched in the stomach. Sumner just stared at the page. Banner couldn't tell what the man was thinking.

"Okay, so we know that her GPS watch is in Ciudad Juarez, but she somehow made her way to La Valle's compound."

"Or was taken there against her will," Stromeyer said.

"Absolutely," Banner said. "Taken against her will. But why the phone numbers in a Range Rover?"

"To get a message to the outside?" Stromeyer said.

Sumner's office phone rang again, and once again he put it on speaker. "Sumner here," he said. This time a woman's voice poured out.

"I've got a call from a sheriff in some small town in the Arizona hills. He wants to speak to Mr. Banner."

"Me? Why?" Banner said.

"He won't say. Let me transfer him."

"This Edward Banner? The man who's looking for a woman named Emma Caldridge?"

Sumner sat forward. Banner felt a twist in his stomach.

"Yes. Who's this?"

"I'm Sheriff Reimer. We had a meth lab in the mountains explode. Two men dead, one seriously wounded and an injured woman."

"The woman is Emma Caldridge?"

"Nope. The woman is Shelby Warren. She's in the hospital and not saying a word. The man is Timothy Conway. He's also in the hospital, but he's saying a lot. He told us that Emma Caldridge and another guy came by his trailer right before it exploded, looking for a lab to make meth. He says they shook up a batch, but did it wrong. It blew up his trailer and his Harley Davidson motorcycle. He's fighting mad and is demanding to press charges."

Banner looked at Sumner, who raised his eyebrows. "Is he well enough to be interviewed?"

"He's got some burns, but he can talk. You want to come on over?"

Sumner leaned into Banner. "I'll fly you. I want

to be present when you talk to him."

"I'll be there."

"Good, because there's something more. The two dead guys are members of the Black Eagles motorcycle gang. Conway claims that the Caldridge woman and two other men went into the house right before the explosion and they ran out with two of the Eagles staggering behind them. Conway says the Eagles were bleeding from everywhere and died on the lawn before the explosion. Bodies are pretty beat up from the explosion, so it's hard to verify his account. There's an autopsy scheduled for tomorrow."

"I'm on my way," Banner said. He and the Sheriff exchanged information and Banner rang off.

"That's an unusual story. Caldridge knows how to cook meth?" Banner said.

Sumner nodded. "I imagine she knows how to make a lot of different substances. The question is, why would she?"

"Perhaps she was coerced." Stromeyer's voice poured out of the cell phone. Banner had forgotten she was there.

"Perhaps," he said.

"I wish I could join you guys, but something's heating up and I have to deal with that. You'll keep me posted?"

"Yep," Banner said.

"Then I'm out." Stromeyer rang off.

"Do you think she would make meth?" Banner said.

Sumner thought a moment. "Perhaps. I can't

tell for certain. But one thing I can tell you, if she did make it, she'd do it right. No explosions when she cooks."

Banner stood up. "Let's go talk to this guy. The situation is getting stranger by the minute."

21

BANNER STOOD NEXT TO TIMOTHY CONWAY'S HOS-
pital bed, with Sumner at his side. He'd already
been briefed on Conway's arrest record. A long
history of theft, some petty and some not so petty,
drug possession, and two arrests for armed rob-
bery, as well as three domestic-abuse calls. The
domestics all were dropped within three days of
filing. Two were filed by Shelby Warren, who was
currently resting in another wing of the hospital. Banner intended to talk to her next. Conway
was also a reputed member of the Black Eagles
motorcycle gang, a small startup enterprise that
dabbled in crime, prostitution, and drug dealing. They were part of the 1 percent, a term used
among motorcycle members to indicate their
status at the top of the gang food chain. Banner
took stock of the man.

Conway's bandaged arms and battered, bruised
face gave testament to the force of the blast he'd
survived. Most of his hair had been burned off

and the rest cut close to his head by the doctors, but the pungent, almost metallic smell still seemed to surround the man. A plastic bag hung from a hook near his bed, with a snaking tube that ended in an IV needle, still unused and wrapped, ready to be stuck into a vein on his arm. Banner noticed the open, red sores on Conway's arms and his jittery affect despite the painkillers he must have received. Meth addict, Banner thought.

His sly, dark eyes looked a challenge at Banner, despite the fact that he couldn't possibly know why Banner was there. He struck Banner as the type that would forever fall on the wrong side of everything.

"Who the hell are you two?" Conway said.

"I'm Edward Banner, and this is Cameron Sumner. We're here to ask you some questions."

"You can ask, but I ain't promising to answer," Conway said. He yanked on the bell cord by his pillow. A nurse's voice came out of a speaker that hung from the wall above the bed.

"Can I help you?"

"Yeah. Come put this IV in and make this damn pump work. I'm in a lot of pain here."

"I can't. You're not due for another dose until five o'clock."

"Screw that, I need it," Conway said.

The nurse stood his ground. "Not until five. There's a cup containing two ibuprofens on the tray by your bedside. Feel free to take those. They should help with the pain." Conway gave the speaker the finger.

"Tell me what happened when Emma Caldridge stopped by your trailer," Banner said.

Conway fixed Banner with an angry stare. "She blew up my bike, that's what happened. If I'd 'a known she was going to cook some meth, I wouldn't have let her in."

"You told the sheriff that she was with a man. Did you know his name?"

Conway shook his head. "He followed her around like he was her lap dog." Sumner, who had been leaning against the wall on the opposite side of the hospital room with his arms crossed in front of him, straightened.

"Can you describe him?"

Conway shifted in the bed. "Not too tall, maybe five ten, eleven. Skinny. Long hair past his ears. Real pretty boy."

"Pretty? In what way?"

"Like them guys on television. Or from the city."

Banner was getting annoyed with Conway's vague description. "Guys on television? Like a news announcer?"

"Nah, like one 'a them models in magazines."

Banner looked at Sumner, who shrugged and shook his head.

"So he was handsome?"

Conway's face twisted in a sneer. "If you can call them sissy types handsome."

Banner tried a different tack. "Did you get the impression she was a hostage?"

Conway snorted. "Hell, no. She was marching around givin' orders like she owned the place."

"The man with her didn't have a gun?"

"No. Listen. You gonna send out an arrest warrant on her or what? She blew up my trailer, killed two friends of mine, and trashed my bike."

"Seems to me that you should be a bit worried about warrants, as you have an outstanding one for possession, and you appear to have been operating a meth lab up there in the hills for some time."

Conway frowned. "You can't scare me with that shit. That warrant is five years old and from a whole different state. I did my time waiting on trial, but it never got recorded. They picked me up already on it once, but this state won't enforce it, and the other said it costs too much to ship me back just for a technicality." Conway grinned. "Piss-poor economy helped me out there. And I told you, I didn't have no meth lab until those two jokers showed up and asked to use my trailer. They musta' brought the stuff with them. You want to arrest someone, you arrest them."

"Do you know where they went?"

Conway shook his head. "How the hell would I? I nearly got killed in the blast. Now get the hell out of here. I'm done talking." Conway reached to the tube by the IV bag, pulled off the sterile wrapping on the needle, and jammed it into the vein on his arm with the ease of long practice. He reached out and flipped the switch on the machine.

"You know how to get this thing pumping?"

Sumner pushed off the wall and sauntered past the foot of Conway's bed. Banner watched

Conway stare at Sumner, as if deciding something.

"You this guy's gofer?" he said to Sumner. Banner sighed. True to form, Conway didn't know when to steer clear of trouble.

Sumner stopped. Turned. And leveled a stare at Conway. Then he strolled over, reached down and grabbed Conway's forearm, squeezing directly over a bandaged portion. Conway's face turned pale.

"Hey. That arm's burned. What the hell you doing?" Conway spoke in a voice tight with pain. Sumner didn't reply. He held Conway's limb in place and yanked out the IV. He turned off the pump, removed the needle from the tubing, and gave the equipment a push with his foot sending the machine rolling away, out of Conway's reach.

"They call you 'Tico,' don't they?" Sumner said.

Tico got a wary look on his face. "Who do you mean by 'they'?"

"La Valle and his crew. The ones that are going to come for you in the middle of the night." Sumner tossed the IV needle onto a nearby tray.

"What you talking about? Coming for me?" Banner continued toward the door, and Sumner started to follow him.

"You know what I mean," Sumner said. "La Valle never lets anyone stay in custody for long. They all end up dead before they can testify before the grand jury."

"Hey!" Tico pulled himself up higher on the pillows propped behind his back. "I ain't in custody. They ain't coming for me. They got no reason.

I didn't blow up the lab, the lady they sent did. They go after anyone, it's her."

Banner put a hand out to stop Sumner from passing him. "What do you mean, 'the lady they sent'? I thought you said she showed up on her own."

Tico leaned forward. "They sent her. Treated her like some queen. She pulls up in a brand new Escalade with two of their best men riding protection and the lap-dog dude, all of them treating her like she was special."

Sumner shrugged. "If that's what you want to believe."

"That's the truth!" Tico said. Now he appeared agitated.

Sumner snorted. "You haven't said one true thing yet. Maybe you start. We can help you."

Tico shook his head in disgust. "I talk to you, La Valle kills me for sure. I'll take my chances with the Eagles."

Sumner shrugged again. "I don't give a damn either way. But just remember, the Eagles are no match for La Valle. None at all. You've already got two dead." He strolled out of the room, and Banner followed.

22

CARLOS PULLED THE AMBULANCE OVER TO THE
side of the road two hours after the explosion at
Tico's lab. Mono waved his gun at Emma.

"In the ambulance. We're meeting up with
La Valle again and he expects you to be inside."
Mono marched her up to the ambulance and tied
her up, this time with her hands secured in front
of her. It would have been easy enough to break
the ties, but two others had joined the caravan in
a beat-up Chevy, and so the possibility of escape
was far less than before. She closed her eyes and
tried to gather her tired thoughts together. She'd
been given a fast-food hamburger and some fries
to eat over an hour ago, and her hands reeked of
animal fat and stale ketchup.

After another hour, the ambulance rumbled to
a stop, and Emma watched the doors swing open.
Sunlight poured into the rear compartment.
Carlos stood in the opening. He waved to her im-
patiently. She scooted to the edge and held out
her hands. Carlos snipped the ties with a scissors.

"To the car," he said.

Emma walked out and looked around. They were on an interstate, parked on the shoulder. Cars whizzed past them. The Escalade idled in front of the ambulance, but the Chevy was gone. Carlos walked to the car and opened the front passenger side door in an open invitation to have her ride there. Mono emerged from the back. Carlos pointed a thumb in the direction of a nearby tree.

Emma gazed around, her eyes stopping on an incredible sight. Fifty feet away was a crooked tree, its limbs reaching to the sky. Clothing hung from nearly every branch. Women's bras, underwear and tank tops hung from the limbs. More clothing lay scattered on the ground.

"What the hell is that?" Emma said.

Mono looked at the tree and a smirk covered his face. "That's the trophy tree."

Emma frowned. "I don't understand."

Carlos appeared from behind a closer tree, still in the process of zipping his pants. He jogged to them. Mono pointed to the trophy tree and said something to Carlos in Spanish. Mono grinned and swaggered up to Emma.

"That's the stopping point for the coyotes and their cargo. We stop here, and take the women. Each time we do, we throw their clothes on the tree." He shoved his face closer to hers. "Once La Valle is done with you, you're next. I got thirty pieces of clothes on that tree."

Emma steeled her face to remain composed, but her stomach roiled at the idea of the helpless women that were raped under that tree. She stared at Mono and watched Carlos chuckle, and at that moment she wanted to kill them both. It was all she could do to stay still. Mono waved at the car.

"You ride with him."

Emma wasn't sure why they were participating in this game of musical chairs, but she was thrilled to be out of the ambulance and back with Oz, especially if it meant that they would be alone and able to talk freely. She slid in the passenger side and settled against the leather seat.

"I'm not leaving until I can be sure that Mono and Carlos are arrested. Or dead," she said. She turned to Oz. He stared out the window, a vacant look on his face. As if he hadn't heard her.

"Why are they suddenly allowing me to ride in comfort with you?" Emma asked.

Oz didn't turn his head. "They don't want to be near me."

Emma felt dread form in the pit of her stomach. "What's wrong?"

Oz closed his eyes, but still didn't turn to look at her.

"Tell me," she said.

Instead of speaking, he held out his hand. Red sores covered the tips of the fingers of his left hand.

"Oh God, no." The words were out of her mouth before she could censor them. Oz closed his eyes again. He leaned his head against the headrest. She stared at his profile while trying to make sense of the situation.

"Did you touch the leaves?" she asked. Her voice broke on the word "leaves," and she swallowed.

He shook his head. "Never. The migrant workers loaded the vehicles."

"From when you smoked some of La Valle's stash?"

"That wasn't from the tainted field. If it had been, I would have died like those Black Eagles did back at Ticos. This disease must be much more contagious then we think."

"Where did the others go?"

"They're ahead. Once Carlos saw my hand, he asked to stop long enough to be able to switch and ride with the ambulance."

Emma fought down the panic that threatened to engulf her. More than ever they needed to get away. To get Oz to a hospital.

"We need to escape. Now," she said.

Oz looked at her for the first time since she'd entered the car. His eyes held a desolate expression.

"*You* need to escape. I'm finished." Emma's simmering anger surged to the surface again.

"What bullshit! You don't give up until you're dead, you understand?" Oz locked eyes with her, but it was clear that he had little fight left in him.

"It's better this way. They're going to kill me at the end of this run anyhow. I decided back at the compound that I wouldn't do what they want. I don't care if they draw and quarter me alive, I'm not delivering this shipment. Somewhere between here and the DOD, I'm going to destroy it."

Emma slammed her hand on the dashboard.

She got some satisfaction from seeing Oz jump at the booming sound her palm made.

"Drive," Emma said. As if reading her thoughts, the ambulance horn gave a loud shriek. "They want you to move. Do it. We're getting the hell out of here."

Oz shook his head. "I'm done. I'm not going anywhere. I told you."

Emma yanked open her door, jumped out, and slammed it closed as hard as she could. The car rocked with the force. The ambulance horn shrieked again and she picked up a stone from the shoulder of the road and threw it at the vehicle. It hit the ambulance with a satisfying bang. Carlos flipped her the bird. She stormed to the ambulance's driver's side and pulled the door open.

"We need to get him to a hospital. Now," she said to a stone-faced Mono.

"No," he said.

"Show me your hands," Emma said.

Mono looked confused. "Why?"

"Show them to me!" she said again. Carlos gave Mono a concerned look. He rattled off a sentence in Spanish. Mono put his hands up in the air. Emma grabbed them and bent them toward her. She analyzed them. Checking the skin color and looking for any sign of forming sores. Mono watched her, a serious expression on his face.

"I didn't touch the shipment," he said after a few seconds.

Emma looked up at him. "Neither did Oz. Not once. It's spreading, but maybe not by contact."

Mono pulled his hands back into the cabin.

"You don't know that. The gringo must have touched it."

Emma shook her head. "Never. And if he has it, we're next. We need to get to a hospital. All of us."

Mono's face took on a stubborn expression. "No hospitals. They ask too many questions."

"What if you get sores? *Then* can we go to a hospital?"

Mono shook his head. "No. Not then. They ask questions, I end up in jail. I end up in jail, La Valle's men on the inside put a knife in my ribs. No hospital. Ever."

Emma wanted to punch the man in his face. If she didn't need his cooperation so badly, she would have.

Then it came to her. "We go to a lab."

Mono shook his head. "There are no more. Tico's was the only one."

"I mean a real lab. Where are we?" Mono's lips formed into a thin line.

"Mono, come on! Where are we? I need to know what labs are in the area."

"We're somewhere in the middle. Why?"

Emma was surprised at how far they'd come in such a short time. She thought of the available labs in the Midwest, and couldn't think of one.

"Do you have access to the Internet?" she asked. Mono nodded.

"Type in 'pharmaceutical companies' on a search. Limit them to the Midwest if you can, but if not, just give me a list."

Mono spoke to Carlos, who nodded and began pressing the keys on his phone.

"You can't go in. La Valle will kill me if you tip off some lab that you're a hostage," Mono said.

"I'm not going to go there in the daytime."

Mono frowned. "Why not? If one is close we can be there shortly."

"Reputable labs won't just let anyone stroll in and use their facilities. They can usually only be accessed by a coded passkey and are protected by security."

Mono gave her a dubious look. "How do you know this?"

"My company makes high-end cosmetics. The formulations are exclusive and proprietary. They, and the recipes for making them, are what keeps the company afloat, and they protect their trade secrets very carefully."

"Eh! Carlos hit Mono on his shoulder before passing his phone to Emma. She was impressed. He had managed to produce a list of pharmaceutical companies, from small to massive, in the Midwest.

"This is excellent," Emma said. Carlos nodded at her.

"Let me see," Mono said. He reached for the phone and took a long look at the list.

He pointed to one on the screen. "We can be there in three hours. But it's famous. Even I know that name. Their security must be very tight." The lab Mono mentioned was a world-class facility. Emma had no doubt security was tight, but she also had no doubt how to get in.

"Let me talk to Oz," she said.

A noise came from behind them. A quick

glance showed her that the Chevy was back. It drove slowly past and pulled in front of the Escalade. She jogged back to Oz.

"Move over. I'm driving."

"Don't touch the wheel. You could get it." Oz pulled his tee shirt up and used it to wipe the steering wheel and shift. His face was set as he slid over the center console and settled into the passenger seat. Once he was in, she hit the gas. The SUV started out.

"We're going to a lab. A world-class facility. It's only three hours away. I'm going to figure this thing out."

Oz shifted in his seat. "Mono agreed to this?"

Emma nodded. "He did."

"Why not a hospital?"

"Because Mono wouldn't agree to that."

"Why not?"

"Hospitals ask too many questions."

Oz snorted. "And labs don't? They're not just going to let you stroll in and get access to their equipment. They're going to want to know what you need."

"I'm not going to tell them."

"So how are you going to get access?"

"We're going to break in."

Before Oz could answer the back door opened and Mono slid in, taking his usual position behind them.

23

EMMA DROVE WITHIN THREE BLOCKS OF THE FACIL-
ity and killed the engine. It was six in the evening, and the lab's parking lot was emptying out.
Car after car passed them, the inhabitants barely
glancing their way as they hurried home. Most
talked on their phone, some appeared to be texting, and none seemed interested in the Escalade.

Carlos had driven the ambulance in a different
direction earlier, with the Chevy following, leaving Mono to guard them in the Escalade.

"Where's he going?" Emma had asked.

"He has a job to do," Mono said. His phone rang
periodically, and though Emma didn't understand the conversation, it appeared as though it
was Carlos.

"What's he doing?" Emma asked.

"You'll see," Mono replied with a sly look on
his face.

That had been three hours ago. Now the ambulance pulled up behind them. Carlos jumped
down from the cabin and sauntered up to

Emma's window. When she rolled it down he waved her out.

"You go and look," Mono said. Oz moved to open his door. Mono waved him off. "Not you. You stay here. Just her." Emma stepped out and followed Mono to the back of the ambulance. He swung open the door.

A man and woman lay tied up on the floor of the cabin. Their wild eyes telegraphed their fear. Next to them lay a bag of adult diapers and a variety of tools, along with a sawed-off broomstick. Emma kept her face perfectly still. She would not show fear in front of Carlos. If she did, he would kill her.

"What's going on here?" she said.

"They're members of a rival gang. We got them, and we play with them. When we are done, they will tell us everything: where they keep their stash, what cops they employ. He picked up the diapers. "They will need these after we start." Emma fisted her hands so tight that her nails dug into her palms. The feeling kept her focused, kept her from attacking Mono right then and there.

"How does this concern me?" Emma said. She was relieved at how cool her voice sounded.

Mono leaned into her, his skinny, pockmarked face radiating evil. "Because how far we go depends on you. You don't come back here, alone, within three hours of entering that lab, then after we torture them, we kill them."

The female hostage groaned and closed her eyes.

"I thought you were coming with me to be sure nothing happens."

Mono nodded. "This is extra protection. And if you mess up, once we are done with these two, we find you and begin on you. You understand?"

Emma understood all too well. "I'm not going to tip anyone off. I'm going to use the lab, then leave."

Mono slammed the doors shut again. "That's right."

Emma kept her stone-faced demeanor the entire way to the SUV. It was only when she returned to the driver's seat that she let her fear show. Mono and Carlos were outside, stretching their legs and smoking a cigarette. Oz glanced at her.

"What the hell did he say? You look pale. Are you going to be sick?"

Emma shook her head. "They have two hostages in the ambulance. Rival gang members. If we do anything to tip off the authorities, they'll kill them."

Oz inhaled a huge breath. "They'll probably kill them anyway. You know that."

Emma shook her head. "I don't think so. The cartel kidnaps, but returns their victims after a payment. They only kill when they don't get paid. I don't want these people's deaths on my head."

"He said they were rival cartel gang members. Why would you care?"

Emma pictured the woman's eyes as she listened to Carlos, and the way she closed them when he said he would kill them.

"I just don't want it to be on my head. Okay? Someone dies here, it'd better be Carlos or Mono or the rest of La Valle's losers."

But Oz persisted. "If they're cartel members they're just as bad. The world would be better off without them. I think we should call the authorities the minute we can. Maybe they can catch Carlos before he does anything to them. I understand that you've never killed anyone before, but—"

"—I *have* killed before." Emma switched on the ignition and gave the horn a slight tap to notify Mono that she wanted to leave. When she was done she looked at Oz. He stared at her in surprise.

"You're not serious, are you?" he said. Emma sighed.

"I've completed a mission for a contract security organization called Darkview. I still take some work from them when they require my expertise. During the course of one mission, I came under attack and was forced to defend myself." Mono was walking back to join them, flicking a cigarette onto the ground as he did. Oz still stared at her, incredulity in his eyes. Emma felt compelled to explain her actions. "Even though I've killed in self-defense, that doesn't mean I'll allow Carlos to kill those two. I have no idea if what he tells me is true. What if they're not cartel members, but innocent hostages? What then?" Emma shook her head. "I'll do my best to get us out of this mess. If I kill anyone, it's going to be Carlos, Raoul, Mono, or La Valle. Not those two in the ambulance."

The door opened and Mono crawled in. Emma pulled away from the curb, glad to have something to do that kept her eyes on the road and away from Oz's horrified stare. She headed to the outskirts of the pharmaceutical campus. A chain-link fence ten feet high surrounded the compound, but that was all. It didn't appear to be electrified, nor was it topped with razor wire. The fence seemed more for show than security. An access road encircled the campus. She circled the campus and then turned onto the main driveway.

A sprawling two-story building with green reflective windows and extensive lawns lit with spotlights loomed in front of her. A granite block engraved with the word MEDICANT sat at the end of the drive leading up to the front door. She turned into the lane. The driveway ended in a horseshoe curve. She entered the curve and stopped directly in front of the entrance. Killed the engine and soaked in the silence. Two men stood on flagstone pavers under a portico, talking to each other. The first wore the dark blue uniform favored by rent-a-cops the world over. The second, a pin-striped suit. In front of Emma the horseshoe branched off onto another path that curved around the main building to the back. A gate blocked it.

"What do we do now?" Oz said.

The pin-stripe-suited man strolled by and gave a slightly curious glance at the Escalade, but continued toward the parking lot. The security guard stood his ground, looking at them.

"Now I go ask a question," Emma said. She jumped out of the car and walked toward the security guard, careful to plaster a smile on her face as she did. He responded to the sight of her with a neutral, professional nod.

"Hello!" Emma said. "We're looking for the lab facility. I'm a chemist and am supposed to meet one of the scientists." The guard, a man of perhaps thirty or thirty-five with sandy hair and a doughy face that matched his rounded waistline, nodded again.

"These are the corporate offices. You want the large cinder-block building in the back. Just follow that branch until you see it. You can't miss it. Huge sign in front says 'Lab.' But you're a little late, aren't you?" He checked his watch. "It's almost seven o'clock, and everyone's gone by now."

Emma gave him what she hoped was a rueful smile. "I am late. But my boss said that the scientist here, I forget his name, always works late, so that shouldn't be a problem."

The guard broke into a smile. "Must be John Raynor. Guy works like a dog. I keep telling him he needs to take a day off, but he don't listen to me."

Emma smiled. "That must be him. I'll head down there."

The guard walked over to the gate, flipped a switch, and the gate rose. She crawled back into the car.

"The lab's in the back. Let's go," she said.

She waved at the guard as she passed through, and he gave her a congenial nod in return.

"There's a scientist working late. I'm not surprised. There's always one. This one's named John Raynor."

Oz gave her a worried look. "What are we going to do with him?"

"Avoid him completely if possible."

It was full dark, but solar lamps lined the road on both sides, illuminating their way. Emma slowed for a frog that hopped across the path.

The lab building was a rectangular structure made out of cinder blocks and with the same green tinted windows of the corporate center. A large, white sign with brass lettering said LAB, just as the guard had promised. Several parking spots, two specially marked "GUEST" and two with a disabled sign, were lined up perpendicular to the front.

"Time to go," Emma said.

"I'm coming with you," Oz said.

"We all go," Mono said.

Emma shook her head at them both. "Neither of you can. You're not dressed appropriately. You won't get past the security desk."

"I go, or you don't," Mono said.

Emma tried one more time to dissuade him. "They'll never let you past. How would you explain your clothing?" She indicated Mono's faded jeans and gray tee shirt. Oz's ensemble was not much different. He was in the same battered jeans he wore when she first met him, and his tee shirt bore the graphic of an English underground rock band. The casual attire, when added to his long hair, made him appear to be exactly what he was, a slightly disreputable roadie making his way through town.

Emma's clothes were in far better shape, although still not appropriate, but she'd been working in labs since college and felt at home there.

She was counting on her familiarity with them to allow her to play off the security desk.

"I go, or you don't," Mono repeated.

"Listen, I saw an entrance with a ramp on that side of the building." Emma pointed to her left. Let me work my way past the guards and I'll head over there and let you in. Deal?"

Mono thought for a moment.

"Come on, Mono, you know they won't let the two of us in, we look like drug dealers," Oz said.

Mono laughed. After a moment, Oz did too. Emma thought it was forced on Oz's part, but he gave it his best shot.

Mono pointed the gun at her. "Remember, you tip them off, and Carlos starts."

Emma just nodded.

Mono jerked the gun to Oz, who gave her a worried look and climbed out of the car. Emma waited until they disappeared around the corner, then took a deep breath. She stepped into the cool evening. Crickets chirped all around her and a soft breeze blew through the trees. She looked up. Stars filled the sky. It was as if nothing bad had happened, would happen, or could happen. How wrong the universe was.

"I NEED TO SEE JOHN RAYNOR," EMMA SAID TO THE female security guard behind the reception desk.

"You'll need a pass. Can I tell him your name?" The guard wore a name tag that said SULLIVAN.

"Emma Caldridge of Pure Chemistry, Miami, Florida." The guard walked to the back of the desk and picked up the phone. Emma heard the woman talk as a low murmuring. She couldn't make out the words. The guard turned to her.

"He says he's sorry, but he thinks you have the wrong person. He wasn't expecting anyone to-night."

Emma smiled. "Tell him I *do* have the wrong person. Seems as though the right one has left for the day. I was hoping to talk to him so that tomorrow he could distribute some information that another team needs. I'm just passing through. This is my only chance."

The guard relayed Emma's response. After a moment, the guard put the phone down and typed on a keyboard. She walked over to Emma with a printed name tag.

"Go through those doors and down the hallway. He's working in Lab Four."

"Thanks!" Emma said brightly. She stuck the badge on her shirt and walked to the glass partition doors that led to a hallway in the back of the lobby. "Here?" she pointed to the partition.

"After I buzz you through go to the next set of doors."

The buzzing sound of the glass doors made Emma jump. Get hold of yourself, she thought. Her heart was racing and her palms were getting sweaty. She slowed her pace and swung through the first set of doors, headed to the second. When she passed through those, she entered a long, wide hallway with doors on either side. To her immediate left was another hall. At the end of that, she saw the doors marked Exit.

She jogged to it and pushed the bar. A beeping noise indicated that the door was breached. She pushed the metal panel wide and found Oz and Mono standing before her. Oz looked as nervous as hell, but Mono appeared excited. To Emma he looked like the loose cannon that he was. She waved them into the hall.

"Let's go. I suspect that the beep you heard was the security system notifying the guards that the door was opened."

She spun and ran back down to the main hall. Here she moved a bit more slowly, checking the doors. The first few were marked sterile and when she tried the door handles they didn't move. Each had a passkey box on the panel. The third sign merely said LAB. This door swung open. Emma fumbled around on the wall to the right of the entranceway. Her fingers found a light switch and she threw it on.

Fluorescent lights hummed to life, revealing a narrow room with counters running the length of it. Various types of equipment sat on the counters, ranging from test tubes to micro-centrifuges.

"My God. A real lab," Emma said. She breathed in the air, with its light scent of alcohol and a mint smell that she couldn't place. "Oz, let's get those sores scraped and analyzed under a microscope." She waved him over to a wheeled stool and rummaged around in the cabinets for a scalpel and a slide. She found both and got to work.

Mono flopped into a chair at a desk in the front of the room to the right of the door. A computer sat on the desk in front of him. He tapped on the keyboard and the monitor sprang to life. He didn't try to use it, but instead just looked around with a bored expression on his face.

Oz's sores had spread to cover the first three fingers of his left hand, and the pinky and fourth of his right. Emma scraped at them, careful to add the pieces to the slide.

"What do you think you'll see?" he said.

Emma wasn't sure. "I'm hoping that this will work as a crude form of a biopsy. Perhaps revealing unusual cells or signs of bacteria. Maybe a type of virulent staph infection or some sort of parasite. Scabies are small bugs that burrow in the skin, as a type of body lice."

THE NINTH DAY

Oz grimaced. "That's disgusting."

"But more common than you'd think, and treatable for the most part," Emma said. "Do they hurt when I scrape them?"

Oz shook his head. "Not at all."

Emma paused. "What do you mean, 'not at all'?"

"Just that. They're numb. My entire left hand is numb. I don't feel anything."

The door to the lab swung inward. A man in navy twill pants and blue-and-white-striped shirt with the sleeves rolled up stepped into the room. Nearing forty, he had brown hair cut short to his head and a slightly craggy face. He looked at Oz sitting on the stool and Emma standing at the microscope. The open door blocked his view of Mono.

"What's going on here?" the man said. He had dark eyes and a low, authoritative voice, as if used to giving orders. The door swung closed, revealing Mono, who stepped up to him. The man towered over Mono, who barely stood five foot seven. Mono reached up to dig the tip of his revolver into the man's head, behind his right ear. "What the . . . ?" The man froze.

"Don't move," Emma said. The man stayed still. Emma watched as his face registered first incredulity, then fear.

"Are you John Raynor?"

"Yes."

"I'm Emma Caldridge. You remember my name?" She very much wanted him to remember it so that he could tell the authorities about her later.

"I do. The guard said that you were a chemist."

"I am. I need to use this lab to . . ."

"Enough! Don't tell him our business. He'll call the police. We need to kill him," Mono said.

Oz rose from the stool so fast that it rolled backward and hit the cabinets. "No, Mono. Don't. We can't afford to have the police crawling up our ass."

Mono nodded. "That's why I'll kill him. He won't talk." Oz took a step toward Mono, who pressed the gun harder against Raynor's head. Raynor bent away from the muzzle, but Mono kept the gun flush with the man's skull. Emma watched Raynor swallow once, and then visibly steel himself. She wished he hadn't gotten involved.

"Come on," Oz's voice held a cajoling tone, "let's just tie him up. Throw him in a broom closet. We'll take off. By the time they find him we'll be miles away. No one dies, and the police don't look as hard for a couple of burglars as they do for a murderer. Especially when all they do is use some lab equipment and leave. You understand?"

"That's a good idea," Emma said. She kept her tone light, as if they were discussing nothing serious. She didn't want to trigger Mono and his wilder instincts. "Do you have the ties that Carlos uses?"

Mono nodded.

"Then you guys tie him up while I finish here. I don't think we should linger." She put some finality in her voice, as if the course of action was decided.

Mono appeared to hesitate, thinking.

"Get down on the ground," Oz said to Raynor.

"I'll help you, Mono." Oz tipped the balance, and Mono began fishing in his pockets for the ties.

Raynor lowered himself to the floor and placed his palms on the tile. He shot Emma a glance before putting his chest and forehead down.

"Here," Emma said. She handed Oz some lab gloves from a box on the counter. "Wear these." Oz put them on, grabbed one of Raynor's hands and waved at Mono to grab the other.

Mono didn't move. He kept the gun pointed at the man's back.

Come on, Mono, just tie him up, Emma thought.

"You do have the ties, right?" Oz prompted.

Mono nodded again.

"Good," Emma said. "Tie him, but then sit him up. I need to ask him some questions."

Oz waved at Mono, who slowly lowered his gun. Emma busied herself at the lab station, all the while doing her best not to look at Mono. The action seemed to help decide him, because he pulled the ties out of his pocket and applied himself to shackling Raynor. When they were done, Emma indicated a chair near the station.

"I need to do a Fite stain. Do you have the material for that?"

Raynor clamped his mouth shut.

"Mr. Raynor, I don't have time to play games. Do you have the tools I need?"

Raynor jerked his chin at a high cabinet next to Emma's shoulder. "Up there."

Emma opened it and found what she needed.

"I don't like the sound of a Fite stain," Oz said, sounding nervous.

"I'll need to cut some more of the sores, and this time I'd like to go a little deeper, but if what you say is true and they're numb, I don't think you'll feel it."

Oz sat back on his stool and rolled over to her. "Okay, but do it quick."

Emma once again applied the knife to the sores. Oz didn't flinch.

"You didn't feel that?" she said.

"Not at all," he replied.

Emma frowned at him. "The sores are numbing your nerves." She glanced at Raynor and found him staring at Oz's hand with a clinical expression on his face.

Emma went to a nearby microscope. It was state of the art, and she admired it for a moment.

"This equipment is fantastic." She powered it on and slid the small piece of glass underneath the lens.

"What do you see?" Oz asked in an anxious voice. "Are there bugs?"

The sore teemed with bacilli interspersed with black hunks of decaying skin. The bacteria triggered some memory in her, as if she'd seen it before, but she couldn't pull the idea forward. She stared at it and tried to concentrate.

"No flipping worm or parasitic beast, and no lice-type insect."

Oz breathed a sigh of relief.

She lifted her head and looked at Raynor, who was leaning forward in his chair, an interested look on his face.

"When did the sores start?" Emma asked Oz.

"Eight hours ago," he replied.

Raynor raised his eyebrows. "That's a lot of growth for eight hours."

Emma inhaled. The bacteria implied that Oz had some sort of mycobacterial infection.

"Do you see anything?" Oz sounded anxious.

She nodded. "Lots of bacteria."

"What could that be from?"

"Tuberculosis. Meningitis." She didn't want to say the other possible infections out loud. "You have any gastrointestinal symptoms? Like diarrhea?" Oz gave her a sharp look, as though he could tell that she was holding something back.

"No."

"Did you dig in the dirt near the field?"

Oz looked confused. "No. Why would I dig in the dirt?"

"Did you dig in the dirt anywhere on the compound?"

Oz shook his head. "No. Come on, tell me. What are you thinking?"

Emma didn't reply. She waved a hand at the computer on the desk. "Does that access the Internet?" she said to Raynor.

"Don't forget Carlos . . ." Mono said.

"None of the lab computers have web access," Raynor said. "They contain research data, searchable reference books, copies of the *Physician's Desk Reference*, things like that."

A voice squawked from the cell phone in a holder attached to Raynor's waistband. "Dr. Raynor? This is Janet Sullivan. Please check in."

Emma, Oz, and Mono stopped moving. Emma

considered then rejected the idea of having Raynor answer. She didn't trust him not to tip off the guard.

"Mr. Raynor?" the guard said. Emma reached down and pulled the cell phone, holder and all, off his belt.

"Time's up, let's go," she said. She pointed at the corner of the room behind the door. "Put him there, and let's get the hell out." Mono and Oz waved Raynor to the corner. He slid his back down the wall until he was seated. Mono tied his ankles together. Emma tossed Oz a roll of gauze. "Gag," she said. Oz wrapped the gauze around Raynor's mouth.

Through it all Raynor stared at her, as if he was memorizing her features. Emma couldn't tell what he was thinking. She hated to let him believe the worst of her, but there was no way of telling him without putting the hostages in the back of Carlo's ambulance at risk. She lowered her eyes while she tossed the slides and scalpels into a hazardous waste container bolted to the wall above a sink. She washed her hands and headed to the computer while she dried them. She tapped a key and the options screen opened. She clicked on the icon for a famous reference manual of diseases. In the search box she typed the words sores, tendon, contraction.

"What are you doing? Let's go," Mono's voice sounded harsh with tension.

"I'm looking up the symptoms. One more minute." Emma kept her eyes on the screen.

"Dr. Raynor? Please respond." Sullivan's voice came through the cell phone. After twenty more seconds that felt like twenty minutes to Emma, the computer screen listed thirty results, with the ten highest ranked displayed first.

"Move!" Mono said. Emma exited the search and went to stand next to Mono.

"I'm ready," she said.

Mono cocked his weapon and cautiously peered around the door into the hall. He waved them forward. Oz went next, and Emma last. When she pulled even with Raynor she glanced at him. He continued to watch her with a hard stare.

I'm sorry, she thought. She flicked off the light and stepped through the door.

They jogged down the main hall and turned into the branch, heading for the side door. Mono hit the bar and Emma heard the beeping noise as it opened. He was gone, with Oz right behind. Emma jogged forward.

"Stop!" A woman's voice gave the order.

Emma sped up. She sprinted the ten feet and slammed the bar against the door. The panel opened so fast that she stumbled through. Emma heard the woman yell again, but she was out and the steel door was closing behind her.

The Escalade idled twenty feet away. Emma put on a burst of speed, yanking open the door and crawling in the back. Oz drove, Mono was in the passenger's seat with the window rolled down and his gun poised on the outside, ready to shoot. A glance at the door revealed Sullivan, her gun in one hand and her cell phone in the other. Emma saw the woman's lips move as she ran toward the Escalade.

"She's trying to get a plate, let's move," Emma yelled the warning.

The Escalade dug in, and then shot forward. Mono leaned out and squeezed off two shots in Sullivan's direction. Emma winced at the loud sound the gun made as it fired. She watched the guard dive to the ground.

"Enough!" Emma said.

"I missed her." Mono aimed anew.

"Stop it!" Oz said. He yanked the wheel to the left and the Escalade skidded into a turn. Emma grabbed at the handrail above her head. Mono fell ten inches backward, into the car. The hand holding the gun flew up, and he hit his knuckles on the top of the window's frame.

"Watch what you do!" Mono said. Oz ignored him. He turned right at the top of the driveway in front of the corporate offices and the car gained even more speed on the straightaway down the drive toward the main road. The Escalade's headlights were off, but low solar street illuminators glowed on either side, making it possible to see despite the darkness. Emma watched behind them the entire length of the road, but Ms. Sullivan didn't appear.

Oz turned the car onto the street and took the vehicle to an even higher speed. Once they were out off the campus, he switched on the headlights and barreled ahead.

"Where are we going?" he said to Mono.

Mono pressed a key on his cell phone and spoke in low tones. After a moment he said, "The interstate entrance is coming up in two kilometers. Take it east."

Oz nodded.

The blue-and-red interstate sign reflected the beam of the car's headlights. Oz entered the eastbound ramp, opening the throttle when they reached the top, and merged onto the highway. The Escalade raced down the interstate, dodging slower traffic that appeared in its path. They continued to drive, Oz keeping the speedometer at ninety and concentrating on weaving in and out of traffic.

No one spoke. Emma sat and worried about the various diseases Oz could have, and the list running through her mind was an ugly one. She felt despair nipping at the edges of her mind. She pushed back the thought. She'd cure him.

She wouldn't let today be his day to die.

25

"EMMA CALDRIDGE BROKE INTO A PHARMACEUTI-cal lab in Nebraska, tied up a scientist working there, used the lab to run some tests on an accomplice, and, when she was discovered, shot at the security guard on duty."

Banner and Sumner were sitting in an all-suite business hotel near the Phoenix Airport when Stromeyer called to deliver this news. Banner was lounging in front of the hotel-room desk, his feet on the top, eating a Subway sandwich, when he'd hit the speaker button to take Stromeyer's call. Now he swung his feet off the desk and stood, unable to believe what he'd heard. Sumner stopped eating his own sandwich and stared at the phone with an expression of surprise on his face.

"Are you joking?" Banner asked.

"No. I have the sheriff of the town on the line, do you want to speak to him?"

Banner sat back down in his chair. "Yes, I believe I do."

"Mr. Banner? Sheriff Carl Wiley here."

"Can you tell me what happened?" Banner said.

"Near as we can tell, Ms. Caldridge lied to gain access to the Medicant Pharmaceutical building. Once inside, she opened a side door, and two accomplices, both men, joined her. She then helped herself to the equipment and supplies in a lab. When a scientist who was working late stumbled upon them, one of the men threatened to kill him and the other tied him up. The security guard for the building intercepted Caldridge as she ran out of the building to join her buddies, and they sped away in a black SUV. They escaped, but not before they squeezed off a couple of shots at the guard."

"Was the guard hit?"

"No. Missed. There's a security camera in the main hallway that leads to the lab. We're looking at it now. Maybe we can get a picture of the three of them. Figure out who the men are."

"Sheriff, I've known Ms. Caldridge for some time now, and she would never allow someone innocent to be attacked. She must have been coerced."

"Doesn't sound like it at all. The scientist said she was marching around the lab issuing orders that the two men followed."

"Do you have any idea where she is now?"

"I do not. Got an APB out on a black SUV. American made."

"I'm on my way."

FOUR HOURS LATER Banner and Sumner pulled up in a rented car in front of the county police station in a town a hundred miles from Omaha. It was a small modern, rectangular brown brick building with glass doors. An empty flagpole held a prominent position on the front lawn. Banner parked at the side of the building.

Once inside, Banner saw a long counter facing him that was covered in some sort of pressed wood veneer. Tacked on a far wall was a large seal with the words E PLURIBUS UNU on it. A tired-looking cop sat behind the counter under a harsh fluorescent light, reading the newspaper. He threw it down when they entered.

"Can I help you?"

Banner introduced himself and Sumner. He pointed at the seal. "You're missing the em," he said.

The cop gave a world-weary nod. Like he'd had that pointed out to him a thousand times before.

"Fell off in the '06 tornado, and the county hasn't authorized the repair."

"Been a while," Banner said. The cop smiled.

"Bureaucracy gears turn real slowly around here." The cop swung open a lower half door that separated the private area behind the desk from the hall and waved them forward. "Josh told me you were coming. He's got the witness in the interrogation room." Banner looked at his watch.

"That's a long time to talk to a witness."

"Oh, they just started. Get a load of this: witness went back to work after the incident. Only came here after. Crazy, huh? I'd be home popping a beer and saying thanks to the Lord. Guy must be a real workaholic."

"Bet if he worked for the county you'd have that em back on your seal by now," Sumner said.

The cop guffawed. "Bet you're right." He pointed them to a door with a sign that read AUTHORIZED PERSONNEL ONLY. "Through there. Second door on your left."

The room contained two men and a long wooden table with four chairs, all of which had seen better days. One of the men, the one that Banner presumed was Sheriff Wiley, was in uniform, the other—Banner knew his name was John Raynor—in conservative clothes. Raynor looked tired, but not nearly as tired as Sheriff Wiley, and a Blackberry phone sat on the desk in front of him. Once again, Banner introduced himself and Sumner, and shook hands all around.

"Can you run down what happened? I know you've probably told the story a thousand times already, but I'd like to hear it from you directly," he said to Raynor. The man nodded.

Banner listened as Raynor gave the same essential facts that Wiley had already relayed.

"Can you describe the accomplices?"

"One Mexican guy, early twenties, and one white guy, maybe late twenties. Both slender. The white guy had hair past his ears and he wore beat-up jeans and a band tee shirt."

"What band?" Sumner said.

Raynor looked confused. "I beg your pardon?"

"What band was on the tee shirt?"

"Uh. Rex Rain."

Banner had never heard of them. "Either of you guys know them?" he said to Wiley and Sumner.

Wiley snorted. "Not me. I like Tim McGraw and Gretchen Wilson. Dolly Parton's good, too."

"They're an alternative rock band out of England. Just completed their first U.S. tour this year. Definitely up and coming," Sumner said. "You like alternative rock?"

Banner liked old rock and new jazz. "You mean like Led Zeppelin or the Stones?"

Sumner smiled. "I mean like Gomez or Phoenix."

"I'll put Stromeyer on it," Banner said. Sumner's smile broadened. Banner turned back to Raynor.

"We've had another witness describe this band guy as handsome, like someone on television with an effeminate manner. That right?"

Raynor shook his head. "He wasn't effeminate at all. He took charge of the Mexican guy and helped him tie me up. When she took a knife to his hand he didn't even flinch."

"She took a knife to his hand?"

"He had sores on his left hand. He said they'd been growing for only eight hours, but they were already pretty extensive. She did a pretty deep cut to get some tissue for a slide."

"Did she analyze the skin?"

Raynor nodded. "She said she saw bacteria, and when he asked her what he had, she said possibly meningitis or tuberculosis."

"I got a call into the CDC," Wiley interjected. "Figured if this guy is running around with tuberculosis, he could be infecting everyone he's coming in contact with."

"Was he coughing?"

"Not at all," Raynor said. "And he didn't look feverish or sick the way meningitis would make him look."

Banner sat back, thinking.

Raynor leaned forward. "I've been thinking about this all night. I went back and dug up the slide that she threw into the sharps container. I put it under a microscope."

Banner was liking this Raynor more and more. "Great. And?"

"It was tainted, but I thought I did see some rod-shaped bacteria. Could be tuberculosis, sure, but the guy wasn't coughing or pale, and that didn't explain the sores. Just by the way she acted, I thought she had a different idea in mind. She hesitated to tell him. It was as if she was holding back. Then she asked him if he had been digging in the dirt at the compound."

Banner threw a glance to Sumner. He was staring at Raynor with as intense an expression as he'd ever seen on the man.

"Is that significant?" Banner said.

"She thought he got the bacteria from the dirt on the compound," Sumner repeated.

Raynor turned to Sumner and nodded. "But not bugs. She told the guy no worms or parasites."

"How big were the sores?" Sumner asked.

"Large ones. They covered his whole hand."

"Does anthrax present in rod-shaped bacteria?" Sumner asked.

Raynor looked triumphant. "Yes, it does."

26

BANNER AND SUMNER WERE BACK IN THE CAR.
Sumner drove while Banner called Stromeyer.
She answered in a sleepy voice.

"I'm sorry to wake you up, but we may be running this Caldridge thing down." Banner filled her in.

"I can't believe Caldridge would try to kill the guard," Stromeyer said. "What I *can* believe is that she's trying to help this guy with the sores."

"I agree, but why not just get him to a hospital? Raynor told us that if it's anthrax and he's reached the sores stage, he's not likely to survive. The good news in all of this is that anthrax is not contagious. The guy isn't spreading it throughout the States on this crime spree of his, or whatever the hell he's doing."

"Did you notify the Mexican authorities? They'd better test everyone who came in contact with the soil in the compound."

"They're on it. Can you check on something for

me? It's an English rock band called Rex Rain. Have you heard of them?"

"Sure. What's their connection?"

"Maybe none at all. The guy with the sores is running around with a tee shirt emblazoned with their logo. Sumner thinks that the only way to get that shirt is to attend one of their concerts."

"You think he picked up the anthrax at a concert instead of at La Valle's ranch?"

"Caldridge asked this guy if he was digging in the dirt. If they had an outdoor concert he may have sat on the ground, come in contact with the dirt that way. I'm told that the only place anthrax exists in nature is in the ground."

Banner heard static from Stromeyer's end as she shuffled around. "I don't like the sound of that. If he got it, then others may have too. It's ten o'clock in the morning in England. I'll track down the band's publicist, find out what outdoor venues they played during their tour, and get back to you."

They had arranged for a hotel near the local airport where Sumner had landed the plane they were using from the Air Tunnel Denial facility. Banner thought it was best that they stay in Nebraska on the off chance that the warrant out for Caldridge and the others was successful and she was apprehended. Banner switched off his phone. Sumner's rang almost immediately. He shoved a hands-free device in his ear and answered it. After a few minutes he rang off as well.

"That sounded like some ATD business. Can we keep the plane?"

Sumner turned the rental car into the hotel parking lot. "Actually, it all dovetails pretty nicely. We've been tracking that rogue pilot. He's currently on a course that has him landing about six hundred miles east of here. They've lost track of him for the moment, but the minute he reappears, I'm going to fly intercept."

"You do what you have to. I'll keep digging around here."

Banner dragged himself out of the car. It was three o'clock in the morning, and exhaustion was gnawing at him. He wished that he could make some sense of Caldridge's actions. Put them into some logical framework that gelled with his view of her, but nothing was adding up. He followed Sumner down the hotel hallway. Their rooms were on opposite sides of the corridor. When they reached their respective doors, he asked Sumner the question that had been preying on his mind the whole long day.

"Do you think she's involved with La Valle in some way?"

Sumner had been sliding his key card into the hotel lock. He looked over at Banner, surprise on his face. "Absolutely not. I have complete confidence in her."

Banner did, too, but he was glad that Sumner, who he considered to be one of the most logical, dispassionate men he had ever met, thought so as well.

"Do you think she's a hostage?" Banner asked.

Sumner nodded. "Yes. I think she's biding her

time. I also think she's doing what she can to help this guy. My concern is that if he has anthrax from the compound, she could have it as well."

"How long does it take anthrax to kill?"

Sumner snapped his fingers. "Not long at all. As far as I'm concerned, the band guy is a walking dead man. I just want to get her freed before she joins him."

FIVE HOURS LATER, Banner's phone rang, waking him from a fitful sleep. It was Stromeyer.

"No go on the Rex Rain publicist. She says they're touring Europe and can't be disturbed."

Banner snorted. "They can't be disturbed? What the hell does that mean? What are they, royalty?" He listened as Stromeyer's laugh came over the phone. The sound made him glad in a way that he didn't want to spend too much time analyzing. He shoved the feeling back.

"Their publicist was clearly stonewalling me. She's a real bulldog. Lots of attitude. If she wasn't sitting safely in England I'd send in an FBI guy to arrest her for obstruction of justice. I don't suppose you know anyone in England who has access to rock stars?"

Banner's phone beeped, signaling another call before he was able to respond. "Let me think about it," he said. He transferred to the second call.

"Wiley here. Just wanted to let you know we got a photo of the three of them as they ran down the hall. We sent some stills to Mr. Sumner by

e-mail. He confirmed that the woman is definitely Emma Caldridge, but was unable to ID the
other two. I e-mailed the photos to you."

Banner flipped open his laptop and pulled up
the still footage. The first showed Caldridge in the
center of the hall. There was no mistaking that it
was her, because the camera caught her full on.
The next photo showed two men just as Raynor
had described them. The Mexican looked keyed
up, edgy. Even in the grainy photograph Banner
could see the whites of the man's eyes.

The second man looked grim. The graphic
on his tee shirt looked like a bit of impression-
ist art, all white lines and spiked edges with
words drawn into the center in an archaic script.
Banner couldn't quite make out the words, but he
presumed anyone familiar with the band might
recognize the image. Banner analyzed the photograph. The white man was handsome in an aes-
thetic, almost artistic way. His bone structure was
classic, refined, and the long hair to his shoulders
gleamed. Banner could now understand why the
drug dealer had interpreted the look as effeminate. Even the fluorescent lights didn't mar his
features.

After a moment, Banner had an idea. He flipped
open his phone and dialed a private number. He
smiled when he heard the woman's voice.

"How was your flight home?" he asked.

"Uneventful. I've been catching up on my
sleep. When I came home no one assured me that
I looked rested. I blame you for that."

Banner chuckled. "Sorry." They chatted a bit

more and he got down to business. "I have a problem that I hope you can help me with," he said.

She paused, and Banner thought she was steeling herself to say no. As if she was afraid he'd intrude on her daily life. After a moment she said, "Of course."

He told her about the Rex Rain publicist's refusal to help them. "Are all publicists like that?"

"Hmmm, they're pretty protective. They have to be, really. It's their job to shield their clients."

"Do you think she'd loosen up if it was you who needed the information?"

"Probably. How about you send me the photo and I'll see what I can do."

Banner sent it from his computer. "It's done."

"That was fast. How soon do you need this?"

"Yesterday."

"Hold tight."

Twenty minutes later, Banner's phone rang. The screen registered an "out of area" number. He picked it up and identified himself. A man's voice, thick with an English accent, came over the phone.

"I'm Richard Carrow, the lead singer for Rex Rain. I got a call. Said you needed some information about the guy in the photograph?"

Banner was impressed with her mojo. Not only did she get access to the band in minutes flat, but the lead singer, no less. Banner poured a cup of coffee that he'd just made in the hotel-room coffeepot. "Yes, thanks. Is that your band's tee shirt that he's wearing?"

"Yes. We sell them at the concerts. Why?"

"We're trying to figure out if this guy attended one here in the States, and where."

"He was in Phoenix. He acted as a substitute technician for one of the shows."

Banner was in the middle of taking a sip of coffee and he almost spit it out. "You *know* this guy?"

"Yeah. That's Oswald Kroger. Nice guy. We have a regular computer tech that tours with us, but he took sick when we reached Arizona and Oz subbed for him. He really helped tune up the sound, and for the first time I didn't have to scream to be heard. I thanked him personally. Saved my voice."

"You know where he might be now?"

"No. Our regular tech got better and we continued on."

Banner thanked the singer, hung up, and dialed Sumner. "The band guy is Oswald Kroger, a computer tech in Phoenix. I don't suppose your guys at the ATD program can muscle up some background?"

"We'll get on him and the Mexican guy. And my rogue pilot's back on radar and nearby. I'm getting ready to fly out."

"Go get him," Banner said.

"I will," Sumner replied.

27

AT FOUR O'CLOCK IN THE MORNING, EMMA, OZ,
and Mono pulled into an RV trailer park and
proceeded to a secluded tree-lined area. Two
RVs of different models sat next to each other.
Mono instructed Oz to park the Escalade near the
second, much smaller, RV. Emma saw the ambulance parked about fifty feet away, near an old
silver Airstream. She crawled out of the SUV and
stretched with a groan. Oz exited slowly. He'd
wrapped gauze around the sores on his hand and
Emma noted that the area of the punch biopsy
was stained red. He was bleeding again.

The lights on the largest RV sprang on. Emma
heard movement from the inside, and a few seconds later, the door swung open. Light splayed
across the grass. A person stood in the doorway,
but Emma couldn't make out the features because the light was shining from behind. From
the shape she assumed it was Serena.

"You found the answer?" she said.

Emma paused. "I'm closer."

"Come inside. All of you." Serena stepped back into the trailer.

Emma felt exhaustion claw at her, but she fought it off and did her best to stay on her feet without swaying. She followed Oz into the trailer. Mono was at her back. His gun was in his hand.

The trailer surprised Emma with its spacious interior and expensive appointments. The galley kitchen area had stainless-steel appliances and expensive countertops that looked like granite, but that Emma assumed were Corian or some other lighter substance. The living room area had a plush sectional couch and a flat-screen television. At the far end of the vehicle was a screen that Emma assumed retracted to reveal a bedroom.

Serena walked to the living area and turned toward them, slowly. Emma gasped when she saw her. The sores covered both her arms, and looked like they were migrating to her face. Her hands were curling into claws, the fingers forming rigid *C* shapes and they, too, oozed with scales and sores. Emma heard Mono make an inarticulate noise. He bolted out of the door, slamming it behind him.

Serena started to cry. "I don't know if I can stand it."

Emma glanced at Oz, who stared at Serena in horror. She could imagine what he was thinking, that this was his future. Emma took a step toward the woman.

"You have to go to the hospital. There's no reason for this. It's time."

Serena shook her head. "I won't. You must cure

me. I must be cured and free. The hospital may not cure me, but they *will* put me in jail. Please, did you find an answer?"

The door to the RV opened and Raoul and La Valle stepped in. Both had grim expressions. La Valle looked stricken as he stared at Serena. He turned to Emma, and his stricken look turned to one of fury.

"You have any answers? Look at her! And now Raoul has it!" Raoul threw up his hand. Sores covered one third of it.

Emma took a deep breath. "It's caused by a bacteria. I started to stain them to see if they were acid fast, and I think they were. There are several that can cause some of the symptoms she has, but not all of them."

"What can it be?" La Valle said.

"Tuberculosis, anthrax."

Serena started keening, Oz gasped and stumbled back onto a nearby chair, Raoul gaped at Serena, and La Valle stilled. He took three steps to the kitchen area, picked up a tumbler from the counter, and threw it against the wall. It shattered and sprayed bits of glass everywhere. Serena cried harder. La Valle stayed in the kitchen, breathing in and out. Emma could see his mind turn. His small dark eyes didn't register as much surprise as she had expected from this revelation. She watched as first his neck, then his face, flushed red. Emma tensed. A gun was attached to his belt in a holster and she didn't trust him not to begin killing them all in a fit of rage. Serena's sobs were the only sound in the room.

"Do the sores hurt?" Emma asked. Serena kept moaning, her body rocking back and forth and tears streaming down her cheeks. She didn't respond, and Emma doubted that she even registered the question. Emma stepped closer. Although she was focused on Serena, she saw Raoul slip out of the RV. Coward, she thought. "Do the sores hurt?" she asked again. Serena inhaled, clearly trying to gain control of herself, but failing. After a moment, she shook her head.

"They're numb." She moved to a nearby couch and fell down onto it, grabbed a towel off an end table and buried her face in the cloth. Emma could see that the towel and some gauze were placed there for a reason. Serena didn't want to spread the sores from her hands to her face.

The memory, still elusive, skittered across Emma's mind.

"Anthrax can be cured?" La Valle said, a hopeful note in his voice.

Emma didn't think either Serena or Oz had a chance to be cured at the late stages that they appeared to be experiencing. She didn't want to say this, though. La Valle would probably kill her on the spot, and she couldn't face Oz after she revealed her true thoughts. Emma decided to ignore the question and focus on Serena.

"Were you digging in the dirt back at the compound?"

Serena looked up from the towel. "Not at all. Why would I dig in the dirt?"

"Maybe gardening? Planting flowers? Something like that?"

Serena shook her head.

Emma started to pace the length of the RV. Something wasn't adding up. "Did you smoke any of the leaves from the infected field?"

Again, Serena shook her head. "I only smoked the healthy leaves. None of us smoked from the diseased fields." Emma resumed her pacing. La Valle watched her.

"What is it?" he said.

Emma paused. "Anthrax isn't contagious. It has to be present, either in the earth or on a surface, for a person to catch it. It can be inhaled, but unless there was a lot of dust kicking up at the compound, I just don't see how it could have infected all those migrant workers. Besides, it doesn't affect plants in the way that the field was affected." Emma continued pacing. She passed Oz, who had his head in his hands.

"Then it's tuberculosis. That's contagious," La Valle said.

"TB sufferers cough, but neither of them show that symptom, and nothing I've ever read about tuberculosis cites a massive physical manifestation on the level of what we're seeing. Besides, TB also wouldn't kill your fields the way this disease is."

La Valle threw open the front door and roared Raoul's name. Raoul appeared seconds later.

"Have you been delivering the shipment as I ordered?"

Raoul nodded. "One fourth in Arizona, some more here." Emma felt sick herself. The idea that people would be touching the leaves and getting the disease was abhorrent. She needed to find an answer before they managed to infect half of the country.

"Did you touch it?" Emma said.

Raoul shook his head. "No. I don't know how I got infected."

La Valle pointed at Emma. "You have one more day to solve this." He looked at Raoul. "Get her to another lab. Tomorrow."

"Mono tells me there's a warrant out for her arrest. For all of them. I don't know how we'll get into another lab."

"You question me?" La Valle roared the sentence.

Raoul put out his hands in a placating gesture. "No, La Valle, no. I'll get her there."

"Where's the pilot?"

"He just landed a hundred miles from here. He's waiting for us."

La Valle inhaled. "Good. You tell him there's been a change of plans. We'll put the shipment onto his plane and tell him to fly it first to Chicago and then to Washington." La Valle looked at Oz, who had managed to sit up. "You're going on the plane with the leaves. I want you to spread them everywhere." He looked at Emma. "You go with them as far as Chicago. If you don't have a cure by then, Mono gets to do with you what he likes." He flipped a hand at Raoul. "Get them out of here."

Raoul waved both Emma and Oz out of the RV. He pointed at the smaller trailer.

"You sleep there," he said to Oz. "You," he said to Emma, "go with Mono."

Mono leaned on a weathered picnic table placed between the trailers. He pushed off and shuffled toward Emma.

"Put her in the ambulance," Raoul said.

Emma wanted to ask about the hostages, but one look at Carlos induced her to bite her tongue.

A calculating look entered Mono's eyes. "She's done?"

Raoul shook his head. "Not yet. La Valle wants us to get her to one more lab."

Mono groaned. "No way. They're watching for us. I told you."

Raoul stepped toward him. "You want to argue? You tell it to La Valle. He gave her one more day to solve this thing, and I . . ." He shoved his infected hand in Mono's direction, causing Mono to cringe backward. "I want this thing solved as well."

Mono grabbed her by the arm, squeezing it as hard as he could. Emma clenched her teeth together but said nothing. She didn't want him to know he affected her in any way. He dragged her to the ambulance, opened the door, and shoved her in. After a moment he followed.

"Move in," he said.

Emma scuttled backward, keeping her eyes on Mono the entire time. His face had a demented look, and he was sweating. Emma could smell him. He gave a quick, furtive look behind him before turning back. He took two steps toward her and put the gun under her chin with one hand. With the other he started to grope at her, snatching at her shirt. Emma curled her hand into a fist. His breath smelled like beer and garlic, and she shoved his hand away.

"What the hell are you doing?" Emma said.

"Trophy time," Mono said.

Emma put up a hand to stop him. "Just let me take my own clothes off. I don't want to tear them. They're all I have."

Mono gave an evil smile and nodded. He stood up in front of her. She shifted onto her knees and adjusted the angle of her body.

She slammed her fist up and directly into his groin.

He collapsed into a heap in front of her, his shoulder hitting her on the temple as he fell.

Fool, she thought. She braced her back against the wall and used her feet to slide his body along the bottom of the ambulance. She had his body almost to the end when Raoul stepped into view. He took in the scene.

"He passed out. Too much to drink, I guess," Emma said.

Raoul shrugged. Emma pushed one more time, and Mono rolled out and dropped the three feet to the ground. Raoul nudged him with his toe, looking unconcerned. He reached to each side of the doors and slammed the panels shut. Emma heard him snap the padlock into place. She settled onto the floor, determined to get some rest. God only knew what she'd be facing when Mono woke up.

28

BANNER WAS EATING A ROOM-SERVICE BREAKFAST when his cell phone rattled on the desk. He recognized Sheriff Wiley's number.

"Mr. Banner? I suggest you turn to the headline news."

Banner picked up the remote control and flipped on the channel. A news reporter stood in front of a ramshackle house that featured a car on cinder blocks to the left of the front door, and a second, this one on tires, to the right. Yellow police tape stretched from the front door handle to a nearby tree. Police in hazardous materials suits were moving in and out of the house and Banner could see a cluster of reporters huddled on the opposite side of the barrier.

"What am I seeing here?" Banner said. He stabbed at the remainder of his breakfast. The television screen changed and Banner saw a picture of Caldridge on a split screen along with the grainy image of Kroger from the lab footage. The image changed to one of the Mexican guy, also from the lab video.

"The Phoenix police just walked into the house of a drug dealer to arrest him on a warrant. They found him, his girlfriend, and two of his buddies dead on the floor. The officer said, and this is a quote, that they 'were covered in sores and looked like they had bled to death from every pore.'" Banner stopped eating. He shoved his tabasco-sauce-covered omelette to the side. He'd just lost his appetite.

"Why are they showing the footage of Caldridge from the lab break-in?"

"Turns out Conway might have been right. The autopsy on one of the Black Eagles that died in the blast showed that he bled from inside before the explosion hit him. The theory is that he contracted some sort of hemorrhagic fever. The second body was too ripped up to make a definitive statement about cause of death. The authorities think Caldridge might know something about it and since she was one of the last people to see the Eagles alive, they're considering her as a person of interest. And there's more. Two of the Phoenix dealer's clients are dead. Same scenario. One was a well-known real-estate broker. He had been tortured to death. His wife was tortured as well, but she's clinging to life. She's also covered in sores that she denies were from the torture. She described her attackers and claims that she saw Emma Caldridge with them."

"The band guy and the Mexican?"

"No, just a Mexican man."

"The woman say that Caldridge was present when she was tortured?"

"They didn't get that far. The woman lapsed into a coma. She's in the ICU."

"Is the Center for Disease Control investigating?"

"Yeah. They're considering anthrax based on what Raynor told us. Or an Ebola-type virus. They're working with the locals. Right now we've put out an arrest warrant for Caldridge, Kroger, and the Mexican guy. We've asked the media to help. CNN should be running the story."

"Can you keep me posted?"

"Sure," Wiley said.

Banner rang off and was packed and ready to go when Sumner knocked on his door at the pre-arranged time.

"You see the news?" Sumner said the minute Banner was face-to-face with him.

Banner nodded. "Think she arranged it? Tried to kill them and get away?"

Sumner looked grim. Rather than answer, he turned and started down the hall toward the far exit. He shoved the bar handle against the panel and they stepped into the morning sun. Banner let it bathe his face a moment.

"If it's a strange and unusual virus, then Caldridge would be the one to have access to such a thing. We have no idea how the band guy got his sores, but these Eagles appear to have what he did, only times ten."

Banner nodded. "I have to agree. Whatever the band guy has might be contagious."

Sumner beeped open the SUV and tossed his

duffel bag in the back. Banner followed with his own. Sumner slipped on some shades and put the car in drive.

"The only thing I can't figure out is, why didn't she just run away? Sounds like whatever this disease is it would have incapacitated everyone in the house in no time. Why does she stay with the band guy?"

Sumner maneuvered the car into traffic. "Who knows? And you're assuming she was at the drug dealer's house when they died. Maybe she wasn't. Maybe they got the disease earlier and died later. I'm headed to the airport. Do you want to fly intercept with me?"

"No. I better get back to D.C. This thing is mushrooming out of control. Good luck with the pilot. How will you force him to land?"

"We ask nicely three times. Then we blow them out of the sky."

OZ PULLED THE ESCALADE INTO A REST AREA OFF
the interstate in the late afternoon. Diagonal
parking spaces lined the front of a small brick
building. A flagpole in the front flew an American flag. Several semi-trailer trucks idled to the
left in an area designated for heavy vehicles and
RVs. Only two cars were parked in addition to
the Escalade, La Valle's BMW, and Raoul's ambulance. La Valle walked to the building, while
Serena stayed in the back of the car.

Raoul walked up and tapped on the passenger-
side window. When Mono lowered it he said,
"Here's where we separate. You take the woman
to the airfield in the ambulance. Load fifty bricks
from the BMW into it along with her. The pilot's
going to fly them first to whatever lab she picks,
then to Chicago."

"You want me to stay with her?"

Raoul shook his head. "The pilot will watch
her. The second batch from the Escalade and La
Valle's is going to D.C. Where you"—he pointed

to Oz—"are going to deliver it right to the DOD's doorstep."

Emma noticed that the sores on Raoul's hand had traveled up his arm. They disappeared under his rolled-up sleeve. He caught her staring at them.

"You find a cure in Chicago," he said. He transferred his attention to Oz. "How bad are yours?"

Oz said nothing. Emma wasn't surprised. When they'd stopped at a restaurant off the interstate to eat, he had ordered a sandwich and eaten half of it. He avoided looking at anyone, including Emma.

"He's not talking," Mono said. "Watch them, I need to take a piss." Raoul snorted and leaned back onto a parking support in full view of the Escalade. When the door slammed, the interior of the car fell silent. Emma inhaled a deep breath, happy to be out of Mono's toxic presence.

"I'll solve this puzzle. I won't let you die," Emma said. "But we need to also keep focused on escape. Once we do, we go straight to a hospital."

Oz turned to her, looking her full in the face for the first time that day. His eyes were bleak, and the exhaustion and despair that showed in them made her want to cry. He moved his arm, and she saw that the sores had crept above the bandage up his arm and under the tee shirt sleeve.

"Are they on your torso?" she said.

He nodded. "Front and back."

"Do they hurt?"

He shook his head. "Still numb, but the skin is sheeting off where they exist."

Emma swallowed. "No bleeding?"

"You mean like the guys at the house?"

Emma nodded.

"No, but I'm not able to straighten my fingers anymore. It's as if the tendons are shortening. My hands are beginning to form claws. Like Serena's were last night."

Emma swallowed again. The tears were welling, and she was damned if she would cry in front of Oz. He would take it as defeat on her part, and she was not defeated. Frightened, but not defeated.

"I will solve this thing," Emma said again.

He gave her a look, and for the first time in hours his face softened into a smile. "I'm glad I met you. I hope to God that you get away from these guys."

Emma reached out to him, and he shrank back against the door. "Don't touch me. You could get it."

"Listen to me. It's not my day to die, and it's not yours either. I *will* find the answer in time."

He shook his head. "No, you won't. But I told you I won't do what they say in D.C., and they'll kill me there. Assuming, of course, that the disease doesn't get me first."

He looked out the window of the car. "There's something you should know. I put a good-bye letter to my family in the lockbox on the back of the Triumph. Sounds like you'll be traveling in the ambulance to the airstrip. Maybe you could get it out and take it with you. Here are the keys." He fished the keys out of his pants pocket and placed them on the seat between them. "Either mail it or deliver it personally when this thing is all over. The bike is yours to keep." He gave her a wan smile.

Emma pocketed the keys without a word. There was nothing to say.

Mono emerged from the building, heading back. Raoul waved her out of the car. Oz looked at her, and she could see unshed tears in his eyes.

"Next time I see you I'll bring a cure."

"Good-bye," he said.

She refused to say good-bye. She got out of the car without a word.

Emma let Mono march her to the ambulance. He shoved her in, but this time he didn't tie her up. She sat on the side with her back to the wall. The Triumph was opposite her, in the same place it had been.

Mono slammed the doors shut, and the back of the ambulance darkened. The ambulance rumbled into movement. Emma scrambled across and applied a key Oz had given her to the lockbox. When she opened it, she felt for the white envelope. She couldn't read the address in the dark. Folding it into thirds, she put it in her pocket along with the keys and settled back to wait.

About an hour later she felt the ambulance slow, and then stop. After another ten minutes she heard the lock on the doors disengage and they swung open. Mono stood in the entrance.

"Move to that side, we need to load the shipment onto the plane."

Emma transferred to the opposite side and sat next to the Triumph. Several men, all Hispanic-looking, began to take apart the ambulance's false walls. She watched them remove the bricks. They were done within twenty minutes.

"You're next. Into the plane." Mono gestured with his pistol.

Emma scooted across the ambulance floor and stepped onto the tarmac. The back of the vehicle faced the end of the runway. She walked around to see where the airplane was parked. It was an ancient Fokker. Next to it stood a tall, lean man with brown shoulder-length hair tied in a pony-tail and a cigarette in his mouth. His face lit up when he saw her.

"Well I'll be damned," he said. "It's Emma Caldridge."

EMMA STAYED STILL AND STARED AT WILSON
Vanderlock, struggling to keep the rush of hope that she felt at seeing him from showing on her face. The last time they'd met had been in Somalia. He looked the same as he did then; about thirty-five, with a rugged, masculine appearance and in perpetual need of a shave. He was dressed in army green cotton chino pants and a loose-fitting black tee shirt, and on his feet were python cowboy boots in a dark green color.

"How do you know her?" Mono's voice was full of suspicion. He kept his gun pointed at Emma's midsection.

Vanderlock removed the ever-present cigarette from his lips and blew out a stream of smoke. He stared a challenge at Mono.

"Who the hell are you?"

"I work for La Valle. How do you know her?"

Don't tell him you know me. Emma thought the words, but wished she could say them out loud. Vanderlock flicked a glance at Emma. She stared back and twitched her head no with a tiny movement. Vanderlock watched her a moment before returning his gaze to Mono.

"Her face is splashed all over the news," he said. Emma let her breath out slowly, quietly. Vanderlock was quick on his feet; she remembered that about him now. He pointed at Mono with the fingers holding the cigarette. "Yours, too, and some white guy. Real good work, getting caught on camera like that." Vanderlock's voice was filled with sarcasm. Mono's face flushed red.

"We needed to get to the lab. She needs another one. It's your job to fly her, and this time you get to break in with her. We'll see how well *you* do."

Vanderlock raised his eyebrows in surprise. "I was only told to deliver the shipment to Chicago. Then I'm out. That was my deal with La Valle."

Mono snickered. "Looks like La Valle changed his mind. Now you have to get her into a lab within the next few hours."

"And if I don't?" Vanderlock said.

"Then he kills you and I get her," Mono said.

"And if I do, do *I* get her?"

Mono shook his head. "She stays with La Valle. For ransom."

"How much?"

"You can't afford me," Emma said.

Mono waved his pistol in her direction. "Quiet!" He looked back at Vanderlock. "You take that up with La Valle. For now you'd better figure out how you're going to get into the lab." Mono walked to the ambulance and began a conversation with the workers as they reassembled the inside of the vehicle.

"What the hell do you need a lab for?" Vanderlock said to Emma. "And, I *can* afford you. Hell, I can afford ten of you."

Emma shook her head. "Still bragging, I see."

Vanderlock snorted. "Still stubborn as hell, I see." He glanced up and took another pull off his cigarette as Mono returned.

"The loading's finished," Mono said. "Get it, and her, out of here." He shoved a piece of paper at Vanderlock.

"What's this?" Vanderlock said.

"Lab sites. Pick one and get going," Mono said.

Vanderlock looked back at Emma with amusement in his eyes. "He wants to be rid of you. Imagine that."

Emma was more than happy to leave Mono behind. She was giddy, almost. Vanderlock had a slippery sense of right and wrong, and she wouldn't have thought he'd associate with killers on the level of La Valle and his crew, but she trusted him not to harm her. She started toward the Fokker.

"Did you fly this thing all the way from Africa?"

Vanderlock turned his attention to the plane. "That's another one. I picked this one up used, in Paraguay."

"Oh great. Does it fly?"

"It'll get you to your lab and then Chicago."

Emma reached the plane's entrance. The plane had two propeller-driven engines and was painted a dirty white. She looked around the landing strip, if that was what it could be called. It was a simple band of asphalt running the length of a field. Dandelions sprouted out of cracks in the pavement, and tall, grasslike weeds swayed on the sides. The setting sun threw shadows that danced in the wake of a breeze, the wind blowing around the branches of the few trees dotting the field. Emma saw no signs of a town or village nearby, but the tall, wheat-type weeds gave her the impression they were somewhere in the prairie part of the middle of America.

"How long to Chicago?" Emma said.

Vanderlock walked up behind her. He bent into her ear. "This guy of La Valle's hurt you?" He kept his voice low. Emma craned her head back and up to look Vanderlock in the eyes. His expression was grave.

"He tried. I punched him in the groin."

"Remind me not to piss you off," Vanderlock said.

"We'd better get into that lab, because I do not want to be left with the guy. He's psychotic."

Vanderlock sobered. "I wasn't joking when I said that your face is all over the news. Every cop from Phoenix to D.C. is looking for you. What the hell is going on?"

Emma started up the stairs. "I'll tell you in the plane, but do me a favor. Do not, under any circumstances, touch the shipment. It's diseased."

Vanderlock put a hand on her elbow to steady her as she climbed into the plane. He followed, and once inside closed the door and the attached stairs behind him. He locked the door and moved to sit in the pilot's seat.

"Do you have a cell phone? Internet access?" Emma said.

"Nothing," Vanderlock replied. Emma wasn't surprised. It appeared as though La Valle's men confiscated cell phones from all their drug runners.

The rear of the plane had been gutted, with only open spaces where the majority of the rows of seats had been removed. This plane did, however, retain the first three rows of seating, which was unlike the plane that Emma remembered from Somalia. She saw the shipment bricks in the back.

"You saved some room for passengers." Emma indicated the three rows of seats.

Vanderlock nodded. "I wanted to use it as a modified cargo plane, but keep the ability to fly some paying passengers if I wanted." He kept his attention on the controls, and Emma saw the propellers begin to turn. "Come on and strap in. We're taking off."

Emma sat down in the copilot seat and snapped on the harness. She knew nothing about flying planes, but in her only other experience with Vanderlock he'd flown her hundreds of miles, and she knew him to be a competent pilot.

After a few minutes the propellers reached a speed that seemed to satisfy him and he turned the aircraft in a slow circle on the ground until it lined up with the runway. He engaged the throttle and the plane started to taxi. Right when Emma thought they'd fall off the end of the tarmac, the plane lifted, almost magically, into the air. They pulsed higher, and Emma was once again struck by the power and beauty of flying when experienced from the perspective of a pilot seat. Her breath caught at the sheer beauty and breadth of the sky, and the image of the ground below growing farther away. Once they reached altitude, Vanderlock turned to her.

"So tell me what kind of mess you're in now."

"I was collecting plants for Pure Chemistry in the desert in Arizona near the border of Mexico and I came upon one of La Valle's coyotes running some illegals into the U.S."

Vanderlock shook his head. "How the hell do you get into these situations?"

Emma rubbed at her eyes. "I was also asked to record any observable trails that the cartels were using to transport their cargo. Just three weeks before, there was a shootout between two rival factions when they crossed each other's paths in the desert. Over twenty people died. The information that I was asked to collect would be useful in the effort to secure the border."

Vanderlock frowned. "Asked by whom?"

"Edward Banner of Darkview."

Vanderlock groaned. "I should have known that he'd be involved in this somehow. If there's a buck to be made in any hot spot in the world, Banner's making it."

Emma bristled. "Darkview pays its personnel well, and not one mission that Darkview has undertaken in Mexico has resulted in civilian deaths. That's saying a lot. Besides, you're here doing something a heck of a lot less reputable. When did you become a drug runner for La Valle? At least in Somalia the drug you ran was legal."

Vanderlock put up a hand in a placating manner. "Calm down. And to answer your question, I got blackmailed into making this run. I was seeing a certain woman in Paraguay . . ." Vanderlock slid his eyes sideways to gauge her reaction.

"So now you're blaming a woman?"

He shook his head. "Not at all. She was great. I just didn't realize that she was related to La Valle. A cousin or so, I never got the exact information on the family tree. Anyway, next thing I know he's up in my grill claiming that she was engaged to someone else and I had convinced her not to marry him."

Emma couldn't help herself. She laughed. "How did you convince her? Or does that fall under 'too much information'?"

Vanderlock smiled. "Wasn't me. She broke off the engagement herself. I had nothing to do with it. But La Valle was furious and she warned me that he was arranging a hit." Vanderlock's expression turned grim. "I don't have to tell you that La Valle is no one to mess around with. Rather than wait for the day that my car blew up, or my plane exploded on takeoff, I went to him. Offered to fly one shipment into the States, and in return he would leave me alone. He agreed, and here I am."

The story was so close to Oz's that Emma thought it was possibly true. What she did not believe was that Vanderlock had actually fallen for any assurances of La Valle's. Vanderlock was light-years more savvy than Oz.

"Do you believe he'll let you go after you deliver the shipment?"

Vanderlock shook his head. "La Valle always lies. He'll let me live only as long as he wants me to, and not a minute more. That's why I'm going to help him keep his promise and be back in the air and gone the second the plane is unloaded."

"Back to Africa?" Emma said. Vanderlock was a South African.

He shrugged. "Maybe. But you haven't told me why you need a lab."

Emma ran down the facts. Vanderlock stayed quiet, but when she was finished, he blew out a long, low whistle.

"Any idea at all how this disease is being transmitted?"

Emma leaned back in the seat. "Clearly smoking the leaves causes the most catastrophic result. From what I can tell, Oz, Serena, and Raoul have the slow-moving version."

Vanderlock shook his head. "There's nothing slow about dying in a matter of days, but I see your point. What kind of equipment do you need?"

Emma sighed. "I wish I knew. I would love access to the Internet in order to search reports of any diseases like this one. La Valle has refused. He's afraid I'll send an e-mail asking for help."

"You would, wouldn't you?"

Emma reached behind Vanderlock and flipped

open a small cooler nestled against the back of his seat. She found cans of soda and a bottle of whiskey. She removed a soda and popped it open.

"Of course I would. As long as it wouldn't mean the death of a hostage. I'd tell you right now to fly to Chicago and I'd go straight to the FBI if I could. But I can't. La Valle's men are threatening to kill two people if I get out of line."

"They'll not only kill them, they'll do it slowly and horribly. Don't get out of line until you're sure what you attempt will work," Vanderlock said. He sat up, all his attention focused on the screen in front of him. "Who the hell is that?"

Emma looked around. "Who?"

"The guy coming straight at us." Vanderlock turned the plane to the left, and Emma saw another aircraft, this one sleek and newer-looking, coming at them head-on.

VANDERLOCK PUT ON A HEADSET. EMMA WATCHED his expression change as he listened.

"Damn!" he said. "It's the Air Tunnel guys. Why the hell don't they just give up already?"

Vanderlock listened a moment, then snorted in disbelief. "Guy's hailing me. He's telling me to follow him and he'll direct me to a runway where I can land. Presumably to be taken into custody. He's crazy if he thinks I'll just fly into the net. Hold on."

The entire plane banked far left, and Emma slid sideways, stopping only when the seat belt held her in place. Now the sky tilted in front of her, and she felt her stomach starting to rebel at the severe angle at which they flew. Vanderlock corrected and turned to the right, seesawing the plane. Emma's stomach barely had time to register this new angle, when Vanderlock repeated the maneuver. Emma watched as the tracking plane kept with them easily. She heard a bang from the rear and glanced back.

"The shipment is shifting. Do you have any gloves or a towel? Anything to cover my hands? I'll need to secure it again. The last thing we want is one of them to break free and open up," Emma said.

Vanderlock jerked his chin to the left. "Look in that toolbox. The one strapped against the wall. Damn, this guy can fly."

Emma unhooked her seat belt and rose up. Vanderlock jerked the controls and the plane banked once again. She lost her balance and fell against him. He didn't react, continuing his laser focus on the task in front of him.

"Sorry, let me get out of your way before you do that again." She made it to the toolbox and opened it. Two rifles and several boxes of ammunition filled the narrow steel case. On top of all the armament was a pair of work gloves. Emma put them on. They were far too large for her, but they covered her hands to the wrist, which was all she cared about. She worked her way to the rear of the jet, grasping whatever she could in order to steady herself. Vanderlock continued to rock the plane from side to side, which caused several of the shipment bricks to become dislodged from the bungee cords that had been used to secure them. The plane suddenly nosedived, and Emma fell forward. She grabbed on to one of the lines to keep on her feet. One of the bricks skittered across the floor, heading straight for her. She lifted a foot off the ground to allow it to slide past. Once the plane righted again, she bent over and grabbed the brick before it could travel all

the way to Vanderlock. She held it far in front of
her as she made her way to the rear of the plane.
Once she reached the stack of bricks, she applied
herself to securing them once again.

"Hey Caldridge, this guy just said if I don't land
immediately he's authorized to open fire on me."
Vanderlock's voice held a mix of incredulity and
anger. "Who does this guy think he is? He can't
just blow me out of the air. This is America. I've
got rights!"

Emma snorted. "You're South African, for God's
sake. You don't have any rights in America. If the
guy says he can fire on you, then he can. Listen,
I know someone who works for the ATD, and I'm
pretty sure they can fire on any suspicious aircraft
arriving over international waters. Perhaps they
can do the same domestically. I don't think you
should assume he's lying." Emma began making
her way back to the copilot seat. The plane bucked
and banked. She slammed against the side wall,
then tumbled forward when Vanderlock pointed
the nose of the plane into another deep dive. She
grabbed at some cage netting strapped to the side
wall and swung around and hit the wall with her
shoulder. When the plane righted, she made a
lunge for the copilot seat and sat down, snapping
the seat belt closed. "Tell him you'll land."

Vanderlock shook his head. "No way. I'm going
to outmaneuver him and get back under radar."

"Forget it! Tell him you'll land, before he starts
shooting at us." A roar came from Emma's right,
and she flinched when the pursuing airplane
passed too close to them. She caught a glimpse of

the plane through the windshield, and then he was in front of them. He pulled up, and Emma watched the plane track higher, gaining altitude. It left her field of vision.

"I land and La Valle kills your hostages first, then me, then you. You think of that?"

"You don't land and that pilot will shoot us down. Either way we die." Even as she said this she felt her stomach tighten. Vanderlock was right. Landing would get them all killed. She wished she had enough expertise to tell if Vanderlock was good enough to outmaneuver the ATD pilot. Emma craned her neck to look in all directions out the window, but all she could see was empty blue sky. "Where the hell is he?"

"He's going to come down on us from above. Probably makes us an easier target to shoot," Vanderlock said. His voice was calm, as if he were discussing a particularly boring subject.

Emma could feel her jaw clench. The combination of the bouncing plane and the stress of knowing that at any minute they might be fired upon was making her stomach turn sour.

"Is the plane outfitted with guns? How will he shoot us?" Emma said.

"He's got a gun mount," Vanderlock said. He nosedived again. Emma braced her hands in front of her, doing her best not to inadvertently hit any controls. The plane appeared again. This time it seemed to drop down from the sky, like a spider lowering itself on a web, and it was flying straight at them. Emma closed her eyes, waiting for the sound of the guns to start. Vanderlock banked hard, left, and the aircraft passed below them.

Emma opened her eyes. She glanced at Vanderlock. His attention was focused on the controls in front of him. He checked the window, dashboard, and maneuvered the plane with a calm professionalism.

"Someone's hailing me on a second frequency," Vanderlock said.

"More law enforcement?" Emma asked.

"Maybe. The ATD guys are chattering on a different channel. They're telling the pilot to begin his final hail."

Emma felt her face go cold and her hands become clammy. She heard the other plane's engines roaring as he tracked with them, somewhere off to the right.

"Does he have to get close to shoot us?"

Vanderlock shook his head. "That's the easiest part of his day. He just needs to lock on."

"If there's any chance of shaking him, then we should take it. Buy ourselves a little more time. Can you outmaneuver him? Because if not, you *are* landing."

"He's good. Really good. Assuming we continue this way, we could be at a standoff. In that case, the guy with the most fuel wins."

Emma glanced at the fuel gauge. "How much?"

Vanderlock banked again, before climbing upward. Emma lost sight of the ATD aircraft, but she assumed it was somewhere behind or above them. Not seeing it was the worst. She hated to think she'd never see the weapon that blew her apart.

"I'm going to fly low. I mean really low. I want him to worry about hitting civilians if he shoots."

Emma glanced at the ground below them. From their current altitude it appeared to be just an expanse of light and dark green in a patchwork pattern. Vanderlock began his dive, and Emma watched as objects on the ground grew more distinct by the moment. Her ears started to react to the pressure, then popped, and filled again.

She heard a creaking sound, then a snap. Thudding noises came from the back of the plane. A brick hit the cooler strapped behind Vanderlock, followed by another, and then another. Emma scrambled back into the gloves as the bricks shifted and slammed into each other.

"One of the bungee cords snapped."

Four more bricks hit the cooler, peppering the backs of their chairs. Bits of leaves flew out of the containers and Emma could see dust motes floating in the air. She wished she had a face mask to cover her nose. She stood for a moment to breathe the air above the cloud of dust, but what she saw through the windshield made her gasp, and she felt the particles enter her lungs.

The aircraft was pointed straight at the ground, which was rapidly looming larger. She forgot about the bricks, forgot about the shipment, forgot everything as she watched the ground approach. She flashed on the airplane landing in the Colombian jungle. Memories of the screams of the passengers filled her head and she felt her own fear

clog her throat. Vanderlock kept his eyes pinned
to the controls, his concentration complete, and
oblivious to Emma's rising distress.

They were over a wide prairie dotted with trees
on the edges of cultivated fields planted with
corn. When they were so low that Emma thought
they'd hit the tops of the tallest trees in a stand,
Vanderlock leveled off. Now the area around
them was easy to see. Field after field passed
under them. The other plane flew alongside on
Emma's side.

"Here's the third hail."

Emma sat back down and grasped the arm-
rests, gripping them tightly. Vanderlock listened
to the transmission.

"We're coming up on a farmhouse, so I think
you'd better shoot at your own risk, guy. Is it
really worth killing people just to stop some weed
from entering the country?" Vanderlock sounded
determined and cool. Emma heard bits of noise
coming from Vanderlock's headset in response,
but she couldn't make out the words. "I know
that runway. I'm going to fly right over it in minutes. I am *not* landing."

Emma strained to see in front of them. Sure
enough, a long passage, banded on each side with
stalks of corn, appeared carved into the field. The
ATD plane pulled even closer.

Vanderlock flipped a switch. "Now I got some
other guy hailing me." He listened some more.
"You again? I told you, I'm not landing! Why
did we have to switch frequencies to have the
exact same conversation? And you should know

that I have a passenger named Emma Caldridge. You shoot me, you kill her, too." Vanderlock listened some more. "What about her?" he said. More noise flowed from the headset in response. Vanderlock turned to her, and waved at a headset placed in front of the copilot position. "This guy claims to know you. Put that headset on." He barked a laugh. "Oh yeah, this guy definitely knows you. Repeat that so she can hear it," he said into the microphone.

Emma felt hope rise in her. "Is it Banner?" She clapped the earpieces on in time to hear Sumner say:

"Tell Caldridge I'm going to strangle her when I get my hands on her."

32

EMMA WATCHED THE PLANE SHOOT STRAIGHT
upward. Vanderlock, though, was cruising even
lower. Her headset was silent. Sumner had
switched off.

"He's taking off," Vanderlock said. "He told me
to land and leave it there. Said it will take the
ATD a few hours to get to the location. The im-
plication being that I have time to get away. Do I
trust him?"

Emma nodded. "He means what he says."

"Then we're landing."

Vanderlock slowed the plane and touched it
down on the runway. They careened ahead, still
way too fast. Screeching wheels and creaking
plane parts echoed in the cabin. They reached the
end of the runway and continued a bit, knocking
through some cornstalks before coming to rest.
Vanderlock switched off the engines.

Emma was breathing fast, as if she'd been running a marathon rather than sitting in a chair.
Vanderlock fiddled with switches and turned

knobs. When he was finished, he reached back toward the cooler. He picked up a brick with his bare hands and tossed it into the hold.

"I told you not to touch it!" Emma said. Vanderlock waved her off.

"Bricks broke open. We're breathing it, so it's done."

He was right. The shipment bricks had all shifted, and the ones closest to Emma and Vanderlock broke open and leaves covered the bottom of the jet around their seats. Vanderlock brushed some off the top of the cooler before opening it and removing the whiskey bottle. He uncapped it, took a swig, and handed it to her. She grabbed it without hesitation and swallowed a mouthful. It burned and she coughed once. She handed it back.

"Wanna tell me about flyboy?" Vanderlock said.

Emma shook her head. "I don't, actually."

Vanderlock raised an eyebrow. "He sure was more than willing to kill me until he learned about you." Emma got up and swayed a bit as the blood moved very slowly to her head.

"Let's get out of this plane. We can talk about it in the fresh air."

They opened the door and Emma stepped down onto the field. The air smelled of newly mown grass and heat and dust, but the good kind, like the type that kicks up in the summertime. Vanderlock tossed a small duffel onto the ground and stepped down himself, with the toolbox containing the guns in one hand and the whiskey bottle in the other. He looked around.

"This is a La Valle runway. I'm surprised your flyboy knew about it."

"His name is Sumner."

Vanderlock gave her a considering look. "The one you went to save in Somalia."

Vanderlock pulled out a pack of cigarettes. He put one to his lips and lit it with a blue stick lighter. "I've been thinking about why he shifted frequencies. I'll bet he didn't want his ATD buddies to hear him ask about you. He had us in his sights but didn't fire and then took off. You think he'll lie? Give the ATD wrong coordinates? Buy us some more time?"

Emma thought about Sumner. She'd depended on him to have her back in other dangerous situations, but in all she'd been on the right side of things. She didn't know if his support would continue if she fell on the wrong side of the law, and right now he must be wondering why she was acting as she was. Just the thought of Sumner losing confidence in her upset her.

"I don't think he'll go so far as to lie about the coordinates."

"Can you convince him to leave us alone?"

"Not forever. Eventually he's going to demand some answers."

Emma checked out the area. There was a small, prefabricated aluminum shed nestled in a corner of the tarmac, amidst some trees. She headed in that direction. The last thing she wanted was to talk, or even think, about Sumner. That he was angry at her was to be expected, but she was bitterly disappointed that he had switched off the channel before she could ask him for help. She swung open the shed doors to find a jumble of airplane parts, old gasoline containers, and several cans of spray paint in various colors, some marked with the word "Neon" and with colors that matched the markings on the makeshift runway. She picked up one with red splattered on its side. She heard rather than saw Vanderlock step in behind her.

"We're going to have to leave the airplane here. Your flyboy"—Emma shot him an angry look and Vanderlock put up a hand—"I mean *Sumner* made it clear he's coming back here. Even if I could fuel up and get airborne, it would be a waste of time. He'd just track me again and start shooting. I'm going to hustle up a vehicle and come back for you."

"We need to lock up the plane. No one should touch the shipment."

Vanderlock shrugged. "Sure, but La Valle's men keep an eye on the runway. They'll see the plane and want to offload the cargo. How much of the shipment did they load?" Emma shook the paint can. It still contained quite a bit of liquid.

"That was one portion. There's more in two other vehicles, and I assume another shipment right behind that one."

"Maybe they'll let this sit, then. Long as they have more. I'll lock it down when I get back."

Emma nodded. Vanderlock disappeared into the cornfield and she headed over to his plane. She walked up the stairs, leaned to the airplane's side, and began to work.

Thirty minutes later she was done. Lucky for her there was no real breeze and she wasn't covered in paint. She reversed down the stairs and headed back to the shed. She tossed the can into a nearby bucket. The sound of a car bumping along the dirt road connected to the tarmac grew louder. A black Dodge Caliber lurched onto the runway, circled to the side of the airplane, and stopped. Vanderlock got out, slamming the door behind him.

"We should hustle. La Valle's guy saw us landing and had the sense to turn on the police band. They're forming up and headed this way. If we move. . . ." Vanderlock flicked a look at the plane and his mouth dropped open. Emma waited while he took in her handiwork.

She'd spray painted a large red skull and crossbones onto the side of the jet. Portions of the bones and skull dripped red paint, giving the effect that the image was bleeding down the white aircraft shell. It looked ominous and deadly and was just the effect that she desired.

"You tagged my plane," Vanderlock said.

Emma headed to the car. "The last thing I need is a bunch of police officers piling into that cabin. Once they inhale they'll be infected. Maybe that will keep them out."

Vanderlock stayed put, still staring at the plane in apparent shock. "What were you thinking?"

Emma spun around and walked up to him. She tugged on his sleeve. "I was thinking about saving a few lives. Now let's go. If we don't get out of here soon, the police will come and lock us both up. By the time I explain everything to them we'll all be dead. We *really* need to get to a lab now that we're infected." Vanderlock tore his eyes from his beloved plane long enough to fix her with an incredulous stare.

"I've been around you for less than two hours and you've managed to nearly get me blown out of the sky, infect me with a deadly disease, and vandalize my plane."

Emma had never seen Vanderlock rattled, but messing with his plane seemed to have done that to him. She wanted to feel some sympathy, but after watching the Black Eagles stagger out of the house with blood everywhere she knew that no one should get into that plane while the shipment contaminated the air inside. She needed to solve the shipment's puzzle, and fast.

"Let's *go*," she said. "We're free, don't you get it? La Valle's men aren't here, and you and I can take off."

Vanderlock shivered. "Okay, right. Where's a lab? Because on top of all of this, I'm not dying in nine days, I can tell you that." He sounded massively pissed, and Emma couldn't blame him. "In fact," Vanderlock stopped at the driver's door, "if we're free, why don't we go to the nearest hospital? Let the professionals figure this thing out. When they do, you give the information to La Valle and I'll let him use my plane to finish the delivery. We all walk away in one piece."

"I'm all for it. Let's go."

Emma climbed into the passenger seat. Vanderlock settled behind the wheel, and he started the car. He shifted into first and hit the gas. The car's wheels spun on the dirt, kicking up bits of earth before gaining traction. Vanderlock hurtled down the road, taking a good bit of his anger out behind the wheel. He'd lowered all the windows and Emma put her head back on the headrest, closed her eyes, and let the fresh air blow over her. Vanderlock turned on the radio.

They were the featured news.

Vanderlock groaned as he listened.

Emma stared at the radio in dismay as she was described as "armed and dangerous." Oz was called an accomplice, and Mono a "drug cartel's henchman with a long criminal record both in Mexico and the U.S." The radio announcer knew to add that she was suspected of having flown in a private plane that had entered the country illegally, and that the appropriate authorities were scrambling to intercept.

"You entered illegally?" she said to Vanderlock.

Vanderlock gave her a sour look. "How else would I enter?"

"Oh, I don't know, register a flight plan like every other pilot?" Emma let him hear the sarcasm in her voice.

"And what would I have put for the purpose of the flight? Drug running? I was bringing in a shipment under radar."

"Well clearly not under enough, since they know about you."

Vanderlock shot her a glare. "Your buddy

Sumner must have told the entire world by now. What did you do to piss him off? You spray paint on his plane, too?"

"Since he works for ATD, it's his job to arrest drug dealers, which apparently now includes me. He must not be thrilled that I'm breaking into labs, shooting at security guards, and flying a load of marijuana cross-country."

Vanderlock turned onto another road, but this one was paved in asphalt. "You think he would have fired on us?"

Emma nodded. "Definitely. He's done it before. He's no one to mess with. I only wish he'd stayed on the frequency long enough to allow me to explain myself."

Vanderlock blew a line of smoke out the window. "We need to get to a road where we can hustle. I only have a general idea of where we are, but I'm pretty sure this will get us to an interstate."

Emma liked that idea. "The sooner the better. Where are we?"

"Middle of Oklahoma, headed east." Farmhouses and barns dotted fields, but the road remained empty of other vehicles. "Tell me straight up. You think a hospital in a small town is equipped to figure out what's going on?"

Emma pondered that question. "Let's put it this way, I think they'll be pretty efficient in telling us what it *isn't*. Figuring out what it *is* will be the challenge, and for that we may need a large teaching hospital with a research facility attached."

"And time," Vanderlock said.

"And time," Emma agreed. "My fear is that they'll spend a great deal of it doing routine tests to rule things out, and all the while we'll be covered in sores and our hands curling into claws."

"Claws? Jesus. Forget that. We're breaking in. I'm putting my money on you."

Emma shook her head. "No. This is *way* above my pay grade. What we need is an infectious disease specialist. First thing we do is find a telephone. I want to call Banner, enlist his help. Warn him about the shipment."

Vanderlock shook his head. "Don't do it. He can't help you, he doesn't have any jurisdiction over this, and there's a warrant out for your arrest. Assuming he can grease some wheels, you're still looking at hours lost in a holding pen waiting for your fingers to fall off."

Emma felt a flash of irritation. Vanderlock's take on Banner always angered her. "He could cut the time spent unraveling this thing in half—" Emma stopped talking as the thought that had been floating in her head, unmoored, suddenly came to the fore. She gasped.

Vanderlock picked up on her sudden stillness. "What? You're as pale as a ghost. What?"

"My God, Vanderlock, did you just say my fingers would fall off?"

"Well you said they'd be claws, I just pictured them brittle and bony. I'm sorry, I didn't intend to freak you out, but . . ."

"We need a lab *right now*," Emma said.

Vanderlock nodded. "That's what *I* say. Grab that piece of paper the cartel loser gave me. It's in the duffel."

Emma leaned into the backseat and searched around in the bag. She pulled out a crumpled piece of paper. She sat back to read it.

"This one." She showed Vanderlock the third lab on the list. "Is it close?"

Vanderlock scanned the paper. "Six hours by car. The second one is better. That's only two hours."

"No, that one won't have the equipment I need. That location is primarily a corporate headquarters, not a lab."

Vanderlock shrugged. "Okay, then we'll go to the other one. But first we'd better lose this car."

"We do that, then how will we get there? This car's great, why would we change?"

"It's owned by one of La Valle's guys. He has a tracking device on it. He'll find us in a heartbeat, and when he does we'll be back delivering a shipment."

"Fine. Anything to avoid La Valle. What about renting a car? The authorities didn't mention your name. Perhaps they don't know who you are."

Vanderlock shook his head. "I wouldn't count on it. The ATD guys have been monitoring me since South America. They have to have my information by now."

"Then what's the plan? Because I can run there, but I'm pretty sure you can't."

Vanderlock took another drag off the cigarette.

"Quit bragging. I'll have you know that I ran cross-country as a teenager."

"In between cigarettes?"

Vanderlock chuckled. "And drinks, and messing with the girls, and . . ."

Emma waved a hand in the air. "Can we stay on the subject here? How are we going to get another car?"

Vanderlock leaned close to her. "We're going to steal one."

BANNER SAT IN HIS HOTEL ROOM FIELDING PHONE calls and working the computer. His crew located in the Caribbean was in the middle of an expanding mission, and things were not going as smoothly as he would have liked. A knock on the door was a welcome interruption. He opened it to find Sumner standing before him.

"Did you get your pilot?" Banner asked.

Sumner stepped past him into the room, a grim expression on his face. "No. He flew low and I wasn't willing to kill a bunch of farmers just to bring him down. I pulled up."

Banner did his best to hide his surprise. He knew that Sumner was not so foolish as to put others at risk just to succeed at a capture, but he'd never known the man to simply pull up and give up. Especially not when he had the pilot in his sights.

"You didn't have enough gas to keep with him?" Sumner popped a coffee pod under the single shot maker and pressed the start button.

"I had enough fuel," he said. He kept his eyes on the cup as it filled.

The other pilot outmaneuvered him, Banner thought. It was the only explanation for Sumner's unsuccessful flight and return empty-handed. Sumner's cell phone rang and he answered it, never taking his eyes from the coffee.

"Yes?" He propped the phone between his ear and his shoulder while he opened a container of cream and dumped it in the coffee. He paused in the preparation as he listened to the speaker. "I heard you. For now, no one enters that plane. Communicate that to whatever local police may be on the scene. We're on the way." He hung up and turned to Banner. "They found the plane in a field on a runway La Valle uses. I'm going to head over there. I think you should join me," Sumner said.

"Sorry, but I can't. I need to finish up with the Caribbean crew and then head back to D.C. I'm no longer any use to Caldridge. With a warrant out for her arrest and every level of law enforcement agency in three states looking for her, I lack any jurisdiction to help her."

"Wasn't she out there to begin with under a contract from the Department of Defense?"

Banner nodded. "Even so, I think I lost control once she crisscrossed the border between the States and Mexico. And I *really* lost control when she started a crime spree. The best I can do is be prepared to assist her once they pick her up. I'll arrange for Ralston, Darkview's lawyer, to be on hand. We'll post bail and then find out what's going on." Banner started collecting his clothes and tossing them into the luggage that he'd opened on the bed.

Sumner stepped closer. "Don't worry about jurisdiction. I have it—or at least the ATD has it—over the airplane. I really think you need to come with me."

"Why? You're just impounding another cartel jet, right?"

"This one's spray painted with a skull and crossbones on the side."

Banner rolled his eyes. "Drug runner art? Trying to scare the locals from getting too close?"

Sumner shook his head. "I think it's more than that. I think it's a serious warning."

"Warning of what?"

"It could be wired to explode. It could be loaded with a toxic gas. I don't know. But I can't help but think it's a warning we should heed."

Banner moved to the bathroom and scooped up his shaving kit. He returned to the luggage and arranged it inside. "I'll concede that you and your organization have a deeper understanding of the cartels in this hemisphere, but why assume they're on the right side of things? Seems to me that they'd love to let some police officers be blown sky high with a booby trap of their making."

"The image wasn't on the plane when I chased it. It was added after they landed."

"Still, I don't think it merits both of us going there. I don't see how I can help you." Banner tossed a polo shirt into the luggage and picked up another.

"I think Caldridge had something to do with it."

Banner stopped in mid-toss. The second shirt landed short of the suitcase. "What in the world makes you think that?"

"Call it instinct."

Banner cocked his head to one side as he looked at Sumner. "I'm not buying that line. What aren't you telling me?"

Sumner downed the rest of his coffee in one gulp. "If you can spare the time, I'd like you to come with me. Let's leave it at that."

Banner locked eyes with Sumner while his mind raced. He immediately reconsidered his earlier assumption that Sumner had been outmaneuvered. Clearly something occurred out there that was not ordinary. He finished piling the rest of his clothes into the suitcase and flipped it closed.

"All right, then. Let's go."

Sumner drove and Banner spent the entire journey wondering about the plane. He sent a short text to Stromeyer telling her that he wasn't headed out just yet. When she asked why, he explained the situation as best he could in the shorthand required by texting. His phone rang.

"I know you're in the car together, so don't say anything, just listen," Stromeyer said. "I just wanted to remind you that he could be violating ATD policy if he knows something that he's not saying." Banner couldn't have agreed more.

"I think we need to see how this plays out and trust that we'll know what to do when the time comes." Sumner stared straight ahead. Banner thought he was doing his best not to eavesdrop on the conversation.

He heard Stromeyer sigh over the phone. "Just don't let him jeopardize his job. There's no sense having two in trouble. Assure him that if he brings her in we'll do everything we can to straighten this out. I still believe that she's being coerced in some fashion."

"I agree and I'll keep you posted," Banner said.

"Great. I'll manage the Caribbean situation for now." When they reached the plane, Banner got out of the car and stood by the door, staring. The scent of wet paint hung in the air.

"It doesn't get any clearer than that, does it?" Sumner said.

Banner nodded. "I didn't expect it to be so graphic." There was a crowd of local law enforcement busy taping off the area. Banner jerked his chin in their direction. "They know not to approach it?"

Sumner nodded. "Look there." He pointed at a group of men dressed in yellow jumpsuits standing next to a truck with lettering that read HAZARDOUS INCIDENT TEAM. Next to it sat an ambulance and one fire truck.

"Ah, I didn't see that. Good," Banner said. He squinted at the plane. "The paint is still wet. She close by?" Banner waited to see if Sumner would pretend as though he didn't know who the "she" was that he was referring to.

"I don't know," Sumner said. Banner contemplated the plane. He hadn't seen a Fokker in quite some time. They were long out of production and used primarily in Europe.

"Only guy I know who flies a Fokker is in Africa," Banner said. "It's not the usual cartel model, is it?"

Sumner shook his head. "I've actually never seen a Fokker this side of the Atlantic."

"Strange," Banner said.

Sumner nodded. "I've given up trying to figure out the cartel guys."

The hazardous incident team waved the uniform police officers away. They turned to the plane and approached it cautiously. One, his head covered with a helmet and an air pack on his back, pulled the door down.

"That's the unlucky guy who gets to go in first," Banner said. "What if it's wired?"

Sumner shook his head. "Bomb squad's already been here. Determined that there isn't a bomb."

The man poked his head into the opening. After a moment, he disappeared inside. He was gone for a few minutes and reappeared at the entrance, holding up a wrapped brick in his gloved hand for everyone to see.

"Nothing more than a shipment of weed," he said. He tossed the brick to a nearby colleague. "Check it?" He descended the ladder and stripped off his helmet. "Let's get it out of there and burn it." The rest of the team lined up to climb the ladder. They removed their helmets, but kept their gloves on. Within minutes they were throwing bricks of marijuana out of the plane into a pile.

"At least it wasn't anything dangerous," Banner said. Sumner, though, looked pensive, his face set in a frown.

"Why would she paint a skull and crossbones for a routine marijuana shipment?" he said.

Banner paused. The question was a good one. He watched the pile of marijuana grow. The officers were milling around, talking, some laughing now that the immediate danger was passed.

"You're assuming she painted it. Maybe she didn't. Maybe the pilot did."

Sumner still looked unsatisfied with the explanation. "Dramatic, empty gestures aren't her style."

"I agree. She's too logical. She wouldn't waste her time unless it was important," Banner said.

The hazardous incident team leader and another officer walked up to Sumner. "You from ATD?"

Sumner nodded.

The team leader waved at the marijuana pile. "The leaves checked out. Marijuana. We're keeping one brick for evidence and some photos, then burning the rest. Take these." He handed Sumner and Banner two packages. "They're temporary face masks with about eight minutes of air pumped into them from that battery pack on the front. Less if you're breathing heavy. You're pretty safe here, but once we light the marijuana you should use these if you want to get any closer."

"No one allowed to get high on the job?" Sumner said.

The man smiled. "Yep. Policy."

Banner watched an officer wearing one of the temporary face masks pour a liquid over the pile. When the leaves were soaked he waved everyone back in preparation for lighting it. He tossed a match and the bricks lit up in flames with a whooshing sound. Smoke billowed into the air, but with the lack of a breeze, it continued straight up in a dark column. Banner watched it burn. Sumner stopped his conversation with the team leader to watch also. Several men hovered around the fire.

"You sure the plane isn't rigged with a bomb?" Sumner asked after a few minutes.

"You mean inside?" The hazardous team leader shook his head. "Nothing there. We'll get the plane's interior fingerprinted. Can you find out who owns it?"

"It's an unusual model. That will make it easier."

There came a choking noise. One of the officers closest to the bonfire grabbed at his throat. He was hunched over in obvious distress. A second ran to him, placing his hand on the man's back and saying something. He staggered back, holding his throat. After a moment, he too, bent forward. His legs buckled and he fell to one knee.

"What the hell?" the hazardous team leader said. He made a move to go to the men, but Sumner held him back.

"Get your helmet on," Sumner said. He cupped his hands to his mouth and yelled at the officers near the smoking marijuana, "Move back. Now!"

Banner ripped at his temporary face mask,

opening the package as fast as he could while still keeping his eyes on the fire. Several more policemen appeared affected. The first two stumbled away. The clearing erupted in chaos, with policemen running to drag the affected men to the ambulance, and the others running away from the fire. The officer that had waited with the team leader started past Banner, heading toward the column of smoke.

"Wait!" Banner grabbed at the fireman's arm. "Take this." He handed the mask to the fireman, who shoved it over his head as he jogged to the scene.

Sumner pulled his own mask over his face and split off in the direction of the fire truck. The ambulance siren blared, underlaid with a beeping tone as it reversed away from the scene.

The team leader, helmeted and covered, reached the fire and used his hands in a push back motion to herd the officers far from the pyre. Two firemen tried to run past him to the fire truck, but their faces were uncovered and the team leader stepped in front of them. They retreated a safe distance away. Two more officers, closer than the others, started to hold their stomachs as if they were going to be sick, but instead drops of blood started from their noses.

Banner jogged backwards as he watched the fireman he'd given his mask to climb into the truck. It began to rumble. Sumner headed toward it and leaped on the running board while he spoke to the fireman. After a moment Sumner appeared at the truck's top. He grabbed a stationary hose mounted on the roof. Water spouted from the nozzle and he directed it at the flames, using both his hands and focused on dousing the fire.

Within a minute the marijuana stopped burning. Two firemen returned to grab additional tanks. They sprayed a tamping foam onto the pile, effectively smothering it. The black column of smoke was reduced to almost nothing.

The ambulance turned around, its wheels churning up the turf, and went screaming down the road. The unaffected policemen hung back, with shocked looks on their faces. Banner could feel his pulse pounding and his breath hitch, but he couldn't tell if it was from inhaling the smoke or the stress of watching the incident go down. He swallowed but his mouth was dry.

Sumner clambered down from the fire truck. He jogged to Banner, ignoring the firemen, team leader, and the remaining police officers. When he reached Banner, he stopped, pulled off the face cover and stood there, his chest heaving and a grave look in his eyes.

Banner leveled a stare at Sumner. "If you know anything about what I just saw, I expect you to tell me. Now."

Sumner hesitated.

That's right, Banner thought, think about what you're doing.

"I don't know anything more about what I saw than you do," Sumner said, his words seemed carefully chosen.

"How much are you telling me? All of it?" Banner pressed.

Sumner gave him a shrewd look. "As much as I think is necessary."

Banner sighed. "I hold her in high esteem, too, but you're doing her no favors protecting her, you know that? She would be safer with us, even if that meant in custody. And something tells me she can explain what it was I just saw, because, I tell you, I can't explain it."

Sumner shook his head. "If she wanted to be in custody she would find a way to get there."

"Maybe, maybe not. I'm going first to Kansas City and then on to the Caribbean before I get back to D.C. You need me, get me there, because I'll be out of contact once I reach the Caribbean."

"Got it. I'll call if I need to, but I think she's deliberately avoiding us, and I'm going to let her work her angle a bit longer."

"As long as she isn't working you in the process," Banner said.

34

"RATHER THAN STEAL A CAR, WOULDN'T IT JUST
be easier to disable the tracking device and keep
the car we have?" Emma said.

They were driving past field after field in Oklahoma.

Vanderlock shook his head. "Those are tough to
find. They're hidden somewhere under the chassis. I don't know that I could locate it if I wanted
to, and then I don't know that I could disable it."
For a moment Emma wished they'd had Oz with
them. She had no doubt he could disable any GPS
device he encountered. Emma saw a combine
working a distant meadow.

"I have a better idea," Emma said. She pointed
at the combine. "I'll bet he left his house unlocked."

Vanderlock snorted. "No way. Anyone could
just waltz in and rob him blind while he's out
working."

Emma laughed. "You were raised in a city, right?"

Vanderlock nodded. "Johannesburg. Why?"

"Because people in the country leave their front doors unlocked, their keys in the car, and if they don't, they always, *always* have a fake rock or concealed jar near the front door that has a spare house key. Just find a small road off this main one and take it. We'll start checking houses."

"I want to see this," Vanderlock said.

"Then we need to find a phone."

Vanderlock flicked her a glance. "I thought the deal was you'd give it one more shot with the lab before you call Banner."

Emma shook her head. "I made no deals. And I'm not calling Banner."

Vanderlock turned down a rutted road, and they bounced along, the Caliber's suspension creaking with each bone-jarring pothole. A sickening smell wafted into the car.

"I know *that* smell," Emma said.

Vanderlock nodded. "Me too. It's a still."

"Can you find where it's coming from?"

Vanderlock kept going, and the smell grew. They came upon another dirt road angling off from the first. A handwritten sign nailed to a tree read, TRESPASSERS WILL BE SHOT. Vanderlock stopped at the intersection and idled there, looking at it.

"Think they have a truck to transport their moonshine?"

Emma nodded. "I believe they just might."

"Well let's go get it. I want you in a lab yesterday. Can you get my gun out of the duffel? We may need it."

Emma twisted around and fished in the duffel.

Her rib cage banged against the seat back as the car continued to jerk up and down. She pulled out the weapon, sat back in her seat, and checked the clip.

Vanderlock flicked her a surprised look. "Since when do you know how to shoot?"

"You taught me, remember?"

"I taught you how to shoot an RPG. I don't recall teaching you how to shoot a gun."

"Rocket-propelled grenades, guns, they're all the same," Emma did her best to keep her voice nonchalant.

Vanderlock hooted. "Yeah, right. One's a bazooka and one's a pistol. Tell me the truth."

"Sumner taught me this year."

Vanderlock drove around another pothole before giving her a shrewd look. "What else did he teach you?"

Emma ignored him and continued to check the weapon, looking up only when the car stopped.

In front of them sat a house that had once been elegant, but was now just tired. A large porch wrapped around the two-story structure with peeling blue paint. The house had the depressing air of a structure long forgotten. The front door, covered by a screen, was closed. To the right of the door was a boarded-up window. The plywood covering was warped at the edges. The stench of rotten corn and moldy yeast assaulted them, and Emma found herself holding her breath. Vanderlock drove the car over a lawn filled with large swaying weeds. They rounded the side of the house to the back and continued down a small path cut between the trees. Branches hit the car's sides and snapped against the windshield. They emerged into a clearing, where a metal still was cooking away. No truck in sight. Vanderlock got out of the car and strolled over to inspect the cooker.

"Hey! There are some finished bottles here." He held up a plastic milk jug filled with a clear liquid. Vanderlock uncapped it and took a sniff. He reared back. "Damn, that's strong! Bet this stuff is a hundred twenty proof, easy." He took a swig. Emma watched in fascination as his face first turned pale, then flushed red. He started to wheeze. She jumped out of the car.

"You okay?" She watched tears form in Vanderlock's eyes as he tried to contain his reaction to the booze.

"Water," he whispered.

She smiled and went to the Caliber, reached a hand through the open back-door window, and snagged a water bottle. She tossed it to Vanderlock. He opened it and started drinking in huge gulps.

"Was it that bad?" Emma asked.

Vanderlock shook his head. "Not bad, just white lightning."

Emma reached out and took the car keys that dangled from his hand. "I'll drive for a while." Vanderlock nodded, picked up the bottle, and headed back to the car. "Wait," Emma said, "you're bringing that swill?"

Vanderlock gave her a huge smile. "Oh yeah. This is *just* what I need. No car here, we're going to have to test your theory and find a house to rob."

Emma turned the car around and bumped across the lawn back to the road. They retraced their path, passing the "Trespassers will be shot" sign, and then she turned onto the main road, a long county highway, well paved, flanked on either side by wheat fields and stretching into the horizon. After ten minutes, she glanced in the rearview mirror. A black Mercedes, followed by a black BMW hurtled toward them.

"Strap in, La Valle's men are coming on fast."

Vanderlock twisted in his seat to look behind them. "Damn, they used the tracking device. Can you shake them?"

"In a Caliber? Not likely. If that's La Valle's BMW, then it has double the horsepower, easy. If it's armored, the plating will add some weight. Maybe slow it down."

Emma pushed the pedal all the way to the floor and the Caliber responded with a surge of speed. The engine started humming, making a high-pitched whine. The road stretched out before them, rimmed by the wheat and offering nothing in the way of cover. Vanderlock pulled out his weapon and kept watch in the side-view mirror.

"You see any side roads, you take them. Wish we had another gun."

"We're not winning this race. Any ideas? Can we negotiate? Tell them you're willing to continue with the shipment?"

Vanderlock shook his head. "La Valle isn't going to negotiate with me after I let a load get confiscated. He'll just shoot me, execution style, which would be merciful by his standards, because he's known for torture. Besides, I'm not going to let him take you hostage again."

In the distance Emma could see the combine working its way through the field to their left, spraying a substance onto the plants from two long poles extending on either side. The road bisecting the fields appeared almost too quickly for Emma to react. She spun the wheel left. The caliber's front tires turned and the entire car started skidding sideways as it was unable to grip the road. They slid down into a small depression on the edge. After a moment the treads regained their traction and the car moved forward again, flinging dirt from the road up in the air. Emma kept her eyes glued to the path and her foot to the floor. The speedometer jumped back up, moving in a smooth motion. The BMW appeared in the rearview, making the turn with little sideways motion. The Mercedes followed.

"We need a plan. They're gaining," Emma said. Ahead she saw a pickup truck parked on the road. It was pulled to the side, but would leave her little choice but to slow down to avoid hitting it when they squeezed past. It grew larger as they hurtled toward it. Emma saw two large round barrels in the back.

"You think that truck has a gun rack?" Vanderlock said.

"Haven't seen a gun rack in a pickup in years," Emma said.

Vanderlock never took his eyes from the side mirror when he answered. "We can only hope this one does, because I have no other idea." As they drew nearer, Emma could begin to see the impression of lettering on the barrels but she was too far to read it. As they approached she saw a propane tank next to the barrels. Seconds later they were on top of the truck. Emma slammed on the brakes. They slid again, this time straight for the vehicle, creating a cloud of dust from the dirt road that tinted the air around them a dirty yellow color. The moment the car stopped she jumped out, leaving her door open. Vanderlock slammed out of his side. Emma grabbed the pickup's gate, stepped on the bumper, and flung a leg over the top to pull herself into the open body.

Both barrels contained common herbicide. Not really flammable, and Emma wrote them off as potential weapons. Next to them sat a twenty-pound propane tank. Out of the corner of her eye she saw Vanderlock enter the truck's cab. He appeared next to the truck's tire, holding his pistol.

"No gun rack. No gun." He aimed his pistol at the oncoming vehicles and fired.

The bullet hit the dirt in front of the BMW. The car reacted immediately, turning toward the field, and drove straight into it, disappearing from sight. The Mercedes behind skid to a stop. Vanderlock shot again, and a little puff of flying dirt near the front tires indicated a miss. The car immediately started reversing, accelerating backward. Vanderlock fired again.

"Out of range," Vanderlock said.

He looked into the pickup and spied the propane tank. "If I shoot the tank, will it explode?"

"No. You'd need a spark. Or incendiary bullets. It would if we threw it on a fire and *then* shot it." She jumped back onto the ground. "Let's go. We don't have the time to build a fire." She reached over and grabbed the propane tank by the top, hauling it over the truck's sidewall. "I'll bring it."

Vanderlock just nodded, keeping his eyes on the road where the two cars were last seen. The Mercedes idled well back and out of range, sitting in the middle of the road, waiting. The BMW remained out of sight, a fact that worried Emma. She half expected it to come crashing from the field at any moment.

"Come on. Time's a-wasting," Vanderlock said. "They're going to start to use us for target practice."

"Back in the car," Emma said. She tossed the propane tank in the hatch and slammed it closed, slid into the driver's seat and hit the gas the moment Vanderlock regained his place.

She drove around the truck and hammered the pedal down as far as it would go. To her left she saw the spraying rods of the combine in the distance. They hurtled down the road. Emma kept flicking looks into the rearview mirror, waiting and dreading the moment when the BMW would appear once again. Vanderlock kept his eyes on the side-view mirror, saying nothing. They sped by bales of hay on the side of the road, spaced in intervals, awaiting pickup. Emma glanced in the mirror. No BMW, no Mercedes, but nowhere to hide, either. They reached another line of hay bales.

"Brace yourself," she said. Vanderlock placed a hand on the dashboard. She slammed on the brakes. "Let's start a fire."

Emma scrambled out of the car and ran a few steps behind it to the nearest hay bale. Vanderlock appeared at her side, his pistol still in his hand. She tugged on the twine holding the bale and lifted it. Vanderlock paused an instant, but then shoved his pistol into his waistband and helped her carry the bale to the middle of the road. Emma started to dig in the straw, making a hollow. Vanderlock snagged the propane tank from the back of the car.

"In the hole?" Vanderlock said. Emma just nodded. She'd hollowed out an area in the bale for the tank. He lowered it into place, twisting it back and forth.

Emma heard the roar of an engine. The BMW was speeding toward them. Vanderlock aimed and fired, though the car was well out of range.

"Throw me your lighter," Emma said. He fished his stick lighter out of his pocket and tossed it to her. Emma flicked it on and held the flame against the hay. Her hand didn't shake as she thought it might. Vanderlock shot twice more, but she kept her eyes on the hay, waiting for it to ignite. She held the lighter steady and a flame snaked upward.

"What the hell is that?"

Emma looked up.

The BMW idled in the middle of the road about 250 yards from them. The doors were open on either side, and Mono and Raoul stood in front.

Both held guns in their hands. Both were pointed at the man who stood between them. It was Oz. His arms and face were covered with masses of angry red sores—so many that it was difficult to tell what he had once looked like. His hands were curled into rigor mortis-like claws, and they, too, were covered in blisters. If he hadn't been wearing his jeans and the familiar tee shirt, she wouldn't have recognized him. He kept his head down, staring at the ground. Anguish tugged at her as she looked at him.

The hale bale continued to burn, the flames spreading.

"That's what the disease does," Emma said. Her voice broke on the word "does."

"Let's get out of here. The propane tank's going to blow," Vanderlock said.

Emma rose slowly. Raoul kept the gun pointed in a straight-arm stance right at Oz's head. Raoul's arm, too, was covered in sores, but they hadn't yet reached his face.

"You see this?" Raoul yelled. "You come back here, now, or I shoot him."

Emma felt rage burble up in her. "You kill him, I'll never cure you! You'll die, too, you understand?"

"Screw your cure! It doesn't matter. La Valle will kill me if I don't bring you back."

"Let's go, the tank's going to blow." For the first time Emma heard stress in Vanderlock's voice.

Raoul swung his arm down and shot at the ground near Oz's feet. Oz jerked, but kept his head lowered, as if he didn't care.

"Let's move, now!" Vanderlock said.

"That's Oz. I won't let them kill him," Emma said.

Vanderlock stepped next to her. "Look at him. Poor bastard would probably rather be dead. The tank is going to blow."

"Give me the gun," Emma said.

"They're out of range, *let's go*," Vanderlock said.

The hay bale flames licked up four feet. They had completed an entire circuit around the propane tank.

"Give me the gun," Emma said again.

"Here." Vanderlock shoved the weapon at her. "Now move!"

Emma snatched the pistol. Vanderlock grabbed her arm and started to pull her back with him to the car. She jerked out of his grasp and broke into a run, heading straight for Oz. She heard Vanderlock yell her name, but she kept going, closing the distance between them. She ran, arms pumping, the gun flashing in front of her as the light hit it.

One hundred yards in, the tank behind her blew.

Emma felt a flash of heat and she dove to the dirt, covering her head with her arms. Smoke and fire boiled into the sky, some of it billowing around her. She looked up and saw Raoul stagger back a few steps, shock on his face as he watched the conflagration. Even Oz looked skyward. She flattened on the ground, aimed, and squeezed off a shot. The bullet entered Raoul at the right shoulder, and he screamed incoherently, hunching over in reaction. She turned her attention to

Mono, but he was already on the move. He leaped behind the BMW's open driver's-side door. Oz turned his head to look, but stayed immobile. He seemed riveted in place. Raoul put his left hand over the wound and raised the gun in his right.

"Damn it Oz, move!" she yelled. Emma shot Raoul again, this time grazing his right arm. The second shot galvanized Oz into action. He ran at an angle, heading for the field. He took a giant leap from the road into the plants, disappearing inside the foliage.

Emma was up and running parallel to Oz, heading to the field. Shots peppered the ground near her feet, she assumed from Mono, but she didn't waste the time looking for the source. She flew, her arms and legs moving in rhythm. She plunged down a small culvert between the field and the road, preparing to plunge into the rows of wheat standing all around her. Off to her left came the noise of the combine, growing louder. It appeared at the end of a row, and stopped. The engine rumbled, but the wheels no longer turned. A man's face appeared in the cab's window.

"Hey, what the hell are you doing there? I could have killed you! Did you set that fire?" He pointed at the smoke from the propane fire. "Get off my property."

The farmer's voice was loaded with fear and anger. He stepped out of the tractor and stared down at her. He wore jeans and a dark tee shirt and stood half in and half out of the cab, with one booted foot on the step. Emma rose. The farmer glanced at the gun in her hand. "Why're you carrying a gun?"

Before she could answer, a shot rang out. The farmer's body was flung backward, and he tumbled down the side of the combine, landing somewhere in the foliage below.

Emma spun and ran back the way she came, moving onto the asphalt toward the still burning propane. She saw the Caliber on the far side of the bonfire, still in the middle of the road facing her. She sprinted toward it, keeping her eyes on it and trying not to look back for her attackers. When she neared the car, Vanderlock pushed open the door.

"Get in!"

She jumped into the car and pulled up her legs. Vanderlock was turning the car in a circle before she could even close the door, and it swung wide with the turn. She managed to get it closed when he straightened out to shoot down the road.

"Have you seen Oz?" she said.

"Why is it that every time I'm around you something is exploding?"

She turned to see Oz, his face and arms a bleeding mass of sores, lying on the backseat.

35

"EMMA CALDRIDGE SHOT A FARMER WORKING HIS
fields. He came upon her by surprise."

Banner sat in a hotel room in Kansas City, participating in a conference call with Sumner in
Oklahoma and Wiley in Nebraska.

"Is he dead?" Sumner asked.

Sheriff Wiley coughed. "No. Bullet missed any
major arteries. He's up and talking."

"He say why she shot him?" Banner said.

"He says she was crouching in his field, a gun
in her hand. Claims he damn near ran her over
with his tractor. He told her to get off his property, and the next thing he knew he was waking
up in the hospital."

"Any idea where she is now?" Banner said.

"Nope. We're still looking for the black SUV she
used at the pharmaceutical company. No luck.
We'll keep you posted. But I gotta tell you, she
gets picked up, ain't nothing you can do. She's
going to get charged."

Banner knew this as well. "I hear you, Sheriff.

Just do me a favor and continue to give her the benefit of the doubt."

"I'll give it to her, but the FBI won't. It's their investigation now, and they want her bad. She's considered armed and dangerous."

Sheriff Wiley rang off and the speaker phone remained quiet so long that Banner thought Sumner had hung up as well. He started when Sumner's voice came over the line.

"I don't believe it. What was she doing crouching in a field?"

Banner sighed. "I have no idea. But we've got another problem. The first responders on the Black Eagles scene have contracted some sort of strange rash. Nothing as dramatic as what we saw at the plane, but we're all going on the assumption that it's related, somehow."

"Is the CDC on it?"

Banner nodded, even though he knew that Sumner couldn't see him. "They are, and still chasing a possible anthrax connection or Ebola-type virus. So far, nothing. They're running a series of tests to rule out everything from poison ivy to virulent measles. We should know something in twenty-four hours. You have any symptoms?" The phone fell quiet again as Sumner didn't answer. Banner closed his eyes briefly. He didn't want to hear what he now thought he might.

"I have a rash forming on my left hand."

Banner exhaled slowly. "You'll need to come in. The CDC is placing anyone with symptoms into quarantine. They can't tell if it's infectious yet."

"I can't afford to be in quarantine. I need to find her. Now more than ever."

"It's not a matter of what you can afford, it's a matter of public health. You need to report in." The lack of a response told Banner all he needed to know. Sumner wouldn't be coming in anytime soon. He tried a different tack. "You, of all people, should do the right thing and report in. You're a member of the ATD, for God's sake."

No response.

Banner threw out the one thing he thought would make Sumner agree. "I'll make you a deal: if you come in I promise to drop everything, get Stromeyer back here, and the two of us will start to look for her. Now will you report in?"

"You told me Stromeyer's in the Caribbean somewhere. How long will it take her to get back here?"

Banner wasn't sure. Stromeyer wasn't operating openly in the islands, and he didn't have instant access to her, as she was maintaining phone silence. Nevertheless, he took a stab at it.

"Twenty-four hours, max."

"Too long."

"Listen to me—"

"—If it was Stromeyer out there, would you come in? Leave the investigation to others?"

The question caught Banner by surprise. His first thought was "Not on your life," and he had to clamp his teeth together not to say it. He said what leaped to mind next.

"There's a difference. Stromeyer is my business partner and whatever she would be doing would fall under Darkview business and I'd have to address it. Caldridge is not related to you or the ATD at all. Also, I know how skilled and resourceful Stromeyer is. She'd solve the situation on her own, or at least do her best to solve it, and she wouldn't call on me unless she thought I could add something to the mix. I think Caldridge is the same. You should assume that if she's not calling you that she doesn't need you."

Banner hated to say the harsh words, but it was true. Caldridge knew Sumner better than anyone else. She had access to him in a way that no one else did. She knew that Sumner would help her in a heartbeat if he could, and the silence from her end spoke volumes. What puzzled Banner is that Sumner knew this as well, yet he continued to place his own future at risk.

"Tell me the truth, here. What happened on that intercept flight? Why are you insisting on helping Caldridge when she hasn't asked for it?"

"For the same reason you'd help Stromeyer."

Banner knew when the game was up. "You're right," he conceded. "I would be the same. But I hope that if the situation were reversed you'd give me some good advice as well."

"That you would ignore." Sumner's voice held a note of humor.

"Fair enough, but here's some more. Stay out of the FBI's way. They won't appreciate it, and your jurisdiction is too thin to win that pissing contest. What are you planning on doing when you find Caldridge?"

"I plan on killing that cartel pilot."

36

"YOU TWO SHOULDN'T BE ANYWHERE NEAR ME,"
Oz said. Vanderlock kept his eyes on the road, a
fact for which Emma was thankful, because he'd
taken the Caliber up to ninety miles per hour.
Luckily the rural county highway held few cars.

"We've already got it," Vanderlock said.

Oz groaned. "What do you mean?"

"The shipment broke free in the plane. We're
definitely infected," Emma said.

"Any sores?"

"No," Emma replied.

"Yes," Vanderlock said. He held out his right
hand, where an angry sore had formed on the
heel of his palm.

Emma sucked in her breath. For a moment
she felt as though she'd lost her equilibrium. The
blood rushed to her head and she thought she
was going to faint. She took a deep breath, keeping her eyes on the road, doing her best to regain
her composure.

"La Valle's got a tracking device on this car. Can you disarm it?" Emma said to Oz.

"GPS or radio tracker?" Oz said.

"I think a cheap radio transmitter," Vanderlock replied.

"Do you know where it is?" Oz said.

"Somewhere on the chassis."

"I'll have to find it first. That will take time."

"We don't have any time," Vanderlock said. "Let's just dump the car. It's our quickest option."

"How are your legs?" Emma said to Oz.

"I get weak pretty quickly. The sores don't hurt, they're just numb."

"How's Serena?"

Oz shook his head. "Serena's dead. She died last night. La Valle went crazy." A stream of blood came out of Oz's nose. He pulled up his tee shirt and held it to his face to staunch the flow. "My nose just won't stop bleeding."

"Who's Serena?" Vanderlock said. Emma sat back in the seat and faced forward. Serena being dead was a very, very bad development for all of them.

"La Valle's girlfriend. She had the disease first. Now that she's dead there's no further reason to keep me—or you—alive."

Vanderlock snorted. "I told you, unless I deliver the shipment I'll be doomed anyway."

"Let's just get rid of this car and find a phone."

Emma glanced back at Oz. He leaned against the side door, his legs stretched out on the seat. She found it was difficult to look at him, his face was so disfigured. His eyes, still lovely, gazed out from the mass. She smiled at him. He watched her for a moment, then a small smile tugged at the corners of his mouth. Maybe it was the best he could do, but Emma felt her throat constrict with tears at the small gesture. She turned away again.

Vanderlock switched on the radio and fiddled with the dials until finding an all-news show. The car hummed along.

"How are we on gas?" Emma said.

"Quarter of a tank. We need to find some."

The radio announcer switched from discussing the price of cattle futures to reporting the news. He said, "Miami chemist Emma Caldridge and two other accomplices are suspected of yet another attack in the last twenty-four hours." The reporter announced that she was implicated in the shooting of a local farmer and was armed and dangerous. They asked anyone having any information to contact the FBI and rattled off a phone number.

Vanderlock shot her a grim look. "They think you shot the farmer?"

Emma felt her stomach tighten. "This is going to take a long time to unravel."

Vanderlock nodded. "You bet it is."

"We need to get Oz to a hospital."

"Forget about me. We need to stop the shipment. La Valle has two more stops: Chicago and D.C.," Oz said. "And it gets worse. They're assembling a meeting of the major gangs in the Midwest who usually distribute the drugs."

"Is he crazy? He'll infect them all," Emma said.

"Good," Vanderlock said. "I hope they die a painful death. Where's the meeting?"

"Somewhere along their usual route. Kansas, maybe. And I think he *wants* to infect them all. I think he wants to eliminate the competition."

"Then who's going to distribute for him?" Emma said.

"He's got a gang in Chicago ready to take over."

Half an hour later they drove into a small town. Oz kept his head low, so as not to be spotted. Vanderlock pulled into a local gas station. The sign said DIXIE GAS, and the entire establishment consisted of one gas and one diesel pump next to a clapboard structure with dirty windows and an ancient Coca-Cola poster in the window. Vanderlock jerked his chin at the sign.

"Bet that's worth something."

Emma scanned the area for a pay phone. She saw a box attached to the side wall.

"Yes! A phone." She jumped out and headed to the side. She got to the kiosk and was immediately disappointed to find that whatever was once there was long gone. The shell contained only a few severed telephone lines and scrawled graffiti in black marker. She came back around to find Vanderlock filling the tank.

"I'm going to ask to use the phone," she said.

"Who we calling?" Vanderlock said.

"Sumner."

Vanderlock snorted. "Flyboy?"

"Don't call him that."

Vanderlock gave her a considering look. "So what should I call him? Loverboy?"

Emma didn't bother to respond, but instead opened the aging screen on the door to the building. It banged closed behind her with a snap.

Faded fluorescent lights bathed the inside of the store with a half light. Beige-colored steel shelving about shoulder height contained the usual travel-size convenience-store items. The largest thing in the shop was a long glass refrigerator unit containing one shelf of water; one of sports drinks, iced tea, and sodas; and three of beer. Emma grabbed a bottle of ibuprofen and a canister of bandages. At a right angle and behind a counter sat a young man sporting a shaved head and a camouflage-green tee shirt. She put the purchases on the counter and placed a five dollar bill next to them.

"May I use your phone? My cell ran out of juice."

The man got an annoyed look on his face. "It's not the battery, you're in a dead zone. Cell phones don't work here."

"What a drag." Emma hoped that she sounded sufficiently sympathetic.

"You're telling me," he said.

"Well, can I use the gas station's?"

The man reached behind him to pick up the phone console.

"Get in the car now! They're coming." Emma heard Vanderlock yell through the screen, his tone urgent. Emma grabbed a pen out of a cup next to the cash register and a newspaper on the shelf below the counter. She wrote a number in the paper's margin.

"Listen, I've got to go. Call this number, will

you? And tell the man who answers Emma was here. I'll call again when I can." She shoved the paper at the man, grabbed her purchases, leaving the five behind, and bolted out the door. Vanderlock was already in the car. He revved the engine. Oz sat up and craned his neck to look out the back window. When she reached the passenger-side door she saw the black BMW less than a half mile away and coming on fast.

The Caliber's wheels spun on the concrete with a squealing sound. Vanderlock put the pedal all the way down. Emma tossed the pills on the floor of the car and grabbed the gun that rested in the console between them.

"You have any more bullets? Or is this it?"

"That's all. What do you have? Thirteen?"

"Just about."

"Not enough," Vanderlock said.

Emma lowered her window. The side-view mirror showed the BMW gaining. Vanderlock kept his eyes on the road. Far in the distance, they heard the sound of a siren.

"Cops," Oz said. He kept a watch out the rear window.

Behind the BMW came the flashing lights of a patrol car. Emma thought she'd never seen anything so beautiful.

"That police car's booking," Oz said.

"Think they'll stop?" Vanderlock said.

"Not a chance," Oz said. No sooner had he spoken, than Emma saw Mono lean out of the passenger-side window and take aim at the patrol car. She heard the reports of two shots. One bullet shattered the windshield's center. The patrol car kept coming on. Mono retreated into his vehicle, screeched into a turn and disappeared down a side road. The patrol car turned to follow.

"Do you think he hit the cop?" Emma said to Oz.

He shook his head. "Don't think so. The guy's probably calling for backup now."

"Lucky break for us," Vanderlock said. Emma doubted that luck had anything to do with it. Sumner must have called the police. She kept the thought to herself, though, while she plotted to obtain access to another phone.

37

HOURS LATER THEY DROVE INTO AN INDUSTRIAL park and killed the engine. Oz's condition was deteriorating fast. He lay in the back, his eyes closed. A line of blood ran out of his nose. The latest lab consisted of one small building, with green-tinted glass windows and an efficient, sterile look to it.

"What does this one specialize in?" Vanderlock said.

"Orphan drug research," Emma said.

"Orphan drugs? What're those?"

"They're drugs that cure obscure, rarely occurring diseases. They're called orphan drugs because most makers don't invest any time or research money in them. The disease they cure doesn't occur often enough to support large sales. Without the payback, they're not worth producing in quantity. Or, in some cases, at all."

Vanderlock kept his eye on the lab. "So why does this lab bother?"

"They get significant tax incentives for researching rare diseases, and they get a seven-year free pass to market them without competition. If they hit the jackpot on a drug, the sky's the limit on the pricing." Emma picked up the ibuprofen from the wheel well at her feet and handed them back to Oz.

"You in any pain?" she said.

Oz nodded. "Starting to be. Mostly a headache." She gave him the pills. "It's the best I can find for you right now."

Oz took the bottle without comment.

"How are we getting into this one?" Oz said.

Emma checked the weapon. "We're going to persuade the security guard that it's necessary."

Vanderlock watched her with a look of approval on his face. "I do believe that a life of crime suits you. Who knew?"

"Don't get your hopes up. I'm not joining you."

Vanderlock leaned closer. "I'm not a criminal, I'm a victim of circumstance. But if you choose to stay a criminal, I might just decide that it would be worth my while to be one, too."

Emma eyed him, but decided not to comment further. "Let's go," she said.

They hit their first obstacle at the front door. It was locked. No guard in sight. Vanderlock put his face against the glass, cupping his hands around his eyes to see inside.

"Nothing. Guess orphan drug research doesn't pay enough to hire a full-time guard." He stepped back and looked up at the building face. "No cameras, either."

"You know how to jimmy a door?"

"Only with a crowbar. Want me to check the Caliber? But I doubt there's one in it."

"Can we shoot the lock?" Oz said.

Vanderlock got a dubious look on his face. "I hate to waste a bullet."

"Break a window?"

"I guess we'll have to," Emma said.

"Once the alarm triggers we won't have a lot of time."

"How about I stay out here?" Vanderlock said. "When the cops come, I'll tear off in the Caliber. Maybe they'll follow. Buy you some more time. I'll honk when they show up. You hear it, you wrap up whatever it is you're doing." Vanderlock gave Oz an assessing look. "Think you're strong enough to run to that Walmart we passed on the way?"

Oz took a deep breath. "I'll do my best."

"Then you two meet me in the back. Once I lose the cops I'll return there for you both."

"And if Mono shows up again?" Emma said.

Vanderlock shrugged. "I'll deal with Mono." He put his hand out for the gun. Emma engaged the safety and handed it to him. He shoved it into his waistband and dropped his shirt over the butt.

They walked around the building, looking for a weak point of entry. They found it at the freight dock. The area smelled of old garbage and grease. A large black plastic trash can sat in a corner along with a small folding table and chair that may have been a station for a guard during the day. Tacked on the wall to the right of the table was a poster from the Department of Labor that said KNOW YOUR RIGHTS. A clipboard with a sign-in sheet hung from a hook within easy reach of the table. Next to that, a wood panel door had a single-pane rectangular glass window at the top.

"Let me go find a rock," Vanderlock said. He jogged toward the end of the parking lot.

Oz heaved a sigh. "I'm going to take a seat under a tree. I'm exhausted. Call me when you need me." He walked to the edge of the lot and disappeared into the darkness. Vanderlock returned, holding a large, gray granite-looking piece the size of a small football.

"This oughta do it," he said.

A minivan turned the corner into the loading bay, its headlights blinding Emma with their white light. Emma froze. Vanderlock moved next to her, holding the rock behind him. He held the other hand up near his eyes while he squinted at the car. The van maneuvered into the loading area and the door slid open. Several women emerged, one after another. The first, a short woman with big arms and hair fashioned into a bun shot with gray, nodded to Emma and gave Vanderlock a quick assessing look. She wore a shapeless gray dress with solid black comfort shoes and a white apron over it all. She shuffled over to the sign-in sheet, pulled it off the wall, scrawled her name and pulled a key card attached to a lanyard around her neck out from underneath the front of the apron.

"The cleaning crew," Emma said under her breath to Vanderlock, who replied with a quiet "um hmm." He still held his hand to his eyes.

Emma smiled the friendliest smile that she could manage and addressed the heavy woman with the key card.

"I'm so glad to see you. I forgot my key card." Emma held her hands out in a helpless gesture. The woman moved past Emma to the door and swiped the card through the reader. She opened the door for Emma and nodded her inside. When Vanderlock made a move to follow, the woman shook her head.

He put his hands in the air. "I'll just wait out here." He smiled at the cleaning lady, who frowned back at him and muttered a word under her breath.

Emma held the door to allow the other cleaning women, all of varying ages, to file into the facility in front of her. They nodded and chattered in a foreign language, which sounded vaguely Eastern European. A couple of the younger women bestowed large smiles on Vanderlock, who smiled back.

"I'll get Oz," Vanderlock said. "Be ready to let him in."

Ten minutes later, Oz and Emma made their way down the first-floor hallway, which was lined with a series of numbered doors. Emma picked number four and tried the handle. The door opened into a small, pristine office space. A computer sat on a desk, along with a picture of a smiling woman and two small children. Emma stepped back out and waved Oz forward again. The hall ended at another, wider, corridor.

"Look left," Oz whispered. To their left was a

set of double doors marked CLEAN ROOM LAB, AU-
THORIZED PERSONNEL ONLY.

"Won't work. That's a sterile room. It has to be
locked," Emma said. She looked right. Another
set of double doors lettered with the simple word
LAB. She headed that way, Oz behind her. She
pushed through the doors to a large, dark area.
She searched around on a nearby wall and found
a bank of switches and turned them on. Fluorescent lights sprung on to reveal a clean, large, im-
personal lab room of the kind that Emma had
worked in her entire life. She felt like she'd come
home.

"Perfect," she said. She hurried to the side counter. "Sit down. Let's move. I want to take another
look at the bacteria on the sores now that they're
so much more severe. Maybe something else will
be revealed."

Oz sat on a nearby stool while Emma fished
around in the cabinets. She found some gloves
and spare slides, along with a small tool to use to
scrape at the sores and several different agents to
use to treat the resulting tissue. She scraped some
more cells from Oz's hand, noting that they were
chewing down into the meat of his palm.

"Still numb?" she said.

Oz nodded.

Once she prepared the slide, she grabbed a
staining solution and began to run through the
steps to complete the process.

"What's that?" Oz asked.

"Something that will help me identify any acid-
fast bacteria."

"What are you looking for?"

Emma shrugged. "Tuberculosis."

"But it doesn't create sores."

"Not usually, no."

Emma finished up and popped one slide into a nearby oven. She turned to the next slide, which she intended to view bare, under a microscope.

"Damn these nosebleeds!" Oz said.

Emma looked up and watched Oz wipe at his nose once again with his filthy, bloodstained tee shirt. She stared at him. He stopped dabbing at his nose and glanced up, catching her look. "What?" he said.

Emma returned to the cabinet and brought out another stain. She took the second slide, added the solution, and waited five minutes. She slid the slide under a nearby microscope and peered through the lens. Millions of red-colored bacteria swam around against a blue background. Emma stared at the stain, stunned. That she, Vanderlock, Oz, Serena, and all the others who had touched the shipment could have what she now suspected, at the virulent level that it appeared to be, was devastating.

"Let's go," Emma said.

Oz stood. "You're done? What about the slide in the oven?"

Emma reached up and turned it off. "I don't care about it now. We need to see their stash of medicines. Look around, tell me what you find."

Oz stood up, a puzzled look in his eyes. "What kind of medications?"

"Antibiotics. Anything that will kill bacteria."

The room, though, contained only laboratory equipment.

"What do you think I have?"

Emma shook her head. If she told him she was afraid he'd shut down, refuse to fight any further. What she suspected was horrifying, but she kept hope that the disease could be reversed. "Not now. Let's get out of here first. I'll tell you then."

She heard, far in the distance, the sound of a honking horn.

"That's Lock," Oz said. "Let's go."

Emma was already moving across the room, heading to the hall. "I'm not leaving without finding their stash of medication. We're in an orphan-drug lab. I may need what they have." Especially now that I know what afflicts us all, she thought. "We're going to have to check every door in that wing."

"We don't have the time," Oz said. "Let it go. I've accepted that I'm dying. Let's just get the hell out of here and stop that shipment."

"You forget that Lock and I have it too," Emma said.

"You have a lot of days left. We'll stop the shipment and you can still get to a hospital."

Oz made a move to grab her, then stopped. "Sorry."

"I don't care if you touch me. Just go. Get to the meeting place and hook up with Lock. Give me fifteen minutes, then leave without me."

Oz stood still.

"Go!" Emma said.

He turned and ran down the hall. Emma kept

up her search, opening the numbered doors on
the way. Nothing. She turned into the main hall,
jogging to each successive door and opening it.
On the sixth she hit pay dirt. She stepped inside
a large room, twice the size of the earlier offices,
and flicked on the lights. Refrigerators lined two
sides of the square-shaped area, and glass-fronted
cabinets lined the others. She ran to the refrigerators first.

Dozens of medications in bottles of all shapes
and sizes filled every inch of the appliance. While
labels arranged by alphabet made finding the
medication possible, Emma wasn't sure if the
bottles were organized by the name of a disease,
the bacteria it fought, or by some other system
with which she was unfamiliar. She'd have to
take as much as she could and sort it out later.

She backed away from the refrigerator and
looked around for something to hold all the bottles. She saw nothing that would be of use. She
briefly considered using the trash can, but discarded the idea. It would be hard to carry while
she ran to the meeting place.

A shrieking filled the room as the alarm system
triggered.

A far corner held a desk and she sprinted to it.
Emma yanked on the lowest, and largest, drawer.
It opened to reveal a set of hanging file folders,
organized and labeled. She opened the corre-
sponding drawer on the other side of the chair
and found a pair of black low-heeled pumps,
neatly arranged in the bottom. They rested on top
of a piece of canvas. Emma pulled the canvas out

from under the pumps and saw that it was a tote bearing the initials BAP. From the hall Emma heard the sound of raised voices and doors being slammed. The sounds drew closer as the searchers checked each room. Emma ran to the door, and turned the lock on the handle before returning to the refrigerator. She held the open tote in front of the first shelf, and used her arm to sweep the medications inside. The noise from the slamming doors came closer. She moved to the second shelf and swept her hand once again. Bottles and plastic containers fell into the tote, making a clinking noise as the ones in glass containers hit the others. Some missed the opening and landed on the tile floor, the glass containers among them breaking with a shattering sound that set Emma's teeth on edge. The rest rolled away.

The door handle rattled. Emma stopped, her heart pounding as she watched the knob. It jiggled again. Emma turned back to the third shelf and started picking up the bottles and placing them inside the tote as quietly as she could.

"Open it, now!" Mono's voice came through the panel.

Emma quit filling the tote and closed the refrigerator door. She needed a place to hide, but the room was devoid of any nooks and crannies. The only possible hiding place was the area under the desk where the desk chair rested.

She heard a woman's voice, speaking in an Eastern European language, pleading with Mono. Emma could tell from the inflection that the woman was scared out of her mind and begging.

"I said, open it!" Emma heard a punching noise accompanied by a woman's cry. She placed the tote over her shoulder and headed to the desk.

Emma rolled the wheeled desk chair to the window and hauled it up by the arms, grimacing as she tried to lift it higher. She staggered backward with the chair's weight, but managed to keep her feet while she swung the metal legs with their steel rollers against the glass with all her might. The hit made a booming sound and the window bounced with the impact, but the double-paned glass held. A bullet cracked through the door and embedded itself into the wall three feet from where Emma stood, creating a dent.

"*Puta*!" Mono screamed through the door. Emma swung the chair again, her arms aching in pain as she tried to both hold the chair high enough and swing it fast enough to crack the glass.

Another boom. This time a long fissure appeared in the pane.

Two more bullets splintered the door. Shards of plywood flew into the room. The shots landed one foot away from Emma, shoulder high. White, chalky pieces of drywall flew into the air. Several bits hit Emma in the cheek.

She swung the chair again. This time the glass broke, shattering into a million cracks. The chair wheels punched out a circular hole in the window about the size of a large dinner plate. Far too small for Emma to climb through. She dropped the chair onto its feet directly in front of the pane, grabbed the bag, moved back, and took a running start.

Mono kicked open the door.

Emma leaped, placing one foot on the chair seat and turning her body so that her shoulder lined up with the pane. The rest of the glass broke open with the force of the hit and she felt herself free falling downward. She landed on the grass below with enough force to knock the wind out of her. Bits of glass showered down.

She rolled up and started running at a forty-five-degree angle to the window. Bullets thudded into the grass around her. She made it to the parking lot and plunged into the surrounding trees. The bag banged against her side with each pump of her arms. She felt a cold liquid soak through her pants at the hip, but she was too engrossed in getting away to stop and check the source. She ran at a breakneck speed down the road in the direction of the store. The high light poles that lit the store's parking lot appeared before her. She kept sprinting in a straight line, scanning the area. She saw the Caliber idling in the back, hiding in shadow. When she reached it she pulled open the door, tossed the tote inside, and followed it in. Vanderlock said nothing, but tore off, driving in the opposite direction of the lab. Oz lay in the backseat, once again with his back against the door, his eyes closed.

Emma snapped on her seat belt and reached up to lower the visor. She slid open the cover to the embedded mirror, which lit up in order to allow her to see her reflection.

A line of blood ran out of her nose.

VANDERLOCK DROVE FOR HALF AN HOUR WITHOUT
speaking. Emma stared out the window, trying
her best to keep calm and keep thinking. The
sight of the blood draining from her nose had
panicked her. She was having a hard time keeping her mind from flying off in a million different
directions.

"Oz, you awake back there?" Vanderlock said.

Oz shifted. "Yeah. Why?"

"'Cause I want you to hear this." Vanderlock
nodded at Emma. "Oz told me that you know
what we have?"

"It's anthrax after all, isn't it?" Oz said.

"I never thought it was anthrax because that's
not communicable between people. This disease
appears to be communicated by touch as well as
inhalation."

"What do you think it is, then?"

Emma paused. Oz sat up, still holding his tee
shirt to his deformed nose, but now looking at
her, a question in his eyes. Vanderlock flicked a

serious glance her way, then returned his gaze to the road.

"I think it's a derivative of leprosy."

The car jerked when Vanderlock did. "Are you kidding me?" he yelled.

Oz groaned from the backseat.

"Damn it, you'd better be right about this. Because if you're not, I'm going to kill you just for scaring the shit out of me." Vanderlock sounded as panicked as Emma felt.

"Is leprosy curable?" Oz said.

Emma inhaled. "Yes. And honestly if *all* you had was leprosy I'd be relieved, because leprosy is completely curable. Take a course of antibiotics and it's over. At least the traditional type of leprosy is. But traditional leprosy takes years to develop and this is a hell of a lot faster growing than that."

"Could you be wrong then?" A thread of hope ran through Oz's voice.

Emma shook her head. "This last look confirmed it. The bacteria appeared strange, as if mutated, but it was still closer to leprosy than anything else. Right now I'm thinking that something La Valle did with his fields, coupled with the herbicide being dumped on them, created this new form of disease."

They drove in silence for a minute. Emma stared out the window, mulling over every fact she'd ever learned about leprosy. "Now we just need to find some antibiotics to cure it. Powerful ones."

"We're driving to a hospital. Right now. Before Mono comes back," Vanderlock said.

"I agree," Emma said. She felt a pang as she thought of Raoul's hostages, but their situation was now so dire that she didn't think there was any way to salvage it and convince La Valle to let them all alone. Not anymore.

"Absolutely not," Oz replied. "No hospital."

Vanderlock looked at him in the rearview. "Why not? We know what it is. We go in there, tell them what we have, get treatment."

"And get killed by La Valle's men when they find us," Oz said. "Or, worse, give this to everyone we touch." He looked at Emma. "You know how this is spread?"

Emma shook her head. "No one really knows how leprosy is spread and this disease is behaving so differently that I don't think we can assume anything. I saw a few cases when I volunteered in India. Contact seems to be required"—Oz appeared ready to interrupt and she held up her hand—"*but* that doesn't mean we can't warn the hospital personnel in advance that we might be carrying a contagious disease. They can prepare for our arrival."

"And La Valle's men?"

"I'll call Banner. He'll send someone to protect us," Emma said.

Oz shook his head again. "I don't know who that is, but I don't want some hospital security guard getting killed by Mono."

"Banner owns Darkview, a contract security company out of Washington. He hires the best. Special forces, ex-military, sharpshooters. You don't need to worry," Vanderlock said. "He and

I don't always see things the same way, but the guy is more than a match for La Valle. I'll get on a major highway. You can still decide if this is what you want."

Oz seemed to mull the thought over.

After thirty more minutes they reached an interstate. An hour later a blue sign appeared giving notice that lodgings, gas, and a hospital were all located at the next exit.

"Go to the hospital," Oz said. Emma breathed a sigh of relief. Their ordeal was almost over.

"Any sign of Mono?" Emma said.

"Not yet," Vanderlock replied.

The sign directed them to a small community hospital on the outskirts of town. Three square buildings, each four stories high, sat in a row, connected by enclosed glass bridges on the third level. The lights glowed in the darkness, and Emma watched as a doctor in blue scrubs walked between the buildings on the bridge. Vanderlock drove into the semicircular driveway following a sign that said ER. He pulled up next to an ambulance.

"You should go in," he said to Emma. "You have the fewest symptoms."

Emma crawled out of the car and entered through the automatic glass doors that slid open with a pneumatic sigh. The waiting area was jammed with people. Adults, children, and babies all occupied the resin chairs. Emma steered away from them, acutely aware of her possibly contagious state. A nurse in blue scrubs sat in a counter area marked with an overhead "triage" sign. She typed furiously on a computer keyboard. Emma stopped three feet away, ignoring the two chairs placed in front of the station.

"Excuse me? I have an emergency. My friend is in my car and he has something that might be contagious. I'm afraid to bring him in and infect the others."

The nurse, a young, friendly-looking woman with a name badge emblazoned with NANCY WALTERS looked up from her keyboard.

"Contagious? What does he have?"

"Leprosy," Emma said. "Or something far more virulent that mimics it. I'm not sure."

Nancy stopped typing. "Leprosy? Are you kidding me?"

Emma shook her head. "I wish I was."

"Where did you say he was?"

"In the car, which is parked in your driveway."

"What's his insurance company? They may require prior authorization."

Emma shook her head. "I don't think he has any."

The nurse got up from her desk. "Wait there."

Minutes later Nancy reappeared, walking fast, this time from another direction. She wore gloves and a face mask. Behind her came a young man in a white lab coat, also with gloves on his hands. His face mask hung on a thin elastic cord around his neck. They both stopped ten feet short of Emma.

"I'm Doctor Emmanuel. You said you have a man in the car with leprosy? That's not an emergency. All you need to do is set up an appointment with a specialist and get some antibiotics."

"It's not exactly leprosy, but a virulent mutation of the disease with fast-growing symptoms that mimic it. Possibly contagious."

"Do you have it?"

Emma nodded. "I think I'm in the early stages."

The doctor put on his face mask. "You need to go to another hospital. We're not set up for hazardous diseases. Our ICU is small, and it's full right now."

"How far is the next hospital?"

He named a medium-sized city in Kansas. "Four hundred miles away."

Emma gaped at him. "Four hundred? Are you joking? He'll die by then."

The doctor put his palms out. "I'm sorry. I'm new. It's July and I just rotated in as a resident. The attending is on vacation, but I called him and he told me to send you to a teaching hospital. He said we don't do highly contagious diseases here. We transfer them."

"That's patient dumping. Someone appears in the emergency room you have to stabilize them before transfer."

He shook his head. "Not if we don't admit them in the first place."

Emma wanted to hit the man. Only the fact that she would infect him as well kept her from doing so. She curled her hands into fists.

"Can you at least get me some antibiotics for traditional leprosy? There are three that work." Emma named them. "Perhaps they'll slow his progress."

The young doctor shook his head. "I'm not supposed to write a prescription without a full workup on a patient. Besides, if this isn't leprosy then the antibiotics won't work."

"Listen to me. He's in a bad way. He'll die. Please."

The doctor still hesitated.

"I'll give you some samples," Nancy said. "Don't go anywhere." She jogged off, back down the hall.

Emma turned back to the doctor. "I need to use your phone."

He shook his head. "You shouldn't touch anything. The attending said to get you out of here. He said if you touch anything the entire hospital will have to run a sterile protocol. We'll have to close. We'll lose days. He said you *have* to leave."

Emma felt her frustration growing. "Then you make the call for me. It's the least you can do. His name is Banner. You need to tell him that Emma was here, that there's a shipment of marijuana crossing the country that is infected with this disease as well, and that he has to stop it. Do you understand me?" She rattled off Banner's number. The resident made no move to copy it down.

"If I report you were here we'll have to close."

Emma took a step toward him, and he took two rapid steps back. "You're a mandatory reporter. I come in here talking about an infectious disease, you damn well better report it." Nancy came jogging down the hall again, a paper bag in her hand. She stopped well clear of Emma, bent down, and slid the bag to her across the floor.

"I got you samples of rifampicin and clofazi-

mine. We didn't have any dapsone, I'm sorry."
Emma opened the bag. Four individual bubble
packs of each drug filled it. The few pills were a
joke, even Emma knew that it wasn't enough to
save Oz, given his advanced condition. Still, she
was grateful to Nancy.

"Thank you," she said. "Can you call a friend
for me?"

Dr. Emmanuel waved her off. "She can't call
anyone. Use your own cell phone outside the
hospital. You have to *leave*."

Nancy nodded her agreement, a sad look on her
face. "I wish you luck. Get him to St. Jude's. They
can help."

Emma turned and stormed out the hospital.
A child ran in front of her and stopped, staring.
Emma slowed, took great pains to avoid him, and
jogged out the door.

39

"WHAT ABOUT THE SHIPMENT? YOU'RE TELLING me La Valle is spreading leprosy?" Oz said in an agitated voice. Emma had recounted the dismal experience in the hospital to both Oz and Vanderlock.

"I'll handle stopping the shipment," Emma said. Oz gave her a dubious look, and Vanderlock gave her a serious one. She handed him the antibiotic samples.

"Take one of each. Maybe they'll slow the progress, buy us some time. You want some?" Emma's last question was directed at Vanderlock. He shook his head.

"Let Oz have them. He's in worse shape." Vanderlock showed his hand to Emma. The sores covered the entire palm and last three fingers. She lifted the tote so both Oz and Vanderlock could see it.

"I've got a bag full of drugs here. All of which treat rare diseases. If there's even one investigational antibiotic, we're going to take it."

"And if not?"

"Then we go to a teaching hospital. To a specialist."

Vanderlock drove on. "You think the traditional treatment won't work?"

"This thing isn't acting like traditional leprosy. There is a resistant strain, though. At least there was when I was dealing with this in India. Several patients came in with it. The ones with the nosebleeds often had the resistant form."

"Okay, we try the new stuff too." Vanderlock was back to his calm self. Emma could hear a slight strain in his voice, but nothing like the shocked reaction he'd just had. "We need to disable the tracking device in order to do this right, without the fear that Mono will come breathing down our necks again, and we need a place to hole up for at least a day."

Oz shifted. "I don't think we should waste time trying to locate and disarm the tracker. They can be hidden anywhere in the car and it would take me the better part of a day to find it. You said it's a radio transmitter?"

Vanderlock considered the question. "I'm pretty sure it is. Not GPS. More like those systems you can buy to recover your car if it's stolen."

"So we need to attenuate the signal," Oz said. Emma raised an eyebrow in a question at him. "Attenuate means to block it. The quick answer is that radio signals hit a certain frequency and travel at the speed of light. Certain materials are 'dielectric,' or excellent at blocking waves. Wood isn't, that's why you can play a radio in your house made of it. Metal has a high attenuation coefficient."

Vanderlock looked at Oz in the rearview mirror. "What did you do before signing on as a mule for La Valle?"

"I was a student at MIT, but dropped out."

"Not the brightest move for an obviously bright guy," Vanderlock said. "Why'd you quit?"

"I followed a woman," Oz said.

Vanderlock nodded. "Now *that* I understand."

"Back to the radio waves," Emma said.

"Without knowing what frequency the tracker's using, I think we'll need to cover the entire car with metal." Emma watched as they drove past a field with a barn in the distance. A thought came to her.

"We're in farm country. Would a chicken coop do it? Surround the car with chicken wire? That's metal, right?"

Oz looked dubious. "It's metal, that's true, but depending on the frequency, the waves could get through the openings in the wire. Better to drive the car into one of those metal sheds you see people use to store their lawn equipment."

"Would be a bit tough to pull up to any old house and ask to park the car in their shiny new shed from Sears," Vanderlock said.

"Following up on your chicken-coop idea, metal-screening material would work. The holes are smaller, dense," Oz said.

"They have rolls of the stuff at every home-improvement store I've ever been to," Emma said.

Vanderlock turned onto a main road. "We'll

buy some at the next one we see. Then let's ask around for an out-of-the-way motel. These small towns have tons of them."

Oz kept low in the car as they approached a larger town. His face appeared almost grotesque. The last thing Emma needed was to attract more notice than they would already.

"Did you know there's blood on your hip? That yours?" Vanderlock said. Emma looked at her pants in surprise. A blood stain, half dried, covered her hip. She touched the skin through the material and felt a wound. She probed it with her fingers. It hurt to the touch, but remained soft. She couldn't feel any metal bullet or piece of shrapnel.

"Mono must have nicked me."

Vanderlock pulled up to yet another Walmart. "Did Sam Walton own the Midwest? These stores are everywhere."

"Maybe not the Midwest, but definitely the South," Emma said.

Emma and Vanderlock entered the store and immediately split up. Vanderlock was in charge of purchasing the screening, Emma food, water, and bandages. She passed a display of faded Levi's and picked up a pair of 501s in her size, doing her best to hold them at her side to cover her own shredded, bloodstained pants. She bought a new shirt, underwear, socks, snatched a baseball cap from a display and also picked up two prepaid cell phones. She hooked up with Vanderlock at the cash register. He put a black tee shirt on the conveyor belt.

"It's for Oz. His is covered in blood." Oz didn't move while they loaded their purchases in the car. He lay in the back, taking short, shallow breaths. "He's falling apart," Vanderlock said in low tones.

"Did you find a motel?"

Vanderlock nodded. "Creek's View. Three miles west, by a local creek. Family owned."

Creek's View consisted of a series of log cabins that stretched into a wooded area lined by a creek. Emma and Vanderlock stepped inside to check in, leaving Oz in the car. The motel office was the smallest cabin and first in the row. A tired-looking woman with faded red hair and rheumy blue eyes smoked a cigarette and watched a soap opera on a small television placed on the counter behind which she sat. Next to the television sat an open register book and a pen. The rest of the single room contained an empty stone fireplace with cobwebs spanning the corner and a wooden trunk used as a cocktail table was placed in front of two armchairs covered in a worn paisley print. A cat was curled up in one chair. It opened an eye to check on them.

"My wife and I would like two rooms," Vanderlock said.

The woman gave Vanderlock a disinterested look. "Why two?"

"She won't let me smoke in hers."

The woman emitted a sharp cackle. "Why not just smoke outside?"

Vanderlock jerked his chin at the woman's cigarette. "I like to smoke in comfort."

The woman rose and pulled the register in front
of Vanderlock. "Sign in." She handed him a pen.
He reached for a separate one lying on the counter. Emma watched him write, "Mr. and Mrs.
Wilson Vanderlock" on the line. He tapped it and
gave Emma a grin.

"Newlyweds," he said to the woman, who just
snorted.

"What's the creek's name?" Emma asked.

"Creek," the woman said.

"Inventive," Emma replied. The woman didn't
respond. She reached behind her and pulled two
keys that hung from hooks on a peg board.

"Do they have telephones?"

The woman shook her head. "No phones, but
your cell should get a signal. No Internet. Take the
two cabins on the end. Last one's a smoking cabin."

"I appreciate that," Vanderlock said. The woman
returned to watching her soap opera, ignoring
them.

"How's it feel to be married?" Vanderlock said
once they were back outside.

"I was surprised you didn't draw a little heart
over the *i* in *Wilson*."

"Smart aleck," Vanderlock said, humor in his
voice. He shook a cigarette out of a pack and
flicked on his lighter. He lit it, taking a deep drag.
They climbed back into the car. Oz still hadn't
moved. His eyes remained closed.

"Let's move. He needs some more medication
fast," Emma said. They drove to the first cabin.

"Can you walk?" Emma asked Oz. He opened
his eyes halfway.

"Not sure. Can Lock help?"

Vanderlock pulled Oz out of the car, wrapped one of his arms over his shoulder, and helped him to the nearest cabin. The interior smelled dusty, as if the room hadn't been aired in a while. A patchwork quilt covered a queen-sized bed and a white lace doily covered the nearby nightstand. Vanderlock lowered Oz to the bed while Emma checked the washroom. It contained a small sink, toilet, and stand-up shower.

Emma sat at a small table placed against a window and surrounded by two wooden chairs. She dumped the contents of the tote and began sifting through the medicine.

"I'll unload the car and cover it with the mesh," Vanderlock said. Emma nodded, not turning her focus from the myriad bottles and pills before her.

The majority of the stolen compounds contained substances that were unfamiliar to her. A couple of the bottles included not only a name, but a suggested use, and none of these were antibiotics.

Eight bottles contained well-known antibiotics found in any pharmacy, including penicillin, and two were broad spectrum and guaranteed to knock any bug out with one punch, but not known to cure leprosy. One bottle contained a powerful antibiotic combined with a second, investigational, one.

"Here, take these." Emma handed Oz two more pills from the samples and one of the new investigational drugs. He swallowed them down without hesitation and followed them with a

swig of water. "I'm giving you a bit of the traditional treatment, but there's a new drug thrown
in there. I don't know about drug interactions,
though."

Oz waved her off. "I don't care. Let's just see
what happens." He closed his eyes again.

She watched him for a few minutes. He fell into
a deep sleep, and she slipped outside.

She stopped a moment on the cabin's front
porch. Crickets scratched, an owl hooted, and a
breeze rustled through the trees. Insects bounced
around a light at the top of a six-foot-high pole at
the end of the circular drive. The cool night air
felt good. She glanced at the spray of stars overhead.

She found Vanderlock and the Caliber a few
feet into the trees on a path that ran from the
cul de sac-shaped driveway. He was engrossed in
unrolling the last of the mesh screen over the car.
He'd run it from front to back and was putting
more over from side to side. He'd taken care to
park the car facing out.

"Considering a quick getaway? No need to turn
around first?" Emma said.

"Can't be too sure. Who knows if this will work."

Emma noticed that he'd bought work gloves to
cover his hands. The rest of their purchases lay
on the ground in front of the last cabin. Emma
grabbed the bag and carried it inside, dumping
most of it on one of the two double beds. This
cabin was larger, with a small kitchenette area.
She separated out the microwave soup and other
food along with the bottles of water and placed

those on the kitchen counter. When she opened the refrigerator to store the bottles of water she found the jug of white lightning already occupying the main shelf. She added the assorted bottles of medicine.

She assembled the prepaid phones, set them on their respective chargers and plugged them into a socket on the wall next to a well-worn toaster oven.

She'd purchased toiletries, toothbrushes, a comb, and shampoo, and these last items she carried with her into the bathroom. A flick of the knobs got the shower started and while the water heated she began to peel the cloth away from the wound on her hip. The oozing red gash hurt, but wasn't deep and not infected. She stepped into the shower and sighed when the hot water hit her back.

Twenty minutes later she emerged from the bathroom wearing the new clothes and bumped right into Vanderlock, who stood in front of the door.

"I thought you'd never finish," he said. He didn't move, remaining a few inches from her. He held a cup of the microwave soup in one hand and a spoon in the other. Emma noticed that he'd kept a glove on the affected one. The smell of hot chicken broth wafted toward her, making her mouth water.

"God, that smells great," she said.

"Have some. I haven't touched it yet." He filled the spoon and held it out to her, bringing it close, sliding it into her mouth. She swallowed the warm liquid, all the while watching him. He paused, his face inches from hers, holding her gaze. He was so close that Emma saw the flecks of gold in his eyes. He smelled of an appealing combination of whiskey and cigarettes and sweat. Emma took a small step toward him, and his look sharpened.

"Your turn," she said, and pointed to the shower.

He gave a nod, but didn't move out of her way and continued to look at her, saying nothing. Emma felt the tension between them rise.

"I'm clearly infected, but you don't have any sores yet?" he said.

"No."

"I shouldn't touch you, then."

Emma inhaled. "That's safest."

He gave her a small smile.

"I'll just take this," Emma said. She reached out and removed the soup from his hand. When she looked up again his face held an amused expression. He moved past her with only inches to spare, keeping his eyes on her the entire time. She gazed back and stayed still. He went into the bathroom and closed the door behind him.

Emma exhaled before walking into the kitchen area. Within minutes she heard the shower kick on again. She finished the soup standing at the sink and in record time, and tossed the carton in the garbage. Exhaustion clawed at her. She set the alarm on her running watch to wake her in two hours and fell onto one of the beds to sleep. Later, she emerged from her sleep state long enough to hear the microwave beep as Vanderlock made another bowl of soup for himself.

Just before closing her eyes she felt a line of blood run from her nose, across her cheek, and into her ear. She grabbed a tissue from the night table and wiped it away.

40

EMMA WOKE TO THE SOUND, NOT OF HER ALARM, but of pounding on the door. She flicked on the nightstand light, and looked at the other bed. Vanderlock sat on the edge of the mattress, checking the gun. She moved to the door and waved a silent "wait" signal to him. He nodded and slipped to her right, getting in line with the door as it opened. He knelt down and aimed. She looked through the peephole.

Three uniform police officers stood on the deck. The one in the lead was the pounder, the two standing behind him were in the same general position as Vanderlock, with guns drawn and prepared to fire.

"Police," Emma whispered. Vanderlock lowered his gun.

"Don't let them in, we'll infect them," he said.

"I don't see that we have much choice."

Another pounding came at the door.

Vanderlock jerked his head at the window in

the kitchenette's wall. "Check the window. Are they in the back?"

Emma tiptoed her way to the opposite end of the cabin, pressed herself against the wall, and peered through the glass.

"Nothing here that I can see." She put her hands on the sash to raise it. Another pounding.

"Police! Your car is being towed. Better get out here and stop it."

Vanderlock joined her at the window. "That means they took off the mesh," he said.

"Perfect. Mono can start chasing the police impound vehicle and leave us alone," Emma whispered back. "I'll talk to them. We have a much better chance of stopping the shipment with their help. You want to leave, you go. I won't tell anyone you were here." The old wooden window stuck. Emma strained to open it. It jerked in the tracks, but moved upward about two feet. She applied herself to removing the screen, pulling the stops and lowering it to the ground. "Time to go," she said.

Mono and Raoul appeared on the rear lawn, thirty feet from the cabin, standing in a half shadow. Mono raised his gun and fired.

The bullet passed through the open window, crossed the room, and punched through the front door. Emma heard a man's cry as the bullet hit him. She grabbed Vanderlock, dragging him to the floor with her. A hail of answering shots hammered through the pressed wood panel.

Emma crawled over Vanderlock, covering him

with her body, wrapping an arm around his head and putting her face against his hair. Bullets flew above her back. She rolled off him and pushed him toward the bathroom, crawling in that direction. Vanderlock lay flat on his stomach, watching the front door. The room quieted. She made it to the bathroom entrance and hovered there.

"We've got to get out of here," she said in low tones to Vanderlock. "Forget the front. If an officer's down they're going to fire first and ask questions later."

Vanderlock nodded. He rose slowly, keeping well away from the window, pointed his gun out the back, and squeezed off two shots. He dropped once again and the firing started from the front door. Emma curled up on the bathroom floor. The moment the shooting stopped Vanderlock crab-walked to the window.

"Mono's gone. Out the window," he said. He threw a leg over the sill, bent his frame in half and slid out. Emma scrambled up and clambered over the sill behind him, dropping onto the ground below. She crouched against the back wall. The lawn appeared empty, but in the dark of the night it was hard to see anything. The weak light thrown by the moon didn't do much to illuminate the area. She thought the worst part would be racing across it without cover. Vanderlock didn't hesitate, and she didn't either. She sprinted the distance, moving as fast as she could. She plunged into the woods and ran toward the creek. From behind came a volley of shots, along with answering fire. When she hit the creek she turned right, jogging alongside it. Vanderlock stayed with her, moving fast. She cut back around the first cabin to the front, sliding up to a tree trunk. Vanderlock came up behind her, leaned against her, and looked in the same direction.

Mono and Raoul stood over the bodies of two of the police officers in the cul de sac drive. The black BMW was there, its headlights on and the engine running. Both police moved slightly, but neither was conscious. Raoul, his arms a mass of sores, chambered a bullet into the gun in his hand.

Vanderlock took aim, his arm extending out next to her shoulder as he did. She heard a sharp intake of breath and he froze. When she turned her head she saw Carlos standing behind them both. She watched as Vanderlock removed his finger from the trigger, clicked a safety in place, and handed back the revolver. Carlos reached around them both to claim it.

"Move away from her." La Valle spoke from behind Emma. Vanderlock stepped away and a metal gun tip rammed into Emma's spine. She felt La Valle frisk her.

"Give me your cell phone," he said.

"You know I don't have one. You just frisked me."

"Serena's dead," La Valle said. Emma briefly closed eyes, unable to believe that she'd come this far only to end up in the exact same position she was in when she started. "Walk over to

Raoul." Emma started forward. Vanderlock and Carlos moved in unison with her. She stopped five feet from Raoul.

His condition, though not as dire as Oz's, was much worse than the last time she'd seen him. He looked at her with wild eyes filled with fear, anger, and a hint of madness. La Valle stepped around to face her, and Emma gasped.

Sores covered his arms, disappearing under the short sleeves of the shirt he wore and creeping up to cover his neck. Three quarter-sized masses covered his right cheek.

"I can cure you," Emma said.

La Valle shot her a look full of hate. "Like you cured Serena? Where's the computer guy?"

"Dead," Emma said.

"Like you cured him?"

"He died before I knew what he had."

"What is it?" La Valle said.

"A virulent mutation of leprosy."

La Valle swung the hand that held the gun and smacked the back of it across her face. Emma's cheek vibrated with the hit, pain exploded across her cheek and she stumbled sideways.

"Liar!" La Valle's face turned red with the force of his scream. The cords on his neck stood up, causing the sores there to undulate. Raoul spit on the ground, his eyes glinting with an ever-increasing frenzy. Carlos took a step back, as did Mono. Both looked repulsed and petrified in equal measure.

Emma fixed La Valle with a stare. "I have pills to cure it in the cabin. Let me go get them."

La Valle hit her again. This time she tasted blood. She'd bitten the inside of her cheek.

In the distance came the sound of sirens.

"Get in the car," La Valle said to Mono.

"Let me get the pills," Emma said. La Valle gave her a massive shove, and she stumbled forward, but managed to keep her feet under her.

"Move."

Emma jogged past the unconscious police officers and stepped onto the porch. There she found the body of the third. Blood pooled around his torso from a still bleeding neck wound that had nicked his artery. Emma stepped over him to the splintered door and pushed it open. La Valle hovered in the entrance behind her, keeping a watch outside as well as on her. She went to the refrigerator, where she'd stored some of the more perishable antibiotics. They were worthless against leprosy and probably even less than worthless against this new strain, but she pulled them out and pretended to read the labels.

"Hurry up," La Valle said.

She placed the bottles on the counter, and used her body to block La Valle's view. She reached up and removed one of the charging cell phones from its base. She busied herself with the bottles with one hand while she pocketed the phone. She jogged back toward La Valle, grabbing the tote filled with pills on her way out. La Valle shoved her forward, toward the BMW. The trunk gaped wide and as she neared she saw that Vanderlock was already there, his body filling the small space. The siren noises grew louder.

"Get in!" La Valle pushed her. Vanderlock moved deeper inside. She climbed in next to him, arranging herself so that they could both fit, spoon fashion. La Valle slammed the trunk closed and darkness descended.

41

BANNER PICKED UP HIS CELL PHONE THAT LAY NEXT to him in his hotel room in Kansas City.

"Banner here," he said.

"This is Oswald Kroger. I need your help."

Banner put down the communique he was reading.

"Is Emma Caldridge with you?"

"No. La Valle abducted her and Lock."

"Lock?"

"Wilson Vanderlock."

Now Banner was on his feet. "*Wilson Vanderlock*? What's he doing in the United States?"

"Listen, I don't have a lot of time. They said you're a match for La Valle. You have to stop the shipment."

"What type of shipment?"

"Marijuana. It's tainted."

"With what?" Banner said.

"Leprosy. Emma called it nontraditional, mutated, and highly contagious."

Banner prided himself on his cool, but the

word "leprosy" activated some ancient, atavistic memory that made the hair on his arms stand on end.

"You sure about this, Mr. Kroger? Because we had some marijuana we found in an airplane tested, and preliminary results from the CDC are leaning toward a virulent form of a fungal infection."

"I'm sure of *her*. She says it's a leprosy mutation, I believe her. La Valle has three tons of the leaves stashed in a storage area somewhere on his usual route between Texas and Kansas. He's preparing to ship it to D.C. and arrange for it to be found by the authorities. He hopes to infect everyone. You need to stop it."

"Where are you?"

"I'm irrelevant. She gave me some pills that she stole. Investigational. I'm still very, very sick, but not dead yet, so that's a plus. My only goal is to stop that shipment before I die."

"Do you know how far along the route it is?"

"Perhaps Kansas by now. La Valle's driving a BMW with some hidden in a false dash, there's a fake ambulance with more, and the rest filled half a semi truck."

And an airplane flown by Vanderlock, Banner thought. He kept this to himself while he jotted down everything Kroger said.

"He's planning a meeting with the heads of all the major Midwestern gangs that distribute his goods. He's going to have them move the shipment, infect them all, then a Chicago crew will take over distribution."

"Any idea where they're stashing her and Vanderlock?"

"There won't be any stashing. They'll kill them both. Last I saw them they were stuffed in the trunk of La Valle's BMW."

"Alive?"

"Yes. I can't tell you where they took her, and I won't be able to help you further. I'm contagious, and I'll be damned if I'll curse anyone else with this disease. I'm going to hole up and take these pills until I die. Here's where I saw them last." Kroger gave Banner the directions to the Creek's View Motel.

Banner rang off and headed out the door.

EMMA SHIFTED so that she could reach the cell phone in her pocket. The trunk's stale air was hot, and the heat from both hers and Vanderlock's body made it rise even more. They could hear Mono, Raoul, and La Valle's voices through the trunk walls.

"You all right?" Vanderlock whispered in her ear.

"I'm okay. I grabbed one of the phones." She pulled it out of her pocket, stabbing Vanderlock in the stomach with her elbow in the process. She dialed Sumner's cell number. It rolled into voice mail, and after the beep she said, "Sumner, it's me. Track this signal, I'll leave the phone on, but be careful, wherever I end up will be loaded with gang members." She got no further. The car stopped, and she returned the phone to her pocket and rearranged herself once again. She heard the crunching sound of shoes on gravel, and the trunk lid flew up. Mono stood before them.

"Get out," he said. Emma unfolded from the tight position to maneuver out of the trunk. Vanderlock followed at a considerably slower pace. They stood in front of a large barn. Mono pushed at her. "Move. Go inside."

She walked through the wide open doors into a cavernous area lit by three overhead lights that hung six feet down on cords. Stacks of marijuana bales filled one half of the chamber, the ambulance occupied the other half. On one wall a long worktable with benches held all the ingredients to make meth, along with a jumble of tools, a blue-canister blowtorch, a couple of stick lighters, and twine. A gasoline can sat on the ground next to some automotive parts. Mono opened the back of the ambulance and jerked his chin at it. Emma climbed in, noting that Oz's motorcycle was still strapped against one wall. Vanderlock moved in behind her. La Valle walked up to the entrance, holding the tote.

"Which ones?" he said.

Emma passed over the investigational pills in the tote. Instead she sifted through the pile and took out one of the broad-spectrum antibiotics. She handed the bottle to La Valle and took the tote back.

"One every three hours to start, then one every four hours."

La Valle snatched the container out of her hand.

He stalked away, and Mono slammed the doors closed. Emma heard the padlock being placed on the handle. She pulled the phone out, lit the screen, and checked the signal.

"No reception in here," she said. She swallowed, hard. She could only hope that Sumner would have had enough time to track a portion of the trip to the barn.

She couldn't see Vanderlock in the dark, but she started to feel for him. She encountered his hand, the one covered with the glove. She ran her palm up his arm and located his face. She stroked the side of his cheek and felt the stubble. He was sitting on the side of the ambulance, his back up against the wall and his legs stretched out in front of him.

"How are you feeling?" she said.

She felt his shoulders move in a shrug. "Not great, but not as weak as Oz."

She tapped the cell phone's screen to light it and fished the investigational antibiotic out of the tote.

"Take this." She opened the bottle and shook out two pills. The cell phone went dark and she reached out to him again, this time running her hand down his side to locate his free hand. She picked it up and placed the pills in his palm.

"Is there a way out of this ambulance?" Vanderlock said.

"Not that I can recall. I've been in this thing so many times over the last days that I must have explored every inch. The padlock Mono is using isn't very large, though. Between the two of us perhaps we could kick the doors open. Given enough time and no interruptions, that is."

"They'd have to leave us alone for that to work."

"La Valle's goal is to get this shipment east. We're bound to hit the highway again once the sun comes up. I imagine they're going to sleep at some point this evening. They have to."

"They'll leave a sentry, though. I would."

"Carlos," Emma said.

"Yep."

"He's mean, but I think he can be manipulated."

Vanderlock snorted. "Only after La Valle is dead. The guy leads by fear and Carlos is way too low in the organization to fight him."

"Maybe when they pull the ambulance out of the barn the phone will get a signal again. They can't mean to leave it here forever. They have to get it to the next stop on the delivery route."

Vanderlock fell silent. She rearranged herself to sit next to him, her back against the wall and her shoulder touching his. She dozed in the darkness, waking only when he shook her.

"Listen," he said.

She heard the sound of voices raised in a heated argument. The conversation was held in rapid-fire Spanish.

"You speak Spanish?" Vanderlock said.

Emma shrugged, then realized that he couldn't see her. "A little. I've been using a computer program. So far I can grocery shop, travel, and ask directions. I have no idea what they're arguing about." She moved closer to the door. One word was repeated twice: *leproso*.

"I think it's Mono and Carlos. They're talking about leprosy," she told him. The padlock rattled against the handles. The doors swung open, and Mono stood alongside Carlos. He pointed a gun at her.

"You said the shipment has leprosy. Is this true?" Mono said.

Emma nodded. Mono looked at the bales and bricks stacked all around them, the fear on his face almost palpable.

"Is it in the air?"

Emma hesitated. She was more than willing to say it was if it meant getting out of the ambulance. She sidled close to the open door, hoping that the cell phone in her pocket would regain its signal. She weighed the options of lying or not and what Mono would do either way.

"I don't know for sure. Why?"

Mono translated the statement for Carlos. "You think we need the pills?"

Emma was starting to see the light. Mono wanted to steal the pills from La Valle to save his own skin.

"I think you do."

Mono waved at the tote. She pretended to look inside, then shrugged. "La Valle has the good ones. You'll need to get them from him," she said.

Mono grabbed the bag from her, tossed it on the ground and waved her out of the ambulance. "You come with me. We'll steal them from a pharmacy." Vanderlock came alongside. Mono pointed the gun directly at Vanderlock's fore-head. "Not you. You stay here."

Vanderlock subsided. Emma shot him what she hoped was a reassuring look before jumping down onto the floor.

"Why not just take some of La Valle's?" Emma said. Mono frowned, and to her surprise, it was Carlos who answered.

"He no give," he said. His face reflected a mulish anger that came through loud and clear in his broken English. Emma drove the wedge in deeper.

"I would think he'd want to protect his best two men."

Mono frowned. "Shut up."

Carlos directed a long string of Spanish at Mono, whose own face displayed a progressively deepening rage.

"I just want to warn you. I stole those pills from the last lab. You know the one, Mono, where you chased me. There's no guarantee that a regular pharmacy will stock the same ones that La Valle is taking."

Carlos hit Mono on the arm and gestured for him to translate. Mono did, and Carlos spit out some more incomprehensible Spanish.

La Valle and Raoul walked into the barn, both holding weapons in one hand, and between them they each held the handles of a cooler, about three feet long. They strode to the long table and placed the cooler on the ground next to it. La Valle lev-eled a stare at Mono.

"You ready for some fun?" La Valle said to Emma. She didn't think she'd ever heard a voice as filled with menace as she did at that instant. Mono blanched and Carlos got a terrified expression on his face as he glanced at the cooler.

"Get the pilot," he said. Mono shot Carlos a look, but did as he was told. He opened the ambulance doors and waved Vanderlock out. Emma stared at the cooler along with Carlos, and a horrible thought started to worm into her brain. The blood rushed to her head, and she inhaled, taking deep breaths to counteract the dizziness. Vanderlock moved next to her. He hadn't yet spotted the cooler, and so threw her a quizzical glance. She held it, doing her best to tear her eyes off the scene in front of her. If she could spare him even one minute of the realization of what La Valle intended to do, she would.

"Tie him up," La Valle said.

Mono moved toward Vanderlock. He put his gun in his waistband and yanked at Vanderlock's wrists, tying them in front with the same twine that was on the long table. Mono jerked the rope. Vanderlock grimaced. Mono tightened it more. Vanderlock's eyes never left Emma's face. It was as if he was memorizing her features. She stared right back, willing him not to look away. Not to see the cooler. She gritted her teeth and the thought came to her, unbidden, that it just might be her day to die. La Valle walked over to the table and swept his hand across it. Empty liter bottles, wrenches, the blowtorch and lighters flew off the top, landing on the beaten earth floor with thuds.

"Lay him down. On his back." Mono shoved Vanderlock toward the table. He broke off staring at Emma and looked La Valle's way. "Bring her with him. I want her to watch."

Carlos pushed her alongside Vanderlock. Mono shoved Vanderlock backward until he was forced to crawl onto the tabletop. As he scooted onto it he looked down and saw the cooler.

His breath came out in a huff, as if someone had punched him in the gut. Mono shoved him back and Raoul tied his ankles together while Mono hauled his hands above his head, stretching him out. La Valle turned to Emma, his eyes glittering with excitement. Vanderlock swallowed once, and then turned his face to Emma, once again holding her gaze. His jaw clenched, as though he was doing his best not to make a sound, but his throat convulsed as if a scream was trying to break through.

He knows, Emma thought.

"You know what a liver sells for on the black market?" La Valle said. "I'll take that first. His heart will still beat. The kidneys are next. The heart last." He lifted the weapon in his hand, a wicked-looking knife that curved upward at the tip. "Bring her closer," he said. Carlos shoved a hand against her spine. Her foot hit the blowtorch canister.

"I'm going to faint." Emma infused her voice with panic, which wasn't difficult, because she was so frightened that she thought she would vomit. She rolled her eyes upward, pretending to faint. She dropped her legs, moving straight down. At the bottom her hand hit the cannister.

She wrapped her fingers around it and knelt on her knees, pretending that she was going to face plant on the earth. She moaned, but collected one of the lighters with another hand. She flicked on the blowtorch, snapped the lighter to life, and hit the nozzle with the fire.

A line of flame, a full eighteen inches, shot out from the metal tube. Emma ran it across Carlos's legs on her way to grab a nearby brick. He yelped and jumped. She had the leaves in her hand and was up, backing away, holding the torch before any of the men had moved. They'd all stashed their guns while they held Vanderlock in place, but the moment they released him to draw their weapons he kicked out with his feet, catching Raoul in the stomach with the heel of his boot. He swung his tied hands down and hit Mono under the jaw. Emma heard the man's teeth clack together with the hit. Vanderlock rolled off the table on the side away from La Valle and scuttled away, moving into the shipment bales.

Emma held the blowtorch and brick in the air. "Everybody freeze or I set the shipment on fire. You all know what happens when you inhale the smoke." The men froze in place, but Emma didn't. She walked backward, stopping next to Carlos, who reared away from the blowtorch and the tainted brick. Emma held the leaves out in front of her and kept the flame within inches of them. The only sound in the room was the roaring of the blowtorch.

"I don't care, I'm a dead man anyway," Raoul said, and he raised his weapon.

A side door creaked open and Sumner walked into the light, holding an automatic weapon. He fired, the noise assailing Emma's ears and making her wince. A bullet hole formed on Raoul's forehead, dead center. Sumner shot Mono next. He dropped into a crumpled heap. La Valle dove between the shipment bales. Sumner's shot entered one and bits of leaves and twigs flew into the air. La Valle made it to the back door, using the bales as cover and was gone. Emma put the blowtorch on Carlos's wrist, forcing him to drop the gun that he was poised to fire at Sumner. He screamed and dropped the weapon. Emma kicked it out of his reach.

"Get down on your stomach. Now!" Emma said. Carlos lowered himself to the ground, face-first. He put his hands up in surrender. Vanderlock regained his feet, standing twenty feet to Sumner's right. Sumner swung the gun in his direction.

"Don't shoot him!" Emma said.

Sumner paused. He lifted his head to look at Vanderlock. "You're the cartel pilot."

Vanderlock nodded slowly.

"He helped me. Don't shoot him, and don't get near him either," Emma said. The look in Sumner's eyes was unlike any she'd seen on him before. Always a determined man, he now seemed like granite, willing to do whatever it took to get his way.

"You okay?" Sumner called to Emma. His voice was remarkably normal in light of the fire in his eyes. "Anyone else in here?"

"No, but don't touch the leaves. They're tainted, and so am I."

Sumner walked toward her, moving carefully around the shipment bales, keeping his weapon high. "Tainted with what?"

"A mutated strain of leprosy," Emma said.

Sumner's eyebrows flew up, but he kept walking toward her. "You sure no one else is in here?"

Emma nodded. She took three steps back. "Sumner, I told you, I have it. It's contagious and may not be curable. Don't come any closer."

Sumner kept coming on, still holding the weapon high.

She danced back farther. He kept walking forward.

"Damn it, Sumner, *stop.*"

Her back hit the side of the ambulance. Before she could get out of his way he was in front of her. He lowered the gun and pulled her to him with his free hand. He bent his head down and brushed her lips with his.

Emma closed her eyes, wanting to weep. "You're an idiot," she said. He pulled away a fraction.

"We have a problem," he said.

She took a shaky breath. "We do now."

He shook his head. "Not the leprosy. The gangs. This barn is surrounded by La Valle's men. I managed to slip in before they formed up, but now we've got to decide how to get out of here."

42

BANNER RODE IN A CHARTERED HELICOPTER OVER
dark Kansas fields. The hired pilot yawned, which
was not surprising as it was three o'clock in the
morning and Banner had hauled the man out of
a warm bed. The pilot pointed below.

"That cluster of cabins is your motel. The police
tell me I can put down over there." The pilot
pointed to an empty lot nearby.

When they were down, Banner jumped out
and jogged to the cluster of police, FBI, and ATF
personnel that milled around the front of the last
cabin in the row. When Banner got closer, he saw
the outline of a body in yellow tape on the deck
in front of a door nearly blown apart from mul-
tiple bullet holes. He looked around for Kroger,
but couldn't see anyone that fit his description.

A slender man with salt-and-pepper hair wearing blue pants and a navy tee shirt emblazoned
with the letters FBI strolled over.

"You Banner?" He held out his hand. "I'm

Agent Roland. Thanks for the Kroger lead, but near as we can tell he never checked in."

"He around here?"

Roland scratched his cheek, where a five-o'clock shadow was heading into its second day. "Nope. Hotel owner said only people who checked in was some slick guy named Wilson Vanderlock and his wife."

Banner couldn't think of a more apt description of Vanderlock than slick. "Hotel owner spoke to him, did she?"

Roland nodded. "Want to see her?"

"Lead the way."

Banner followed Roland into the hotel office. FBI agents filled the small space. Roland shoved through the crowd and stepped up to a woman sitting on a chair, her hand on the back of a cat that sat in her lap. The woman looked him up and down.

"This is Mr. Banner. He's going to ask you some questions about the slick guy and his wife," Roland said. The woman just nodded.

"They check in alone? Was there no one else with them?"

The woman shook her head. "Was just them. He signed for two rooms. Said his wife didn't like him smoking in hers. I knew they weren't married, though."

"How did you know that?"

"He was too slick and sure of himself. Good-looking and knew it. A real cowboy. And she just stood next to him and let him do all the talking. A wife woulda' said something. Put her two cents in."

Banner was amused at the woman's observation of married life. "You think?"

"I *know*. You're not married, or you'd know, too."

"You're right. I'm not married. Guess I'll find out."

The woman cackled. "Yes, you will."

Banner asked her to describe the woman. She gave an accurate description of Emma Caldridge.

He headed back out, not sure what to do next, which, he thought, was probably for the best since he lacked the jurisdiction to make any real decisions. Banner's cell phone started to vibrate. He pulled it from his pocket and saw "Sumner" displayed on the screen. He punched the button and glanced up while he put the phone to his ear.

"I need backup. I'm in a barn in Kansas that's surrounded by La Valle and his cartel buddies."

"Give me coordinates. You alone?"

"No. Caldridge is here, and the cartel pilot. He might be on our side. Caldridge vouched for him."

"His name is Wilson Vanderlock, and I've never known him to work for the cartels. I'd take Caldridge's word on that."

"I already have." Sumner rattled off the coordinates.

"Stay put. I'll be in touch."

Banner waved Agent Roland to him. "I got a guy who says he's in a barn that's surrounded by La Valle's cartel. Seems to be pretty close to here." He gave Roland the location.

"That's ten minutes east. Tip was just called in

as well. Says they're in a parking lot on the far side of town. You coming?"

"Sumner said they were surrounding a barn he was in, not a parking lot. I wouldn't assume the tip is correct," Banner said.

Roland considered that. "Who's in this barn?"

"My guy's in the barn, along with Emma Caldridge and a pilot."

Roland looked disgusted. "Far as I'm concerned Caldridge is one of them. She's been running with them the whole way."

Banner shook his head. "Never. I know this woman. She's one of ours."

"Who are the other two?"

"One's the pilot of the cartel plane the ATD impounded, but I think he was coerced too."

Roland gave Banner an incredulous look "My heart isn't exactly bleeding for either of them. And the third? He a good guy gone bad, too?"

Banner hesitated. Sumner's actions since intercepting Vanderlock could give rise to questions about his loyalties. He dodged the question.

"Listen, I think you need to consider both angles. Maybe split up the teams?"

Roland shook his head. "Not necessary, and possibly dangerous. We'll come in from the west and pass the barn first. Give it a quick check, then head to the parking lot. You coming?"

Banner nodded, even though he wasn't thrilled with the idea of driving straight to the barn. He climbed into the passenger side of a black Mercury Marquis sedan with Roland and two other agents. The tension in the car ran high. Agent Roland kept a running discussion with another officer while he drove, detailing the plan. He took the curving country lane at sixty miles per hour.

Drives like a native, Banner thought.

A state patrol officer led the procession, his siren quiet. The other cars remained silent as well. Three more FBI vehicles, two SUVs and one more sedan followed, backed up by three police cars. More patrol cars approached from the opposite end.

Banner's phone vibrated again and he looked up as he put it to his ear.

He saw the ambush too late.

Several men stepped from the trees, the guns in their hands silhouetted by the headlights. They opened fire on the procession.

Roland jerked the wheel left, which only caused the car to turn in to one of the gunmen in the semicircle. He fired, pelting the car. Banner saw the muzzle flashes and heard the reports. Bullets punched through the windshield.

"Back up!" one of the agents in the rear yelled. Roland slammed on the brakes and threw the car into reverse. Banner braced his hands on the dash while they shot backward. His phone flipped out of his hand, dropping somewhere at his feet. The Marquis nicked the corner bumper of a following SUV, but only tilted with the hit and then kept going. The lead patrol car barreled past the circle of shooters. It drove a block and a second set of assailants appeared. They hammered the sides with shot. The car drove off the road and smashed into a tree. The assailants turned, heading toward the disabled vehicle.

Roland slammed to a stop. All three agents flew out of the car. Banner, too, was out and used the door as cover. The agents began firing, scattering the gunmen. Banner's own weapon was back in his home in Washington. He kept low, and reached over to the glove compartment. It refused to open. Locked. Now Banner was sure Roland kept a gun in there. The firing stopped and the sudden silence seemed eerie.

"You looking for a weapon?" Roland said, his voice low. He stayed in his position crouched behind the driver's-side door.

"You have an extra?"

Roland tossed Banner a keychain. "In the glove box."

Banner located the proper key and opened the compartment. A gun case nestled inside. It, too, was locked, but the keychain contained the answer and Banner removed a Glock from the case. He checked and found it fully loaded. He tossed the keys back across the car.

"You see anything?" Banner whispered.

"Nothing." Banner didn't either. He reached up and turned off the interior light.

"No sense putting a spotlight on us," he said.

Roland punched off the headlights. The resulting dark interspersed with moonlight made the smashed car recede into shadow. Banner stayed still, straining to hear the sound of a twig snapping or foot crunching on stone. His phone vibrated and lit the car's foot well area when the screen sprang to life with a text message. It was from Sumner and said, "Heard shots, you OK?" Banner stared at the message. He retrieved the phone from the floor and hit the call button. Sumner picked up on the first ring.

"I'm outside that barn. They just ambushed your backup. An FBI convoy."

"I heard the shots. Anyone left besides you?"

"About ten, maybe eleven. Any idea how many we're facing?"

Roland looked over, a question in his eyes.

"It's my man inside the barn," Banner explained.

"I saw at least ten when I came in. I killed two in here, but La Valle got away. And Caldridge says the leaves in the barn have leprosy. She says to be sure not to do anything that might ignite it."

He looked over at Roland, who was whispering into his own phone. When he was done he turned a grim look on Banner.

"Three more squads are hidden on the far side of the barn. We're going to drive them forward, toward the barn. Get them contained and demand surrender."

"These guys will never surrender. They'll hole up inside that barn."

"Fine. It'll be their choice. Either they surrender or we take them out."

"Caldridge says the leaves in the barn are contaminated with a fast-growing form of leprosy. Whatever you do, don't burn the barn down. The smoke will sicken everyone in the immediate area."

Roland looked aggravated. "Again, I ask you, do we believe her?"

Banner put his hands out. "They were here and not at the parking lot, weren't they? So the information given by my people was correct. Can you run this plan without burning the barn down?"

Roland shrugged, irritation clear on his face. "We'll do our best. Maybe we just blow it sky high. Burn it fast and quick."

"Give me twenty minutes. Buy me some time to get them out before you do this."

Roland shook his head. "You see that car?" He pointed to the smashed SUV. "I've got two men in there. We've got to get them out and to a hospital. That means we do this now."

"Ten minutes, then."

Roland hesitated.

"If it was one of yours in there, would you wait ten minutes if it meant saving his life?"

Roland rubbed his face with his hand. "Fine. You've got ten. After that we drive them toward that barn and either they surrender or we blow their asses to kingdom come."

EMMA FINISHED TYING UP CARLOS AND FRISKED him, looking for spare ammunition. She found one cartridge, which she pocketed, and a switchblade. She grabbed his gun, a serviceable weapon with a filed-off serial number, and shoved it into her waistband after setting the safety. She strode to Vanderlock, flicked open the knife, and cut his bindings.

"That Sumner?" Vanderlock indicated Sumner, who was talking on his phone.

Emma nodded. "Yes." Vanderlock rubbed at his wrists with his healthy hand while he looked at Raoul's body. It lay face up, and the eyes remained open. A line of blood ran from the hole in the forehead.

"He's a hell of a shot."

Emma picked her way over to Raoul, bent down next to the hand that still clutched the gun. She pried the fingers off the handle.

"You with him?" Vanderlock said. Emma

checked the gun's clip while she thought about how to answer. Vanderlock's question was understandable in light of the kiss he'd just witnessed, but she had no time to devote to considering why Sumner acted the way he did.

"I'm with myself," she said. She handed Vanderlock Raoul's weapon. He took it without further comment. "Wish we had more."

Vanderlock nodded his agreement. "You hear those shots?"

Emma had. "Sumner says we're surrounded." While they talked, she watched Sumner lock the barn's side door. He cut across the room and did the same to the large double doors at the barn's middle, sliding a bar into place.

Sumner strode over to them. "Banner's outside."

Emma felt her spirits rise. "Thank God," she said.

Sumner grimaced. "The cartel ambushed an FBI convoy. Near as I can tell, we're in the center of two concentric circles. First are the cartel members I saw, second the authorities."

Sumner's cell rang. He answered, and listened. Emma and Vanderlock watched him, and though his expression didn't change, Emma knew him well enough to tell that whatever he was being told was not good news. He hung up.

"FBI's running a pinch. They're going to drive the cartel guys in this direction, then order a surrender."

"La Valle would rather die than surrender," Vanderlock said.

"They don't surrender, the FBI is going to take them out."

"Take them out how?" Vanderlock said.

"I imagine they'll line up some sharpshooters."

Emma paced back and forth, wishing she could run instead. She sorted through her mind the possible outcomes of the FBI's pinch maneuver, and none left her, Sumner, and Vanderlock any room to get out of the barn and past the cartel. A worse possible outcome came to mind.

"These cartel guys get close, they're going to want to hole up in here."

Sumner gave her a serious glance. "The thought had occurred to me," he said. "And the FBI is not quite buying the leprosy story."

Now Emma was angry beyond her already extreme agitation. "Can I borrow your phone?" she said to Sumner, who handed it to her. She used it to access the Internet and typed in two words on a search engine. The results came back and she showed the screen to Sumner. "You tell Banner to show the FBI this."

Sumner read from the screen. "Armadillos?"

"They're natural leprosy carriers. Some carry massive bacterial loads in their system. It doesn't hurt them and most people in contact with the animal don't get the disease either, which is why I didn't put it together right away." Emma rubbed her forehead, where a headache was forming. "La Valle keeps a barn full of them, feeds them to his crew for strength, grinds their carapace into dust and uses it to line the compound. Said it acted as a magical barrier. He probably sprinkled it in the fields as well. I think the herbicide dumped by the DOD mingled with the ashes and triggered a virulent form of the disease."

"I already told them not to burn the leaves, because I've seen what that does firsthand, but I don't think telling them about the armadillos will stop the maneuver."

"How much time do we have?" Vanderlock said.

"Ten minutes."

"Generous of them." Vanderlock sounded disgusted. "You got a plane nearby?" he said to Sumner, who nodded.

"About a mile north. On an improvised runway. A runway set up by a guy La Valle controls, actually, who's currently sitting in jail on a parole violation."

"We have two vehicles. The ambulance and the motorcycle inside. What if we just drive the thing right through the doors and out?" Emma said.

Sumner walked over to the ambulance, looking at the walls. "Some rounds might pierce this."

"Let's line them with the bales. Might add another layer." Emma strode to one of the bales of marijuana and lifted it. Vanderlock reached her side and helped toss it into the back of the ambulance. With Sumner's help they tossed in three more, placing them in two stacks and leaving a center section open.

"I'll drive it," Sumner said.

Emma shook her head. "No you won't. I will."

"Not a chance. Whoever drives is at the most risk. Once they figure out what we're up to, they're going to open fire."

"I'm not as good a shot as you are. And I'm pretty sure Vanderlock is better than I am, too."

"Thanks for the overwhelming vote of confidence," Vanderlock said in a dry tone. Sumner looked down while a smile played around his lips.

"You guys will have to be prepared to cover me when they disable the ambulance. I'll run it on the rims if I have to, but when it stops it's done," Emma said. Sumner opened his mouth to argue. "I'll sit below window height and maneuver it that way. Will give me some measure of protection."

The last seemed to mollify Sumner a bit. "Okay. But I'll ride along, shoot from the passenger window. You cover the rear?" Sumner said the last to Vanderlock, who nodded.

"And if they do manage to kill the ambulance, I'm going to drive that motorcycle right out the back."

"That should be a last resort. At least the walls of the ambulance give you some protection. Once you're on that cycle you're completely exposed," Emma said.

"Agreed. Only as a last resort."

"Then let's go."

Emma ran to the table and grabbed a heavy hammer that she could use as a weapon and headed to the discarded tote. She fished out the bottle of the investigational antibiotic pills and emptied it into her hand. She shoved the handful into her pocket. On her way back to the ambulance she passed Sumner, and overheard him talking to Banner.

"Just tell the FBI not to shoot at the ambulance. I don't want to get clear of the cartel and then face another round."

Emma reached the driver's side and checked for the keys. They weren't hanging in the ignition as she expected. Vanderlock appeared next to her.

"You know where the keys might be?"

"In Raoul's or Mono's pocket? I'll get them."

Emma moved the driver's seat all the way back and crawled into the space between the wheel and the seat, checking to see if she could get below the window line. While wedged in between them, a pair of keys entered her line of vision.

"That is a beautiful sight," she said to Vanderlock.

"Let's turn it around to face out." When they were in position, Vanderlock took a deep breath. "No time to waste." Sumner walked to the passenger side. "You ready?"

Emma nodded. Then a thought came to her. "What about Carlos?"

"I dragged him to the side door and untied him. Told him that we're leaving and he's on his own. He said he's not interested in us, but getting as far away from La Valle as possible," Sumner said.

Emma nodded. "Then I'm ready."

"I'll open the barn door," Vanderlock said. "Be sure to drive slow at first, give me time to jump in the back."

A booming noise at the side door made Emma jump. "What the hell was that?"

The noise came again. Emma stood on the ambulance's running board and looked over the bales of hay. The side door shivered with each hit.

"Someone's trying to get in," she said.

The hits started in a rhythmic pattern.

"They're battering it down," Vanderlock said. Sumner moved back around the ambulance, lifted his weapon, and shot directly into the door. The bullet pierced through the wood, and a man's cry came from the other side. A hail of gunfire followed, punching holes in the door in a crazy pattern. Emma dove to the packed earth. Out of the corner of her eye she saw that Sumner had done the same.

More gunfire came from the direction of the double doors in front of the ambulance and Sumner crawled on his belly to the vehicle's side. The double door shook when some large object hammered into it from the outside. Sumner reached the driver's-side front wheel, rolled onto his back and fired up and into the door. A boom signaled return fire, but this time the bullet ripped a large hole in the heavy wooden double doors. Sumner returned to his stomach and crawled toward Emma. Vanderlock moved up to crouch on her left.

"That must be a fifty caliber," Vanderlock said. He hovered at the rear of the ambulance, aimed and fired at the side door, where the banging had stopped briefly. Vanderlock's shot resulted in another volley. Several bullets pierced the bales of marijuana stacked nearby. Emma saw a small wisp of smoke emanate from one.

"One of the bales is on fire," Emma said. "We've got to get out of here, now." More bullets peppered the double doors, shooting holes in the wood. Emma waved at it. "Forget about opening the door," she said to Vanderlock, "I'm going to drive right through it." She got behind the steering wheel, keeping her head low while she waited for Sumner and Vanderlock to take their positions. "Stay low until I clear the door," Emma said to Sumner, who had made his way around the back and reappeared on the passenger side. He slid into the seat and bent his frame to keep low. A quick glance at the marijuana bale told Emma that she had no real choice. The small wisp of smoke had turned into a steady, upward column.

Emma started the engine, lowered herself to the floor and grabbed the wheel. She put her foot on the gas.

EMMA PUSHED THE GAS PEDAL ALL THE WAY DOWN.
The ambulance started to roll, slowly at first, but
quickly building speed. She felt the jerk of the
transmission as it shifted from first to second
gear. Emma peered over the dash, doing her best
to keep low but still steer the van. She aimed for
the double door edge, near the side that opened,
where she thought was its weakest point. Splin-
ters flew from the panel where the bullets were
still hammering into it. A cloud of dust hung in
the air from the pulverized wood. They plowed
into the door.

The ambulance shuddered with the impact
and the hinges ripped from their supports with
a creaking, squealing sound. Three bullets hit
the windshield, creating a long crack in the glass.
Two more bullets pinged off the hood. A dirt path
led from the barn to a nearby road, and Emma
used it. The van hit thirty miles per hour and was
one hundred yards from the barn when the real

shooting began. It came from all sides. The windows were lowered and she could feel the bullets zipping past. Muzzle flashes lit the trees, and Emma felt panic rise as the lights revealed the full number of gang members that hid in the trees. The side walls gave off metallic pinging sounds as the ordnance hit the van. Sumner pointed his rifle out the window and began laying down return fire, sweeping the area near the trees. She heard Vanderlock firing from the back.

It was impossible for Emma to stay as low as she wanted and still drive. She rose slightly, keeping her foot down. Her headlights bounced with the ruts in the road, occasionally illuminating a shooter in the trees. The hammer bounced at her feet in the foot well.

Holes punctured the windshield, multiplying second by second until it finally shattered and showered down on Sumner and her. She closed her eyes and felt the bits of glass hit her face. Fear focused her mind, making her stare at the darkness around her, but keeping her foot frozen on the pedal. The ambulance picked up more speed.

Emma kept driving. The van lurched when the front, then the back, tires deflated. Sumner fell against her, and she pushed him back to his side. He aimed and continued to fire. The ambulance hit the rims and the entire vehicle slowed on the inadequate wheels. She heard a booming noise and a bullet hammered into the engine. Flames erupted from the front.

"Someone's got another fifty caliber. We've got to get out of here before the gas tank blows up," Sumner said.

The van still moved forward, but was slowing. Emma grabbed the hammer and put it on the gas pedal. Sumner jumped out his side, and Emma rolled out of hers. She hit the ground, bent her knees, and kept moving to absorb the shock of the fall. The ambulance shot past her. She started to race toward the trees, with Sumner hot on her heels. She heard a second engine start up, and seconds later Vanderlock came roaring past on the motorcycle. The van picked up speed, shimmying from side to side, fire spouting from the engine. Vanderlock waved them to him, braking the cycle to wait. Emma ran for it, with Sumner in front of her. A car pulled next to Vanderlock and Emma saw a swarthy man aiming a weapon at her. She veered off, leaping over a small bush into a stand of trees. Behind her she heard Sumner's rifle fire, followed by return fire. She kept moving, running at an angle through a stand of trees.

She was 150 yards in when she saw movement in front and to her right side. She slowed, moving from trunk to trunk, using them as cover, trying to figure out if the movement came from a ring of FBI agents or from the gang members. The darkness all around made it difficult to see anything. She glanced at the sky, and could see a lightened area of wispy clouds that covered the moon. The breeze was soft. The moon would emerge from its cover, but not immediately. She had time.

She moved from tree to tree, keeping low and doing her best not to make noise. The battle at the barn continued, with bursts of staccato gunfire cracking through the night. She huddled by a large trunk, the last in a row. The next grew a full forty feet ahead, across a small expanse of grass and two-foot-tall wildflowers. Emma paused, hating to reveal her position for even the short time it would take to get across the area.

A volley of fire to her immediate left made her crouch lower, tighter against the bark. She slid around the trunk to keep it between her and the source of the noise. The clouds moved, and a weak pool of light illuminated the clearing.

La Valle stepped into sight, and it was all Emma could do not to gasp at his sudden appearance. He held a gun in one hand and the wicked looking knife in the other. Four men materialized to his right from the trees, pushing a man in front of them. The man looked to be in his late thirties, wore dark clothes and had an empty gun holster attached to his waistband. La Valle raised his own pistol to aim at the man's face.

"I'm Agent Roland of the FBI. You don't want to do that," Roland said.

La Valle didn't move, but he didn't fire, either. "You think I'm afraid of you?"

Roland shook his head. "It's not a matter of being afraid, it's a matter of position. We've got the barn surrounded."

Emma thought the man showed courage, but she doubted the barn was surrounded. If it had been, she would have hit the line of FBI already.

The fact that she had run as far as she had without encountering any meant there were holes in
the perimeter. She removed Carlos's weapon from
her waistband and flicked off the safety while she
analyzed the men in the circle, deciding what
would happen to Roland if she fired first.

Five men, including La Valle, all armed and
all prepared to kill her and Roland. If she fired
they'd likely dive to try to save themselves, but
someone would surely take out the FBI man in
the process. She thought La Valle was the player
most likely to eliminate Roland. Roland repre-
sented authority and La Valle wouldn't allow
anyone in his vicinity with higher status than
he thought he commanded. The other gang
members would protect themselves, because in
Emma's experience to date she'd never seen a
group of criminals risk their lives to save each
other. Once their leader was down the organization inevitably splintered.

La Valle waved the gun. "Give me your walkie-
talkie and get down, face-first." Roland handed La
Valle a small transmitter and then slowly lowered
himself to the ground, keeping eye contact with
La Valle as long as he could. When he was on the
grass, face-first, La Valle spoke into the walkie-
talkie. "I have Agent Roland. He's alive, but only
for three more minutes. Either agree to let us pass,
or I kill him. Not fast, but slow. You can all listen."
La Valle shoved the walkie-talkie into Roland's
face. "Tell them to lower their weapons. We get
safe passage to the airplane on the runway."

Agent Roland hesitated. La Valle kicked him in

the side. Roland flinched, but remained silent. La Valle put his knife to the back of Roland's ear and pressed. Emma saw a dark line of blood run down Roland's cheek. She swallowed, but her throat was dry. She didn't want to watch La Valle cut off the man's ear, but she couldn't look away, either.

"They have me hostage," Roland said into the walkie-talkie. La Valle kicked him in the side.

"The airplane. Tell them!"

Roland looked up at La Valle with a confused expression. "We don't have an airplane nearby. I don't know what you're talking about." La Valle pressed harder and the blood trickle behind Roland's ear became thicker, wider. He groaned.

"Liar! There's an airplane on the runway not a thousand meters from here. On *my* runway."

"This is Cameron Sumner of Air Tunnel Denial." Emma heard Sumner's voice pour through the transmitter. "That plane is mine. You want it, come get it, but you'd better have Roland alive when you step on the tarmac. Because if he isn't—"

"If he isn't, then what! You kill me? You think I'm afraid of you?" La Valle screamed into the small walkie-talkie. The cords on his neck bulged with the force of his anger and spit flew from the edges of his lips. Emma watched as a drop of blood ran from his nose down his face, over his lips. He wiped it away with his arm.

Emma looked at the base of the tree. Roots rose from the edge, and a few large rocks sat a foot away. She reached her arm out, slowly, straining to collect a rock. She grasped it and held it in her left hand, feeling its weight. She rose in a fluid movement.

She raised her weapon and took aim at La Valle's torso with her right hand while she threw the rock with her left, flinging it as hard as she could in the direction behind La Valle and his crew. It hit a small bush with a thudding sound and making the branches shudder. As she'd hoped, the entire group spun in that direction.

Emma fired, hitting La Valle in the midsection, the bullet entering through his side, but not in a vital location. She doubted the hit would kill him. La Valle bellowed in a mixture of anger and pain. His body jerked sideways and he squeezed off a shot that missed Emma and her tree by inches. Roland catapulted himself to his left, toward Emma. She fired three more times in rapid succession, making sure to hit La Valle again, this time in the calf, and then aiming at the fleeing cartel members. Predictably, the gang members scattered. La Valle, though, was still standing.

"Agent Roland, get over here!" Emma called to the man. He gained his footing and started toward her. La Valle staggered from the bullet in his calf, but raised his weapon toward Roland. Emma shot again, hitting him in the shoulder. Another hit not guaranteed to be fatal. But La Valle jerked as the bullet slammed into him and he landed on the ground, hard. He didn't move.

Roland reached her tree and crouched in position next to her. He gave her a searching look.

"You're Emma Caldridge," he said.

Emma nodded. "How many are we facing and where do you think they're located?"

"We're in the ring. I'd say there's about thirty. Less now." He indicated La Valle lying in the field. "He has my gun in his waistband. I need to go get it."

"Don't touch him. He's got a disease. I'll get the gun. I'm already infected."

Roland looked at her. "With what?"

"A fast-moving, mutating bacteria that mimics leprosy."

Emma could feel Roland steel himself not to recoil from her. She gave him some more points for courage.

"I'd have you cover me while I go out there, but you'll have to hold my gun. Do you have a piece of cloth? Anything we can wrap the handle with? Just as a precaution. I don't think the disease is transmitted quite that easily, but I'd hate to take the risk."

Roland pulled his shirt up, and unbuttoned the bottom. "Hand it over."

Emma placed the gun's butt in his palm, which was now covered by the shirt. "I'll be right back."

She jogged to La Valle's body and turned him over. His knife stuck out from his stomach, where he'd fallen on it. He was still breathing in short, shallow gasps, and opened his eyes to look at her.

"You fell on your knife," Emma said.

La Valle grimaced at her. "I won't die," he said. "I can't die." Blood ran from his nose. Emma didn't respond. He would die, and by his own hand. She thought of Octavio's claims that La Valle was cursed. At that moment, staring at a man riddled with sores and with his own weapon piercing his body, Emma believed.

His eyes closed and he stopped breathing.

Emma searched his pockets and found a second weapon. She removed it and jogged back to Agent Roland, leaving La Valle's body where it lay.

45

EMMA PLACED THE WEAPON ON THE GROUND NEXT to Roland. "This yours?"

Roland nodded.

"Maybe you wipe the butt before you handle it," Emma said.

Roland returned Carlos's weapon to her before wiping off the butt of his Beretta.

She heard a massive explosion from the barn's direction.

"They blew the barn," Roland said. "What about the leaves? Banner said burning them spreads the disease."

"*Now* you ask me?" Emma was aggravated and didn't bother to hide it.

Roland gave her an apologetic look. "I didn't trust your report to him."

Emma pulled out her compass and checked her direction. "And now?"

He nodded. "I saw the sores on La Valle's arms. Now I do. Should we evacuate?"

Emma handed him the transmitter. "Yes. Tell

everyone to move as far away from the barn as possible." She jerked her chin at the walkie-talkie. "Wipe it first."

Roland gave the order.

"Let's move," Emma said. She waved him forward, moving quickly in the direction she thought would be parallel to the road. They jogged a full minute without coming upon any cartel members.

They took off. Cowards, Emma thought. She ran faster, cutting between trees and jumping over low-lying bushes. Roland stayed with her, and after five minutes was breathing heavily in her ear. She kept going, not willing to slow down until she was sure the remnants of the barn's smoke couldn't reach her.

After ten minutes she emerged from the trees onto the road. Emma turned onto it, running faster now that she had a flat surface to use. Roland picked up his pace, too, but he was breathing heavily in and out, sounding like a bellows, and clearly would be stopping soon.

"You go. I'll catch up," Roland said.

Emma slowed. "I think we're far enough away."

Ten minutes farther, and Emma saw the runway off to her right. She and Roland turned off onto a beaten earth path that led straight to it.

A small plane sat on the runway. The waning moonlight hit some reflective sections, and they glowed. Oz's motorcycle was parked next to it with Vanderlock still sitting on the seat. Seconds later a car pulled up, driving past them and stopping about twenty feet away.

Banner stepped out of the car. Emma thought it was the second time that evening that she was profoundly happy to see someone. Sumner came out of the passenger side and his eyes went right to her. He looked relieved, then glanced at Roland. Banner walked up.

"Everyone all right?"

Emma nodded, not sure she could speak normally quite yet and wondering how it was that Banner could.

"Surprised to see you in the States, Vanderlock," Banner said.

"Not as surprised as I am to be here," Vanderlock replied. He took a package of cigarettes out of his pocket, lit one, and inhaled.

Banner turned to Roland. "Glad to see you got out alive. How'd you do it?"

Roland jerked his head at Emma. "Your operative was hiding in the trees. Lucky break for me."

"In that case, can you vouch for her? Cancel the warrant?"

Roland nodded. "I'm pretty sure I can. Especially if the leprosy story pans out." Emma opened her mouth to protest and Roland put up a hand to stay her. "Which I know it will. The biggest problem I'm facing is you." Roland indicated Vanderlock. "By rights I need to arrest him for the illegal importation of drugs."

"As do I," Sumner said.

Vanderlock rolled his eyes. "I was coerced. Does no one care?"

Banner pointed at Sumner's plane sitting on the tarmac. "You want to fly me to St. Martin in the Caribbean? You do that and then technically you're working for me. Gives you some credibility and gets you out of the country, fast."

"I'll fly you wherever you want to go, but I'd rather do it in my own plane," Vanderlock said. "You still have it?" he said to Sumner.

"It's at an impound center in Nevada, so this one will have to do. Nice paint job on the Fokker, though."

Vanderlock took another drag off his cigarette. "Blame the chemist."

Banner tossed Sumner the keys to the Marquis. "You and Agent Roland deal with the rest of the Bureau when it gets here? Tell them the truth?"

Roland nodded. "I'll back them down. But what about the leprosy? Or whatever it is?"

"We'll all need to be tested. But I have these," Emma pulled the investigational antibiotic out of her pocket. "I need to find Oz. See if they worked."

"They work. Oz sent me a text saying they did. He's still keeping low, but promised to keep his phone on in case we needed him," Banner said.

Banner pointed to Emma but spoke to Vanderlock. "Let Emma take the motorcycle." And to her he said, "Why don't you head home? I'll have the Darkview attorney contact you to straighten out any loose ends."

Emma nodded. She shook a few pills out of the bottle, placed them in her pocket and handed Vanderlock the container. "Keep taking these, then." She gave the rest to Banner. "For you and

Sumner." She looked at Agent Roland. "Can you arrange to get me some more?"

He nodded. "Of course."

"Come on, Vanderlock. Let's go," Banner said.

Vanderlock lowered the cycle's kickstand and stood up. "Key's in the ignition. You still have that cell phone?"

Emma withdrew it from her pocket and gave it to him. He stepped next to her, took the phone, and used one hand to manipulate the buttons while the other kept the cigarette in play. Emma peered at the screen, and saw that he was inputting his name and a phone number at the Contacts page. When he was finished he hit "save" and handed it back to her. "You need anything, ever, you call me."

Emma nodded.

He stepped up to her and bent his head down. When his face was inches from hers he paused. "Why don't you come with me to St. Martin? You'll like it, I promise you," he said.

Emma understood exactly what he was saying. She shook her head. "Maybe next time."

He smiled. "I'd show you a preview, but God knows what I'd give you right now and Sumner is still holding that gun."

"Discretion is always a wise move. Especially when Sumner has a gun in his hand."

Vanderlock stepped back and smiled a large, happy smile. He sketched a wave at Sumner, who was leaning against the Marquis, his arms folded across his chest. Sumner nodded back. Banner glanced between the two men and at Emma, raising his eyebrows just a touch in a question. She lifted her shoulders. Banner gave her a devilish grin, which surprised her, coming from him. He followed Vanderlock to the airplane.

She turned her attention to Sumner. "You shouldn't have kissed me. Now you have it."

"I'll see you in a few days. We should talk," he said.

Emma put up a hand. "I don't want to talk."

He gave her a slight smile. "You can't run forever."

She walked to him, stopping only when her body hit his folded arms. She looked into his eyes, which held humor, as if he was enjoying the moment.

"I can run for a very, very long time," she said.

46

EMMA SAW A MAN TRUDGING ALONG THE ROAD
in the early-morning light, just where the GPS
phone tracking system said he would be. He wore
battered jeans and a black tee shirt. She pulled
alongside.

"You need a lift?" Oz took in the motorcycle
and her driving it. His face broke into a huge,
beautiful smile.

"Nice ride," he said.

"You like it? It belongs to a friend of mine. I'm
bringing it back to him."

"I've been hitchhiking, but no one will pick me
up. Guess I look a little scary."

Emma cocked her head to one side. He must
not have looked in a mirror recently, but the sores
on his face had diminished from an angry red to
pale pink, and portions of his neck were clear.

"You look much better than you think. How do
you feel?"

He tipped his hand from side to side. "Less
numb, but that's both good and bad. As the

nerves come back I'm feeling all sorts of pain. I do okay as long as I take the ibuprofen. And the prednisone seems to really help."

"Climb on," Emma said.

Oz hesitated. "You look normal. What if I infect you?"

Emma shrugged. "I'm taking the pills, too." Oz swung a leg over and settled in behind her. "Where you going?" she said.

"East. I want MIT to take me back."

"Now *that's* a plan."

She opened the throttle and brought the motorcycle up to speed, feeling the wind in her hair and the sun on her face.

AUTHOR'S NOTE

Once again, I seem to have stumbled upon research that was just at the tipping point. This time: leprosy and armadillos. I started writing this novel with an incorrect belief that leprosy had been eradicated worldwide. While it has been greatly reduced, the disease, now called Hansen's Disease, persists. Lucky for us, leprosy is now completely curable with a course of antibiotics, and bears little resemblance to the fictional disease in the novel. My thanks to Dr. Carlotta Hill for her explanation of the real disease and its treatment. For further information on Hansen's Disease (leprosy), you can go to www.hrsa.gov/hansens or call 1-800-642-2477.

Dr. Hill also confirmed my suspicion that one

might be able to become infected with leprosy from contact with armadillos. Armadillos carry massive bacterial loads but are unaffected by the disease. Their proliferation in the American Southwest and Mexico made them the perfect animal upon which to hinge my fictional disease. Imagine my surprise when, several months after speaking with Dr. Hill, I happened to read an article in the *Chicago Tribune* about researchers having confirmed that armadillos can transmit the disease to humans. I've never eaten armadillo meat, and after that article you can be sure that I won't!

EMMA CALDRIDGE FOUND THE BLOODY OFFERING on her credenza just before midnight. She had been working late, preparing samples and organizing slides in the makeshift lab set up in the rented villa's spacious garage and had returned to the main house for another cup of coffee.

A small votive candle flickered next to the pile of feathers and hacked off rooster foot, all arranged in a triangle on top of a pentagram drawn in a red substance that looked like blood. Emma's employer, Pure Chemistry, was located in Miami and Emma had seen Santeria altars before, with their animal sacrifice and elaborate rituals, but this was nothing like that. This was voodoo. She pulled a pencil out of a cup next to the phone and used the eraser end to lift the mass of feathers. Underneath she found the doll. The body was fashioned of hastily stitched burlap, that sported brown yarn for hair and two black felt dots for eyes. A toothpick jutted from the center of the doll's forehead.

Emma snorted at the crude scare tactic. She was a scientist, unafraid of ghosts or demons and unbelieving of things that went bump in the night. If it made noise, then a human, animal, or physical element created it.

She heard the sound of breaking glass in the distance. The intruder was in the garage.

She dropped the pencil and ran through the darkened house, out the French doors at the back of the kitchen and onto the lawn. As she neared the garage she saw the shape of something that may have been a man, working his way through her carefully prepared slides. He swept something across the table and Emma watched in disbelief as bottles, jars and the containers holding a week's worth of work went crashing to the cement floor. She ran toward him, the sharp gravel of the drive cutting into the soles of her feet.

The garage's overhead light cast a yellow glow over the tables that Emma had set up in order to form the workspace. The man, if that what the humpbacked shape was, pushed over the nearest table, upending it and sending another set of petri dishes, test tubes and even a microscope tumbling to the floor.

"Stop it!" Emma's voice was harsh. The man froze. As she neared she could see the machete in his hand. It was this that he had used to sweep the bottles off the table. "That's my work. You have no right to be here." The man stayed still, saying nothing and keeping his face turned away. Emma heard the gravel crunch behind her.

"He responds only to me."

Emma turned around. A woman stood at the corner of the drive. The weak moonlight lit her dark skin. She wore a scarf wrapped around her head and a sarong skirt was knotted at her hip. The woman smiled and her teeth, straight and white, glowed in the night, giving her a feral appearance. "He's my slave. A zombie."

"He's a trespasser. And so are you," Emma said. Her anger fizzed at the deliberate destruction of her work. She leveled a stare at the woman. So here's the source of the voodoo offering, she thought.

The woman moved toward Emma, walking in an exaggerated, swaying motion. "*You* are the outsider on this island. We belong here. Leave. And take your bottles and experiments with you."

Emma glanced at the man, but he remained still, not moving a muscle. His stillness was strange and Emma felt a frisson of a chill run through her. She wished that she had thought to bring her cell phone. She was loath to leave these two even for the time it would take to retrieve it. If she did, she was afraid they would destroy even more.

"You don't belong here either. This island has no history of voodoo," Emma said. "I saw the mess you made in the entrance hall. I'll be sure to let Island Security know about your breaking and entering."

The woman chuckled, but the noise sounded evil, wicked. "Island Security knows better than to interfere with a Bokor Priestess."

Emma was glad that the man stayed frozen during this exchange. She didn't want to grapple with both and the machete in his hand made him the more dangerous of the two. She took a step toward the woman.

"But *I* don't know better, and I'm telling you one more time to leave. Now. And take your companion and ridiculous talk of zombies with you." The woman raised an eyebrow.

"Ahh, the scientist in you doesn't believe? Be warned. You have no idea what you're dealing with here. With one word from me he'll cut you to ribbons. There's no negotiating with him."

"I don't recall offering any negotiation. I said leave. Both of you." Emma kept the man in her peripheral vision. With the machete in his hand he didn't need to be a zombie to hurt her. Flesh and blood human would be enough.

The woman flicked her hand. "Kill her," she said.

The man burst into motion. He raised the machete and sprinted to her, closing the distance between them in seconds. His hair hung in thick rasta braids down his back and his face was contorted in a strange spasm. His eyes pointed straight to the sky even as he ran toward her swinging his machete. It was as if his body was responding to a force outside of his mind and even less controlled by it. His tongue whipped right and left, adding to the horrific sight. He started screaming in a high pitched wail.

Emma spun and started to run toward the villa. She heard the priestess's harsh laugh and the man's pounding feet on the driveway behind her. She had the fleeting thought that the man was insane and if he were to catch her he would show her no mercy.

She made it to the French doors and wrenched them open, tumbling through the entrance and slamming them behind her. She turned and flipped the deadbolt just as he crashed into the glass with his hands. The machete's blade made a clanging sound on the pane.

He stood there, breathing heavy, his weirdly canted eyes still staring upward. She crossed to the phone on located on the kitchen counter, dialed the emergency number and glanced back.

He was gone.

CAMERON SUMNER SAT AT THE BLACKJACK TABLE and watched the croupier deal out the cards. The woman to his left watched as well. She had long, blond hair, a full figure, pretty face with brown eyes, and wore no wedding ring. He estimated her age at about twenty-eight. It was unusual that such a young woman played the Casinos alone. Perhaps she had a gambling problem, he thought, but rejected the thought as soon as he had it. She didn't appear desperate or stressed at all, and wasn't sweating with the thrill of the game, as most chronic gamblers did. Sumner had noticed that whatever table he joined, she inevitably appeared. She didn't speak to him, but played her hand with intelligence and calm, hitting when the odds were against the dealer and sticking when they weren't. She won three out of four hands.

He kept playing, scratching the table slightly with his cards to indicate to the croupier that he wanted a hit, making a small wave to stick and watched the woman do the same. When the cocktail waitress appeared Sumner ordered a Maker's Mark whiskey, the woman seltzer water with lemon. It was at that moment that he knew she was staking him out. She was on duty and not drinking.

He completed the hand, tipped the croupier, took his chips, and pushed away from the table. The Maker's Mark came with him to the roulette wheel where he played his favorite number: 32.

Twenty minutes later the blond joined a nearby wheel. Close enough to see him, but not at the same table. She would move closer, he was sure of it. After twenty minutes more she strolled over and took the empty seat next to him. He smiled inwardly. After a few moments she made an attempt to reach across the roulette wheel to place her chips on a number located at the far side.

"Excuse me," she said as she leaned over him. He smelled her perfume and was treated to a full view of her chest in her low, but not too low, blouse.

"Of course," he said. He shifted his chair back to allow her access. The wheel turned and landed on 32. The croupier doled out Sumner's winnings and pushed them across the felt table top with his stick.

Sumner was on the small island of St. Maartin

on business. As a supervisor in the Air Tunnel Denial program, he flew intercept planes for the United States Southern Hemisphere Drug Defense program. Generally he and his crew operated out of Key West, but the recent upsurge in the areas of the Caribbean and West Indies islands had altered the ATD's focus. Sumner's job was to locate suspicious flights, usually flying under radar, warn them against crossing into the United States' territories, and, once they did, arrest or intercept the planes before they landed. He was also charged with investigating the origin of the flights and putting an end to the drug operation.

He figured the woman could either be an undercover security officer hired by the casino, a member of the small island's police force undercover, or a foil hired by the drug cartel to compromise or eliminate him before he had a chance to shut down the operation. He hoped she wasn't part of the cartel, but he thought that to be the most likely scenario.

He won two rounds in a row, decided that was the best he would do against the house, and once again collected his chips. He swallowed the last of the whiskey before strolling to the window to cash out. After pocketing his winnings he headed to the exit. The blond woman intercepted him.

"Leaving already?" Her voice was low and husky. She stood in front of him holding a stack of chips in one hand and her drink in the other.

He nodded. "Quitting while I'm ahead."

"The house isn't going to like that." She smiled at him.

"It's such a small amount, I doubt they'll care."

"Maybe you should stay and have a drink in the bar. It's quite early by island standards." Her words were light but her gaze pointed. Sumner had the fleeting thought that perhaps she was a call girl working the casino, except for what he saw in her eyes. Sumner thought he read a warning in them.

"Do you work for the casino?"

She looked surprised and shook her head. "Not at all. What gave you that impression?"

"You seem reluctant to let me leave."

She raised an eyebrow. "Just thinking that you'll enjoy yourself more here than at home."

"I have a good book." She looked a bit stung and he said, "But I thank you for your concern. I'll enjoy the quiet."

She shrugged. "I hope you do. Goodbye." She turned and walked back into the maze of tables.

The balmy air smelled of salt water and engine grease, a combination that wafted off a nearby pier. He crawled into the small rental car and started back home. He drove carefully, keeping with the flow of traffic on the narrow road with one lane in either direction.

His rental was actually the beach house for a much larger estate. St. Maartin's crime rate had been escalating in recent years, and as a result the estate was gated, with three large dogs that roamed the grounds. Sumner hit the button and watched behind him in the rearview mirror while he waited for the gate to open. In the distance he heard the dogs barking. He'd have a few minutes if he was lucky to drive through before they swarmed over the road. The gate swung closed behind him just as the dogs appeared. They were in full howl and the largest, an Akita with an impressive ruff around his neck, began snapping at the car tires. Sumner proceeded ahead at a slow pace, using the car bumper to nudge the dogs out of the way. One, a large Rhodesian ridgeback incongruously named Susie, put her paws on the drivers' side window and peered in at him, her big nose sniffing at the glass. Her bark turned to a sound of welcome once she recognized Sumner.

The big house sat on the bluff above with lights blazing, and even at the distance of four hundred yards Sumner could hear the beat of heavy dance music as the inhabitants partied. He drove through the palm trees on either side and down the winding road to the beach. His house was considered a small guest house despite its three bedrooms, dedicated pool, and location on the water. He killed the engine and stepped out of the car.

He was alone. The dogs had followed him halfway down before heading back to the entrance. A sliver of moonlight shot across the gently moving waves and he stood a moment, enjoying the sound of them lapping against the shore. He heard a padding noise and Susie loped into view, her long tail wagging as she approached. She pushed her head against his knee in greeting. He reached down to scratch her ears before turning to the door. He was three steps away from the entrance when Susie began to growl.

He paused, straining his ears to pick up any hint of what Susie had noticed. He focused his senses around the heavy bass still pounding from the house above. Hearing nothing else he took another step toward the door. Susie's growls grew louder and she began to pace in front of him. He kept moving forward and the dog subsided, walking alongside him. When they reached the entrance Susie began to sniff at it in loud inhalations, her sides heaving as she did. She snorted and shook her head, stepping back.

Sumner paused again. The back of his neck tingled and he wondered if something, or someone, was waiting for him on the other side of the panel. He reversed away. The beach house had a second, rarely-used rear door off the laundry room that led onto the backyard where a clothesline stretched. Sumner headed that way, keeping his head down and moving with as much silence as he could. Susie stayed with him. He reached the door and slid his key into the lock. It turned with a snick and he slipped inside. Susie pushed in after him, knocking the door wider with her big body. He grabbed her collar to hold her in place.

He decided against turning on a light as he worked his way down the hall, holding Susie's collar. Her nails clicked against the floor and for a moment he wished he'd left her outside, except he had no weapon other than Susie. In full howl and enraged she made a formidable sight. He peered into the darkened living area. A far bank of windows faced the ocean, taking full advantage of the view. To his left was the front door.

A glance at it told him everything he needed to know. A tangle of wires ran from what looked like a car battery to the door handle. An LED display glowed red. Sumner couldn't see what it was and he didn't bother to stay. He spun around, dragging Susie with him, and ran back the way he came. His heart beat in a crazy rhythm and his hand on the leather collar was suddenly slick with sweat. He had made it into the laundry room and had managed to slam the door closed when the bomb exploded.